W9-ADI-867

FOR THE LOVE OF SUMMER

Also by Susan Mallery

The Summer Book Club
The Happiness Plan
The Sister Effect
The Boardwalk Bookshop
The Summer Getaway
The Stepsisters
The Vineyard at Painted Moon
The Friendship List
The Summer of Sunshine & Margot
California Girls
When We Found Home
Secrets of the Tulip Sisters
Daughters of the Bride

Wishing Tree

Home Sweet Christmas
The Christmas Wedding Guest

Mischief Bay

Sisters Like Us
A Million Little Things
The Friends We Keep
The Girls of Mischief Bay

Blackberry Island

Sisters by Choice
Evening Stars
Three Sisters
Barefoot Season

…and the beloved Fool's Gold and Happily Inc romances.

For a complete list of titles available from Susan Mallery,
please visit susanmallery.com.

SUSAN MALLERY

FOR THE LOVE OF SUMMER

mira

Recycling programs
for this product may
not exist in your area.

ISBN-13: 978-0-7783-6820-5

For the Love of Summer

Copyright © 2024 by Susan Mallery, Inc.

All rights reserved. No part of this book may be used or reproduced in any manner whatsoever without written permission.

Without limiting the author's and publisher's exclusive rights, any unauthorized use of this publication to train generative artificial intelligence (AI) technologies is expressly prohibited.

This is a work of fiction. Names, characters, places and incidents are either the product of the author's imagination or are used fictitiously. Any resemblance to actual persons, living or dead, businesses, companies, events or locales is entirely coincidental.

For questions and comments about the quality of this book, please contact us at CustomerService@Harlequin.com.

TM is a trademark of Harlequin Enterprises ULC.

Mira
22 Adelaide St. West, 41st Floor
Toronto, Ontario M5H 4E3, Canada

Printed in U.S.A.

For Andrea. I always knew you'd inspire a character one day
and here she is. Erica shares your drive, your smarts
and most importantly, your warm and giving heart. To you, my friend.
With love and the hope that your dreams will always come true.

1

"But it's orange!"

"I saw."

"I didn't know hair could turn that color of orange."

Erica Sawyer glanced from her laptop to her partially closed office door, her focus on monthly product sales overtaken by the conversation from the hallway. Two women spoke in hushed voices. The calmer of the two was Daryn, a level-six stylist at Twisted. Erica didn't recognize the other voice.

"Did you ask the client if she'd been using box color at home?"

"I did! Twice!" Tears thickened the unknown woman's voice. "She lied."

"It happens." Daryn sounded more resigned than surprised.

The conversation continued, but the stylists had moved out of earshot.

Erica looked back at the spreadsheet, telling herself Daryn was more than capable of handling whatever disaster had been brought down on them because a newbie had thought she was better than she was. Oh, and because a client had lied. If Daryn got into trouble, then she would go to *her* supervisor and if she couldn't help, there was still the salon general manager. There were layers and layers between Erica and the hair drama du jour. Part of running a successful empire meant trusting her staff to take care of business. And that meant staying out of the day-to-day issues.

Three minutes later she swore under her breath as she walked out of her office, apparently unable to be the boss she should be and let it go.

"I'm not going to meddle," she murmured to herself as she headed for the main salon. "I'm on a fact-finding mission."

She spotted the client instantly. The bright orange shoulder-length hair was hard to miss, as were the tears. Everything about the body language warned Erica the day was going to take a turn for the complicated.

She continued to the back room, where stylists mixed color. Daryn was already doing a color test on a swatch of orange hair. Next to her was a petite blonde with a blotchy face and tear-filled eyes.

"How bad is it?" Erica asked as she entered.

Daryn shrugged. "Bad. She used box color regularly and lied about it. Plus I think she switched products. See how some of the strands are lighter than the others? She wanted to go blond. Not happening. We just have to get the color close to normal and hope her hair doesn't turn to spaghetti."

Erica glanced at the other stylist. "I don't believe we've met. I'm Erica Sawyer."

The blonde—maybe twenty-five and shaking—swallowed before she spoke. "I'm Poppy. I know who you are."

"That's gratifying. What's your level?"

Stylists were rated on a scale from one to six. Those fresh out of beauty school started as associates, aka assistants. They washed hair, held the foil, swept the floor. Every few days they were allowed to work on a client, supervised. If they were smart, they listened and learned. If they weren't, they complained about the drudge work, then quit.

Depending on their enthusiasm and talent, they graduated to a level-one stylist in six to nine months and began developing their own client list. If they worked hard, followed the company rules and gave a damn about their career, they could quickly work their way up the food chain. Somewhere between levels two and three, stylists at Twisted were clearing a hundred thousand a year. Once a stylist hit level four, he or she was given an associate of their own.

"I'm a two," Poppy said, staring at the floor.

"How many color correction classes have you attended?"

Poppy seemed to shrink a little. "I haven't." She raised her head and looked at Erica. "She swore she hadn't colored her hair before."

"Did it feel like virgin hair? Did you believe her?"

Poppy slumped. "No, so I asked again."

"And she lied again."

"I thought it would be okay." Tears poured down her cheeks. "I'm so sorry, Ms. Sawyer. Please. I'm sorry. I love my job here. I messed up but I can make it right."

"No, you can't and that's the problem." Erica turned her attention to Daryn. "Can you fix this?"

Daryn grinned. "I'm offended you have to ask." Her humor faded. "I'm booked all afternoon and this is going to take a while."

"When's your next client due?"

Daryn glanced at the large clock on the wall. "Ten minutes. It's an easy cut and color. Just roots. We did highlights last time. Her hair's in a classic bob." Daryn jerked her head toward Poppy. "She could do it."

"You're very trusting."

"I don't understand," Poppy said. "You want me to take Daryn's client?"

"Right now I want you to stay here. Once we figure this out, you can stop by my office at the end of your shift."

Erica swung by reception to request notification when Daryn's client checked in, then she returned to the main salon and walked over to the orange-haired liar.

The woman was in her early forties, pretty enough. Her Botox wasn't great and whoever had injected her lips had added way too much filler, but her jawline was good.

Erica introduced herself to the woman, who stared at her blankly.

"Oh my God! You're Erica Sawyer."

Oh, good. A fan—or at least someone who was starstruck. That would help the situation.

Erica leaned against the counter and shook her head. "Well, we messed up, didn't we?"

The tears returned as the client stared at herself in the mirror. "I can't believe what happened. That girl—I didn't get her name—said she knew what she was doing. Obviously not. I'm surprised you let someone like her work here. I thought Twisted was better than that."

Erica shifted behind the client and lightly touched her hair. "How long have you been coloring your own hair?"

"What?" The woman flushed. "I would never do that."

"The problem isn't the color so much as the minerals some companies use. I could explain the chemistry, but as you can see, box color doesn't play well with others. When Poppy went to lift what she'd been told was virgin hair, the minerals revealed themselves. You must admit, it's a spectacular orange."

She rested her hands on the other woman's shoulders. "Our biggest worry is your hair falling out."

"What!" The single word came out as a shriek. Several clients turned to stare. "No. No! You can't let that happen."

The tears flowed hard and fast. "Please, help me. Okay, yes, I've been coloring my hair myself for years. I didn't think it was a big deal. I'm sorry. Just save my hair. Please."

Erica had little patience for the client. Just tell the truth. If she'd come clean, Poppy would have known she was over her head and could have rescheduled her with a more experienced stylist. End of problem.

"We're going to get you back to a more normal color," Erica said, her tone soothing. "I would suggest going a little shorter until the damage grows out. We'll send you home with some treatments that will strengthen your hair. If you're careful, in a few months, you'll be as good as new. Then we can take you from a fabulous brunette to a gorgeous blonde."

She let her expression harden. "If you color your hair before it's grown out, it will break and break until you're left with about an inch all over. Understand?"

The woman nodded. "Yes."

"Good." Erica paused. "Color correction is six hundred dollars, triple what you were quoted. Sometimes clients lie to get cheaper service, but I'm sure you'd never do that."

The woman flushed again. "No, I wouldn't. I'll pay what it costs."

Erica held her gaze in the mirror for another couple of seconds before offering a faint smile. "We'll stick with the quoted price. Daryn will be here shortly to walk you through the process. She's one of the best. You're in good hands."

Erica stopped by reception again and tagged the account so the client would only pay the original price. Hopefully she had enough class to tip Daryn well. She sent her office manager a quick note to let her know Daryn was to be fully paid for the service, then she introduced herself to Daryn's client and explained about the crisis.

"If you'd like to reschedule with Daryn, we'll get you in as soon as we can. If you're willing to take a chance on Poppy, I think you'll be happy with her work. It's totally up to you." Erica paused. "Either way, I'd like to give you a complimentary hair mask treatment. As a thank-you for understanding."

The client glanced past Erica toward the salon. She flinched.

"Is it the woman with the hideous orange hair? What happened?"

Erica smiled. "Trust me, you don't want to know. So you'll give Poppy a try?"

"Sure. Thanks. I'm looking forward to the hair mask."

"The lavender one is my favorite. I'll make sure you get that one."

"I'm excited."

Twenty minutes later Daryn was dealing with orange hair and Poppy was mixing color under another stylist's supervision. Erica retreated to her office, where she typed up notes on what had happened and sent them to her office manager.

A little after four, Erica heard a tentative knock on her door. "Come in."

A very pale and red-eyed Poppy entered. "You wanted to see me?"

Erica pointed to one of the chairs opposite hers. "How did it go with Daryn's client?"

"Good. She loved the hair mask." Poppy twisted her hands together. "I thought I could do it, you know. Before. I wasn't trying to mess up."

"You knew the client lied. You knew she'd used box color on her hair and that you haven't been trained on color correction. Did you do a color test before starting?"

Poppy stared at her lap. "No. She was in a hurry and she said it would be fine."

"And it wasn't."

"No."

"You broke several salon rules today, Poppy. Is this usual for you?"

"No. I would never..." She wiped away tears. "I love my job. I want to do better. I work hard. I just thought it was okay."

Erica leaned back in her chair. In the past couple of hours, she'd looked up the young stylist's employment record at the salon. Poppy was young and eager. She'd done well in her training and she was well-liked on the floor. Her rebooking rate was excellent and she sold a lot of product. Just as important, she excelled on social media, which brought attention to the salon.

"Do you know why salon policy prohibits talking about your personal life with clients?"

"Because it takes too much time?"

Erica offered a faint smile. "Not exactly. Clients come to Twisted for an experience. There are cheaper places for hair color and a decent cut. Oh, we're the best—that's always the goal—but we do more than excellent work. Our mission is to make every client feel important and beautiful. We brighten their day and make them feel good about themselves."

Poppy looked confused. "Okay."

"Let's say you meet a great new guy. Both you and your client are so excited for the possibilities."

Erica leaned forward. "But three months later he dumps you and you're crushed. Obviously your client cares and commiserates with you. So instead of focusing your time together on her experience, everything is about you and while your client leaves happy with her cut and color, she's not leaving feeling like we were the best part of her day."

"Because she's worried about me?"

"Exactly. It's why we suggest you talk about your client rather than about yourself. It makes things easier."

"I get that." Poppy raised her chin. "Are you going to fire me?"

"No. I'm going to demote you to a level one and send you to an intensive color seminar in three weeks. For the next three months, you'll run every color formula past a senior stylist. If you do as well as I think you should, you'll return to level two and be on track to be a color specialist. How does that sound?"

Poppy's eyes widened. She jumped to her feet and circled the desk to hug Erica.

"Thank you so much!" she said, squeezing tight. "I'll do better. I promise."

Erica stood and smiled at her. "I know you will. We all make mistakes. It's whether or not we learn from them that makes the difference."

"I'll learn so much, you'll be shocked!"

Poppy practically danced out of her office. Erica watched her go, then sat down. While she wasn't thrilled with being less than two years from fifty, she had to admit she never wanted to be as young as Poppy again.

Her phone buzzed. She glanced at the screen, smiling when she saw a text from her daughter.

I'm hanging with Jackson and A tonight. Dad's working late with clients. I'm getting takeout. Want me to get extra to bring home to you?

Erica felt the smile fade as her lips formed a tight line of disapproval. Summer wanting to spend time with her stepmother and half brother was a good thing. Her daughter had a big heart and she adored little Jackson. The annoyance of having to hear about Peter's second family was ever present, but not anything she would ever discuss with her daughter. As far as Summer was concerned, Erica lived in constant anticipation of yet more news about little Jackson and the impending arrival of his sister.

Enjoy yourself, she typed with fabricated graciousness. I'll get something on my way home. Be back by eight. You're a new driver and you shouldn't be out too late.

Oh, Mom. You're such a worrier. I'll be home by 8.

The text was followed by several heart emojis.

Erica returned them, then set her phone on her desk and

shifted her attention back to her computer. Her daughter was thriving and happy, and a business crisis had been averted. So far it was turning out to be a very good day.

2

"When are you due?"

Allison Jenkins smiled at her customer as she continued to scan groceries.

"Three months."

"Your first?"

"Second. My oldest is eighteen months."

The other woman, a fiftysomething with a kind expression, winced. "That's close together. You won't get much sleep for the next few years."

Allison laughed. "I haven't been sleeping for the past two, so I probably won't notice."

Yes, she was having her kids close together, but she was already thirty-four. Through a series of circumstances no one could have foreseen, she hadn't been able to even think about having a baby until the last few years. Now that she was married to a great guy, she wasn't putting off anything.

"It's a girl," she added happily. "We're naming her Bethany."

"Beautiful. Congratulations."

"Thanks."

Allison finished ringing up the order, then waited while the credit card payment processed before handing over the receipt. Thankfully she had a brief lull in her line. She took a second to try to stretch out her back. Only twenty more minutes until her shift ended, then she would collect Jackson and head home. Peter, her husband, had said he would be in client meetings until after seven. Summer, her stepdaughter, had mentioned dropping by with takeout. Most sixteen-year-olds preferred to hang out with their friends, but Summer was a sweet young woman who adored her half brother and looked for reasons to spend time with him. As Allison adored her, she was happy for the company. Not to mention the takeout. With a toddler and another on the way, money was tight. Plus, their rental house was being sold by the landlord, meaning they were saving to move right before the baby was due. Takeout was a treat.

Allison clocked out right on time and started the thirty-minute drive to pick up Jackson from his day care. Halfway there, she pulled into a gas station. She inserted her ATM card at the pump and waited for the machine to okay her purchase. Seconds later the keypad buzzed at her while displaying a single word. "Declined."

Allison frowned, then tried the card again. The keypad buzzed a second time. That didn't make any sense, she thought, knowing there was plenty of money in their checking account. She put in the credit card she tried never to use and it went through just fine.

After making a mental note to call the bank, she filled her tank. She pulled into the day care parking lot at her usual time and went to collect Jackson.

Her son spotted her instantly and beamed. He was a happy, friendly kid who liked everyone and was rarely moody. He'd been a cheerful baby and so far only had very mild toddler tantrums. She could only hope she was just as lucky with Bethany.

"Hey, you," Liz, her friend and manager of the co-op day care, called. "Ready to take your little man home?"

"I am. How'd he do?"

Liz pressed a hand to her chest. "He was perfect. I wish they were all as good as him."

The report wasn't a surprise—Jackson did well with the other toddlers. He wasn't yet fully playing with them, but he enjoyed the company and often watched the older kids doing things together.

Allison signed out her son, then crouched so she was at his level, her arms open wide.

"How's my favorite boy?" she asked as he flung himself at her. "Mama!"

He was warm and sturdy. His little hands held on tight. Love filled her, warming her from the inside. This, she thought fiercely. This child, this moment. She'd been so blessed.

He stepped back and patted her belly. "Bethany here."

"She is. Just three more months."

Three long months, she thought, knowing the worst of the pregnancy was still ahead of her. At least for now, she was able to sleep well and her back only hurt on days she worked at the grocery store. But before she knew it she would ache all the time and be counting the minutes until her baby was born.

The quick drive home was uneventful. She parked in the driveway of their small rental house before releasing Jackson from his car seat. Once they were inside, she changed his diaper then got out his favorite blocks and a toy bucket. She sat on the floor, across from him, and put the blocks in the bucket. Once Jackson was busy with the game of taking them out and throwing them on the carpet, she went to the banking app on her phone to find several alerts.

She opened the first one and stared in disbelief. She'd heard the phrase "She felt her heart stop beating" but had never experienced the sensation herself until this very second.

Your bank accounts have been frozen.

There was more writing and a phone number to call, but all she could see were those six horrible words.

Frozen? What did that mean? How could an account be frozen? Was that why her ATM card hadn't worked?

Her stomach lurched as chills rushed through her. She felt herself starting to shake as she struggled to call the number on the notice. A recording walked her through the process of verifying her identity, then she had to wait seven minutes to get a representative.

While music played and a voice kept saying, "Due to unexpected call volumes, wait times are longer than usual," she helped Jackson stack blocks and told herself there had to be a mistake. Everything would be fine. If the representative couldn't help her, then Peter would handle everything when he got home.

Her husband was a numbers guy. He had his own accounting business. He knew about finance and investing and doing taxes. He was the smartest man she'd ever known—and he was college educated. No one in her family had ever gone. In the small town where she'd grown up, money had been tight for nearly every family she'd known, and going to college wasn't something she and her friends ever considered. In her circles, only those lucky enough to earn sports scholarships or smart enough to be a superbrainiac went. Everyone else got by learning on the job or maybe by going to trade school or into a family business.

But Peter was different. His meeting tonight was with a potential new client. He was always doing things like that—finding new clients and growing the business. His now thriving company had been decimated by his divorce. Not only had his horrible first wife, Erica, taken her business away, but she'd bad-mouthed him all over town. He'd had to start from practically nothing. But he'd done it because Peter always did what was right. He worked hard and he loved her. Of that she was sure.

"This is Mia at Northwest Bank of the Pacific. How can I help you?"

Allison clutched her phone tightly. "I'm having a problem

with my account. I have a notice that it's frozen. I don't even know what that means. What's going on?"

Despite her fear and sense of panic, she was careful to keep her voice calm. Jackson played happily next to her and she didn't want to upset him.

"All right, Mrs. Jenkins, give me a second and I'll—"

She paused. "Oh. Well, yes, you're right. Your accounts are frozen. There's not a lot of information here. It seems the Treasury Department notified our bank about an investigation. That's all I know. If you want more details, you should talk to your branch manager."

"I don't understand. What are you saying?"

"Every account you have with us is frozen and until we're told to release the money, you won't have access to it."

What? No! "You can't do that. It's our money. Our paychecks. We need that money for rent and food. You can't just take it from us."

The customer service representative's voice tightened. "We haven't taken it, ma'am. The accounts are going to be locked until they're released by the government. That's all I know. I'm sorry. You might want to talk to a lawyer."

A lawyer? Like she had one on retainer? "I need to get groceries and diapers. How do I pay for that?"

The representative sounded uncomfortable. "I can't answer that. There's nothing I can do. I'm sorry."

Sorry? She was sorry? Allison fought tears. This wasn't happening—it couldn't be. "But it's our money," she repeated. "You have no right to keep it from us."

"I'm afraid we do. When there's illegal activity, we have to—"

"Illegal activity?" Allison's voice came out in a shriek.

Jackson stared at her wide-eyed. "Mama?"

She forced a smile. "I'm okay, sweetie. Sorry. It's fine."

"Talk to your branch manager," the representative said. "I really can't help you with this. I'm sorry."

The line went dead.

Allison dropped the phone on the carpet. She was beyond scared. Her stomach roiled, and her breathing was shallow. Terror gripped her. Their money was gone? Maybe not permanently, but it was unavailable now? That couldn't be legal. Everything the representative had told her had to be wrong.

She grabbed her phone and pushed the button to call Peter. He wouldn't want to be disturbed while with a new client but this couldn't wait. Her call went directly to voicemail.

"Peter, it's me. Call me as soon as you get this. Something's really wrong. Our bank accounts are frozen." She brushed away tears. "Peter, call me."

She followed the call with a text urging him to call her right away. Once it was sent, she waited for the small "Delivered" to appear, but it didn't. Had Peter turned off his phone? He never did. He would silence it for a meeting, but that was all.

"Mama?"

She smiled at Jackson. "Let's go play in the backyard for a few minutes."

Anything to occupy herself until Peter called.

She rose to her feet and helped Jackson to his. Her stomach continued to churn. Her heart thundered in her chest and fear clutched her so tight, she could barely breathe. She couldn't begin to imagine what was going on with the bank. Nothing made sense. Obviously there had been a mistake, but until she talked to Peter, she wasn't sure what to do.

She and Jackson took turns chasing each other. She helped him roll the big ball they kept for him. After a few minutes he stopped and looked at her.

"Hungry now."

"I know, sweetie. I'll start dinner."

She spoke automatically only to realize she wasn't making dinner. Her stepdaughter was bringing takeout.

She pulled out her phone, trying to remember when Summer

had said she would stop by. Maybe there was time to tell her not to bother. No way could Allison make pleasant conversation while freaking out about what was or wasn't happening with the bank.

But before she could text her stepdaughter, she had an incoming call from an unfamiliar number.

"Let it be the bank!" she murmured. "Hello?"

"Will you accept a collect call from SeaTac Federal Detention Center?"

The voice was mechanical, followed by a pause, then "Peter Jenkins," in Peter's voice.

"What?"

At first her mind went blank as she tried to process the information. Federal Detention Center? Was that like jail?

The mechanical voice began again. "Will you accept—"

She gripped her phone, tears burning in her eyes. "Yes. Yes! Peter? Peter? Are you there?"

There were several clicks, then a message stating "This call is being recorded" followed by a hoarse, "Allison?"

She dropped to her knees, unmindful of the damp grass. "Peter? Where are you? What's going on? I tried to call. Our bank accounts are frozen. They have it all and when I called, they wouldn't tell me anything. Peter?"

"I'm sorry." His voice was ragged as if he'd been crying. Which wasn't possible. Her husband never cried.

"I'm so sorry," he continued. "God, I never wanted this to happen. I wanted to take care of you."

Jackson tugged on her sleeve. "Hungry, Mama."

"I know," she said. "Just a minute." She shifted away from him. "Why did you call me collect? Where are you?"

She heard the sound of a sob. "I've been arrested. I'm sorry. I thought I had more time. This isn't—" His voice crackled. "Allison, listen to me. I'm going to figure this out. I love you so much and I would never hurt you."

She heard a loud buzzing followed by the sensation of the

world falling away. She had a feeling that if she'd been standing, she would have fainted.

"Arrested?" She could barely speak the word, let alone comprehend it. "You're in jail?"

"Yes. I'm working on getting a lawyer. It's going to take a bit."

"But why? You didn't—" She tried to make sense of what he was saying. "Did you commit a crime?"

"No. It's a misunderstanding. Things got complicated and there was some confusion with a few accounts. I'll get it straightened out. You have to believe me."

She did. He was her husband and she loved him. He'd never been anything but honest with her, with their money, his business. "But you're in jail and the banks have frozen our accounts."

"I know. I'm sorry about that."

Sorry? That was it? "Peter, I have to pay rent and buy food. We're nearly out of diapers. How am I supposed to do that?" She touched her belly where Bethany had decided to practice her soccer kicks. "I'm pregnant. Are you telling me you're in jail and I'm pregnant?"

Her voice rose with every word until she was nearly shrieking. In the background all she heard was Peter saying he was sorry.

"I'll call you tomorrow," he said. "I'll have answers by then, I swear. I didn't think this would happen so fast. I wasn't ready. But I'll make it up to you. I love you, Allison. You and Jackson and Bethany. You're my world. I'll make this right."

And then he was gone. She stared at her phone, unable to process what was happening. None of this could be real. She had to—

The sound of Jackson's sobs broke through to her. Her son stood in front of her crying and pointing at her. She touched her face and realized she was crying, too. She hadn't known. Obviously her shrieking and tears had frightened him, which made two of them.

She lumbered to her feet, then picked up Jackson and held him tight.

"I'm sorry," she said, walking back into the house. "I didn't mean to scare you. It's okay. We're okay."

A lie, but what else was there to say to her eighteen-month-old?

In the small kitchen, she set him on the counter, then lightly touched his nose.

"What's that?"

Jackson stared at her, wide-eyed. "Dada."

Her body tensed. "Your dad's busy. He won't be home for a while."

Jackson shook his head, then pointed toward the front door. "Dada." He drew in a breath for a full-throated howl. "Dada!"

She reached for him, but he shrank back.

"Dada!"

"He's not here. He's not coming home." Not tonight and who knew how many nights after that.

The truth of that statement slammed into her. Peter wasn't coming home because he was in jail. He'd been charged with some crime that was serious enough to cause their bank accounts to be frozen. He'd been arrested and she had no idea why. He'd talked about getting a lawyer. Could he do that from jail? What happened after that? The only thing she knew about people going to jail and to trial was from TV and movies. That sort of thing simply didn't happen to anyone she knew.

The panic returned, along with fear and trouble breathing. No! she thought frantically. She couldn't have a panic attack. She had to take care of Jackson. She was fine. She could breathe.

She made herself consciously inhale and exhale, but the sensation of the air going anywhere but her lungs only got stronger. She was alone with a toddler, she was pregnant, and she had no money or way to talk to her husband. She didn't even know where he was. Okay, yes, SeaTac Federal Detention Center, but where was that? And while she wanted to believe this was as bad as it was going to get, she was afraid it would get worse.

What was she supposed to do? How could she protect herself and Jackson while helping Peter? Should she call a lawyer? Should—

Jackson began to cry again. As she gasped to suck in air, she wrapped her arms around him. He hung on to her, sobbing so hard his little body shook. She gave in to her own tears, crying just as loudly.

Ten more seconds, she promised herself, then she would pull it together. At least the act of crying had eased her panicky feeling.

She and Jackson clung to each other. Allison told herself she'd gotten through worse, but nothing in her past had prepared her for this.

"It's me!"

Allison looked up in time to see her stepdaughter walking into the house. It was a straight shot from the front door, through the open living room to the kitchen—something she'd always liked about the small rental, although less so now. There was nowhere to hide, no way to keep Summer from seeing her and Jackson.

The sixteen-year-old's smile faded instantly. She hurried forward, set the takeout on the table, then reached for Jackson.

"Summy!"

He held out his arms as she pulled him close. Summer rubbed his back, but her attention stayed on Allison.

"What's wrong?"

Allison wiped her face and did her best to fake a smile. "Nothing. It's nothing. Just, you know, ah, pregnancy hormones. I started crying, then he started crying." She waved her hand. "You know how it goes."

Summer, tall and slim in that way of teenage girls, stared at her intently. "You're lying." Her tone was flat. "Tell me what's wrong."

Allison had always admired Summer's honesty and fearlessness when it came to confronting emotions. Today, however, she found that characteristic incredibly inconvenient.

"We're fine."

Summer's eye roll told Allison she hadn't been convincing, but honest to God, she was too exhausted to try again.

"Look, this isn't a good time for us," she said bluntly. "Why don't you take the food and go home? I'll make something for Jackson and we'll have an early night."

"That's not happening."

Summer carried Jackson to the bathroom. Seconds later Allison heard running water.

"Let the water get a little warm," Summer said, her voice cheerful. "Uh-huh. We *are* washing our hands together. This is fun. Are you hungry? I think you're going to love dinner."

Obviously the teen wasn't leaving anytime soon. Allison gave in to the inevitable. She blew her nose, then washed her own hands. Once that was done, she unpacked the meal. Summer had gone to their favorite Mexican place and ordered for what seemed like twenty. There were a dozen chicken street tacos, along with a huge salad with chopped vegetables and avocado, and sliced oranges on the side. One container was full of rice, another, pinto beans. There were two trays of enchiladas, and the quesadilla Jackson liked.

Summer returned with Jackson on her hip. "Someone's hungry."

Allison tried to smile. "You or your brother?"

"Probably both of us."

Summer set Jackson in his high chair, then collected plates from the cupboard. She put chicken from a taco on a plate, then tore a quesadilla wedge into small pieces. She added a few of the diced raw vegetables and two orange slices.

When she'd placed the food in front of Jackson, she glanced at Allison. "Did you want to get his milk?"

"What? Oh, right. Sure."

Allison poured whole milk into a sippy cup and gave it to her son. She grabbed a bottle of some weird fruit-coconut drink that Summer kept in their fridge and handed it to her stepdaughter. She poured herself water as Summer stuck the enchiladas in the refrigerator.

"Those will heat up great for lunch or dinner tomorrow."

Allison couldn't imagine ever feeling well enough to eat, but nodded. "Thank you. I appreciate it."

At least that part was true, she thought. Summer was always like that—bringing extra food or little gifts. She was thoughtful and kind.

When Allison had first started dating Peter, he'd told her horror stories about his cold, cruel ex-wife. The details had been so vivid, she'd been terrified to meet his daughter. But Summer was apparently nothing like her mother. From the first second, she'd been so sweet and caring. She'd been thrilled when Allison had gotten pregnant and even more delighted when baby Jackson had been born. She was the perfect stepdaughter. Peter was rightfully proud of her. He—

Without warning, the tears returned. She tried to blink them away but they flowed down her cheeks. She mumbled something and raced the few feet to the bedroom she and Peter shared. But before she could close the door, Summer was right there next to her.

"There *is* something," the teen said, her voice low. "I knew it." Worry darkened her brown eyes. "What is it? Are you feeling all right?" She went pale. "Is it Bethany?"

"It's not the baby."

Jackson called out. "Summy! Eat!"

"He shouldn't be alone," Summer said. "But after dinner, you're going to tell me what's going on."

Allison nodded, not sure how she was going to come up with a convincing lie. And if she didn't, she was going to have to tell Summer that her father was in jail and she didn't have a clue as to why.

3

Erica checked her calendar, then added her availability to her email. While she no longer saw clients, she refused to let her hair skills atrophy. In addition to attending classes the salon offered the stylists, she did the hair of several employees every month. Between the four salons she owned, it took her a while to work through everyone, but she kept at it. Not only was it a good way for her to stay current with trends, but the time she spent with her staff also allowed her to get to know them and them to feel more connected with her. In the next few weeks, she would do a cut and color for a massage therapist and a nail tech. A level-four stylist was getting hair extensions. For that appointment, Erica would act as the assistant. While she was certified in hair extensions, she hadn't done them enough to be good at them.

Most months she managed to get to around four employees, but this time of year, that was impossible. Summer's softball season was starting and that meant at least twenty games in less than three months. Erica did her best to get to every game, so the season seriously ate into her work time. Still, she wanted to be supportive and that meant showing up every single time.

Her calendar updated, she closed her computer, then glanced at the clock. Nearly eight. Summer should be getting home soon. Her daughter wasn't usually one to ignore curfew.

Erica prowled her home office, more restless than usual. If

she was by herself in the evening and wasn't working, she often didn't know what to do. Watching a movie alone wasn't very fun and while she read most nights, that was more of a before-bed activity.

She needed a hobby, she thought for possibly the eighty-seventh time—although she had no idea what. Crafts had never been her thing. She supposed she could text her mother and see if she wanted company. Mara lived in the carriage house at the rear of the property. Not that it was likely her mother was home. Mara was the most social of the Sawyer women with a large cadre of friends and a rotating selection of men with whom she did the wild thing on an uncomfortably regular basis. Erica often tried to tell herself she should be happy her seventy-year-old mother had a healthy sex life. While on an intellectual basis, she was okay with it, emotionally, she was still a little grossed out by knowing her parent had sex. She supposed there were some things a child never outgrew.

She walked toward the family room. Once she knew Summer was safely home, she would take a bath and maybe give herself a minifacial. That would fill the rest of the evening. Tomorrow, she would spend some serious time thinking about a hobby. Or making a list of female acquaintances she thought might be possible friends. A transition she frequently found awkward and uncomfortable.

Peter had always teased her about being slow to warm up to people. No, she corrected silently. At first he'd teased her. At the end of their relationship he'd accused her of being a heartless bitch who refused to trust anyone.

"Not going there," she murmured to herself. While she was long over the man, thinking about the end of their marriage always depressed her. She'd come to terms with the divorce, but even after four years, she still didn't know what had gone wrong, nor could she understand the speed with which everything had changed between them. From her point of view, one day they'd been perfectly happy together and the next he'd told her he wanted a divorce. When she managed to recover from the shock enough to ask him why, he'd claimed that he no longer loved her, that he found her sexually repugnant and regretted every second he'd spent in her presence. But not to worry. His loathing was quickly changing to indifference.

They'd been standing in the main bath. She remembered how the chandelier over the large tub had almost created a halo over his head. Then he'd crossed to his vanity and pulled out a drawer. He'd tossed a prescription bottle toward her.

"I have to take these to get it up," he'd said coldly. "I'm not willing to do that anymore."

He'd walked out then, leaving her staring after him, unable to grasp what had just happened. She'd picked up the bottle and read the label. Viagra.

Shame flooded her, then and now. But with the passage of time, Erica was better at shaking it off. Peter had changed. He'd fallen out of love with her. Her job had been to accept that and move on, which she had. The cruelty wasn't her fault or her responsibility. While *that* lesson had taken longer, she'd been determined to learn it.

"Why am I even thinking about the man?" she asked herself, not that she had an answer. She supposed it was because Summer was spending the evening with him and his family, as she often did.

Summer burst into the house from the garage.

"Mom! Mom! Where are you?"

Erica heard the tension in her daughter's voice and hurried toward the kitchen.

"I'm here. What's wrong?" Her chest tightened as a thousand possible disasters filled her mind. "Were you in an accident?"

Her daughter came running around the corner and barreled toward her. She'd been crying. Her face was blotchy and her eyes red.

She dropped her bag on the floor and flung herself at Erica. "Oh, Mom, it's so awful. We have to do something."

Erica grabbed her daughter's arms and shifted back enough to see her face. "What are you talking about? Are you all right?"

"I'm fine. It's not me. It's Dad and Allison. Dad's in jail!"

Erica stared at her daughter. "What are you talking about? Peter can't be in jail." It was a ridiculous thought. He was an ordinary person. He rarely drank, wasn't much of a gambler and ran an accounting business, for heaven's sake. Accountants weren't wild enough to go to jail.

Summer twisted free of Erica's hold. "He is! It's horrible." Tears pooled in her eyes. "Allison was so upset, which freaked out Jackson. Mom, it's awful. The accounts are frozen and there's no money and Allison couldn't eat. She's scared and I am, too. We have to *do* something!"

Summer wasn't making sense. Erica pointed to the stools at the island. "Sit down and take a breath. Then start at the beginning."

"Mo-om! You're not listening!"

"That's because you're not making sense. Please sit down. I'm going to listen, but you have to calm down a little so I can understand what you're saying."

Summer groaned but did as she was told. She slumped on a stool, the ratty flannel shirt she wore as a light jacket hanging off one shoulder.

Erica allowed herself a second to lament, yet again, that her only child had no interest in anything related to her appearance. Aside from showering and wearing sunscreen, Summer did nothing to take care of her skin. She eschewed makeup of any kind, dressed in jeans and sweatshirts in the winter and shorts and T-shirts in the summer, and refused to do more than tie her long hair back in a ponytail or braid. She was a beautiful young woman but acted as if she were invisible. Or indifferent.

Peter's doing, Erica thought grimly. A few years before the

divorce Peter had started dismissing Erica's business as frivolous and superficial. At first the comments had been teasing but over time they'd gotten more pointed. Eventually they'd taken root.

She held in a sigh—yet something else not to think about.

"You saw Allison," she prompted her daughter. "She was upset."

Summer nodded vigorously. "They were both crying and she tried to tell me it was nothing, but I knew something had happened. She said it was pregnancy hormones." The tears returned. "She couldn't eat, Mom. Allison always does what they say to take care of the baby. She's a really good mom."

Erica told herself to ignore the admiration in her daughter's voice. It was nice that she got along with her stepmother. Erica should be proud of her, and she would be. Later.

Summer detailed how Allison had tried to hide a problem, but after Jackson went to bed, she'd confessed the truth. Peter had been arrested and the family bank accounts had been frozen, leaving Allison with no money and no husband.

"She's pregnant, Mom. Bethany is due in like three months. She already works two jobs, but she can't stay at the grocery store much longer because it's too hard on her. And now Dad's in jail and we're all so scared."

Erica took a seat as she tried to process the information. Peter in jail? She couldn't imagine it. He wasn't a stellar businessman but he wasn't dishonest. All right, he'd taken money from her company, but she'd assumed that had been more about bitterness and wanting to hurt her than because he was a criminal.

"She doesn't know what's happening or how to contact him," Summer continued, pushing a strand of dark hair off her face. "She's alone and pregnant and there's no one to take care of her."

Erica tried not to show her annoyance at Summer's insistence on protecting her stepmother.

"Allison is very capable and together," she said, her tone

soothing. "She'll figure it out. I know this sounds awful, but it's probably not as bad as it seems. This has to be a misunderstanding. Your father isn't a criminal. He can get out on bail."

Summer wiped her cheeks. "How? There's no money. Everything is frozen by the bank. I didn't even know they could do that. It's not right. She has to buy food and diapers. They're going to starve, Mom!"

"Not today. Let's give Allison some time to figure out what's going on."

"But she doesn't know how. She's not like you, Mom. You can do stuff like that. Or Killion can. Please. She's so scared."

Erica held in a sigh. Obviously Summer wasn't going to let it go.

"I'll talk to Killion," she said, hoping she didn't sound as grudging as she felt.

Summer pushed off the stool and hugged her. "You're the best! Thanks, Mom. It's just Allison is all alone and Dad's in jail and I don't know what to think."

Erica nodded. "It's a lot, but we'll figure it out. Allison will be fine. You'll see."

"I hope so." Summer picked up her backpack. "You'll come talk to me after you call Killion?"

"I will."

She waited until her daughter had gone upstairs, then pulled her phone out of her pocket and scrolled through her contacts.

"It's me, Erica," she said when Killion answered.

He chuckled. "I have you in my contact list, Erica. I know that it's you."

She smiled. "I'm happy to hear that."

She liked Killion. He was a good guy—successful, low-key emotionally. He worked hard and liked that she did the same. Trust had come slowly, after her divorce. She'd waited nearly two years before going out with a man. Her first forays into the dating scene had been a disaster, so she'd given up on the idea, only to meet Killion a few months later. While theirs wasn't a conventional relationship, she enjoyed having him in her life.

"I need your help with something," she said slowly. "Summer came home nearly hysterical from dinner with her stepmother."

She detailed what her daughter had told her.

"Your ex-husband is in jail?" He sounded more amused than shocked.

"Yes, there is an interesting karmic element, but Summer is worried about Allison and her father, so I'm trying to get some information. I don't even know where to start. I thought you might have some ideas."

"Of course."

She heard him typing.

"He's being held in SeaTac."

"By the airport? There's a jail?"

"He's in federal custody. Let me make some calls. I'll get back to you within the hour."

"Thank you, Killion. I appreciate the help."

"Of course."

She went upstairs and told Summer what he'd said. Her daughter was sitting on her bed, phone in hand. Her eyes widened.

"Dad really is in jail? I was hoping Allison was wrong. What happened?"

"I don't know, but we'll find out. I'll let you know as soon as I hear from Killion."

She went back to her home office. As she waited, she thought about texting her mother, but she was fairly sure Mara was out with one of her male friends. So she played computer games until the phone rang thirty minutes later.

"He's been arrested on several charges, including money laundering and wire fraud."

"What?" Her voice was more of a yelp than she'd expected. She cleared her throat. "Are you sure?"

"Yes. There's also something about threatening the police with a gun, but I can't get specifics on that."

"Peter doesn't own a gun." He never had. "Threatening the police?"

"That's what I was told. Someone in his office tipped off the FBI about illegal activity and the FBI got in touch with the Secret Service."

"Why? He didn't threaten the president, did he?"

Killion chuckled. "They're part of Treasury."

As in the Department of Treasury? "None of this sounds right."

"More charges are pending. I'm guessing they want him to flip on a bigger fish. I hope he has a good lawyer."

"This can't be true. Peter isn't the criminal type. All of this sounds terrible. Did I mention the bank has frozen all of their accounts?"

"Given the charges, I'm not surprised."

"But half the money belongs to Allison. Shouldn't she be able to access it?"

"The government doesn't work that way. Plus banks tend to overreact at the first sign of trouble."

"It doesn't seem fair."

"They would tell you if he hadn't broken the law, he wouldn't be in this mess in the first place."

Erica nodded slowly. "You're right, of course, but I still can't take it all in. None of this feels real. Peter was never ambitious. I can't imagine him putting together a plan to steal or whatever and then executing it."

"I doubt he was in it alone."

"You think he's working with someone?"

"Or for someone."

Peter, a criminal? "I still can't believe it."

"Imagine how the wife feels."

Not anything Erica wanted to think about. "She'll be fine."

"As long as Summer thinks so. What are you going to tell her?"

"I genuinely have no idea." She sighed. "Thank you, Killion. I appreciate the information."

"Anytime."

He hung up. She tucked her phone into her pocket before heading down the hall. Just outside her daughter's open door, she paused, still not sure what to say.

Summer jumped to her feet as soon as she saw her. "What did he say?"

"He doesn't know much. Your father is being held in a facility in SeaTac. There are several charges. I don't know the specifics."

Summer's brown eyes widened. "I can't believe it."

"Me, either. None of this sounds right. I was with your dad over ten years. He's not a criminal."

"What are we going to do?"

We weren't going to do anything, she thought grimly. "You can tell Allison what Killion found out. I'm sure your dad is already talking to a lawyer."

"How is he supposed to pay for one?"

An excellent question. "He can't be the first person this has happened to. The lawyer will take him on with an agreement they'll get paid when the accounts are released. I'm still having trouble believing this isn't all a big misunderstanding."

Especially the part about Peter pulling a gun on police. He just wasn't the type.

"But we have to help!"

"We don't know what the problem is. Try not to panic. We'll know more in a few days."

Summer drew in a breath. "You're right. It's just hard not to freak out."

"I know. This is difficult." She hugged her daughter. "Are you going to be able to sleep? I know you're worried but the season starts soon. You need your sleep so you don't let down the team."

Because the team mattered.

"I'll be okay," her daughter murmured. "Thanks, Mom. And thank Killion for me. I'm going to text Allison right now."

Erica nodded and left. When she was in her own room, she shut the door and turned on the TV. What a mess, she thought as she walked to the bathroom. Thank God it wasn't her problem.

4

Allison showed up at ten to six for her morning shift at the day care co-op. She hadn't slept much the night before. Between what Summer had told her and the worry haunting her, she'd been unable to relax. Telling herself to rest for the sake of the baby hadn't helped.

She couldn't wrap her mind around what had happened. Her husband, the man she loved and trusted and lived with and had children with, was in jail. He was being charged with crimes. Peter!

Worse, she didn't know what to do. She had no life experiences to fall back on, no one she could ask. She kept thinking she should talk to a lawyer, but how would she find one, let alone pay him or her? She wasn't the kind of person who was supposed to need a lawyer.

"Just focus on being here," she told herself as she got Jackson out of his car seat. He was all smiles, excited to spend the day with people he knew.

She walked inside, Jackson grasping her hand as he toddled along with her.

The bright yellow building was a converted house in eastern Kirkland. The yard, front and back, was completely fenced. Tall trees provided shade in the summer and all the plants were nontoxic. There were plenty of toys on the huge covered patio.

Artificial turf meant nearly year-round play, even in Seattle's rainy winter months.

Inside, the twenty-four-hundred-square-foot house had been converted to day care paradise where kids were segregated by age and ability. There was a room for the infants and babies, with several changing stations and an area with thick mats for crawling time.

Around ten months, students went into the middle group, with toys, scheduled naps and story time. At about three and a half, toddlers transitioned to pre-K with even more socialization and some early learning.

The kitchen had been modified for the kids. The children ate in shifts with the meals catered by a local grocery store deli that provided child-friendly, organic when possible, meals and snacks.

But the real appeal of the day care, at least for Allison, was the hybrid co-op model they used. Parents could pay the hefty monthly fee, just like anywhere else. Or one or both parents could work as a caretaker in the day care. For every hour worked, you earned two hours of day care.

Parents who chose the latter option were vetted, just like any other employee, and had to complete a comprehensive online program. Once done, they signed up for shifts at the day care a month in advance so Liz, the manager, could have plenty of staff on hand.

Allison had been working in the day care since Jackson was a baby. She spent her mornings there, then went to her afternoon job, clerking at a grocery store. It was the best of both worlds—Jackson had quality day care that she didn't have to pay for, plus she had a regular, albeit small paycheck from the grocery store. She always worked more hours at the co-op than she needed, so was able to bank the time for a rare afternoon off.

She greeted the other staff member on duty as she signed in her son. Once he was settled, she clocked in for her shift. Now that she was over six months pregnant, she mostly worked with the babies. Feeding and rocking babies and changing diapers was a lot easier on her body than herding energetic four-year-olds, although she still did story hour a few times a week.

She stored her handbag, wishing she could keep her phone with her, but Liz had a firm no-cell-phones rule. Hopefully she wouldn't miss a call from Peter. After washing her hands, she slipped on an apron, then went to check in the first of the infants to arrive.

By seven thirty she had five babies, from six weeks to seven months. The former, a little girl, had been reluctantly handed over by her sobbing mother.

"I'm not ready to go back to work," she said, wiping away tears. "But my maternity leave ended last week. I asked for more time but my boss is a heartless bastard."

Allison had offered as much comfort as she could before taking baby Sabine. "She'll be fine."

"I know, but I still want to call every hour."

"Absolutely."

The day care also offered remote camera access through a secure server.

She got Sabine settled in her bassinet and checked on the other four. Little Michael, nearly seven months, was going to need some playtime. He was on the cusp of crawling. Jessie, her partner for her shift, tickled Michael's tummy, making him laugh and wave his hands and feet.

"Want me to play with this one?" she asked, glancing at Allison's large belly. "It's easier for me to get on and off the floor."

"I hate to give up the fun, but getting to my feet is a challenge these days." In her current condition, she was better suited for sit-down duties.

The first hour of settling everyone helped distract her from the disaster that was her personal life. A little before nine, Liz, her boss, stopped by.

"Everyone happy?" she asked.

Allison had baby Sabine in her arms. Jessie had taken Michael to the young toddler play area and the other infants were sleeping. She looked at her friend-slash-boss, prepared to say everything was fine. Instead she found herself fighting tears.

Liz immediately hurried toward her. "What's wrong?"

Allison struggled for control. "It's personal, not work. Can we talk on my break?"

"Of course. Come get me when you're ready." Liz touched her shoulder. "Are you okay? Do you want to go home?"

"No. Being here is better." Not only was caring for the babies a wonderful distraction, but also she wanted to bank as much day care time as possible. Who knew what horrible thing was going to happen next?

Once it was time for her break, Allison hurried into her friend's office and closed the door, then took a seat.

Liz's expression was concerned. "Tell me," she said gently. "I've been worried."

"I don't know what to say or how to explain." Allison drew in a breath as she tried to figure out how to talk about what was happening. "I just found out yesterday and it was a shock. I mean I..." She pressed her lips together before blurting, "Peter's in jail."

Liz's eyes widened. "What? No. He can't be. Your Peter?"

"I know it seems impossible. I can't believe it myself." Allison quickly filled her in on the details of the last eighteen or so hours. "I don't know what to do or who to talk to. I'm scared and Peter and I barely had any time on the phone so it's all a mess. And with my bank accounts frozen, there's no money. I can't even call him to ask what to do. I have to wait for him to call me."

"Money laundering? What is that? Taking money from crimes and somehow making it legitimate?"

"I guess." Allison hadn't thought much about it. "Peter wouldn't do that. He's an accountant. His clients trust him. He doesn't lie. He's a good husband and father." The tears returned. "He loves me."

"You must be so scared. How can I help?"

Allison wanted to ask for a loan, but didn't think that was a good idea. Liz was her friend but also her boss. That meant there was also a line between them.

"I'm okay. It's good to just talk about what's happening. This is so not what I'm used to in my life. I've never known anyone arrested."

"Me, either. You might want to talk to a lawyer."

Allison nodded because on the surface it was good advice… assuming one ignored the fact that SHE HAD NO MONEY! But she kept the shrieking inside her head, where it was much less scary for her boss.

"I'm thinking that, too," she murmured with a confidence she didn't feel. "I need to eat and get back to work. Thanks for listening."

"Of course. Anytime. And I meant what I said. Let me know if I can help."

"I will. Thanks."

Allison returned to the babies. After changing a couple of diapers and feeding one of her charges, she settled in for some serious cuddle time with another. Holding a baby, rocking back and forth, comforted her. After the cuddle session she would start playtime with the infants. They used brightly colored soft toys to encourage them to focus on the object and try to grab it. If they were old enough, there was also supervised tummy time to help with balance and strength in the precrawling stage.

About thirty minutes after her break, Allison saw Liz walking toward her. Her shoulders were set, her expression determined.

"We need to talk."

Allison returned her charge to his crib. "What's going on?"

Liz looked around. "Let's go to my office."

Allison followed, a knot of worry tightening in her stomach. When they were in the office, Liz shut the door and faced her.

"You can't work here," she said flatly.

Allison stared at her. "How can you say that? I'm one of your best people."

"I know that, but given what's happening..." She looked away. "If the other members found out about Peter, they wouldn't like it." She returned her gaze to Allison. "They wouldn't want you around their children."

The unfairness of the statement was like a slap. "But I didn't do anything wrong. We don't know that Peter did, either."

"He's been arrested and is in jail. We're talking about people's children. I'm not willing to risk the business. I don't mean to be cruel or pile it on, but the truth is I wouldn't want my kids taken care of by someone so closely connected to a criminal."

Tears burned, along with a growing sense of unfairness. "He's not a criminal! It's all a mistake. I can't believe you're doing this. I'm great with the kids."

"I'm sorry. I wish I didn't have to do this."

"You don't have to do it," Allison said bitterly. "You know me. You're going to be shorthanded now."

"I'll deal with that. I'm sorry, but you need to leave."

Allison turned away. "This is your idea of helping?"

Liz flinched. "I know it's awful, but I'm doing my job."

This wasn't happening, she thought grimly. It couldn't be. How could she be losing her job when she hadn't done anything wrong? If anyone was the injured party in all this, it was her.

She reached for the door handle.

"Wait," Liz said. "You can still bring Jackson here for day care. You have a lot of credits."

Allison was sure her former boss was trying to be helpful, but the words weren't the least comforting. Yes, she had credits for now, but when they were used up, she would have to pay for day care if she wanted to keep working, and that sure didn't come cheap.

She collected her things, signed out Jackson, then drove home. Once she got there, she pulled out her phone and stared at it, willing Peter to call. But he didn't. There was only silence and the knowledge that everything was going to get a whole lot worse.

Three of Erica's salons were on the Eastside of Seattle—that area defined as between Lake Washington and the Cascades. Bellevue (of course), on the lake in Kirkland at Carillon Point and Issaquah. The fourth was in the U District—the area around the University of Washington, just a few miles north of downtown Seattle. The salons were all sleek, modern facilities featuring clean lines and minimalistic decor, with comfortable furniture and luxurious treatment facilities. Hair care was the largest chunk of income, but the spas at each Twisted location did a thriving business.

The Bellevue salon had been her first, followed by the one in the U District. Issaquah had come third, and while she'd wanted to open in Kirkland earlier than she had, she'd been waiting for the perfect location. Once that had come available, she'd snapped up the spot and opened her fourth salon and spa.

She'd chosen to use the same color palette and furnishings in all of them, so clients always knew they were in Twisted, but there were little quirks to each of the stores. Bellevue's pedicure rooms were all private, set up for one or two clients. At Carillon Point, there was a large lake view space upstairs where private parties could book group treatments for say a wedding party or a girls' day out. In Issaquah, three of the treatment rooms opened onto private walled gardens. When the weather was nice, the French doors were left open and the tables could be moved outdoors.

While Erica considered Bellevue her home base, she had a small office in the other three salons and she spent at least one day a week in each of them. Even after all this time, walking into one of her salons gave her a flush of pride and a strong sense of achievement. When she'd bought out her mother twenty-five years ago, Mara had owned a three-chair salon in a run-down building long since demolished. Within two years, Erica had moved to a better location in Bellevue, had changed the name to Twisted and hired someone to do nails. Within five years, she'd had nearly forty employees, had added a thriving spa and moved to her current location. She'd signed the long-term lease on her twenty-eighth birthday. Two days later, the location in the U District had become available. She'd already been stretched thin, but she'd taken a chance and had signed that lease, as well. Two years later, she'd met Peter. They'd married and Summer had quickly followed. On her daughter's first birthday, Erica had opened the Issaquah location.

Now she pulled into that parking lot, driving to the far end so as not to take a spot a customer might want. She'd planned to be in Kirkland but had awakened that morning thinking she needed wise counsel.

After Erica had bought out her mother, Mara had spent nearly a year traveling with one of her men. When she'd finally returned home, she'd gone back to work at another salon, saying she loved her daughter too much to work for her. But when Erica had bought the Issaquah store, Mara had insisted on moving there. She found the setting restful and loved that her station was next to the window with the view of the mountains.

Erica walked into the bright, open reception area and nodded a greeting at the two young women checking in clients. Three more were in line. Midmorning, midweek should have been a quiet time, but the hair salon was more than half-full and a quick glance at the spa schedule told her that nearly every treatment room was booked.

Erica unlocked her office and booted her computer, then went onto the salon floor. Her gaze settled on her mother, who was chatting with her client, a woman of a certain age. They had an air of familiarity about them—as if they'd known each other for years, which they probably had. Mara's clientele was intensely loyal.

Like Erica and Summer, Mara was a tall brunette with brown eyes. She'd just turned seventy but could easily pass for someone in her late fifties. She stayed in shape with what Erica considered an unnatural affection for her Peloton bike, but whatever worked. Last summer Mara and one of the men in her life had taken some kind of barge-bike European vacation. They'd cycled from stop to stop most days and had slept on the luxury barge at night. It wasn't Erica's idea of a good time, but if it made her mother happy, then yay her.

As Erica approached, her mother smiled at her. "Annie, you remember my daughter, don't you?"

Annie, a sixtysomething with stunning gray hair, nodded. "Of course. Good to see you."

"You, too. I still envy you your hair."

Annie laughed. "It's about the only thing I enjoy about my age."

"I doubt that." Erica looked at her mother. "Do you have a break anytime soon?"

"When I'm done here." Her mother's brows rose. "Have I broken any rules? Am I going to get lectured?"

Mara and Annie laughed at the thought, while Erica wished what she wanted to discuss was that simple.

"Nothing so dramatic, Mom."

"Then I'll come see you in your office."

"Thank you." She lightly touched Annie's shoulder. "So good to see you."

Erica excused herself and took a quick tour of the store before returning to her workspace. After clearing her email, she found herself unable to concentrate. Usually work was her refuge, but not this morning.

She hadn't slept well and when she had finally dozed off, she'd had bad dreams about Summer being held captive by someone who wouldn't tell her what it would take to get her daughter back. Apparently the Peter situation had affected her more than she'd realized.

No, she amended mentally. Not Peter problems so much as how upset Summer had been.

"I knew you'd find out I'd been stealing towels," her mother said cheerfully as she walked into Erica's office.

"Very funny."

Her mother took one of the visitors' chairs on the other side of the desk. "What couldn't wait until tonight?" She paused, her eyebrows drawing together. "You didn't sleep well and you're tense. What's going on?"

"Nothing with me or Summer. Not directly at least." She paused. "Peter's in jail."

Her mother's eyes widened as her jaw dropped. "What did you just say?"

Erica explained what she knew about the very bizarre situation. "Obviously I haven't talked to him, so I don't know much. Killion found out what he could. According to Summer, Allison doesn't know anything either." She looked at her mother. "Allison being the second wife."

"I know who she is. In jail?" Mara shook her head. "I can't see it. He's not that driven. I would think money laundering and wire fraud require more effort than he puts into most things." She sighed. "Which sounds mean and unfair, but he was cruel to you and I'm never going to forgive that. So what are you going to do?"

"There's nothing *to* do. I'm sure he has a lawyer."

Her mother stared at her without speaking.

"What?" Erica shifted in her seat. "I'm not married to him anymore. This isn't my problem."

Her mother smiled. "If it's not your problem, why did you want to talk to me?"

An excellent question, Erica thought. "Nothing like this has ever happened to our family before. It's hard to know what to think."

"I can see that." Her mother studied her. "Isn't Allison pregnant?"

"So I'm told." Summer was far too thrilled about the impending birth of her half sister.

"And she has a toddler."

"Jackson. Yes. He's, I don't know, eighteen months."

"So Allison has one child, another on the way, her husband is in jail and her bank accounts have been frozen."

"I'll admit it sounds bad, but Peter and I are nothing to each other."

"I don't see Peter as the main issue."

Unfortunately her mother was right about that. "Summer's upset," she admitted. *Hysterical* was a better word.

"I can imagine. She's a tenderhearted young woman who loves her stepmother and half brother. They're in trouble and she wants to help. And her father is in jail." Mara's tone was pointed.

"It's not my rock. I'm not getting involved."

She thought her mother might try to convince her otherwise. Instead Mara rose and smiled at her. "Good luck with that. I'll be home tonight in case you need me."

"I know she's worried, but there's nothing we can do. I'm sure Allison already has a plan and she'll be fine."

Amusement brightened her mother's eyes. "Keep telling yourself that and maybe it will be true."

5

The Washington West (otherwise known as Wa-West) high school fast pitch softball season lasted twenty regular games, not counting postseason. There were two games a week, plus invitationals, for ten weeks, equally divided between home and away. Games were seven innings, unless there was a tie, or one team was ahead by more than fifteen runs at the end of the fifth.

Start time ranged from three thirty to five, depending on the location. Home games started promptly at four. Summer had been on the team since her freshman year and in all that time, Erica hadn't missed a single game. Peter came to a couple a year, Mara stopped by to see her granddaughter play at least a few times a month, but no matter what else was happening in her life, Erica showed up to cheer on her kid.

As she walked from the parking lot to the playing field, she glanced at the gray sky. Rain was common in March, but according to the local weather app, it should hold off until around seven, giving the team plenty of time to slaughter their opponents. The temperature was in the upper forties—not exactly ideal outdoor viewing weather, but she'd grown up in the Pacific Northwest and knew how to layer with the best of them. Her jacket had a hood and she'd brought a scarf and a blanket. Unfortunately, she'd forgotten to change out of her high-heeled boots into something more sensible, so had to cross the few feet of muddy grass with her weight on her toes.

The stands were half-full, mostly with clusters of moms sitting together and talking. Erica recognized a few of them as other mothers of Wa-West players. Several of the team members had been playing since they were eight or nine, so the families knew each other well.

Summer had gotten interested in softball when she'd been around ten. Peter had wanted her to find a sport she liked—anything to keep her out of Erica's salon-based world. In the beginning play had been casual and Erica hadn't gotten involved. But in middle school Summer had joined a local league and started to shine as a player, and Erica had begun attending games.

The other moms, most of them stay-at-home types, had been friendly, inviting Erica to sit with them. But after the games, when they'd hung out over barbecues or potlucks, Erica had needed to get back to work. The start times had been even earlier then, cutting into her hours at the salons. She'd been unable to join them on afternoons of shopping or DIY projects. Eventually they'd stopped inviting her to sit with them, or maybe she'd stopped saying yes. At this point, she wasn't sure which.

Which explained why, although she smiled and waved at the women she'd known for six or seven years, she didn't head in their direction, nor had they saved her a seat. Instead she sat, as she always did, by herself.

This was fine, she told herself, draping the blanket across her lap. She was here to support her daughter and watch the game. Nothing else was important. All her life she'd had to follow her own path—it was the price of success. She didn't want anything different.

Despite her brave words, she found herself glancing at the other moms. They were talking and laughing, obviously comfortable with each other, and why wouldn't they be? They'd been close for years. Their daughters were friends, and they were friends. Erica was the only outsider.

Summer's team was first at bat. Erica watched, then cheered as her daughter hit a double, which scored a run. By the end of the first inning, the Wa-West Raptors were ahead by four. By the third, they were ahead by ten. Erica found herself hoping for a few more runs and an early wrap-up to the game.

"Hi, Erica."

Erica turned and saw Crystal, one of the softball moms, approaching. Behind her, the other moms watched carefully, as if they wanted to judge Erica's reaction to whatever was going to be discussed.

"Hi." Erica smiled brightly. "Could it be colder?"

"I know." Crystal, a pretty blonde with delicate features, smiled as she sat down. "It's freezing. I was torn between hoping for rain so the game was canceled or dressing in more layers."

"A missed game just means a tighter schedule at the end of the season."

"That's what I told myself, so I picked the layers." Crystal laughed. "Not that I have weather superpowers. So, um, how are you?"

"Good. Busy. What about you?"

"The same. Declan, my youngest, is going to be seven, if you can believe it. Probably time for me to get a job or something." She wrinkled her nose. "I haven't worked since Jeff and I got married and it's not like we need the money, but I need a little more in my life than taking care of the family and the house." She tilted her head. "Not that you can relate, right? I mean you've always been a tycoon."

"I'm not sure tycoon is the right word," Erica murmured, unable to relate to Crystal's description of her day. Of course her own schedule—running four spas while being a single mom—would be just as foreign.

A crack of a bat had them both glancing at the field.

"Another run," Crystal said. "Maybe this game will end early." She held up a hand. "I don't mean that in a bad way."

"I know. It's a weather thing."

Crystal smiled, then looked away. Erica waited, not sure why the other woman had stopped by. Crystal gave her yet another smile.

"So, um, we were wondering about the spa packages at Twisted. We were thinking about having a girls' day out. We've heard there's a special room at the Kirkland place that you can't book online, so we, ah, thought maybe I should talk to you."

"A spa day?" Erica repeated before she could stop herself. "With the other softball moms?"

Crystal's gaze dropped to her lap. "Yes."

Because those women were friends, Erica thought, refusing to acknowledge any reaction on her part. Friends who got together and did things like spa days. It was normal and good for business.

"You're right—there's a treatment area for private parties. It's on the top floor with a beautiful view of the lake. There's a lovely patio, although this time of year we don't use it. The dressing area and bathrooms are separate, but all the treatments are done as a group. We can do massages, facials, mani-pedis, along with hair and even makeup, if you want. We cater lunch."

The sales pitch was easy and practiced. No thought was required. As she spoke, she told herself to stay relaxed, to not feel anything. This was business and nothing more. She and those women had never been close. They wouldn't think to invite her and if they did, she would never accept.

She pulled a business card out of her handbag. "Here's my contact information. Email me a few dates, along with the services you're interested in, and I'll see what I can do."

Crystal took the card. "Are you sure?"

"It's what I do." She faked humor. "Sort of a tycoon thing."

Crystal laughed. "Thanks for this. We'll figure out what we want, then be in touch."

With that, she got up and made her way back to her friends. Rather than watch her go, Erica returned her attention to the game. The Raptors had scored another two runs. At this rate, the game would only last an hour or so, and wouldn't that be nice. When it was over, she could escape back to one of her salons and get lost in a world that made a lot more sense to her.

Allison counted the diapers on the shelf. Thank goodness she'd just bought two boxes with a coupon she'd found online. Each box lasted about three weeks. With those and the loose ones in the drawer, she figured she was good for at least seven weeks.

She'd decided to prioritize her expenses. Until Peter called, she was still pretty much in the dark, but whatever happened, they were still going to be in trouble, money-wise. At least until the bank released their accounts.

Diapers, food, medical insurance, electricity and water. Those were the most important items. She'd already canceled the cable and internet. There were two more rent payments until their lease ended, so she supposed she should add those to the list. She'd never once not paid a bill. When she'd been a kid, money had been tight but somehow her dad had found a way. When she and Levi had been married and she'd been putting him through HVAC tech school, they'd struggled to survive financially, but somehow had always made it work. It wasn't in her nature to deliberately stiff someone. But the rent was so high and the landlord was tossing them out whether they wanted to go or not. Perhaps more to the point, she didn't have anything to pay him with. The twenty-two dollars she had in her wallet wouldn't go far. She'd requested more shifts at the grocery store, but she could only do that as long as she still had day care credits.

The fear she'd been living with for the past twenty-four hours cranked up a couple of degrees, fueled by reality and bitterness over how Liz had treated her. Everything about what was happening totally sucked. She hadn't done anything wrong. She didn't even know what had happened, but here she was, having to deal with it.

She touched her belly and told herself she had to keep breathing and try to relax for the sake of the baby. Her credit card, if it kept working, would cover the huge medical insurance premium for at least two months. If she used part of her next paycheck to cover the minimum credit card payment, she could string that along for even longer. The rest of her paycheck should cover food and utilities. It wasn't ideal, but it might be enough to make sure she and Jackson got by until Peter returned home to fix everything.

Allison went into the living room, where Jackson sat on the floor, happily playing with his farm playset. There was a barn, a farmer and several animals. Jackson loved opening and closing the plastic doors, putting the animals inside, then taking them out.

Knowing he was all right pushed away some of the fear. She continued into the kitchen, where she did a quick inventory of the food she had on hand. Jackson needed milk, along with fresh fruits and vegetables, and she had to worry about eating healthy for Bethany's sake. Healthy didn't come cheap. Still, she could supplement their diets with a lot of what was in the pantry. She had plenty of cereal, packages of rice and pasta, canned soups and beans. She'd always made a point to shop the sales—now she would put those skills to good use.

As she returned to sit with Jackson, she carefully avoided looking at the certified letter that had been delivered shortly after she'd gotten home from being thrown out of day care. She didn't have to open it to know what was inside. Their landlord was once again reminding them to vacate in about ten weeks. She and Peter had started looking at places last weekend and were going to make their decision this weekend. In less than three months, she would have nowhere to live. Worse, she didn't have any money for a security deposit or the move.

"It's okay," she whispered. "Peter will be home soon and everything will be fine."

She pulled her cell phone out of her pocket and set it on the floor. Eventually Peter would call—he had to. He was the only one with answers.

It rang a few minutes before four. The same mechanical voice asked if she would accept a collect call.

"Yes," she said, trying not to sound frantic so as not to upset Jackson. "Yes, I will."

"Allison."

Relief poured through her. She hung on to her phone. "Peter! Are you all right? What's happening? How can you be in federal custody? Why are you suspected of money laundering and wire fraud? Peter, what's going on? I'm so scared."

"You know about the charges?"

"Summer told me."

"You told her where I was?" His tone was accusing.

"I didn't have a choice. She walked in while I was terrified and sobbing last night. I tried to pretend it was just pregnancy hormones, but she wouldn't believe me. So yes, I told her."

She felt her temper rising. "What your daughter knows and doesn't know isn't the point. Peter, you've been arrested. How is that possible?"

"It's all a misunderstanding. You have to believe me. One of my clients is a criminal and they think I was involved with him, but I wasn't. I only handled his legitimate businesses. I'm working on getting a lawyer who can help."

She desperately wanted to believe him. "You didn't do anything wrong?"

"Of course not." His voice softened. "Allison, I love you and Jackson so much. You know that. I would never do anything to hurt you or put you at risk. I'm sick about this."

"Me, too. So when can you come home?"

"I don't know. Like I said, I'm working on getting a lawyer who can help."

"But we don't have any money!"

"There are ways around that. If we can pull together the retainer, they'll usually wait for the rest of it."

"I only have twenty-two dollars."

"I know. It's okay. I'll figure it out. You know you can use your credit card, right? It's with a different bank, so it shouldn't be frozen."

She nodded, even though he couldn't see her. "If I pay the minimum payment, I can keep using it for a while. I was thinking I would put the medical insurance on it. We can't lose that." Not when she was going to have a baby in a couple of months.

"Don't do anything for a week or so," he told her. "Let's see how things settle."

Her breath caught as hope filled her. "You think you'll be released in the next week?"

"No, not that. Just some other things."

Hope died. "What does that mean?"

"I can't explain it now. Just trust me, Allison."

"I need you to explain things. Peter, I'm scared. I don't know what to do. Why won't you be honest with me?"

"The calls are recorded." He sounded frustrated and unhappy. "I have to be careful."

But if he was innocent, why would he care about them recording the call?

She shook off the question. "What should I do?"

"Live your life. I'll stay in touch. This will all blow over, you'll see. I love you, Allison. I'll always take care of you."

Right now he wasn't taking care of anything, she thought bitterly.

"I need you to do a couple of things for me."

She brushed away tears she hadn't felt fall. "Like what?"

"I have dry cleaning. The receipt is in my blue blazer. Can you pick that up?"

He wanted her to get his dry cleaning? "You're in jail and you're worried about your clothes?"

Her voice was a shriek. Jackson stared at her. She faked a laugh and a big smile.

"It's okay," she said quickly. "Look at that pink pig. Oink."

Jackson giggled, then returned his attention back to his play. She drew in a couple of breaths.

"I'll get your dry cleaning."

"Thank you. I also need you to go by the office. I'm sure they served a search warrant, so it's probably a mess. I want to know how bad it is and if anyone is still working."

She resisted the need to curl up in a ball. His business. She hadn't thought about what was happening there. Peter was the person in charge. He ran everything. Without him, she wasn't sure it could survive.

"Why wouldn't they be?" she asked. "Won't Gail handle things?" Gail was his office manager and had been with Peter practically since he opened the business.

"I hope so," he said cautiously. "But I need to be sure. Can you go in the morning? You know where the spare keys are."

"I'll go. Peter, none of this makes sense. Why is it happening?"

"I wish I knew. I have to go. I'll call you tomorrow. In a few days, you can come see me and we'll be able to speak more freely."

Of course she had to go see him, she thought, stunned that the possibility hadn't occurred to her before. Visitors were allowed, weren't they? She knew where he was being held—she would have to look up the rules.

"Peter, wait!" She paused, not sure what to say. "I miss you."

"I miss you, too. More than I can say. I'll call tomorrow."

The call disconnected.

She sat there for a few seconds, telling herself she would give in to the fear and dread later, when Jackson was asleep. She didn't want her breakdown to upset him and she didn't want to trigger a panic attack, so she sucked in a couple of breaths, then plastered on a smile.

"What about the chicken?" she asked, picking up the white plastic piece.

He pointed to the front of the barn. "Here."

"That's a good spot for our chicken."

They played until dinnertime. She put together an easy meal of chicken over pasta with a few cut-up vegetables for him and ate one of the enchiladas with salad. She'd just put Jackson to bed when she remembered Peter's request that she get his dry cleaning.

Seriously, how could the man be worried about his wardrobe while he was in jail? Although she supposed it would be foolish to not get the clothes. It wasn't as if they could afford to replace them.

She found his blue blazer in their closet. When she stuck her hand in the right-hand pocket, she felt several pieces of paper. But not a dry cleaning receipt—a wad of twenty-dollar bills.

She sank onto the bed and spread out the money. She counted five hundred dollars. Given how grim things were right now, it felt like all the money in the world. Five hundred dollars! She could buy the fruits and vegetables Jackson needed. She could buy meat! And pay the utility bills and put gas in her car. If she didn't have to use the credit card for that sort of thing, she might squeeze an extra month of medical insurance out of it.

She flopped onto her back and smiled up at the ceiling. Peter had known about the money and wanted her to have it. He was right—he was taking care of her. He was a good man who loved her. Somehow they would fix what was going wrong and they could be together again. For always.

6

Erica chopped the zucchini into even cubes. She'd already done the carrots, onion and celery. Once she'd finished with the red peppers and bok choy, she would steam the carrots for a few minutes so they were nearly cooked and ready to be tossed into the Thai-inspired stir-fry. Summer's rice was in a bowl, ready to be popped into the microwave, and the peanut sauce was made.

Erica eyed the fluffy white rice she batch-cooked for her daughter. As a rule, Erica avoided carbs. Not only did she feel better when she ate less of them, it was easier to keep her weight in check. When she indulged it was on things she really loved like pasta or great bread—neither of which she was serving tonight.

Dinner was ready to go, but one key element was missing. Summer.

Erica glanced at the kitchen clock. They ate at six the nights they were together and her daughter was always on time. But at quarter 'til, there was no sign of the teen. Their only communication had been a text around three saying Summer was going to stop off to see Allison and Jackson before coming home.

"She better not have stayed for dinner without telling me," she grumbled aloud. They had a schedule. Erica made sure she was home for dinner at least one school night and every Sunday. Mara had her granddaughter over one or two nights a week.

In addition to spending every other weekend with her father, Summer ate dinner there at least once a week. There were also the evenings she spent with friends, although so far, not with a boyfriend.

Erica wasn't sure why her daughter didn't have someone special in her life. She was well-liked, pretty and while smart enough to be interesting, not intimidatingly smart. Boys her age were often wary of someone too smart. Or too goal oriented, she thought, remembering how when she'd been in high school, she'd been busy working on a business plan to buy out her mom and launch her empire. The guys in her class hadn't found her drive the least bit appealing.

She heard the mudroom door open, followed by rapid footsteps. Summer burst into the kitchen, her ratty oversize plaid shirt hanging off one shoulder, her backpack slipping to the floor.

"Sorry, sorry, sorry," she said. "I wasn't watching the time."

The teen shrugged out of the shirt jacket and let it fall on top of her backpack. She quickly unlaced her very ugly construction-style boots before stepping out of them and hurrying over to Erica. She wrapped her arms around her and hung on.

"I'll wash my hands, then set the table."

Erica stroked her back. "We're having stir-fry. We're not on a tight schedule. Are you all right?"

Summer stepped back and shook her head. "No. Oh, Mom, it's so awful. Allison is totally freaked about what's happening with Dad. She tried to make me feel better by telling me she has a credit card she can use and stuff, but it didn't work. She knows how many diapers she has!"

Erica held in a sigh. Obviously the issue with Peter wasn't going away anytime soon, so she would have to be patient. Unfortunately patience when it came to her ex-husband was in short supply.

"Knowing how many diapers you have isn't earth-shattering,"

she said calmly. "When you have a baby or toddler, you need that kind of information. The last thing you want is to run out."

She put her hand on her daughter's shoulder. "I know this is really hard for you. Everything about the situation is upsetting and confusing. Allison is dealing with a lot right now, and it doesn't seem fair. She has little Jackson and is pregnant."

"I know. It's horrible." Summer's eyes filled with tears. "She doesn't have anyone, Mom."

"She has friends and coworkers, and she has Peter." She deliberately softened her tone. "Sweetie, you're so caring and softhearted, plus we're talking about your dad, so of course you're processing emotion. Nothing about what's happening makes sense to any of us. But give it time. In the next couple of weeks, we'll find out what's really going on and then we can deal."

Summer nodded slowly, then wiped her eyes. "I'm so scared."

"I know. But we'll get through this. Can you let it go long enough to enjoy dinner?"

She nodded again. "I'll try."

"Good. I'll steam the carrots, then start the stir-fry."

"I'll set the table."

Summer disappeared down the hall to the half bath. Erica heard the sound of running water, as her daughter washed her hands. She dumped the carrots into the steamer. The water was already boiling, so the cooking time would be short. She gave the sauce a quick stir.

By the time the carrots were ready, Summer had set the table and poured herself a large glass of milk. She set ice water in front of her mom's place mat.

Erica heated her wok and quickly seared the chicken pieces. Once they were done, she dumped them into a clean bowl, then began adding vegetables. She kept everything moving, adding the next group as the first ones began cooking through. The bok choy went in last, followed by the cooked chicken. A minute later, she stirred in the sauce. She heard the microwave beep as Summer finished heating her rice.

Erica transferred the stir-fry from the wok to a serving bowl and topped it with cilantro. Peanuts were already on the table.

"How was school?" Erica asked when they were seated across from each other at the table by the window. Most meals were taken in the kitchen. The dining room was for special occasions, entertaining or holidays.

"Good." She scooped rice onto her plate, then wrinkled her nose. "We have to read *The Great Gatsby*. Ugh. I loved *The Color Purple*. That was so interesting, but this book is about a bunch of rich people. Why should we care?"

Erica tried to recall what the book was about. Or the movie— there'd been a remake several years ago. At least she thought there had been. Plus that old one her mother had made her watch a couple of times.

"Gatsby doesn't really love Daisy," she said, remembering a discussion in high school. "He wants to possess her, or what he thinks is her, but he never truly knows her. His feelings for her aren't about love, they're about acquisition."

Summer stared at her wide-eyed. "Go, Mom!"

Erica laughed. "I know it sounds impressive, but honestly that's all I can remember. I didn't love it, either."

"Shouldn't literature be interesting? And relevant?"

"The basic themes of great literature are relevant. But you're right—the setting, the way people act, that's all out of step with our lives. *The Great Gatsby* was written a long time ago. Part of understanding it is to understand the times the author was living in. Everything changes with perspective."

"Maybe."

"How does everyone feel about the next game?" The team was playing the Bellevue High School Wolverines, typically a tough opponent.

"We're going to kick Wolverine butt. Player for player, we're better." Summer paused. "But they do have a better outfield."

As her daughter spoke, Erica wondered (for the eight-thousandth time) why Summer wouldn't put a little effort into her appearance. Her hair was thick and shiny, but she wore it back in a ponytail or braid all the time. She had no interest in skin care or makeup. Her clothes were equally utilitarian. Summer had never wanted to experiment with different looks or go shopping. She never wore dresses or skirts unless it was a special event and Erica insisted.

Several of her friends dressed well, wore makeup and even asked Erica for tips. But not her own daughter. When pressed, Summer would roll her eyes and say she couldn't be bothered with something so unimportant. Erica tried not to take the remarks personally, but it was difficult. Helping women look more beautiful was the entire point of her business.

Summer helped herself to seconds. "I don't know what to do for Allison."

Erica ignored the flash of impatience and resisted the urge to point out they'd agreed not to discuss the topic at dinner.

"You're being supportive. That's your role in all this. You don't have to *do* anything. I'm sure your dad's giving her advice."

"I guess. She's going to go see him. I wonder what that will be like. I don't know anything about prison or jail or stuff. Do you think Dad's scared?"

"I doubt he's happy where he is, but I don't think he's in any physical danger."

"Do you think he did the things he's charged with? Dad's not a bad person. He's so great with Jackson and I know he loves me. Allison is his world. They fit together, you know?"

Before things had gone south in her marriage, Erica would have said Peter loved her very much, but she wouldn't have ever thought of herself as "his world." They simply didn't have that kind of relationship. No one should be anyone else's world. That was too much pressure and it sounded incredibly codependent.

"They must miss each other," she said, going for the neutral response.

"They do. Remember after the divorce, when Dad was so down? I worried about him. He wasn't himself, but then he met her and it was like a light went on inside. She makes him happy."

Erica told herself that her daughter wasn't being cruel on purpose, that the teen's insistence at seeing things from her father's point of view was more about her being the stronger parent, more successful. Summer saw her as capable, determined and rarely bothered by the emotions that laid the rest of humanity bare. There was no thought that Peter had initiated the divorce, and she'd never told Summer that she'd been blindsided.

The unfairness of it all made her push away the rest of her meal. Part of her wanted to point out that she'd suffered, too. That the divorce had been hard emotionally, although unlike Peter, Erica hadn't shared many of her feelings with her daughter. She'd felt Summer was going through enough on her own without having her mother dump her disappointment on her.

"He was working so hard to grow his business," Summer continued. "Practically starting from scratch."

Because once Peter had said he was leaving, she'd pulled her account from his business. Twisted had been his major client, so she knew the move had hurt him financially, but given what was happening at the time, staying had been out of the question. Finding out he'd stolen a hundred thousand dollars from her over the years had only solidified her decision. Thank God she'd had the brains to insist on a prenup before they married. She'd started Twisted before they'd ever met and was the sole owner of the business. Despite being in love, she hadn't been willing to risk her salons.

"Allison is so scared," Summer said. "Mom, we need to do something to help her."

"We talked about this. Let's wait until we know more."

"But she's broke and pregnant. There's no internet anymore—she canceled that. What about when Bethany's born? How is she going to do that, on her own? What about Jackson?"

All good questions, Erica thought. "She'll figure it out. She's not a twenty-year-old with no life experience. She's what? Thirty-four, thirty-five? She has resources."

"Not financial ones. Mom, why aren't you taking this seriously?"

"I am. I'm sorry Allison and your father are dealing with this, but it will get straightened out. By now your dad has a lawyer and—"

Summer's mouth twisted. "He doesn't. She told me. I think it's because there's no money. How is he supposed to pay?"

"We talked about this before. The lawyer will be paid when the money's released. It's fine."

"It's not." Summer pushed back from the table and stood. "It's not fine. Stop saying that. What about the move?"

"What move?"

"The landlord is selling their house. They were going to pick a place this weekend, but now Dad's in jail and there's no money. How is Allison supposed to rent another house or even an apartment? Mom, she's pregnant!"

Erica did her best not to react. Having to move in the middle of all this did make the situation worse. She felt a small twinge of pity for the other woman. In a matter of days her entire life had gone to crap.

"She has friends or maybe family who can help." At least she assumed Allison did. Honestly, Erica didn't know that much about the woman. There was no reason to—she wasn't one of those sick people who stayed friends with an ex.

"I'm her family," Summer shouted. "*I'm* her family. She's my stepmom and Jackson is my brother. You've always said it was our responsibility to take care of those we love. I love them and we have to *help!*"

The flinch was involuntary. Erica knew her daughter cared about Allison, but the knowledge was nowhere near the same as a shouted declaration. Her first instinct was to say the other woman was nothing to her, but she knew that would be problematic. No matter how Summer's words stung, she had to react in an understanding and thoughtful manner. The important person here was her daughter.

"Screaming at me isn't communication," she said quietly. "I know you're concerned. Anyone would be. Allison and your father are dealing with a difficult situation."

She motioned to the chair. Summer hesitated before sitting down.

"But they are dealing," Erica continued. "You're sixteen years old. Mature for your age, but still not an adult. There are things they're not going to tell you. So while I respect your feelings and understand why you feel freaked out, you need to take a step back and see that you don't know everything happening."

"What if what I don't know makes it worse?"

"What if it doesn't?"

"Mo-om! That doesn't help."

"You're not helping, either. You're assuming disaster and ruin are the only options and you're also assuming Allison doesn't have anyone in her life but you. This isn't your problem to fix. It's theirs."

"But they're my family!"

"Yes, they are and it's great that you're being so supportive. I'm not saying that has to change. Instead I'm pointing out that it's only been a couple of days. Let's give everyone a little time to figure out what's really happening before you start yelling at me."

Summer slumped in her seat. "I didn't mean to yell."

"I know. You're worried. But again, they're handling the situation. Give them space to do that." She thought about mentioning maybe it would be better if Summer didn't run over to her father's house every fifteen minutes, but decided not to go there.

Her daughter looked at her. "Will you talk to her?"

"Excuse me?"

"Will you talk to her? Come on, Mom, you're the most to-gether person I know. You're successful, you have employees, there's always money. You know things. You could give Allison advice."

"Not about Peter being in jail."

"No, but about life and stuff. I know she'd want to talk to you."

Erica doubted that. And on a different, yet oddly related topic, why hadn't she had wine with dinner?

"Your stepmother has no interest in speaking with me."

"Why would you say that? She likes you."

Oh, to be that young and naive, Erica thought grimly. Or not.

"I'm not having a conversation with Allison."

"Why not? Don't be mean. You have everything and they have nothing and my dad's in jail." The tears returned. "I can't believe you won't help! They're family. Our family."

They weren't her family, a thought Erica kept to herself.

"She's pregnant and alone and what about Jackson? Mom, please just go talk to her."

She knew her daughter could keep going like this for hours. She'd never been a fan of circular arguments, but Summer was a teenager and an expert. She didn't want to demand a change in subject or imply she wasn't equally distraught about Allison's problems, although she wasn't. And the comment about her being mean had stung.

"Stop badgering me," she said, careful to keep her voice calm. "I had nothing to do with what happened and I'm not the bad guy."

"I'm sorry." Summer reached her arms across the table. "Mom, please. Please, for me."

Ugh. Children—what had God been thinking? Because re-sisting her daughter had always been impossible.

"Give the situation a few days to settle down," she said grudgingly. "After that, if your stepmother wants to speak with me, then I'll go talk to her." She held up her hand to keep her daughter from interrupting. "I mean that. You aren't to push her into saying yes. Me showing up uninvited won't make anything better. This situation is difficult for her, and your job is not to make it worse. I know you think you know what's best, but please consider that every now and then you're wrong. Don't play games with Allison's life."

Summer's eyes widened. "That's a really good point, Mom. I don't want to make things harder. I'll wait until we know more, then I'll ask her if she thinks talking to you would help."

Summer rushed around the table and hugged Erica. "Thank you, thank you. You're the best. I'm sorry to be such a pain, but it's all so scary."

Erica held her close. "I know. I wish this wasn't happening, too."

7

Allison spent a restless night, falling to sleep only to wake up, her heart pounding, her body damp with sweat. A little after five, she gave up and stepped in the shower to start her day. By five thirty, she was on her phone, trying to make sense of the visiting rules for the Federal Detention Center, SeaTac, Washington.

There was a pdf that detailed much of the information, but it wasn't easy to understand. From what she could tell, Peter would qualify as a pretrial inmate, so he could have visitors on either odd or even days, depending on the fifth number of his register number.

"What?"

She blinked at the screen, then read the example. Hmm, if his register number, something she would think of as a prison number, was 12345-086, he had visitors on odd days. Which meant she needed to know his number.

Social visits were up to two hours long, he could only have one social visit per visiting day and there were no visits on Tuesday, Wednesday or Thursday. And before she could schedule a visit, she had to fill out an application.

The times of visiting hours varied. Some days it was 7:30 a.m. to 2:30 p.m., and some days it was 2:00 p.m. to 9:00 p.m. She continued to read. There were exceptions for holidays. On those days everyone could have visitors. She scanned the list.

Memorial Day, July 4, Christmas and New Year's Day. It was late March. Surely Peter wouldn't be in jail on Memorial Day, or worse, Christmas.

She felt the familiar flicker of fear and panic and immediately looked away from the screen. She was fine, she told herself as she took a deep breath. She would be fine. She had enough money to get through the next couple of weeks. She was going to get paid and that would help. She still had to solve her housing crisis, but not today. She missed Peter more than she could say, but she was figuring it out as she went.

She'd promised herself she would get through the day without giving in to the terror that lurked just under the surface. She needed a break from that. Today was about being practical. Later this morning, she would go by the office so she could tell Peter what was happening there. This afternoon she was working. This weekend she would go look at apartments.

Not that she had a clue as to how she was going to move—not just physically, but money-wise. She might be able to swing a security deposit, but wasn't sure she could qualify on her own. With Peter's income, getting a place wouldn't be a problem, only there was no paycheck anymore and all their money had been frozen. Just as frightening, how was she supposed to have a baby with no one to care for Jackson?

A few days ago, she would have considered Liz a possibility. They were friends—at least she'd thought they were, although she'd been wrong. So if not Liz, then who? She supposed Jessie, her shift partner, was a maybe, but she didn't know her that well and leaving Jackson with her was a huge ask.

An ask that got bigger if she allowed herself to consider the possibility that something went wrong and she had to stay in the hospital longer. Even if everything went well, how was she supposed to care for a toddler and a newborn by herself?

A cold knot formed in her chest. Once again she consciously slowed her breathing and told herself she would be fine. "Not today," she whispered. "Not today. I'll panic later. Today is going to be a good day."

She put down her phone and woke up Jackson. The early morning passed quickly as they ate breakfast together, then had some playtime. A little before ten, she put him in his car seat and drove to Peter's office building.

His accounting firm was on the third floor. When she got there, she tried to open the door but it was locked.

A sense of foreboding trickled down her spine. Shouldn't the business be open? Gail, the office manager, always got in early. Peter used to joke that one day he was going to beat her there and then he would celebrate. And what about the other employees?

Questions without answers, she thought, grateful she'd thought to bring the spare office keys. She shifted Jackson to her other hip and fished the keys from her pocket. The door opened easily. She walked into the small reception area. The desk was still there, along with a couple of club chairs for waiting clients. But nothing else was the same.

The two framed prints were askew and beside them someone had posted a notice claiming a warrant had been served. Every drawer in the desk was open and the contents were spilled onto the floor. It was as if a tornado had swept through the room.

Still holding Jackson, she walked down the short hallway. In all of the offices, desk drawers and cupboards were open, contents tossed to the floor. No space had been spared, not even the break room. On her return trip, she realized there were no computers anywhere. She saw printers and scanners, even a sad old fax machine, but no laptops.

She sank into one of the chairs and set Jackson on her lap. He immediately squirmed to get down. She set him on the floor and he ran to a pile of paper and tossed it into the air, then laughed. She looked around, trying to make sense of what had happened, only she couldn't.

After a few seconds, she pulled out her phone and logged in to the company's Wi-Fi, then went online and typed in "What happens when the police have a search warrant." She clicked the first link.

She learned that the police, or whoever was executing the search warrant, didn't have to be especially careful with the belongings, and depending on what they were searching for, they had every right to rip the place apart.

"But what would they be looking for here?"

She glanced around. They'd taken the computers, so what was left? She continued reading about how if it was something small, like a stash of drugs, the search could take hours and be more physically destructive to the location. Other examples were given. And then she saw the answer. A thumb drive.

The police or whatever agency had been here had been looking for financial information, so they'd been searching for a thumb drive or maybe a backup hard drive. Anything where Peter could store records of his supposed illegal activities.

The phone on the desk began to ring. Allison stared at it but didn't pick it up. Jackson looked from her to the phone, then returned his attention to a pencil holder he'd found. He rolled it on the carpet, making sputtering noises. The phone went silent.

Despite her promise to herself not to fall into despair today, she felt the heavy weight of uncertainty and worry. Her husband was in jail, his office had been trashed and no employees had shown up to work. No business, no income. Which left her totally on her own. And even if he did get out on bail, how was he supposed to get things up and running again if all the computers had been taken by the police or FBI or whomever?

Her chest tightened and her breathing quickened. The panic returned. She was in so much trouble and didn't know what to—

The phone rang again. Allison stared at it for a couple of seconds, then walked to the desk and picked it up.

"Um, Jenkins Accounting, may I, ah, help you?"

"What's going on there? I've been calling for two days. I need my quarterly deposit number and no one has sent it to me."

The woman on the other end of the call sounded furious.

"Okay, that's not good."

Allison spotted a loose pen on the desk, then grabbed a random piece of paper, turned it over and wrote, "Needs quarterly deposit numbers."

"Let me get your name and number so someone can call you back."

The woman gave her the information. "I need to hear today. You got that? Today."

"Yes, I understand. I'm sorry you have to wait, but I'll get you something."

"You'd better."

The woman hung up. Allison replaced the phone in the cradle, then stared at the message. How was she supposed to get the information the client needed? Ignoring the no-computers problem, she didn't know what a quarterly deposit was. When Peter called, she would ask him what to do, but until then, she was stuck. They were all stuck.

The phone rang again. Allison ignored it. She tucked the message into her bag, then collected Jackson and made her way out of the office. As she reached the elevator, she could still hear the phone ringing.

"You're distracted."

Erica looked up from her salad. "Am I?"

"I'm not complaining, just observing."

Killion smiled as he spoke, which deepened the lines around his eyes. What would have been aging on any woman on the planet made him look gorgeous. Yet another unfair advantage for men. Where a woman of a certain age and means would be talking to a dermatologist about slowing the ravages of time, men just looked good as they got older.

"I have things on my mind," she admitted.

"Should we talk about them or pretend they don't exist?"

"I'm not sure."

He picked up his glass of champagne. "Let me know when you decide. I'm happy to listen, offer advice or act like nothing is wrong." He took a sip. "Usually our dinners are a prelude to sex, but if tonight isn't a good night for you, then it can just be dinner."

He was being so kind, she thought, both appreciative and annoyed. A testament to her being unsettled. While the correct response was to say *Thanks, I'll let you know*, what she really wanted to say was *Don't pretend this is a real relationship. It's not.* Only that would sound incredibly bitchy and she didn't mean it that way.

She held in a sigh. All right, yes, she *did* mean it that way, but knew she would immediately regret saying it and she really, really hated having regrets.

"The salad is lovely," she said instead.

"Thank you."

"You're wonderful in the kitchen. Much better than me. I don't have the patience."

"Cooking relaxes me." The smile returned. "As long as I don't have to do it every day."

The first time he'd offered to cook her dinner, she'd been skeptical. In her experience, a man "cooking" implied really good takeout. But Killion had surprised her with an exquisite meal. Usually they went out to eat but every couple of months, he made dinner. She always offered to help, but he preferred to do it alone. He did tell her what wine to bring. Tonight's was Peter Michael Mon Plaisir Chardonnay, which they would have with their entrée. The champagne was for the appetizers and salad.

They'd started with prosciutto-wrapped melon with a balsamic glaze, followed by an arugula salad with shaved parmesan. Dinner would be seared scallops with brown butter and lemon sauce and an oven risotto with crispy roasted mushrooms.

The risotto made her nervous. She wasn't afraid it wouldn't be good. On the contrary, she was terrified it would be so delicious, she would eat it all and gain five pounds. Although given what she knew about Killion's skill with risotto, it would probably be worth it.

"Is it Allison?" he asked.

The change in topic caught her off guard and before she could stop herself, she said, "In a way. Summer's worried about her." She leaned back in her chair. "She wants me to talk to her."

"Summer wants you to speak with Allison?" He stood and collected her salad plate along with his own. "Interesting."

She followed him into the kitchen. "What does that mean? Allison's in a difficult situation. Summer thinks my business experience might help her."

His kitchen was large, with an eight-burner stove and beautiful copper cookware hanging from an overhead rack. There were miles of counter space, tons of cabinets, but the real eye-catcher of the room was the man who owned it.

Killion was conventionally handsome—tall, fit, with dark hair and green eyes. He had an easy smile, an air of confidence and a velvety chocolate kind of voice. He was smart, intuitive and funny. The latter trait caused more than one foolish person to fail to recognize he also came with a killer instinct—at least in business. He was a ruthless venture capitalist with a reputation for swooping in when a company was close to being profitable but couldn't quite get there on its own. He brought in cash and sometimes resources. And he insisted on profitability.

If a member of the existing management team wasn't pulling their weight, firing them became a condition of the deal. If a division was losing money, off it went. He got in for the least he could and left with as much as possible. Erica wasn't sure of his actual net worth but had done a preliminary investigation on him when he'd first asked her out. Word had come back that a hundred million was a low estimate. As that amount had put her personal net worth to shame, she didn't have to worry about him being in it for the money.

"While I think you'd have a lot of advice Allison could use," he said, before opening the oven to check on the risotto, "I'm not sure I see the two of you sitting down over a cup of tea."

"There wouldn't have to be beverages." She leaned against the counter. "I don't *want* to talk to her. We barely know each other. I've met her at a few school events and she comes to the occasional softball game. We're not friends so getting together would be awkward."

"Very few first and second wives are close." He heated a pan for the scallops. "Let me guess. Summer didn't just mention it, she's insisting."

"Yes."

"And you can't tell her no."

"I tell her no all the time."

"Not when it comes to matters of the heart and this is a heart problem."

He was right, of course. In addition to the aforementioned charms, Killion was also insightful, which both impressed her and left her, once again, annoyed. A testament to the stress caused by the situation, she thought. None of this was her problem, yet here she was, reacting.

"Everything about what Allison's going through sucks," she admitted. "I get that. I can't remember what she does for work, but I doubt it pays much. She's pregnant, her husband's in jail, the bank has frozen everything. She's got to be scared. But it's not my issue. I don't mean that harshly, but it isn't."

"Except Summer's making it your issue."

"She's trying."

"Doesn't Allison already have a kid?"

"Yes." She crossed to the refrigerator and pulled out the chardonnay. After setting it on the island counter, she collected foil cutters and a wine opener, along with an ice bucket. She added ice to the latter until it was about half-full, then poured in water. Once she'd expertly opened the bottle, she tucked it into the bucket and draped a white linen towel across the top.

"A little boy. Jackson. Summer adores him." She paused. "I think he's about eighteen or twenty months. He's under two for sure."

"So the pregnancy isn't Allison's only complication. He's probably still in diapers, right?"

She eyed him. "Are you working with Summer to guilt me into doing what she wants?"

His easy smile never wavered. "Not my style. Just gathering information."

She believed him, but she didn't like the way the conversation was going. While Allison had many problems, none of them were Erica's fault.

"I don't like how much she's telling Summer," she admitted. "Yes, they have Peter in common, but Allison's the adult. She shouldn't lean on Summer so much."

"I agree. I'm sure some of it is the shock of the situation."

"That's probably true."

Erica carried the ice bucket into the dining room, then removed the champagne bottle and glasses. When she returned to the kitchen, Killion was plating the scallops, and the dish of risotto sat on a trivet next to the stove.

They carried everything into the dining room and resumed their seats.

"Did you want more children?" he asked, pouring the wine. "Or was one enough?"

She paused to consider the question. "I wanted one for sure. I thought about having more, but I knew my limitations. The business has always taken the bulk of my time and I wanted to be there for my child."

"Every school event, every big moment."

"I believe in showing up."

"And doing the work."

"It's the only way to achieve. Or in Summer's case, have her know that I love her. Words are fine, but in the end, actions matter."

Which was why she attended every softball game and made sure she and her daughter had dinner together a few times a week. It was why, when she'd been married, she'd cleared her schedule for regular date nights and had made sure to keep track of how often she and Peter made love. So nothing important got forgotten.

She tasted a scallop. "Delicious, as always."

"Thank you." He watched her. "You're lost in thought again."

"Sorry. Apparently I'm in a mood."

"I don't mind. I'm just noting there's a difference. Thinking of the past?"

"Some. I always knew what I wanted to do with my life. I was going to go to beauty school and business school, then save every penny and buy out my mom."

"Your first step toward your empire." His voice was gently teasing.

"It was. In high school, I didn't want to do the same things as the other girls. Oh, I was happy to play with hair and makeup, but I didn't spend hours sitting around talking. I had things to do."

"What about boys?"

"They weren't interested in me. I was too driven."

"You scared them."

She wrinkled her nose. "That sounds awful."

"You intimidated them," he amended.

"Which isn't much better, but you're probably right. I was on a path and I wasn't interested in distractions. My mother used to tell me I was ahead of my time, that the boys would catch up." She reached for her wineglass. "It took a while for that to happen."

She was happy with her success and wouldn't change any of it, but she was clear that she'd paid a price.

"Do you have friends?" she asked. "People you're really close to? Not family. Genuine friends."

"Yes. A couple of guys. One I've known since high school." He looked at her over his glass. "You?"

"Not really. There are acquaintances, but no real friends." Her lips pressed together. "I work with women all day. You'd think it would be easy to click with someone, but everyone I know is either an employee or a client. When I started Twisted I went to a lot of local entrepreneur events, hoping to meet other women doing what I did."

She offered him a rueful smile. "The problem was we were all juggling work, marriage and kids. There wasn't any time to simply hang out. I've always thought success would be easier to deal with if I were a man."

"You're right, but I'd find the change disappointing."

Her smile turned genuine. "I'm sure that's true."

"Are you lonely?"

The unexpected question stopped her. She resisted the urge to snap that it crossed a line and there was no point in pretending they were in an actual relationship. They didn't discuss feelings. Their encounters were limited—good conversation, followed by good sex.

Only she liked Killion and she couldn't summon the energy to be bitchy.

"Sometimes," she said slowly, not looking at him. "I have work and my mother and Summer, and that's mostly enough." She raised her gaze to his. "It's just every year at this time, when softball season starts, there they are. The other mothers. They're all so chummy—laughing and talking. They've been tight for years and while I don't care, sometimes I feel... Oh, I don't know."

"Left out?" he offered.

She saw him watching her. There wasn't any judgment in his gaze or derision. If anything, she would say Killion was listening and concerned.

"Yes," she admitted. "When Summer started playing softball years ago, I met them and they were very nice. They invited me to do things with them." She waved a hand. "Girl stuff. Lunch and shopping or lunch and a movie. A few things were at night, but mostly they were during the day, when I was working."

She picked up her wineglass. "They're all stay-at-home moms. Most of them have never worked. A couple have part-time jobs." She sipped. "I can't relate to that. I always wanted to own my own business. I wanted to grow it and work hard and make money and be proud. But they don't get that and I don't understand how they can spend their days doing nothing."

"Judge much?" he asked, his voice teasing.

"You know what I mean. My God, they're dependent on a man. If any of them were to get a divorce, they'd be screwed with no money of their own, no skills beyond raising kids. Statistically, a woman getting a divorce is one of the most likely reasons for her to fall below the poverty line."

"But you still wanted to go to lunch with them."

"Maybe." She looked past him. "Sometimes. But I was busy so I kept saying no and eventually they stopped asking. Most of the time I don't care, but..." Her voice trailed off.

"The season starts and it feels like they're rubbing your nose in it," he finished.

She glared at him. "Don't be insightful. I don't like it."

He laughed. "I'm stating the obvious. Don't accuse me of being insightful."

She sighed. "Sorry. Apparently the topic puts me on edge." She pushed her fork through the risotto. "Crystal, one of the moms, asked me about a spa day at the Kirkland location."

"In Carillon Point?" His brows rose. "For all the moms?"

"Yes. It's a great way to spend a day with friends. We cater and..."

He reached across the table and touched her hand. "It's not about the treatments, Erica."

"I know."

"You want them to invite you."

She squirmed in her seat. "I don't. Why would I want to have a spa day in my own store? It's ridiculous."

"You want them to invite you," he repeated.

"I do and that makes me feel stupid."

"You're many things, but you're not even close to stupid. Maybe you could divide and conquer. Invite one or two of them to lunch."

She pulled her hand free of his. "I don't need you to tell me how to make friends."

"I was offering a suggestion. I'm a guy—I can't help it."

"We should change the subject."

His gaze met hers. She read indecision there. He wanted to continue the conversation and yet he wanted to respect her request. She was sorry she'd brought up the topic. She wasn't lonely and she didn't care if those women had a thousand spa treatments. More business for her.

Later, she would have to deal with the fact that she'd been reduced to lying to herself to get through the evening, but for right now it was enough.

"Do you go to every game?" he asked.

"Of course. Always. The season is only about ten weeks, but they cram in at least two regular season games every week, plus invitationals. It's a lot. And of course they always make the play-offs. But I'm there."

"You're a good mom. It's one of the things I admire about you."

She stared at him. "You admire me?"

"Yes. Why are you surprised?"

She didn't have an answer for that. He leaned toward her.

"Why would I want to be with you if I didn't admire you?"

"Because the sex is good."

He grinned. "Yes, it is." His humor faded. "But good sex isn't that difficult to find. Someone I can be friends with, someone I can respect and admire, with whom I also have good sex, is pretty rare. Plus, you play fair. You say what you want and you're not into games."

Was that how he saw her? The words felt good. "Thank you. You're not into games, either. It makes things much easier." She hesitated. "I've been told I can be difficult."

"You are, but I can handle it. I travel a lot and I can be moody."

"I don't mind the travel and I ignore you when you're moody." She picked up her fork. "And you can cook."

He raised his glass. "A partnership of equals."

"It is." She smiled. "And after dinner, if you'd like, we can have sex."

His eyes brightened. "I'd like that very much."

8

Allison worked her way through the rental application. The questions were fairly straightforward, but she didn't find the process easy. Take the first line: "Name of applicant(s)." Obviously she was married and she would lease an apartment with her husband. Only she wasn't sure if she should put Peter on the lease or not. Would he be out of jail in time for him to sign it? And if he wouldn't, was it legal for her to lease the place in just her name? She simply didn't know.

She left him on the lease, thinking she could take out his name later if she wanted and continued to fill out information, only to stumble over a question about arrests and convictions. While Peter hadn't been convicted of anything, he had been arrested.

She skipped that question and scrolled down to the next section of the application, then held in a groan. She told herself she wasn't going to cry, that she would get through this, no matter what, but no matter how she blinked, she felt tears filling her eyes.

Applicants must provide proof of income that is at least three times the monthly rent. A W-2 plus the last three paychecks is sufficient. If income comes from another source, proof of income must be provided, along with two years of tax returns.

She didn't have enough proof of income, mostly because she didn't have enough money coming in. At the day care, she'd mostly been paid in childcare credits and her job at the grocery store was only part-time. By herself, she didn't come close to qualifying.

With Peter's income, she would be fine. His company was a corporation so he got regular paychecks. She could provide pay stubs and his last W-2, only he wasn't around to sign the lease. And what about the whole "Have you been arrested?" question? Not to mention there wasn't going to be a current paystub.

The unfairness stole her breath. She'd gone online looking for the cheapest one-bedroom apartment she could find. It was a piece of crap, with hardly any room, but she still couldn't afford it. But in less than two months, she had to move out of the leased house. She had no money, no home, nowhere to turn.

Nothing about the situation was fair or reasonable or right. Desperate didn't begin to describe her circumstances and the worst part was, she couldn't figure a way out.

Jackson was busy playing with his farm. She figured she had about five minutes until he demanded attention. She shut the computer and closed her eyes, willing herself to stay strong. After she played with him for a bit, she would go back online and look at other options for housing. Maybe there was some organization that could help or—

The doorbell rang. Jackson looked up expectantly. Immediately the door opened and Summer stepped inside. Allison held in a groan of dread. While she loved Peter's daughter, today was not a good day for a visit.

"It's me," Summer called, then spotted Allison on the sofa. Her smile faded as she walked inside. "You've been crying."

"I haven't."

The lie was automatic. Allison wiped her cheeks. "I'm good." She glanced at the clock. "It's barely eleven. Shouldn't you be at school?"

"We don't have school today, so I came by to talk to you. I'm worried."

"You don't have to be. Jackson and I are fine." She faked a smile. "Really. It's all good."

Summer didn't look convinced by the statement, but just then Jackson squealed, waving his arms. Summer dropped to the floor and pulled him close for a hug.

"How are you, little man? Is that your farm? I love playing with the farm."

He reached for one of the sheep and handed it to her.

"For me? Thank you. That's so nice."

Summer's tone was upbeat and friendly, but she kept glancing over. Allison told herself to rally—that the teen wouldn't stay long. She could fake being okay for an hour.

"When are you going to visit Dad?"

"Saturday."

He'd given her his register number, so she'd figured out when she was allowed to go see him. Her application had been approved and even though all the Saturday appointments were full, the warden had given her permission because she hadn't seen Peter since his arrest.

She'd also been given a detailed list of clothes she could and couldn't wear, and what she could bring. Basically she was allowed to carry in her car key, a small amount of cash for the vending machines and her ID, along with a diaper and toy for Jackson. Lockers were provided for her handbag. Everything else stayed in the car.

"I'm off work so I can drive down and spend the full two hours with him."

Summer's large brown eyes widened. "Are you nervous?"

Yes, she thought. Visiting her husband in jail had never been part of her life plan.

"I'm sure everything will work out," she lied. "I need to see

Peter and he needs to see me and Jackson. I'll get a lot more information." At least that was the plan.

"You have to be so scared." Summer's voice was thick with concern. "You should talk to my mom."

Allison wasn't sure if she should bolt or laugh hysterically. Talk to Erica? That was never going to happen.

"Why? She has nothing to do with this."

Given how horrible Peter always said his ex-wife was, she was probably gloating. A depressing thought, but most likely an accurate one.

"She can help. She's really good with business and all that. She'll have ideas."

Spoken with all the earnestness of a sixteen-year-old who had never had to deal with the real world. Allison fought against exhaustion. There was too much going on. She wasn't sleeping, she could barely bring herself to eat. Everything about her situation was hopeless and she didn't see a way out. The last thing she needed in her life was quality time with Erica.

Allison drew in a breath. "I know you're trying to help, but I'm not going to talk to your mom."

"But what about Dad's clients? You don't know what to do with them." She pressed her lips together. "I'm not badgering you—I want to make things better for you. Easier. Mom knows what she's doing and she's family. She *wants* to help."

Your mother isn't any family to me. Only she couldn't say that—not to Summer. Mostly she adored the teen, who was always so wonderful with Jackson. And while she appreciated the support, she didn't actually care about Peter's clients.

Only without them, there wasn't any future income. Once Peter was out of jail, he would need a business to go back to and she didn't know the first thing about bookkeeping and taxes. Her eyes burned as she realized no matter where she turned, she was trapped.

"I can't deal with his clients," she admitted, wondering when she was going to hit bottom, because right now it seemed like the disasters just kept on coming. "I can't deal with any of this."

Summer slid Jackson to the floor, then hurried to the sofa and sat next to Allison. She put her arms around her and squeezed tight.

"We're going to get through this," the teen said fiercely. "We will. I'm scared, too. He's my dad and I don't know what's happening. Thinking about what to do for you really helps me but you don't have that."

Allison managed a smile. "You understand a lot for just being a kid."

"I know, right?" Summer bounced to her feet. "Let me text my mom right now and we'll figure out a good time to get together. Do you want to meet here or at our house?"

Exhaustion joined worry, leaving her with a case of *I don't care.*

What did it matter where they met? Nothing would come of the moment, with the possible exception of Erica doing her best to make her feel awful, stupid and small. Something Allison was perfectly capable of doing on her own.

"I doubt she'll be able to do anything," she murmured before she could stop herself.

Summer waved the comment away. "Don't tell her I said this, but she's really amazing. She has all kinds of people working for her and they mostly love her." She flashed a grin. "Okay, they're a little scared of her, too, but they would do anything for her."

Allison couldn't reconcile that statement with what she knew to be true about Peter's ex-wife, so she ignored it. She slid onto the floor, next to Jackson, who beamed at her. He grabbed a cow and a chicken, then climbed onto her lap and waved his arms.

"I see them," she said, faking a happy voice. "Chickens give us eggs."

"And KFC," Summer added, while typing on her phone. "Okay, so let's get together tomorrow. We'll figure out a plan, then you can talk to Dad about it on Saturday. You can tell Mom any specifics he shares and she'll get it all managed." She looked up with a smile. "One problem solved."

Allison wished it could be that simple. Erica was a hairdresser with a few employees. How did that compare to Peter's large accounting business? She had never done her own books—in fact Peter had been her accountant. That was how they had met.

But Summer meant well and Allison didn't have it in her to refuse the kind offer. Especially when Summer was pretty much the only person she knew who was totally on her side.

Allison's regrets about meeting Erica were immediate and only grew overnight. By the next morning, she was making lists of reasons it was a bad idea and wondering how to convince Summer to call the whole thing off. But between getting ready for her shift at the grocery store and dropping Jackson off at day care, she didn't have time to do anything, and after six hours on her feet, she hurt too much to think, let alone act.

She collected her son, avoiding eye contact with Liz as they passed in the hallway.

"Are you all right?" her former friend asked, sounding concerned. "I've meant to call."

Have you? Have you really? Allison could hear the snippy words in her head, but she didn't say them. She had to assume that the horror of her current situation was temporary, and everything would work out. When that happened, she would want her job back.

"I'm hanging in there," Allison lied, ignoring the throbbing in her lower back and the pounding headache. She shifted Jackson to her other hip. It felt like the kid had put on twenty pounds in a single morning.

"We miss you here," Liz admitted. "The parents are asking after you. Any news about—" she paused "—the situation?"

Is that what they were calling it?

"Not yet, but I should know something soon." Yet more lies, but why not?

Liz offered her a tentative smile. "As soon as everything goes back to normal, please come talk to me."

"I will."

"I'm really sorry about having to let you go. I didn't want to."

Allison smiled tightly, nodded once, then left, all the while thinking Liz hadn't had to do anything. She knew Allison's character and how great she was with the babies. They could have kept the information quiet, at least for a couple of weeks. But there was no point in dwelling on that tiny issue when she had whale-size ones swimming right at her.

She got Jackson into his car seat and started for home. She had just enough time to get him fed and herself changed before Summer and Erica showed up. No way she was facing Peter's first wife wearing a bright pink T-shirt with the name of the grocery store blazoned across the front and stylized cantaloupes on the back.

But of course everything went wrong. Jackson threw more food than he ate and refused to drink his milk. He squirmed in his high chair, constantly looking at the door and asking for Dada. He kicked, he screamed, he wouldn't look at her. Allison did her best to stay calm, but she wanted a little tantrum of her own. She wanted to scream that this wasn't easy or fair, that her back hurt, her feet were swollen, she was scared, she was exhausted and in less than an hour, she would have to sit politely with the woman who had taken Peter for every penny he had during the divorce, forcing him to start over. In fact, excluding her husband being in jail, every bad thing that had happened in the past few days was practically Erica's fault!

"Jackson, please! Just one more bite."

He looked at her and burst into tears, then tossed his plate onto the floor. Food went flying, hitting cabinets and the floor. Applesauce oozed into a puddle. Bits of chicken and cheese piled together in the corner. Allison looked from the mess to the clock on the wall and knew that she just didn't have it in her to care.

"Fine," she said, taking off the tray and unstrapping him. "You want out? Get out and do whatever you want."

She set him on the floor, then turned her back on him. Despite her large belly, she got down on her hands and knees and began clearing up the mess. Jackson stood where she'd left him, crying harder, but she ignored him. She'd reached her crisis limit and simply couldn't deal with him this second.

It took fifteen minutes to clean up the worst of it. She lumbered to her feet and put the high chair back against the wall. After putting the dishes in the dishwasher, she rinsed out the sink, then risked a glance at the clock.

She only had ten minutes and Summer was never late.

She hurried into her bedroom. Jackson followed, his tears quieter now. He held out his arms to her, but she didn't have time to make him feel better. She replaced her ugly comfort shoes for semicute clogs, tore off her work T-shirt and put on a pretty white blouse that was cut large enough to drape over her belly. She combed her hair, knew makeup simply wasn't happening, then turned to her son.

He sat in the middle of her bedroom, butt on the floor, arms outstretched. His cries had become tired little mews and he looked miserable.

"All right," she said, kneeling in front of him. "It's okay."

He got up and flung himself at her, his hot sweaty arms clinging hard.

"Shh." She rubbed his back. "I know you weren't trying to be difficult. Somehow you always know when I'm in a hurry and act up. It's a gift. I wish you had a different one, but we need to work with this one."

He was going to be hungry later, she thought. They both were because she hadn't had time for dinner. Soon, she promised herself. Soon she would figure out something they both could eat, then they would spend a quiet evening on the sofa. They would listen to music while they played with a puzzle, then she would read to him until they were both sleepy.

"You'll see," she told him.

He took a step back and shook his head. "Tum-tum."

"What?" The word was unfamiliar. What was he trying to say?

She reached for him just as his face twisted. Seconds later he threw up all over her shirt. He burst into tears, she wasn't far behind and then the doorbell rang.

Allison knelt there, unable to believe what had just happened. Could the situation be any more unfair?

"It's me," Summer called. "I have my mom with me. Allison?"

"In here."

But her voice was a resigned whisper and there was no way Summer could have heard. But Jackson recognized his precious Summy and shrieked for her. Summer walked into the bedroom.

"Are you—" She pressed a hand to her mouth. "Oh, no. What happened?"

"He didn't like his dinner."

"Let me help."

"Is everyone all right?"

Erica followed her daughter into the bedroom. Allison held in a groan as she looked at the tall, perfectly dressed, un-vomited-upon woman who had been Peter's first wife.

Erica's dark hair was cut short in a soft, yet spiky style that brought out her incredible bone structure. Her makeup was subtle but perfect. She had on slim-fitting jeans, boots that looked house-payment expensive, a sweater and a chunky necklace that probably wasn't costume jewelry. A brown bag covered with the initials LV was casually slung over one shoulder.

"Well, this is a mess," Erica said, shaking her head. "All right, let's get this under control. Summer, help Allison to her feet, then we'll leave her to get changed. I'll handle handsome Jackson here."

She crouched down in front of the toddler and smiled broadly. "Hello. I'm Erica. We've met but I bet you don't remember. Did you throw up? Are you feeling better or is your tummy still upset?"

Jackson stuck his fingers in his mouth as he moved close to Erica. His eyes were wide as he studied her, then he thrust both arms toward her. Erica reached for him.

"Oh, you shouldn't do that," Allison said. "He might have vomit on his shirt."

But it was too late. The other woman had pulled him into her arms and rose with a graceful movement Allison could only envy.

"Not to worry. Clothes wash." She nodded at her daughter. "Help your stepmother. I'll get this one changed."

Allison found herself pulled to her feet. She moved with all the ease of a mud-bound hippo. Summer collected a washcloth and a clean T-shirt.

"Why is Jackson sick? Was he feeling okay after day care? I wonder if they gave him cheese sticks for his snack. Sometimes that really messes with his tummy."

Allison tried to appreciate the concern, but she was out of answers and low on patience.

"Could we not talk about that now?" she asked. "Please. I just need to get through this."

Summer stared at her. "Okay. Are you mad?"

"No, just stretched really, really thin."

Summer's shoulders slumped. "I'll wait with my mom."

She left, closing the door behind her. Allison went into the small attached bath, telling herself she would deal with her stepdaughter's trampled feelings later. She cleaned up as best she could, replacing the soiled blouse with a slightly too small T-shirt.

As she quickly brushed her hair, she saw the dark circles under her eyes and the blotches on her cheeks. She looked awful and felt worse. And now she got to face someone who defined perfect.

"Why am I being punished?"

But there was no answer. Just the faint sound of conversation from the other room.

She braced herself for what she knew would be an uncomfortable half hour, then went into the living room. Erica sat on the sofa with Jackson. He held her chunky necklace in his small hands. He was studying the stones and the metal, turning it over and over, before putting it in his mouth.

Allison nearly shrieked as she lunged for him. Erica waved her back.

"It's fine. The piece is just back from the jeweler. A stone had fallen out. They made sure everything was secure and then they steam cleaned it. He can't hurt it and the materials are perfectly safe for him." She smiled. "I'm not suggesting it should be in a line of toys, but for the moment, it's okay."

Allison eyed the necklace, not sure how much it had cost. If it was real—gold and semiprecious gemstones—then possibly more than her car. Without meaning to, she looked around the small living room, wondering how Erica must see it. The furniture was inexpensive and a little worn. The paint was relatively fresh, and the hardwood floors were nice, but the window covers were the cheap blinds landlords favored and there wasn't any artwork on the wall. Just a few photographs of the family, with an emphasis on Jackson.

"Thanks for changing his shirt," she said, settling in one of the club chairs.

"Of course. His room is so cute. I love all the stuffed animals." Erica smiled at her daughter. "Remember that lion you loved so much? You wouldn't go to sleep without it."

Her daughter grinned. "That was like twelve years ago, Mom. But yes, I remember."

"Is your room on the other side of the house?"

At first Allison didn't understand what Erica was asking. What room? Then she got it—Erica wanted to know where her daughter slept.

Summer shook her head. "I don't have my own room. That cabinet across from the crib is a Murphy bed. It pulls down."

"You sleep in the same room as Jackson?"

Erica sounded faintly outraged. Her gaze slipped between the toddler and the teen.

"It's fine," Summer told her. "Once he's out, he's out. Plus when I'm here, I take care of him in the morning so Dad and Allison get to sleep in."

"I see."

Allison had no idea what Erica was thinking, but it couldn't be good. Worse was her faint sense of guilt, which she tried to ignore. The house was small and they were doing the best they could with what they had. Maybe if Erica hadn't taken every single dollar she could in divorce, she and Peter wouldn't be in such dire financial circumstances. He hadn't gotten a penny from the house and she'd ripped away her business, all the while bad-mouthing him to his other clients. She was evil, Allison reminded herself. An awful person.

Only she wasn't particularly awful with Jackson. She deftly distracted him with a large teddy bear and when he dropped the necklace, she casually slid it into her bag.

"When are you due?" Erica asked her.

"In ten weeks."

"Have you seen Peter?"

"I'm going tomorrow." The city of SeaTac wasn't that far, but visiting the jail was going to be a challenge. She'd never been and didn't know what to expect. "Getting in for visitation is harder than they make it look in the movies."

"I'm sure there are hoops to jump through." Erica pulled a small pad of paper out of her bag, along with a pen. "Summer mentioned you went by the business and all the computers are gone."

Allison nodded. "No one was there. I don't know if they all quit, or what."

"Is Gail still the office manager?"

"Yes."

Erica made a few notes. "She and I always got along. Let me get in touch with her and find out what she knows. Even with the computers confiscated, all the accounting records should be backed up somewhere. Possibly on the cloud or with a company like Carbonite. She should have the information. Does Peter have a lawyer yet?"

Allison told herself the questions made sense and she wasn't being grilled, even if it felt as if she was. "I don't know. He hasn't said."

Erica frowned. "He needs a lawyer."

"I'm sure he's aware of that."

"These are serious charges. This isn't some problem he can ignore, hoping it will go away."

There was something in her tone—judgment and a touch of derision.

"Peter's not like that," Allison snapped. "He's a good man."

"All evidence to the contrary."

"Mom!" Summer's expression was pinched, her tone sharp. "You're supposed to be helping."

Erica stared at her daughter, then exhaled audibly. "You're right. I'll talk to Gail and see what's happening with the business. I'll text you what I find out and send along any suggestions I have. With the bank accounts frozen, the company can't pay the bills or the lease. I wonder how long until they get thrown out."

She sounded more intrigued by the question than worried by the answer, Allison thought bitterly.

"And the house," Summer said. "Don't forget Allison and Jackson have to move because the house is being sold."

"I'll find something," Allison said, avoiding looking at either of them.

"But how will you pay for it? You don't have any money. You're pregnant and you have Jackson and Dad's in jail." Summer's lower lip quivered. "I'm scared and I know you are, too."

Without thinking, Allison held open her arms. Summer rushed to her and hung on.

"This is going to work out," Allison said, knowing she was lying, but not wanting the teen to worry. "It's going to be fine."

"That's what my mom keeps saying, but I don't believe you *or* her."

Involuntarily, she glanced at Erica. The other woman's expression was unreadable, but there was tension in her jaw. Allison didn't care about Erica being uncomfortable, but Summer was a different matter. She touched the teen's shoulder.

"We're going to get through this. Your mom is going to help with the business and I'll handle the rest."

Lies, all lies, she thought, hoping she was doing a good job of faking it. Summer was right—she was terrified. She was trapped in a horrible situation with no way out. Every day the news got worse. In a matter of weeks, she was going to be homeless and then she would have a baby. At some point she was going to have to give in to the inevitable and start looking at women's shelters. And what happened to Jackson when she went into the hospital?

The fear churned in her belly, making her worry that it might be her turn to throw up. She forced herself to breathe, trying to let it go. Once Erica and Summer left, she could freak out, but until then, she had to stay calm.

Summer moved back to the sofa. She wiped her face, then smiled at Jackson. "You feeling okay?"

He grinned at her.

Erica slipped her notepad into her bag and rose. "We should get out of your way. You have to be exhausted from work and now that Jackson's doing better, he's probably going to be hungry." She offered a tight smile. "Once I find out what's going on at Peter's office, I'll be in touch."

Allison pushed herself to her feet. Her back screamed in protest, but she ignored the discomfort. "Thank you."

"Of course."

Summer hugged her again, then scooped up Jackson and kissed both cheeks. "See you soon, big guy!"

He put his head on her shoulder. "Summy."

Summer held him for several seconds before handing him back to Allison.

"Talk soon."

Allison nodded and opened the front door. When they were gone, she walked over to the sofa and sank down. Jackson crawled off her lap and reached for his teddy bear.

"Hungwe."

"I'll bet you are. Just give Mommy a second and I'll fix you another dinner."

Something simple, she thought, fighting weariness and a growing sense of dread. Something cheap. She would give herself the evening to not deal with the crap storm that was her life, then face it all in the morning.

9

Erica sat at her kitchen island, watching her mother rinse black-berries.

"They were insanely expensive," Mara said with a laugh. "But the produce guy said they were delicious."

She set them on the cheese plate she'd prepared. "All right, I think that's everything. I put a very nice pinot grigio in the re-frigerator. It should be chilled by now."

Erica waved at the different cheeses, her favorite stuffed olives, the rosemary crackers. "This isn't spontaneous. You planned it. Why?"

Her mother patted her arm. "Darling, I knew you were meet-ing with Allison, and that wouldn't be easy." Her expression was kind. "Now open the wine and join me at the table. We'll eat, we'll talk, we'll have that second glass."

Erica's throat got a little tight. "Thanks, Mom."

"Of course. You're my baby girl." Her smile turned teasing. "Even if you are closer to fifty than forty."

"Let's not talk about that."

Erica retrieved the wine and two glasses. As she sat at the table, she felt a rumble of hunger. On the way home from Al-lison's she and Summer had stopped at Taco Bell. Her kid had put away three tacos and two burritos, but Erica had only sipped water. Normally she enjoyed a Crunchy Taco Supreme as much as the next person, but she'd been too rattled by the visit to eat.

Now, with a little time and distance, she thought she might be able to eat something, and she was definitely up for wine.

Mara waited until they'd both filled their plates.

"So, how was it?"

"Awful." Erica put a little Brie onto a cracker. "The house is small. Maybe a thousand square feet." She thought about the furniture in the living room, the battered coffee table and the worn sofa.

"There are only two bedrooms. I didn't know that. When Summer spends the night, she sleeps on a Murphy bed in Jackson's room."

Her mother picked up her wine. "You sound outraged."

"Per the parenting plan, she's supposed to have her own room."

"Yes, but that's not the real problem, is it? What you don't like is that she doesn't mind the arrangement. When she's home with you, she's mostly a good kid, but she has her bratty, entitled moments. She disses what you do, won't bother with her appearance and makes it clear she's very much her father's daughter. Now you're afraid that isn't as much of an act as you'd hoped. She really does like being there."

Erica did her best not to wince. "You could at least try to be less blunt."

"What's the point? It's what you're thinking."

"I was actually trying not to think it." Erica felt her mouth twist. "She loves her and is worried about her. The way they hugged. It was like she never wanted to let go. It hurt."

"You're the mother," Mara told her. "You're dependable. No special care needs to be taken. Plus you've always been the strongest person Summer knows so she never has to worry about you. I don't know anything about Allison, but I'm guessing she's nothing like you. And now she's in a pickle."

"That's one way of describing her situation." Erica picked up an olive. "I'm going to talk to Peter's office manager and find out what's happening with the business. It sounds like the police had a search warrant and took everything."

Her mother's eyes widened. "Then how can you help? If the computers are gone, there won't be any records."

"The cloud, Mom. Peter has to have backed up his files. Gail should have that information, too." She shook her head. "The records are easy—it's the lack of money that's going to be a problem. I assume they froze the business accounts, too."

"What are you going to do? And what about Allison? Does she have any options?"

Erica did her best to ignore the whisper of guilt. "I don't know what her plans are."

"Is that because you didn't ask, or because she doesn't have any? If she has no money, she's in worse shape than the business. She and Peter rent, don't they?"

Erica was careful not to look at her mother as she piled meat onto a cracker. "The landlord has sold the house. She has to be out in a couple of months."

"But isn't the baby due then? The woman has a toddler, a baby on the way, no money and she has to move out of her home?"

"You sound like Summer." She stared at the cracker only to realize she suddenly wasn't hungry.

"The woman is living a nightmare."

"She's going to see Peter tomorrow. Hopefully he'll have some answers. If he can get out of jail, then he'll be around to help."

"How is he supposed to make bail? Didn't you say he shot at the police when they came to arrest him? If that's true, bail won't be cheap." Her mother looked at her. "To quote Princess Leia, you're their only hope."

"No, I'm not. I empathize, but she and I barely know each other. I'll help with the business. As for the rest of it, I'm sure she'll figure out something."

Her mother patted her hand. "I'm sure you're right."

Erica eyed her. "You don't mean that."

"Of course not, but I'm a warm, generous person. I'll let you have your delusions for as long as you can. Because in the end, it's not an Allison issue, or even a Peter issue."

Her mother was right. It was a Summer issue and Erica couldn't do anything about that.

Allison read the instructions for the eighth time, then checked her reflection. She'd dressed in black maternity pants and a plain gray crew neck sweater that barely covered her huge belly. She wasn't wearing any jewelry except her wedding ring and she hadn't bothered with makeup. There was nothing provocative about her appearance.

She'd reduced the contents of her handbag to her wallet, her cell phone and her keys. She had a separate tote for Jackson that included extra diapers, a couple of toys, juice, a sippy cup, crackers and paper towels and wipes. She would leave her handbag in one of the lockers. Jackson's tote, save a diaper, would stay in the car.

Despite going to bed right after she'd put down Jackson, she was exhausted. She'd tossed and turned, worrying about the upcoming visit and what to expect. She had a feeling TV and movies hadn't prepared her for the reality of seeing her husband in jail.

She glanced at the clock on the wall. She still had a few minutes until she had to leave. Timing the drive was awkward—she wanted to arrive early, but not too early. Waiting outside for too long risked having her show up with a cranky toddler. But being late cut into her time with Peter.

"It's not supposed to be this hard," she murmured to herself, turning her attention to her son, who played with stacking rings on the living room floor.

At least he didn't know what was going on, she thought. He

still occasionally asked for his father, but was mostly happy hanging out with her. She was lucky that he was so easygoing and—

Someone knocked on the front door. Instantly cold rushed through her. It was nine thirty on a Saturday morning. Summer never showed up this early and Allison wasn't expecting anyone. For a second she wondered if the police were here to trash her home the way they'd trashed Peter's office. There was a second knock.

She crossed the small living room and opened the door, only to stare in surprise when she saw her former boss on the doorstep, several grocery bags on the porch by her feet.

"Liz?"

"Hi. Yes, it's me. I thought about calling, but I didn't know if you'd answer, so I risked stopping by." Liz offered a tentative smile. "I hope that's okay."

It wasn't, Allison thought in a rush of anger. Liz had fired her for no good reason. Now she had no way to earn childcare credits, which meant when hers were used up, she could no longer afford day care.

Liz bent down and picked up a couple of the bags. "I stopped by the grocery store. Just to pick up a few things." Her smile wobbled. "To help."

Some of Allison's mad faded. "You didn't have to do that."

"I wanted to. I'm sorry about what happened. I know it seems like a harsh decision and you have every right to be pissed, but I'm hoping I can still be your friend."

Ambivalence didn't begin to describe what she was feeling, but she felt like she was alone in the world, so having someone on her side seemed important. Not that she could fully trust Liz, but maybe something was better than nothing.

"Thank you."

Liz's smile turned genuine. Together they carried in the groceries. There was a gallon of milk, lots of fruits and vegetables, cereal for Jackson and a couple of packages of raw chicken.

"This is too much," Allison said, thinking Liz had to have spent at least seventy-five dollars.

"Just say thank you and I'll sleep better at night."

"Thank you."

While Allison put away the groceries, Liz sat down with Jackson.

"Are you doing all right?" Liz asked her.

"Mostly. I'm going to see Peter in a few minutes."

"He's still in jail? I would have thought his lawyer would have gotten him out by now."

Allison didn't want to admit she wasn't sure if Jackson had a lawyer yet. "All our bank accounts are frozen. There's no way to pay bail."

"Oh. I hadn't thought of that. I'm so sorry. You must be terrified."

She finished with the groceries and walked into the living room. "I'm getting by."

Liz's expression turned concerned. "How can I help?"

Give me my job back! But she didn't bother saying that. Nor could she ask for a place to live or a loan.

"The groceries were very generous. Thank you for those." She glanced at the clock. "Jackson and I have to go. You have to make an appointment to visit the jail and I don't want to be late."

"Sure." Liz scrambled to her feet. "I'm here if you need me. I mean that."

"Thanks."

Liz gave her a quick hug, then left. Allison collected what she needed for the trip and carried the tote, along with Jackson, to the car.

As she buckled him in, she told herself she was excited to finally see Peter. It had been so long and she'd missed him so much. She wanted to know he was okay and find out what was happening. She wanted him to hold her and tell her everything would be all right. She wanted him to say that all this was a mistake, that the charges were being dropped and he would be home by Monday to fix everything.

If only, she thought grimly. If only.

Allison didn't consider herself a very nervous person, but she couldn't remember ever being so ill at ease. Nothing about going to a federal detention center was meant to be family friendly—at least not in her limited experience.

The multistory gray building was surrounded by fencing, with gates everywhere. Visitors were asked to park at the light rail station and walk—not easy when she had to leave the stroller in her car.

She stood in line with over a dozen other women—some with kids, some without. They were quiet mostly, their expressions more resigned than happy.

She'd already had her ID checked, her appointment confirmed and her small bag searched. She'd had to walk through a metal detector. Jackson had wobbled along next to her. They went into a room with lockers that could be rented. She put her bag in there, but kept her ID with her, along with a single diaper and cash. She would use the latter to buy a card that could be used in the vending machines. Peter had asked for a cola drink and some doughnuts.

On the way out, they had to pass by a large German shepherd that sniffed each of them thoroughly. Probably for drugs, Allison thought, so out of her element as to be inching close to hysteria. Her sense of unease skyrocketed when Jackson lunged for the dog, obviously intent on hugging it.

"Puppy," he managed, flinging his arms around the thick neck.

She held in a shriek as she pulled Jackson back, all the while trying not to imagine what those sharp teeth could do to her son. "Don't! That's not a puppy. That's a working dog."

The guard holding the leash barely gave her a look. "Get back in line."

Fortunately the dog was much more friendly. He turned his head and gave Jackson a quick swipe of his tongue on his cheek. His tail wagged twice and his expression softened. Then he turned to the next visitors and immediately went on alert, sniffing the woman and the teen.

Allison's heart was pounding in her chest as she went into the holding area. She used her cash to purchase a card for the vending machines, then waited with everyone else. After a few minutes, Jackson raised his hands.

"Up."

Her back already hurt, but she didn't want him to get upset, so she tried to lodge herself into the corner, to get as much support as possible, then lifted him into her arms.

Her lower back screamed in protest, but she ignored the pain. She held him, rocking slightly, willing her name to be called, so she could go in and see her husband.

After what felt like hours but was probably only twenty minutes, she and the other visitors were allowed in. She was the sixth visitor who passed through the guarded door into a big open room.

There were plastic chairs pulled up to low tables. The overhead lighting was harsh, the room sterile. Vending machines lined the far wall, surrounded by a barrier along with a sign saying no prisoners were allowed in that part of the room.

She searched the men filing into the room, looking for—

"Allison!"

She saw him and immediately rushed toward him. "Peter! Peter!"

Jackson saw his father and began to shriek. They closed the distance between them and then Peter's familiar arms were around her, holding her so tight. She hung on, letting her fear fade, feeling only this minute and how much she'd missed him.

"Hey, Jenkins. That's enough. Back off or you're out of here."

Peter immediately stepped back. "Sorry. It's my first time having a social visit."

The guard glared at him. "You know the rules. One hug, one kiss. That's it. Otherwise keep your distance. I'm not going to tell you again."

Allison stared at Peter. "I don't understand."

He looked at her. "We can't hug like that. I'm sorry. I got carried away." He offered her a sad, awkward smile. "There are a lot of rules. But I am allowed to hold Jackson."

He took their son and settled him easily on his hip, then motioned to some chairs. "Let's have a seat."

He said something else, but it was difficult to hear because an airplane flew directly overhead. It was a reminder of how close they were to the airport. Did Peter hear that noise all the time?

She studied him as he smiled at his son. Peter looked pale and thin. His clothes hung on him. She squeezed the card she held.

"Did you want me to get the drink and some doughnuts?" she asked.

"Please." His mouth turned down. "I have to eat them here. I can't take anything back to the cell with me."

She had no idea what to say to that. Everything about this experience was awful. The bright lights, the air of desperation. More and more people poured into the visiting room, raising the volume. Another plane flew overhead.

She bought the cola and a small, plastic bottle of juice, along with two packs of doughnuts. When she returned to her seat, Peter frowned.

"You didn't want anything for yourself?"

"I have water in the car."

He opened the can and took a long drink, then sighed. "This is good." He opened the juice bottle and helped Jackson take a drink. "Hey, little man. How are you doing?"

"Peter, we have to talk," she said. "What's happening? What's going on? Where's your lawyer? When are you getting out? How are we going to get our bank accounts unfrozen?"

He kept his attention on his son. "I'm so sorry, Allison. I never wanted this to happen." He paused as a guard walked by. Once they were (relatively) alone, he looked at her. "It's not what you think."

She stared at him. "I think you're in jail. I think I have no money and I'm about to lose my home. Peter, I'm over six months pregnant. Bethany is due in ten weeks. You have to get out of here so you can be with me."

"I know. I'm sorry." He swallowed. "I never wanted to hurt you."

"You haven't hurt me, you've terrified me. I can't handle this. I can't."

"It's going to be okay." He paused as another plane flew over. "There have been a few misunderstandings, but—"

"Misunderstandings," she shrieked, interrupting him. "This isn't a misunderstanding. You've been charged with serious crimes. You shot at police. We don't own a gun."

He stared at the ground. "I kept one at the office for self-protection."

What? He'd owned a gun?

She thought about the money in his jacket and the search warrant and the gun. "Do I even know you?"

He flinched as if he'd been struck. "Please, Allison. Don't say that. I love you with my entire heart. The things I did, the chances I took, they were for us. I wanted you to have a good life."

"I did until this happened. We were fine. We were happy."

He leaned toward her, his expression intense. "You were living in some crap rental. I wanted to give you the world, or at least buy you a house. That's what I was doing. There was going to be an inheritance. I nearly had that worked out. Then there was some trouble with a client and the feds showed up. You know the rest."

"I don't know anything. You're not making sense. Peter, what happened? What did you do?"

"Nothing bad. I give you my word."

But he wasn't looking at her as he spoke and while she knew innocent people could be arrested, she had a bad feeling that there was so much more she didn't know.

"Do you have a lawyer?"

"I'm working on it. I've been interviewing them."

She nearly came to her feet. "Interviewing? What does that mean? Shouldn't you take the first one you can get?"

"No. I need the right sort. Someone who understands what's happening and can help me. I'm getting close."

He sounded so casual, she thought bitterly.

"I don't understand. Why aren't you doing everything in your power to be home with your family?"

His gaze shifted, as if he were trying to see who was nearby, then he leaned close and lowered his voice.

"I'm cooperating. I don't want to go into details, but I have information they want. That's part of why I need the right lawyer. It's all a negotiation. I need to stay here until the details are worked out. If I just walk out of here without a good deal, there could be real problems."

She tried to make sense of what he'd just told her. "If you're cooperating, then that means you have information about a crime that the authorities want. You said it was a misunderstanding."

"It was." He held her gaze. "Just because I know something doesn't mean I was doing it myself. I have information that's useful. You have to believe me, Allison. You're the reason I get up in the morning. I love you. I'll figure this out and things will be better than before."

How could they be better? If he was cooperating, then he'd obviously been involved in some serious crimes.

"When are you getting out on bail?"

His gaze slid away. "I don't know."

"Before I have the baby?"

"I want to be there."

The fear returned, making her sick to her stomach. "Peter, I'm alone out there. I have nothing. Jackson and I will be homeless." Tears burned in her eyes. "I need you to come home and help me."

"Just hang on a little longer."

"'Hang on'?" Anger and fear twisted themselves around each other. "'Hang on'? That's easy to say from in here. What do you have to do in a day, except wait for your next meal and call me collect? 'Hang on'? This is all your fault. You did this to me, to us. We're married. You're not supposed to keep secrets and you're not supposed to ruin our lives. This is on you. All of it."

She had more to say—about how she'd never thought he was capable of committing a crime, but now she wasn't sure, and how she was reduced to taking food from friends and asking his ex-wife for advice—but she couldn't find the words. She was enraged, she was terrified, she was exhausted and every single part of her life was out of her control.

She stood and circled around the low table, then took Jackson from him.

"Allison, what are you doing? Don't go, please. Don't. I love you. I'm sorry. I'm going to fix this, I swear. I can make it right."

She ignored the words and marched steadily to the exit. Another plane flew overhead.

When she reached the guard, she showed her ID. He glanced from his clipboard to her.

"Once you leave, there's no coming back until your next visiting day."

"That's fine with me."

She walked out, Jackson on her hip, the boy waving back at his father. Peter called out her name, but she didn't turn around. After getting her small purse from the locker, she started the long walk to the light rail parking lot. It was only when she was in her car that she realized what she'd done. She'd let her temper get the better of her, and had walked out on her husband, leaving him alone. Worse, she hadn't gotten a single answer— at least none she could use. She'd wasted gas, time and energy, and she was one day closer to the coming shitstorm. And there wasn't a single thing she could do to stop it.

10

Gail, Peter's office manager, had been difficult to pin down but Erica had finally convinced her to meet by bribing her with a free facial. Or, as Erica had put it, "We have some new products we're using. I'd love to get your thoughts. Any interest in being a beta tester for us? Of course the facial will be complimentary."

Gail had gone for it and was now seated in the small conference room at the back of the Bellevue store. The space was generally used for vendor meetings or discussions between management and employees. Or in this case, finding out what had happened at Peter's office.

"You're not working for Peter anymore?" she asked, pouring the other woman tea from a lovely porcelain pot she'd picked up at a charity auction. "When Allison went to the office, no one was there."

"What's the point of anyone going in? The feds took all the computers and trashed the place." Gail, a fiftysomething with graying hair and absolutely no sense of style, sniffed. "I hear Hillary is trying to do some work from home, but she's the only one. Everyone else left. I walked out the day they arrested him. I left a letter of resignation on his desk."

"Which he never saw," Erica murmured, wondering about the timing.

"That's not my problem. He's the one who broke the law. If you ask me, he got what was coming to him."

Erica had always thought of Gail as efficient and hardworking. If she had to guess, she would have said the other woman respected her boss. Obviously she would have been wrong on that account.

"It was a shock to find out he's in jail," she said, her tone neutral. "At least to me. Were you surprised?"

Gail's thin lips pressed together. "I had my suspicions about what he was doing. People would come to the office. They didn't look right."

"In what way?"

"They weren't regular clients. They'd ask to see him, but wouldn't give anyone the name of their business. They looked—" she leaned forward "—shady."

Gail was starting to get on her nerves, but Erica told herself to be patient. She needed information and as of right now, Gail was her best option.

"That must have made you uncomfortable. You understand the business world." Erica offered a warm smile. "You've been Peter's right-hand person for over a decade. He'd be lost without you."

Gail shifted on her seat. "Thank you. I always tried my best. I've been handling people's books for over thirty years. I know what's legal and what isn't. He got into some things." There was another pause. "It's her fault."

Her? What her? "Excuse me?"

"The wife. Everything changed when he married her. I don't know what he sees in her. She's useless. Did you know she works in a grocery store?"

There was something in Gail's tone that set Erica's teeth on edge. What was wrong with working in a grocery store? People needed jobs and it was honest work.

"She has no ambitions, no training for anything, but he didn't care about that. She was young and pretty enough, if you like the type. One second he'd met her, the next they were married and she was popping out babies. That's when it all changed. He got into things."

Erica was still wrestling with Gail's assessment of Allison. Erica didn't know Peter's wife very well, but from what she'd seen, she was handling an incredibly difficult situation with a lot of grace. Gail seemed to be looking for the worst.

"Illegal things?" Erica asked, striving for a normal, friendly talk-to-me tone.

Gail nodded. "That's when I found he was keeping two sets of books on certain clients. Plus, I saw him putting lots of cash into a safe he'd had installed. We don't handle cash—not ever. He got nervous and snapped at everyone. I knew something was up."

Erica suddenly understood what had happened. "You're the one who turned him in."

Gail stiffened, color rising on her cheeks. "What? Why would you think that?"

"Oh, I'm not saying I disagree with your decision," Erica lied, wanting to get to the truth. "If Peter started down a dark path, you'd be the one to know." She feigned concern. "How hard this must have been for you. You'd known him for years, trusted him, enjoyed working with him. Then he turned on you."

Gail nodded vigorously. "It was exactly like that. I felt so betrayed. And to do it for *her*! He told me once he wanted to give her a better life. A big house and fancy cars. I wanted to say that wasn't the important part of life, but it wasn't my place."

She picked up her tea. "And I didn't state the obvious—that you were the only reason he had those things in his other life. You'd owned the house before you two married and there was a prenup on Twisted. You convinced him to start his own business, then paid all the up-front costs. He owes you everything, and then he left. Just like a man."

Erica was more caught up in the fact that Gail knew so many personal details about her marriage. Had Peter told the other woman or had Gail used her trusted position to snoop into their private files?

Questions she wasn't likely to get answered, she told herself. And they weren't the point of the conversation.

"You mentioned Hillary was still doing some of the accounting work? Do you have her contact information?"

"I do." Gail's tone was grudging. "With the computers gone and the office shut down, there's not much she can do."

"Isn't everything in the cloud? She can access it from there."

"I suppose but I don't know why she'd bother."

Erica felt Gail was being difficult on purpose, but there was nothing to be done about her attitude. Erica needed to get in touch with Hillary and Gail was her best option.

"You and me both," she said with a smile as she picked up her phone. "Her number?"

Gail gave it to her. "She's not going to work for free, you know. The bank accounts are all frozen. There's no way to get any money."

"We'll figure something out." She rose. "Thank you, Gail. You've been very helpful. I look forward to your feedback on the facial."

"I'm sure it will be nice."

Erica walked her to the reception desk and checked her in, then excused herself. Once back in her office, she quickly called Hillary.

"Hello?"

"Hillary, this is Erica Sawyer, Peter's first wife. I was hoping I could talk to you."

"About what?"

Erica couldn't read her tone, so had no idea what the other woman was thinking. Did she like Peter? Hate him? Hate her for reasons that had nothing to do with reality?

"As you know, there's been some trouble at the office. I was told you're still trying to work with clients, which is just amazing. Thank you for that. Peter has asked me to step in and help with the business as best I can."

"Peter wants your help?" Her tone turned a little more friendly. "I didn't know. Actually I don't know anything. One second we were working, the next, the police were everywhere. They took everything, then they searched the place. I was afraid they wouldn't let me leave with my handbag. I had to empty it and show them."

"They were probably making sure you didn't take a thumb drive with you."

"Oh. I hadn't thought of that."

"Are you able to access the business accounts remotely?"

"Yes. I'm doing that from home. My little laptop is old, but I'm doing my best. It's hard with the kids around, but I'm making it work."

Her voice cracked. "I have to. Not just because I need the job, but also for Peter and Allison. They're such good people. When my mom died, Peter let me take off as much time as I needed and Allison brought a few dinners. They don't deserve this."

Allison didn't, Erica thought. But from all she'd heard, Peter had totally screwed up and was getting exactly what he'd earned.

She thought about all the accounting that needed to be done to keep his business running. One person couldn't possibly do it by herself, and she doubted Hillary was a CPA, so there were legal limitations on some of the reports and filings. But she could do some things and right now that was better than nothing.

"Where do you live?" she asked.

"North Bend."

A town just a few miles east. That could work, Erica thought.

"I can give you an office in my Issaquah salon. It's not fancy, but it's quiet and we can get you a direct phone line for clients to call. I'll text you my IT person's number. Tell her what you need. A new computer, probably a printer and scanner. She'll have it waiting for you. In the meantime, email me the hours you've worked since Peter was arrested and I'll cut you a pay-check. Moving forward, report your hours and I'll cover you until—" Erica realized she didn't have any idea how this would play out "—until we get the situation straightened out."

Hillary's breath caught. "You'd do that for me?"

"Of course. You have children to feed. Plus, Peter and Allison are family."

She half expected to be struck by lightning for saying that, but fortunately the powers that be were busy elsewhere.

Hillary took down Erica's email address, along with the info for her IT person. Erica gave the other woman her work cell number and the call quickly wrapped up. That done, she sent an email to her office manager in Issaquah to tell her what was happening. There were at least a couple of small empty offices that Hillary could use. As for paying her, well, that was annoying but inevitable. Plus now she could tell Summer how much she was handling. Maybe that would calm down her daughter.

Wishful thinking, she knew. Without someone in charge, Peter's business would quickly spiral into disaster. Clients would find out their CPA was in jail and move elsewhere. Even if the charges were dropped, his firm would be significantly diminished and his income reduced. It would take years for him to recover, assuming he could.

She leaned back and thought about what Gail had said about his illegal activities. She had trouble reconciling that with the man she'd known. Or did she? After they'd split, she'd moved her accounting business to another firm. Within a couple of weeks, they'd discovered Peter had been skimming money from Twisted. No single amount had been huge but it had added up to over a hundred thousand dollars.

She'd been shocked and hurt by the revelation. That pain had quickly been followed by anger at her soon-to-be ex. She'd considered talking to a lawyer, but hadn't wanted the mess that would create. At the time she'd assumed he was acting out of spite—trying to hurt her in a passive-aggressive way rather than confronting their problems head-on. Once she took her business away, he couldn't get access to any accounts, so she hadn't been worried about future theft.

But maybe she'd been wrong to think of his actions as a one-time thing. Maybe instead they'd been a statement of his character. Something she hadn't seen in him at all. She wasn't sure what that said about her judgment and she didn't know what would happen next. But one thing she knew for sure—it was going to be one wild ride.

At this point in her pregnancy, pain was a constant companion. The longer shifts at the grocery store didn't help. Worse, Allison knew she couldn't keep them up much longer. Not when every day she got bigger and bigger. Standing put so much pressure on her joints and her back. But she needed the money.

She tried to shut down the familiar litany of worry and fear, but her brain refused to cooperate. Adding to her sense of discomfort was guilt. She felt awful for walking out on Peter when she'd visited him. They could have had a full two hours together, but she'd gotten upset and once she'd left, she hadn't been allowed back in. Now she had to make another appointment and wait to be approved again. Not only did she miss Peter, she needed answers.

She sat across from Jackson on the living room floor, playing with several stuffed animals. In a few minutes she would start dinner, then wait for Peter's call. At least she'd arranged for a calling card through a vendor that served the prison. She wouldn't have to deal with the expense of a collect call every time.

"I'm thinking spaghetti," she said, hoping it wouldn't trigger too much heartburn. She had leftover chicken she could throw in, along with some steamed vegetables. It was a meal Jackson would eat and it was relatively healthy. These days she had to force herself to eat—for the sake of baby Bethany.

Someone knocked on the front door. Both she and Jackson looked up. Allison half waited for Summer to burst in, calling her happy "It's me!" Only her stepdaughter had a game that day.

"Ugh."

She tried to get to her feet, which was tough going. She grabbed the sofa arm and used that as leverage, then lumbered to a standing position.

"Can I help—"

Allison stared at the man standing on her porch. She'd never seen him before and, given a choice, she never wanted to see him again. He was big and mean-looking, with too many muscles and tattoos, and an air of menace. He had a big knife sticking out of his right boot.

"You Peter's wife?" he asked, his voice gravelly.

"I, ah, yes."

He thrust a brown envelope at her. "He asked me to give this to you. It's all there. You need to remember that. Tell him Cappy gave you every penny."

As he spoke, he stared with such intensity that she instinctively stepped back. "Okay."

He shook the envelope again. "Here. Take it. It's for you."

She took the thick package. "Thank you."

He nodded and turned away. Only then did she notice the battered truck parked behind her Subaru. Seconds later, he drove down the street. She was shaking when she closed and locked the door.

Her heart pounded in her chest and her breathing was ragged. How could Peter know a man like that? Okay, maybe he was nicer than he looked, but he'd scared her. Worse, he knew who she was and where she lived.

She glanced down at the envelope in her hand. When she lifted the flap, she saw hundred-dollar bills. Lots of them. She hurried to the kitchen table, where she dumped them out and began to count.

Seconds later, she was ten thousand dollars richer than she'd been five minutes before. Ten thousand dollars! She couldn't believe it. She didn't know where the money had come from and despite everything, couldn't bring herself to care. While she still didn't have proof of income for an apartment, this covered all her other expenses. She could pay the minimum on the credit card and keep that going. She could pay for medical insurance through Bethany's birth. She could afford diapers and gas and still have money for any emergency.

She sank into a chair and gave in to tears. Jackson walked over. She pulled him close and hugged him.

"It's okay," she said, doing her best to smile. "I'm just tired. Everything is going to be okay."

She had resources—at least for the moment, and as long as she didn't think about the fact that in less than two months she would be homeless, then she had a lot to be grateful for.

Summer's game had been called on account of weather, but not before everyone got soaked. Erica peeled off her wet jeans and hung them over the tub in her bathroom. She was damp and shivering. It felt like one of those nights when she would never get warm.

She replaced her wet underwear with dry panties, then slipped on thick leggings and a pair of Uggs. The fleece lining would eventually warm her feet. She'd already put on a cashmere sweater over a long-sleeved T-shirt. She didn't bother with her hair. She wasn't going anywhere tonight—it could dry as weird as it wanted. She was about to walk out of the bathroom when she heard music over the house's sound system. The opening beats of Queen's "Another One Bites the Dust" made her smile.

"Oh, Mom, you do have your fantasies."

Practical Magic was one of her mother's favorite movies and she was forever trying to recreate the scene where the adult characters all danced together in the kitchen. Their song of choice had been something about a lime and a coconut. Mara had chosen the Queen song for their dance party. So far only she and Erica were drinking the margaritas, but Mara was counting the days until Summer could join them.

Erica found her mother and daughter dancing together by the kitchen island. She joined them, laughing and singing along. The ingredients for margaritas were by the blender and burger fixings were on the island.

This was good, she thought, clapping her hands. This life with her family. Summer, cleaned up from her game, spun in a circle, her damp ponytail swinging out behind her. Erica stared at it.

"You cut your hair!"

The words came out louder and more forceful than she'd intended. It didn't help that the song ended at that exact moment, leaving the kitchen silent.

Mara avoided her gaze while her daughter put her hands on her hips. "Oh, Mom, please. I asked Reese to cut off a few inches. It was getting too long. Don't make a big deal about it. Come on. It's just hair."

Erica ignored the sense of rejection and dismissal that came with every conversation about her daughter's appearance. Summer was basically a good kid, but she did seem to go out of her way to diss what Erica did for a living.

"You could have asked me or your grandmother," she said, going for the judgment-free, conciliatory tone and falling a little short. "I'm sure Reese meant well, but the edges are uneven and you could use some layers."

Summer rolled her eyes. "Really? Layers? I don't do layers. I don't care about my appearance. I'm not like you. I care about important things."

The slap came out of nowhere. Erica stiffened. Before she could think what to say, her mother stepped between them.

"No," Mara said sharply to her granddaughter. "Neither of us is willing to accept that kind of disrespectful attitude. If it makes you happy to not care about how you look, then go for it, but insulting your mother will not be allowed."

Mara pointed at Summer. "It's just hair? Is that what you said? It's just hair? Well, young lady, the 'just hair' you dismiss is the reason you live in a nice house and have a car you didn't have to pay for. It's the reason you don't worry about paying for college. It covers all the fees so you can be on your softball team. Your mother is a gifted businesswoman who built what she has from almost nothing. You claim you're not interested in the beauty industry, that you want to study business. I'm not sure I believe a word you say. You have a living example right here in your own home and instead of appreciating that and trying to learn from her, you act like a rude little brat. I'm very disappointed in you."

Erica blinked at her mother. For the most part, Mara didn't get involved in disciplining her granddaughter, but every now and then she took charge. Today was yet one more excellent example of why you didn't want to ever cross Mara Sawyer.

Summer seemed to crumple. "Grandma, don't."

"Don't what? Tell the truth? Am I wrong about any of it?"

Summer's lower lip quivered. "You were so mean."

"So were you."

Erica had to consciously keep herself from comforting her daughter. But she knew that would dilute the message.

"Grandma!"

Mara stared at her. "You're welcome to run to your room and pout, or you can apologize and we can move on."

Erica looked at her daughter. "I'd like you to stay."

Summer rushed toward her. "Mommy, I'm sorry."

Erica held her, smoothing her hand over her head. "For real?"

"Yes. I'm sorry for what I said. Grandma's right. I was being a brat."

Erica fingered the edges of Summer's uneven hair. "Why do you hate layers?"

Her daughter laughed. "I don't know but I do." She raised her head. "I am sorry."

"Then I forgive you. Ready for burgers?"

Summer smiled. "I'm starving." She stepped back. "Can I help with the grill?"

Mara moved to the cooktop and ignited the burners. "Go wash your hands, please."

Summer hurried down the hall to the half bath. Erica watched her go, then moved close to her mom.

"Thanks for coming to my defense."

"I don't usually, but every now and then she pisses me off and I can't hold back."

Erica smiled. "That's a good flaw. When you're on a tear, you scare us all."

"I'm happy to know I still have it in me."

Erica collected sliced cheese for the burgers, along with condiments. Summer returned and, under her grandmother's supervision, lowered the burgers onto the heated grill.

Order had been restored, Erica thought. At least for now. But even with the apology, her daughter's comments still stung.

When her daughter had been little, she'd assumed that Summer would grow up and join her in the business. She'd loved playing with her daughter's hair and dressing her like a princess. But that wasn't who Summer was, and she was the antithesis of being interested in Twisted. Something that would make Peter happy. He'd won that battle.

Given that he was still in jail, it was unlikely he was enjoying the victory and she was just petty enough to take a little pleasure in that.

11

"I'm concerned about your blood pressure," Dr. Gerstenberger said, a frown pulling her brows together. "And you haven't gained any weight since your last visit. The baby is doing well, but I'm worried about you. Tell me how you're feeling."

Allison told herself to stay calm and answer the question in the most neutral way possible. If she actually told Dr. Gerstenberger how she was *really* feeling, she might start crying and never stop. Or start laughing hysterically and *then* start crying. Either way she would end up in tears and her lovely doctor would consider admitting her for a psych evaluation.

"Peter's, ah, traveling on business," she lied. "I'm nearly seven months pregnant, working, and I have a twenty-month-old at home. You can imagine how I'm feeling."

"It's tough," her doctor said. "You're not going to like this, but you have to take care of yourself. You're not twenty-three."

Allison managed a genuine smile. "I know, I know. I'm having an old-lady pregnancy. I have to be careful. I'm being careful about what I eat." When she could eat, she added mentally.

"You need rest and nutrition. I know your son makes relaxing difficult, but you need to do that, as well. I don't want to put you on bed rest for the last few weeks of your pregnancy."

Bed rest! Allison held in a shriek. Oh, sure. Bed rest. Why not? By the end of her pregnancy, she would be homeless, so hey, she would just hang out in her car. Resting would be absolutely no problem.

"I'll do better," she said, hoping she meant the words.

"Good. I want to see you in three weeks. Eat more, put your feet up and hang in there. We'll get through this."

Allison wished that was true, but she had her doubts. The situation that was her life seemed unsolvable. The only bright spot was she got paid today. The money would help for sure. At this point, she wanted to save as much as possible for whatever hit was coming next. If nothing else, she would need it to survive the few weeks after Bethany was born.

She ignored the fact that she would probably be homeless by then. Why think about the most depressing thing?

She dressed quickly, made her next appointment, then left her doctor's office. She was going to swing by the grocery store before picking up Jackson. Yes, that would burn up precious day care credits, but it was so much easier to shop without him, especially when the store would be crowded. She would stock up on staples and replenish their fresh fruits and vegetables. She'd downloaded as many coupons as she could find and pored over the weekly ads. Pork tenderloin was on sale at a buy-one-get-one-free price. That would provide the two of them with at least ten protein servings, maybe more.

Forty minutes later she loaded her grocery bags into the back of her Subaru. There'd been a pop-up sale on the hot cereal Jackson liked, so she'd bought three boxes. She wasn't too exhausted and if she ignored the threat of bed rest, she was kind of having a good day.

As she drove home, she wished Peter was with her so they could talk. She missed his arms around her, his gentle voice, the way he took care of her and Jackson. Her anger from the visit had long faded and now she was just left with her loneliness and worry.

She told herself not to dwell on the bad. She had to stay positive, if not for herself, then for the baby. Better for her to speculate on how much her paycheck would be. She'd put in a lot of extra hours and had the back pain to prove it. She was hoping it was at least two hundred more than usual. Maybe a little more. The taxes were always confusing and—

Her breath caught in her chest as her entire body went cold. Panic seized her and her hands started shaking. No! Just no!

"Don't you dare," she screamed out loud. "Don't you dare!"

She checked her rearview mirror before pulling into a fast food parking lot. Nausea joined the fear, and she was trembling so hard, she could barely pull her phone out of her bag.

She unlocked the screen then swiped to the banking app. After opening it, she quickly navigated to her checking account.

"No," she moaned, staring at the screen until her tears blurred everything.

There it was, as always. Her monthly paycheck, sitting right where it should, after being automatically deposited. It was nearly three hundred dollars more than she usually earned, in a bank account frozen by the government.

She'd worked her ass off for nothing, because she'd never once thought to stop the automatic deposits. She could see the money, but it was just out of reach—held in an account she couldn't access. It wasn't fair, it wasn't right and she couldn't do anything about it.

The shaking went away and the tears dried up. Even the nausea subsided. Allison felt herself drifting into a gray place of nothing. She was in her body, yet not. There was simply too much, she thought dully. Too much bad and no way out.

She tossed her phone into her bag, then checked for cars before backing out of the parking space. She drove home and parked in the driveway, then managed to carry in all the groceries. She made it all the way to the living room before the emotions crashed into her.

She dropped the bags and sank to the floor, covering her face with her hands and screaming as loudly as she could.

"Make it stop! Make it stop!"

She couldn't do this anymore. There was no way. Just when she started to think she could get through this, something else happened. She could probably manage if Peter was here to help, but he wasn't. Bad enough to miss him, worse to manage this on her own.

She cried until there were no tears left, then rocked back and forth, trapped in a hell she couldn't escape. She was out of ideas, out of options, out of hope. Worse, she thought maybe she didn't even care.

"Knock, knock. It's me."

The front door opened and Summer stepped inside. The teen's wide smile instantly faded as she stared at Allison.

"Oh my God! What happened?" Her stepdaughter was at her side in an instant. "Allison, are you all right? Is it the baby?"

Allison stared at her, knowing there was nothing to say, no way to explain why she sat in the middle of the floor, surrounded by groceries. She was too tired to come up with a lie.

"They took my paycheck," she said dully. "I worked all those extra hours for nothing. Swollen ankles, aching back—for nothing. I did it to have a little extra and they took it."

Summer crouched next to her, rubbing her arm. "Who took it?"

"The bank. It was automatically deposited and the accounts are frozen, so it went in but I can't get it out." She tried to smile and was pretty sure she failed. "The doctor's threatening bed rest if I don't take care of myself. Isn't that funny? When am I supposed to do that? Peter's in jail. I don't have anyone. I'm responsible for all of this and I don't know what to do. When the lease is up, we'll be homeless. Jackson and I will be living in my car."

She stared at the wide-eyed teen. "I didn't think my life would be easy, especially after I lost Levi, but I thought it would be okay. That I'd work hard and save money and have a little happiness. Then I met your dad and he was so great. He took care of me and loved me and I was happy. Now it's all gone."

Summer reached for Allison's hand. "You're scaring me."

"I'm scaring myself." Allison pressed her lips together. "Sorry. I know I should say something comforting, but I don't have anything left."

"Don't say that. We'll figure this out."

Allison patted her shoulder. "You're sweet and very young. I know you care, but this isn't your problem. You should go, Summer. You don't have to take this on."

"I want to help."

"You can't. It's okay." A lie, but what was she supposed to say? "You really should go."

"I'm not leaving you." Summer sounded determined. "There's a solution. I know it." She frowned. "Where's Jackson?"

"At day care. I need to go get him."

"You can't drive right now." She stood, then pulled Allison to her feet. "Wash your face, then put away the groceries, then sit."

She crossed to where Allison had dropped her bag and fished out her car keys. "I'll get Jackson. We'll get takeout on the way home. We'll have a nice evening and when Jackson goes to bed, we'll talk."

Honestly, Allison would rather be alone, but she didn't know how to say that to the teen. And Summer was right—she shouldn't drive right now.

"If you could pick him up, I'd appreciate it, but I can manage the rest."

"Not happening." Summer grabbed her backpack. "I'll see you in about forty minutes."

Allison forced a cheerfulness she didn't feel. "I'll be here." She paused, then walked over and hugged her stepdaughter. "Thank you. I know you worry. I wish I could fix that."

Summer hung on. "You can't. You're my family, too. We'll figure this out. I know we will."

If only, Allison thought. If only.

"I need to circulate," Erica said without a lot of energy.

Killion kept his hand on the small of her back. "I'd rather you stayed close."

She smiled up at him. "I thought I was here on a reconnaissance mission. You know, discover the enemy's weaknesses."

"I don't need you for that." He paused. "Just to give me a sense of who they are."

"Isn't that the same thing?"

He grinned. "You're sexy when you're powerful."

"I thought I was sexy all the time."

"You know that's true." He lightly kissed her. "All right. Go forth and discover. I look forward to hearing your report."

"Is that all you look forward to?" she asked, her voice bright with amusement.

He glanced around. "You know, we don't have to stay."

She laughed. "Yes, we do. Think of what we're going to do later as your reward. It's been on my mind all day."

He groaned. "You're killing me."

"Good."

She turned and studied the room. The cocktail party was in full swing, with nearly fifty people. Killion's company was sponsoring the casual get-together with executives and their spouses from potential acquisitions. Technically the event was billed as a business networking opportunity, and she was sure most of those attending believed that. But Erica knew better. Killion believed that character was a big part of success. More than one deal had been scuttled because the president of the company was a jerk.

If the person in charge was a bad boss, growing the enterprise would be that much harder. Killion only bet on sure things.

At events like this, he liked her to talk to the executives

without him around. It was a little game they played—one she enjoyed. Much information could be found in casual conversation. When she introduced herself, she offered no more than her name. If the other person didn't bother to ask what she did, assumed she was simply the wife of someone more interesting, that was a black mark for them.

Should they find out she was the owner of Twisted, did they dismiss her because it was just "a salon"? Did they ask questions, listen to her answers? If she walked up to a group of men, did they engage or ignore her? Which married men tried to pick her up? She never approached a man alone, but that didn't stop men from coming on to her. Less now that she was in her late forties, but enough to be both annoying and occasionally gratifying. She wasn't looking for anything beyond what she had with Killion, but it was nice to be admired.

She approached a group of three women and two men. During a brief lull in conversation, Erica turned to one woman and said, "I love your earrings."

She smiled. "Thank you. My daughter designed them."

The gold hoops with offset diamonds glimmered in the light.

"She's incredibly talented. Where does she sell her work?"

The woman named a local jewelry store, then held out her hand. "Bonnie Winter."

"Erica Sawyer."

The other people introduced themselves. One of the men asked where she worked.

"I own a company called Twisted. It's a—"

"I know it," another man said. "Salons, right? My wife loves the Bellevue location." He gave her a self-deprecating grin. "I keep a gift certificate in my desk. If I mess up and she's mad, it's my go-to get-out-of-jail-free gift."

One of the women laughed. "You're a good husband."

"I try. She's amazing."

Conversation shifted to sports. Erica excused herself to freshen her drink. As she walked to the bar, she made a mental note of the man's name. He was a senior executive at a local tech firm. Killion would want to meet him. Not because he shopped at her salon, but because he was organized, willing to admit he was wrong and cared about someone other than himself.

"White wine," she told the bartender, then took the glass.

The volume continued to climb. In an hour it would be loud enough that real conversation would be difficult. At that point, Killion would find her and they would leave.

Her gaze drifted across the crowd until she located him. He looked good, she thought. Not just handsome, but also at ease. He knew who he was and what he was capable of. He was the kind of man others instinctively looked to for leadership. Yet he didn't dominate—not her or anyone else. He didn't need to announce himself or draw attention, and she liked that.

He was so different from Peter, she thought. Peter had been funny and kind when they'd met. A little younger, a lot less experienced. She supposed she'd been attracted to his awe of her as much as his smile. After men telling her she was too driven, too determined, too everything, it had been nice to find someone who admired her.

She'd always known theirs wasn't a level playing field. He'd been a junior accountant and she'd been a business owner planning to acquire an empire. She bought the house on her own. After the wedding, he'd moved in. She'd always meant to put him on the deed, but somehow never had, so the house was never community property. He'd come into the marriage with no real material assets and had left with little more beyond half their joint bank accounts. She'd signed off on her half of his business—because that *had* been considered community property. In return he'd released his share of her retirement plan.

Once she'd pulled her account from his business, he'd been struggling. Of course after finding out about the money he'd stolen, she had no reason to feel guilty. But sometime after the divorce, he'd changed.

She shook off the past and told herself to focus on the party. She glanced around, searching for another group to join, when she felt her phone buzzing in her small clutch. She pulled it out and glanced at the screen.

We're both okay physically but Summer is nearly hysterical about Allison and I can't calm her down. Can you come home early?

Erica walked quickly to the foyer, where it was quieter, and called her mother.

"What's going on?"

"I don't know. She's not making any sense. Something about Allison and the baby and a paycheck. She won't stop crying. Summer can be moody, but I've never seen her like this. I'm worried."

Considering Mara was basically unflappable, her concern wasn't happy news.

"Let me tell Killion goodbye, then I'll be there."

"Thank you. I wouldn't normally bother you, but under the circumstances…"

"You did the right thing. Tell Summer I'm on my way."

She hung up and turned to find Killion, only to see him walking toward her.

"Something happened," he said when he was in front of her. "I saw it on your face when you looked at your phone."

"Later we'll discuss your ability to read me from a distance. Summer's upset. My mother described her as almost hysterical, which isn't like my daughter. She's worried about Allison. They're so close."

He took her hand in his. "She loves you."

"I know that."

"She loves you," he repeated, then tugged gently. "Come on. I'll take you home."

Because he'd driven her here, she didn't have a car. "Stay. I'm fine. I'll get an Uber."

"I'm not sending you home with someone I don't know. I have a car waiting here in case someone is too drunk to drive. He'll take you."

"Thank you. You're being silly, but thank you."

"Let me know what happens with Summer."

"I will."

Thirty minutes later, she was tipping the driver. She'd barely started toward the front walkway when Summer burst out of the house.

"Mom! Mom! You came home."

Her daughter ran to her, arms outstretched. Tears streaked her face.

"It's so bad. If you'd seen her. She was on the floor and I thought she'd lost the baby. They took her paycheck and she doesn't have anywhere to live and we have to help. We have to!"

Erica put her arm around the teen. "Slow down. I don't know what you're saying. Who took Allison's paycheck?"

"The bank. It was automatically deposited."

Erica held in a groan. Of course. Most paychecks were, but with the accounts frozen, there was no way for Allison to get it out. She could cancel the automatic deposits going forward, but her current check was gone, at least in the short term.

"Her doctor is worried about her. Her blood pressure is too high and she's not eating, so she's not gaining weight."

They went inside. Erica stepped out of her three-inch heels. Summer faced her. Her skin was blotchy, her eyes red. As she spoke, she squeezed her hands together.

"Plus the house. Allison can't get an apartment. She can't show enough income on her own. Dad's in jail and she's pregnant and she's going to be homeless." Tears dripped down her cheeks. "It was so awful."

Erica agreed the situation was dire but where did Allison get off dumping all this on a sixteen-year-old? But before she could figure out what to say, Summer repeated, "We have to help."

She knew there was no response possible beyond "We do and we will."

"She's my family, too."

"I know."

"I've been thinking and I've come up with a plan. Don't be mad, Mom, but I want Allison and Jackson to move in with us."

12

Work had always been Erica's happy place. Even when there were problems, she enjoyed every second of every day. Her salons were temples of joy and possibility. Yes, there were always crap things to be done, but they were a means to an end. She loved the high ceilings, the buzz of conversation, the scents in the spa area, the whir of the air purifier. She'd worked sick, pregnant and hungover. She'd worked while falling in love and while dealing with the fact that her husband didn't want to be married anymore. She'd worked through disappointments and a false positive on a mammogram. Until today, until this very moment, she had always been able to work. But right now, she couldn't.

Her mind was like a hamster on a wheel, circling around and around, not going anywhere, instead churning over the same thing.

I want Allison and Jackson to move in with us.

Summer's words still haunted her. They'd kept her up most of the night and now they sat with her, repeating themselves over and over again.

Oh, there had been more. Her daughter had an entire plan to make an impossible request seem reasonable. She would give up her beautiful corner en suite with the giant walk-in closet for Allison and the baby, and move into a still very nice but smaller bedroom with a Jack and Jill bathroom shared with the room next door. That was for Jackson, when he was ready to be on his own. Summer had said for the first few weeks they should put his crib in with her so he wouldn't get scared.

Living with them would mean Allison wouldn't have to work, freeing her to care for her toddler and her newborn. When Peter was finally out of jail, they could go live together, happily ever after, as God intended. Or some such nonsense. Then life would return to normal.

It was, her daughter had informed her, the perfect plan. Except for, you know, the part about Erica's ex-husband's second wife and her child moving into *her* house and mooching off her for who knew how long. Sure, it was great. Erica couldn't imagine being happier.

Her mother knocked on her half-open office door, then walked inside. Mara's expression was sympathetic.

"You still look shell-shocked."

"Good, because that's how I feel."

"Want to go get a drink?"

Erica glanced at the clock on her computer. "It's quarter to ten in the morning."

"Still, desperate times."

"Thanks, Mom, but I don't think day drinking is the best solution. Not that there is a problem. Allison isn't moving in with us."

Mara sat down and leaned toward her. "You're going to tell Summer no? She'll be heartbroken. The situation really is dire."

"I know that and I'm not completely heartless. I'm going to rent her an apartment. She'll pay me what she can and I'll take care of the rest."

"What about when she has the baby? Who's going to take care of Jackson?"

"She has friends. Someone can step in."

"How is she supposed to manage with a newborn and a toddler? What if there's a problem with the birth or the baby? How does she deal with all that?"

"She's not the only single woman on the planet having a baby."

"But she's the one Summer knows."

Erica glared at her mother. "I thought you were here to help."

"I am." Mara's tone gentled. "You're ignoring the heart of the situation. I understand that you don't like it and don't want to deal with it, but as far as Summer is concerned, Allison and Jackson are her family."

"So she tells me daily." And every time was a little dagger to her heart.

"This isn't an argument you're going to win. Summer will wear you down."

Erica didn't want to address that. "She's asking for the impossible. That woman isn't moving into my house."

"It solves a lot of problems."

"Not for me." She narrowed her gaze. "You want this. You think Allison *should* come live with us."

"It's not the worst idea in the world."

"How can you even say that? I don't know her. She's Peter's wife. The man left me. Explain to me why I should give a rat's ass about my ex-husband's wife and his child."

"It's the right thing to do and you've never been comfortable being a bitch."

"I have employees who would disagree with you."

"No, you don't." Her mother's mouth flattened. "It's a huge ask. Years from now Summer will be shocked that she insisted and even more surprised that you said yes. The woman has nowhere to go. She's not your family, but she is important to your daughter. You have to be the bigger person and say yes."

Erica turned away, hating that she'd been put in this position and resenting the possibility that her mother might be right.

"I don't want to talk about it anymore." She needed time to think. She needed to figure out another option and she needed more information.

"I'm going to see Peter," she said.

Her mother stared at her in surprise. "In jail?"

"That's where he is. I need more information and Peter is the only one who has it."

"Can you do that? Just go see him?"

"No. There's a whole process. I had to fill out an application and be approved. When I talked to Killion last night, he said he'd help. He knows someone who knows the warden, so I can go see Peter this afternoon."

"It's good to have powerful friends," her mother said with a smile. "Or sleep with a powerful man."

Erica tried not to grimace. "I don't like using him this way, but I didn't know who else to turn to."

"You're not using him. You're asking for help. Trust me. The man is thrilled he can do something for you."

"Killion isn't like that."

"All men are like that. You're successful and self-sufficient. I'm not saying it's a bad thing, but when a man loves a woman, he wants to take care of her. You don't make that easy."

Erica dismissed her words with a flick of her wrist. "Killion doesn't love me any more than I love him. We're friends who have a convenient sexual relationship, nothing more."

Her mother ignored her. "My point is, he's not thinking you're taking advantage of him."

He had been gracious when she'd called. He'd listened while she'd ranted and had been the one to suggest she go see Peter to find out what was going on, then had offered to smooth the way.

"Do you want me to come with you?" her mother asked. "I'd probably have to wait in the car, but I'd be there for moral support."

"You're sweet but no. I'm just visiting Peter. It's not a big deal."

"Have you been to a federal detention facility before?"

"No. Have you?"

"I haven't and that's how I know it's a big deal."

"I'll be fine."

"And I'll be around if you want to talk."

Erica found herself regretting her dismissal of her mother's offer as she waited while a male guard went through her purse.

"It's not a visiting day," he grumbled, opening a lipstick and staring at the color. "And you're not a lawyer."

She had no idea what to say to that, so kept her mouth shut and hoped this would be over soon.

The drive hadn't been too bad. She'd been told to park in the closest visitor lot, so had been able to walk right up to the entrance. But the gray multistory building had looked plenty intimidating, as had the signs posted on the tall fencing.

The guard put everything back in her bag and returned it to her, then motioned for her to proceed. She'd already gone through a metal detector and been sniffed over by a large German shepherd.

She followed the guard through several doors, each with a big lock, into an open area she would guess was the general visiting area. There were plastic chairs and low tables. Vending machines sat against one wall. The guard pointed to a chair.

"Wait there."

"Thank you."

She took a seat, grateful she'd worn pants instead of a skirt. She hadn't thought of what to wear while visiting her ex in prison, but Summer had a game that afternoon, so pants had made the most sense.

As she waited, she wondered if Peter would refuse to see her. She hadn't been in touch with him and had no idea what he was thinking or going through. All she knew was her name had been added to his visitor list, but given the special treatment she'd already received, she wasn't sure that meant he'd approved it.

Despite the fact that she was the only person in the large room, the space was anything but quiet. She could hear shouts

and loud conversations. Metal doors clanged, guards issued orders. She had a sense of being watched and it made her uneasy,
even though when she glanced around, she didn't see anyone.

After what felt like an hour but was probably ten minutes, a
different guard appeared with Peter. Erica rose, mostly out of
shock as her ex-husband shuffled toward her, leg irons around
his ankles, hands cuffed.

He looked thin and tired. The lines around his brown eyes
had deepened since she'd last seen him and his skin had a pallor
that said he hadn't seen sunlight in days.

"We're not prepared for visitors," the guard said, his tone accusing. "And you're not an officer of the court."

"A what?"

"A lawyer," Peter said, avoiding her gaze. "You're not a lawyer."

"I can't stick around to make sure you don't get into trouble,"
the guard continues. "He stays in restraints."

"It's fine," Peter said, kicking a chair out from the table so
he could sit down.

Erica started to help, but he shook his head. "Stay back. It's
better that way." His gaze finally met hers. "They'll be watching remotely. We don't want them thinking you're passing me
drugs."

She wasn't sure if he was trying to be funny or telling the
truth. Regardless, she settled back in her seat.

"You're a surprise," he said. "I was told you would be visiting and that I would be fine with it."

"I can leave if you're not."

"No, it's okay. Visitors break up the routine. Plus Allison can't
get here as often as I'd like."

At the mention of his wife's name, he seemed to shrink a little, his face crumbling. "This is so hard for her and it's all my
fault. God, I've hurt her. I've put her through so much and I
only wanted things to be good for her, you know. Better than

what we had. I would lie awake at night in that shit rental and think about the house you and I had. I wanted something like that for her. Beautiful things, never worrying about money."

He turned away. "She looks for coupons online. Did you know that? My wife has to clip coupons."

The conversation had taken an unexpected turn and Erica didn't know how to respond. She understood that Peter wanted the best for his current wife, but the way he was talking about the house confused her. It had never been theirs. She'd been the one to buy it and she'd been the one to arrange for it to be taken care of. Peter had shown no interest in repairs or maintenance. He'd come and gone with the ease of a man living in a hotel.

"Peter, what happened? Why are you here?"

He tensed at the question, looking around, as if expecting to see someone nearby, listening. "I'm not going to talk about that. They're probably recording this conversation."

Could they do that? Was it legal? She had no idea and that wasn't the point. "The charges against you are serious. Allison isn't sure you even have a lawyer yet. You need a lawyer."

"I have the newly minted court-appointed lawyer for now, but I'm working on getting someone decent. Once I figure out who, everything will change."

She had her doubts. "You threatened police with a gun. I didn't know you owned a gun."

"Just for work stuff."

"You're an accountant! Why would you need a gun?"

He looked at her. "Please lower your voice."

There was something in his tone. More than a request— almost a demand. But Peter never demanded anything. He went along to get along. He never got that involved. His easygoing nature had been such a contrast to her drive and she'd liked that. She'd thought he would help her get more balance in her life and she thought she would... Well, looking back she wasn't sure what she thought she brought to the table.

Her determination? Her success? With a little perspective, she saw that he'd admired both of those until he hadn't. That the very thing that had drawn him to her had ended up pushing him away. Or maybe she was fooling herself. Maybe she'd fallen for a charming, slightly awkward but sweet facade. Maybe it had all been an act, a way to access a very nice life.

Yes, they'd been divorced for over four years now, but she had a feeling the reason she didn't know him now was because she never had.

"Have they set bail?"

His gaze slid to the floor. "It's a million dollars."

"What?" Her voice was a shriek. "That's insane. So you need to come up with what? Ten percent, so a hundred thousand. Why is it so high?"

"They want to make sure I cooperate. I'd need a guarantor. For the million. So ten percent in cash or property and a guarantor."

The hundred thousand was bad enough but finding someone to guarantee the million dollars? "I don't know how that's going to happen. Your business is basically shut down. Once the police trashed it, everyone quit but Hillary."

He frowned. "Gail quit?"

"Gail's the one who turned you in."

In other circumstances, his shock would have almost been comical. He stared at her wide-eyed, his mouth working without him making a sound.

"Gail?" he asked finally. "It was Gail?"

"She figured out you'd crossed a line and she wasn't happy."

"But we'd worked together over a decade."

"Probably why she was so shocked to find out about the illegal behavior." Erica realized too late she probably shouldn't have mentioned Gail. "You're not going to hurt her, are you? You're the bad guy here, not her."

He stared at her. "Hurt her? I'm in jail. What can I do to any-one?"

"You could have an associate kill her."

He swore and looked away, then back at her. "Is that what you think of me?"

"I don't know what to think, Peter. The last time you and I had a conversation this long, you were explaining how much you didn't want to be married to me and how horrible I was." She forced herself to hold his gaze when she really wanted to turn away and find a corner to hide in.

She squared her shoulders. "When we were married, you had your flaws, but not money laundering and wire fraud. At least not that I know of. You're different, so maybe I get to be worried about telling you Gail turned you in."

"Nothing's happening to Gail. She's the least of it. Allison is the only one I care about." He leaned toward her. "Have you seen her?"

Erica hesitated. "Briefly. We talked about the business and I said I would handle things. I found Hillary workspace in one of my salons and I'm paying her salary. She'll keep things limping along for as long as possible."

After that, Erica would write Hillary a glowing recommendation, give her a generous severance and ask her current accounting firm if they had any openings.

"How did she look? How is she doing?" His shoulders sagged. "Did you see Jackson?"

Erica assumed the "she" in question was his wife, not his accountant.

"She's struggling," she said bluntly. "You might have had some grandiose plan but it's all gone to hell." She leaned toward him. "What the fuck were you thinking, screwing with her life like that? You claim to love her and this is how you treat her? You abandon her to what? Live in her car?"

She thought Peter might blow up at her. He didn't get angry

often, but when he did, it was a serious event. But instead of pushing back, he crumbled, sagging in his chair, his head down, his shackled hands covering his face.

"You're right," he said, his voice thick with emotion. "I did that to her. God, I've ruined her and it's all my fault."

He looked at Erica. Tears filled his eyes. "She's everything to me. My world, and look at what she's going through. I never wanted that. I wanted her to live like a princess. She's my princess."

His eyes squeezed shut. "And now she hates me."

The intensity of his emotion made Erica squirm. She wasn't used to Peter sharing so much, or feeling so deeply. Oh, sure, when they'd been married, he'd told her he loved her, but the words had always seemed casual. She knew for a fact she'd never been his "princess." He used to joke that she didn't need him for anything.

"Crying doesn't help," she snapped. "It makes you weak and then one of the other inmates is going to make you his bitch. Do you really want that?"

He sucked in a breath. "That's the Erica I know. Always able to get to the heart of the problem."

"You being someone's bitch isn't a problem that concerns me right now. In addition to your princess wife, you also have a sixteen-year-old daughter who's pretty frantic with worry. It would be nice if you asked about her."

He wiped his eyes. "How is Summer?"

"How do you think? Her father's in jail, her stepmother and half brother are about to be homeless. She's not planning a long weekend at a theme park."

She stood and circled the chair, then faced him. "I can't believe you did this. I can't believe you were so stupid, not only that you got into something illegal, but then you got caught. I hope it's worth it."

He stared at her. "Tell me you'll help Allison."

"What?"

Her outrage was more pretense than real, but she went with it.

"You came to see me for a reason."

"I wanted to know what was going on."

He waved his hands. "Now you know. This is where I am and this is where I'll be staying until I can make bail. Finding the right lawyer takes time." His mouth flattened. "It's not like I have a home office and can make calls whenever I want."

He leaned toward her. "You've talked to Allison. You know what she's up against. She's pregnant, Erica. She's alone with Jackson and she's scared. She doesn't have a lot of friends. It was always the two of us. I didn't give her enough. You have no idea how sorry I am about that. I wanted to give her the world."

"Right now all she needs is an apartment, but I guess that was too much to ask."

He ignored the slam. "Please. Help them."

"They're not my problem."

He slid off the chair, his knees hitting the floor. His dark eyes met hers. She read regret, determination and a couple dozen other emotions she couldn't name—probably because she was in shock from seeing her ex-husband supplicating himself to her.

"I'm begging you," he said quietly. "Erica, I'm begging you. If you ever loved me, help Allison. Do it for Summer, do it because it's the right thing to do. You're the only one who can save her."

She stood there, unable to move, unable to speak. Everything about the moment was surreal. A voice in her head whispered that at no point in their marriage would he have begged for her. With the realization came a stab of pain, but she ignored it.

"Us," she said quietly. "Did it begin falling apart because I pushed you to start your own business or was it before that?"

"The business thing didn't help, but it was before that."

Another blade carved through her heart. That long ago? She'd had no idea, no hint they were anything but happy.

"Will you help her?"

She picked up her bag. "I don't know. But if I do, it won't be because of you."

13

Erica sat alone in the stands, trying to focus on the game. Summer's team was up by three in the second inning.

She tugged her trench coat more tightly around her body, once again grateful she'd remembered to wear pants and low-heeled boots, along with a turtleneck and blazer. Suitable attire for both a high school softball game and a visit to prison, she thought, still processing her meeting with Peter.

She'd spent less than twenty minutes with him and still felt traumatized by everything that had happened. No, she amended. Not everything. The part where he'd begged.

No man had ever gone on his knees to her before. When Peter had proposed, it had been on a beach in St. Barts. They'd been walking along, after a wonderful dinner. The sky had been the cliché of an artist's sunset paint palette, the air warm. She'd been happy, content and maybe a tiny bit drunk.

"I wonder if you'd like to marry me."

She could hear the words now, slightly hopeful, a little chagrined. No wild declaration of love, no promise to make her the happiest woman in the world. Just Peter being Peter. Or at least the man he'd presented to her and the one she'd fallen in love with.

She'd looked at him, surprised by the unexpected question. "You're proposing?"

He'd given her that lopsided grin of his. "Badly, if you have to ask. I have a ring back in the room and I was going to do the whole champagne-flower thing, but you're just so beautiful here on the beach and I want us to be together."

"You bought me a ring?"

"Yes. Your mom helped me with the size." The bashful expression returned. "I hope you like it."

She'd faced him then, taking his hands in hers. "I love you, Peter. So much."

"I love you, too."

He'd kissed her then, in that way of his. Kissing him had always given her butterflies in her stomach. Even years later, when she'd sensed he was distant but didn't know why and didn't have the time to find out, she'd felt the flutter. Shortly after that, he'd announced he wanted a divorce—shocking enough but not as horrifying as his cruelty as he severed every connection between them.

He'd certainly never begged her for anything, had never declared that she was his princess—something to be treasured. Maybe he'd never loved her at all, but he did love Allison.

She tried to figure out what she was feeling. She didn't want him back. She just couldn't stop wondering how things would have been different between them if just once he'd loved her enough to beg.

The crack of a bat brought her back to the game. Summer's hit sailed over second base, allowing her to make it to first and two teammates to score.

Crystal made her way across the bleachers and sat next to Erica.

"At this rate, we might be done early," the other softball mom said with a faint smile. "You doing all right?"

Erica didn't know what to do with the question. "I'm fine. How are you?"

"Good. I was just wondering how you were handling everything. I know it's been tough. Poor Summer, with her dad and all. She's staying strong, but the whole family has to be shattered."

Erica stared at her, wondering how Crystal had ever found out what was—

Of course, she thought, mentally slapping herself on the forehead. Crystal and her friends were the mothers of Summer's friends. Her daughter would talk to her girlfriends about the trauma of her father's arrest and what was happening with Allison. The teens would tell *their* mothers, who were also friends and would talk.

She glanced past Crystal and saw the other mothers watching them. When her gaze met theirs, they quickly looked away.

"I don't know him well," Crystal said in a low voice. "Peter, I mean. I've met him. We all have. Dropping off our girls at his house or when he dropped off Summer on the weekends. And of course from before the divorce. I always thought he was just a regular father. One of the guys. It's shocking."

"It is," Erica admitted. "I don't know very much. Peter and I have been divorced over four years."

"You had no idea about his—" Crystal paused, then dropped her voice to a whisper "—criminal intentions."

"Do you think I would have stayed married to him if I thought he was breaking the law?" Erica snapped. "Do I strike you as that kind of person?"

Crystal cringed. "You're right. I'm sorry. I'm saying this all wrong. I've never known anyone who did anything like this. I just wanted to say I'm sorry and ask if I can help."

Erica held in a sigh. None of this was Crystal's fault. As for Erica being the object of curiosity and pity, well, that couldn't be helped.

"Thank you," she said, trying to sound gracious. "This has nothing to do with me beyond how it affects Summer. I'm fine. I just want to make things right for her."

"Of course. I know she's worried about her stepmother. I guess she's pregnant and really scared."

"Wouldn't you be?"

"Yes. It's an impossible situation." Crystal offered her an awkward smile. "Anyway, I just wanted to say I'm here."

"I appreciate that."

She told herself Crystal wasn't the problem and blaming her was silly. She should accept the offer in the spirit in which it was meant. If Crystal and her friends also got a little thrill from the salaciousness of it all, who could blame them?

"If you hear Summer say anything that catches your attention, please let me know. If she seems overly upset or worried. She's only sixteen and this is a lot." And Allison was taking advantage of her willingness to listen.

"I will," Crystal promised. "Absolutely."

"Thank you."

They smiled at each other. Erica was about to mention she could stay here for the rest of the game when Crystal said, "I'd better get back." She paused. "I won't tell them what you said. I know this is a private matter."

"I appreciate that."

The promise was nice, but Erica couldn't help wondering how long it would be until Crystal broke it. She didn't care what the other women knew. They could talk about Peter and his issues for days. As long as word didn't get back to her kid, they could talk about her and Peter and Allison, speculating as they liked. Just leave Summer out of it.

Allison paced in her living room, glancing at the wall clock every time she made a circuit. In exactly two minutes—assuming Erica was going to be on time, and didn't she seem the type?—her husband's first wife was going to show up to talk to her. At least that was what Erica's text had said. Or more precisely:

I'd like to stop by tonight after Jackson's in bed. How's 8?

Allison had wanted to say that wasn't a good time. That they had nothing to say to each other, etc. etc. But she hadn't because Erica was Summer's mother and she'd offered to find out about the business. Maybe she had good news. Maybe a bunch of clients had paid and Erica had managed to intercept the money before it got deposited in the bank, where it would sit, frozen and inaccessible.

A few hundred would really help. A few thousand would mean she could try to rent a small apartment by paying a six-month lease in advance. She had the ten thousand from the scary guy and she had her credit card, but until she got paid again, that was it. She had medical insurance to worry about, co-pays for the doctor and hospital. Assuming she could somehow convince someone to rent her an apartment, she had to pay for movers and ask Liz if she would please keep Jackson during the birth. All of which assumed she could keep working the whole time and nothing went wrong.

What if she was put on bed rest? What about after Bethany was born? How was she supposed to survive with two kids under the age of two? Day care would be prohibitive, but she needed day care to work.

The familiar panic returned. She told herself to take a couple of breaths, to relax so she faced Erica calmly and in control. Unfortunately just then there was a light knock.

She opened the front door. Erica offered her a tight smile as she walked in, looking put together in a turtleneck and blazer, with expensive-looking pants and gorgeous boots. She was tall, thin, and had perfect hair and makeup. Plus the designer handbag. Allison, on the other hand, had nearly outgrown all her maternity clothes and hadn't even thought about doing something with her appearance. These days it was all she could do to stay upright.

"Thank you for seeing me," Erica said, moving to the sofa. "We have a few things to discuss. I'll be brief. I'm sure you're exhausted and would like to get to bed early."

Bed sounded wonderful—if only she could actually sleep instead of worrying and missing Peter.

They both sat.

"Do you have news on the business?" Allison asked eagerly.

Erica stared at her blankly. "The business? Oh, yes. I spoke to Gail, the office manager. She's the one who turned in Peter. She found out about the illegal activity and reported it. The day the police showed up, she resigned."

Allison stared at the other woman, unable to process the blunt words. "Why would she do that? She's worked with Peter for years."

Erica looked away. "I can't possibly know all her motives, but as I said, she figured out what he was up to and wasn't willing to ignore it."

"You're saying you think Peter committed a crime? You're wrong. He said it was a mistake. When he gets the right lawyer he's going to—"

"Do you actually believe that? No one with any resources simply sits in jail, waiting for the justice fairies to free him. Of course he's guilty. I don't know what all he's done, but it's enough that your bank accounts are frozen. That should have been your first clue."

"He's innocent," Allison protested, fighting tears, knowing Peter was a good man. He had to be. They loved each other, they had dreams. "He would never hurt me."

"Yet here you sit." Erica sighed. "I don't mean to be blunt."

"Yes, you do."

Erica gaze sharpened. "Maybe it's because right now you're not one of my favorite people."

"What does that mean?"

"Summer is sixteen years old. I understand your situation is dire and you're afraid, but you have no business dumping on her. You shouldn't be sharing all the details with her and you shouldn't be asking her for help. She's not *your* child, but she is still a child and this is way beyond what she can handle."

Allison felt her face flush as a rush of shame washed through her. Erica was right—of course she was. Peter wasn't just Allison's husband, he was Summer's father. The teen was worried about him, about her little brother, all of it.

"I didn't mean to hurt her."

"Now you sound like Peter."

"If you're going to act like this, then we have nothing more to say to each other. You're right about Summer. She shouldn't be handling this, but I didn't set out to tell her. It's like she knows when there's a crisis and she shows up. It's hard to keep the truth from her when she walks in on me curled up on the floor sobbing. You can believe me or not, but that's what happened."

Erica stared at her. Allison had no idea what she was thinking. According to Peter, the woman was heartless—only caring about business—something she'd always believed. Until now. She could see Erica loved her daughter very much.

Allison sagged against the sofa back. "I love her and I wouldn't hurt her. I'm sorry for what happened. It's just been so hard. Everything's happened so fast and I don't know what to do or how to manage. Peter won't tell me everything."

"He wants to protect you." Erica sighed. "I saw him today."

"What?" Allison leaned toward her. "You did? But it's not a visiting day."

Erica brushed away that comment. "I wanted to look him in the eye and find out the truth."

"Did he tell you?"

"No. He was concerned about our conversation being recorded, plus I'm not exactly someone he wants in his life."

There was something about the way she spoke the words—as

if there was more going on than Allison could know, but had no idea what.

"His bail's been set at a million dollars. He's not getting out of jail anytime soon."

Allison felt herself starting to crumble as her hopeless situation just got worse. "That much? I didn't know." A million dollars? That was impossible.

"Bail requires ten percent in cash, plus someone to guarantee the rest, so basically a million dollars is at risk."

"No one has that kind of money," Allison whispered, then pressed her lips together. "He's never coming home, is he?"

"He will. I just don't know when," Erica said, meeting her gaze. "Try to remember he loves you and he would do anything for you." She paused. "What is your plan for Jackson when you go into the hospital?"

The question caught Allison off guard. "I, ah, am going to ask a friend to take care of him."

"Does this friend know she'll be asked?"

"Of course." Allison had never been a good liar and wasn't sure she'd pulled off this one.

Probably not, she thought when Erica didn't look convinced.

"And your living situation? Isn't the lease ending a couple of weeks before your due date? Where are you going?"

Allison raised her chin. No way she was showing weakness in front of this woman. Well, not more than she already had. "I'll be fine."

"You're not answering the question."

"I don't owe you an answer."

"You're not in a position to have attitude."

"Right now attitude is all I have."

Erica stared at her for a long time, then rose. "You need to get your rest. I wanted to tell you about seeing Peter. Whatever happens, the man loves you." She offered a faint smile. "He called you his princess."

Allison tried to find comfort in the words as she struggled to her feet. "I'd rather have him home."

"I know. I wish I could make that happen. Believe me when I say I want nothing more than Peter back in regular life."

"Why would you care?"

"Because of Summer. She's very worried."

"Right. I am sorry about telling her too much."

"I know." Erica walked to the front door and pulled it open. "Get some sleep. You need it and so does the baby."

With that, she was gone.

Erica walked into Killion's kitchen still groggy from oversleeping. She was usually up before him, but last night she'd been restless. He sat at the table, drinking coffee. He was already showered and dressed and the smell of coffee mingled with the scent of something with cinnamon baking in the oven.

"Good morning," he said when he saw her. "How do you feel?"

"About how I look."

"Then you feel good."

She laughed before collapsing on a chair at the table. "I hate when I wake up looking my age but I've reached the point in my life where sleep really matters."

He poured coffee from the carafe and set it in front of her. "You did have trouble settling."

"I told you I should go home. I didn't mean to keep you up, but you were warned."

He flashed her a sexy smile. "It was worth it. I like when you spend the night."

Something he requested she do every month or so. She tried to coordinate those visits with Summer's frequent sleepovers. If that wasn't possible, then Mara stayed with the teen.

"Despite your cutthroat reputation, you're a traditionalist," she told him.

"About some things, although I will point out there are very few straight men alive who wouldn't want you in their bed."

"You're being kind. Certainly no one under forty."

"You underestimate yourself."

"And you're being silly."

"Only for you."

A timer dinged. Killion removed two baking dishes from the oven and carried them over to the set table. He'd already put out a large bowl of cut-up fruit and glasses of water. Now he set down what looked like a vegetable frittata and a gooey, delicious-looking coffee cake.

"What is that?" she asked, telling herself not to calculate the calories.

"Sour cream coffee cake. You'll like it."

"I'm sure I will. Too much."

He dismissed her concern with a flick of his fingers. "It's one breakfast."

"I was thinking I'd take some with me for later, so it's two breakfasts."

"Good."

They served themselves. The frittata was perfect—light, flavorful and something she could tell herself was healthy—but the coffee cake was the real star.

"What time did you get up?" she asked. "It had to be close to five for you to do all this."

"I'd prepped it last night, before you came over."

She'd gotten to his place close to nine, directly from Allison's house. Unfortunately, thinking the other woman's name brought back memories of the previous day.

"What?" he asked. "You just thought of something."

"I don't want that woman living with me. There. I've said it and I'm sure that makes me a horrible person, but I don't." She set down her fork. "I feel like my life is a moving train that's going faster and faster and I don't know how to jump off. It's not just Allison, it's Peter and everyone else."

"Who else is there?"

She grimaced. "The softball moms. Summer is friends with their daughters."

He nodded. "She tells her friends and her friends tell their moms. Someone said something."

"Crystal. She was very nice about it and I don't care what they think, but you know what's going to happen." She changed the pitch of her voice. "Yes, my ex-husband's second wife has moved in. How droll."

"You don't care what they think."

"I tell myself that. They're nothing to me. I barely know them and we're not friends." She looked at him. "But maybe I care a little. It's all so complicated."

His smile was gentle. "You know you don't have a choice in this. Not anymore. Allison has nowhere to go and Summer wants her to move in."

"So I should give my daughter everything she wants?"

"This time, yes. It will be difficult and messy and you'll face questions and gossip, but that's not the point. It's the right thing to do, which is your default position. More important, it's something for Summer to experience. She'll always remember this. For the rest of her life, you will have done this for her. Years from now, she'll look back and be in awe of your actions."

"I wish. My daughter doesn't feel awe when it comes to me."

"She will this time."

Nice words, but she wasn't sure they were true. She was more inclined to believe that it was the right thing to do. She'd always had trouble walking away from that.

"I want to say no."

"But you won't."

Erica felt the weight of the inevitable on her shoulders. "Did it have to be that woman moving in? Couldn't I just give her a kidney?"

"You're unlikely to be a match."

"But I could offer and that would be my good deed for the year."

His gaze was steady. "You'll get through this, and I'll help as much as you'll let me."

She laughed. "You make me sound difficult."

"In a good way."

"Why are you so nice to me? I'm not sure I'm worth it."

"We're good to each other."

An evasive answer, she thought, unwilling to push. Right now she was already at her limit with the whole Allison issue.

"I really don't want her in the house."

"I know. Let me know the date and I'll arrange for packers and movers."

Erica cut herself a large piece of coffee cake. "Ugh. Details. Yes, I'll need movers, but not just for Allison and Jackson. Summer's going to move into the Jack and Jill guest bedrooms across the hall. Jackson will take one and she'll take the other. So all that furniture has to be moved out and hers put in."

She took a bite of the coffee cake and did her best not to moan. "This is delicious."

"Thank you. Don't forget about babyproofing the house."

"What?"

"Jackson is only going to get faster as he grows. He'll be into everything."

She thought of her beautiful home and her comfortable life and that she didn't even like Allison.

"I don't want to do this."

"I know. But you're going to anyway."

14

For the second time in as many days, Allison found herself in the presence of Erica Sawyer. This time the request to stop by had come from Summer, with no mention of her mother, leaving Allison wary when the two arrived together.

"We brought food," Summer said, handing a large to-go bag to her mother and hugging Allison. "It's fried chicken and stuff that will keep until tomorrow."

"Thank you," Allison said, not sure what was happening. She'd been hoping to speak to Summer alone so she could apologize for dumping on her, as her mother had said the previous evening. Knowing she'd hurt the teen had been yet another reason why she hadn't slept. But exhaustion was hardly news.

"Unless you haven't eaten," Erica said as she walked into the small kitchen and began putting containers in the refrigerator.

"It's after eight. I ate with Jackson."

Summer led her to the round table by the window. "I wanted to come by earlier so I could see him, but my mom said we needed to wait so we could all focus."

Allison glanced between them, her senses immediately going on alert. "Focus on what?"

Summer sat next to her, obviously dying to say something, but she only looked at her mother. Erica, once again stylishly dressed in a dark green knit dress and stunning leather boots with a four-inch heel, sat across from her.

The older woman leaned forward, then sat back and looked away. Allison felt her tension rise.

"Did something happen to Peter?"

"As far as I know, he's fine." Erica looked at Summer, then back at her. "Your situation is unsustainable. You have Jackson, you're pregnant, you have no money."

Allison immediately felt defensive. "Thanks for the recap but I know this. Why are you here?" *And how can I get you to leave?*

"Believe me, I don't want to be having this conversation any more than you want to hear it," Erica snapped.

"Mom!"

"It's true. The whole thing is ridiculous."

Summer's mouth trembled. "Mom, you said it was okay. We have to help."

Allison glanced between them, unsure what was going on, but not liking it.

Erica looked at her. "You need a place to stay while you have the baby and get back on your feet, so to speak. We don't know what's happening with Peter, but nothing about his situation speaks to an early release. Not with bail that high. Once he gets a better lawyer, maybe they can negotiate with the court or—"

"Mom! Get to the point."

Erica seemed to steel herself. She nodded once, then said, "You and Jackson should move into my house. There's plenty of room and you'll be safe."

Allison blinked several times, unable to process the words. They'd sounded like they were in English but she must have misheard them.

"Move in with you? Are you insane?"

"Debatable."

Summer rolled her eyes. "Mom, you're not helping." She smiled at Allison. "It's a perfect solution. I'm going to move out of my bedroom. It's really big and on the corner, so you get lots of light. It has a private bathroom and plenty of room for Bethany's crib and changing table. Right across the hall are two bedrooms with a connected bathroom. I'll take one of those and Jackson can have the other. So I'll be right there if he needs anything."

"No," Allison said automatically. Move in with Erica? Live with her husband's first wife? "I don't know you and you don't know me. You can't offer me somewhere to live."

"And yet I just did." Erica smiled. "I'm as shocked as you are."

"If you're playing with me, it's really crappy."

"She's not." Summer grabbed her hand. "We want you to move in. It's the best idea. You won't have to pay rent or worry about your credit. You can stop working right now. You know how hard it is for you to stand all day and now you won't have to. We'll look after Jackson while you're having Bethany. Oh, my grandma's there. She lives in the carriage house, but she hangs out with us all time."

Summer laughed. "Okay, when she's not on a date. Grandma is very popular with her gentlemen friends. I used to think that was gross, but now it's kind of sweet. She's like Mom—she loves kids and babies."

Allison didn't know what to deal with first. That Erica had a house large enough that it came with a carriage house—not that she knew what that was—or that there was a grandmother in the mix. Peter had never mentioned his former mother-in-law. The offer was incredibly generous and if anyone else was making it, she would be tempted. But living with Peter's first wife? She couldn't.

"There's no way it would work," she said firmly. "I can't move in with you." She paused. "Thank you for being so kind, but no."

"You're being ridiculous," Erica said, her voice thick with annoyance. "You don't have a lot of options. I get having pride, but this isn't the time."

Allison glared at the other woman. "You don't know anything about me. Judge me all you want, but you don't know me."

"I know you married a man who's sitting in jail with bail set at a million dollars and no decent lawyer. I know he's not going anywhere for months, possibly years, and if you don't stop waiting for him to magically appear and fix all your problems, you'll find yourself living in your car with child protective services knocking on the window to take your babies away from you."

"Mom!" Summer glared at Erica. "Stop."

Allison tried to blink back tears, but she couldn't. They leaked down her cheeks, despite her attempts to brush them away. She felt sick and scared and the worst part of that horrible woman's words was they were true. All of them.

She just wanted all of this to go away. She wanted her life back. It had never been especially big or fancy, but it had been hers and she'd been happy. Right now, she couldn't imagine ever being happy again.

She pushed herself to her feet and walked to the counter. After getting a glass from the cupboard, she filled it with water and pretended to drink. Anything to keep from returning to the kitchen table.

"Mom! You were mean. You have to fix this."

"Her inability to face reality is as big a problem as frozen bank accounts. I can't fix the latter, but I can make her deal with the former."

"That's not your job."

"Summer, you don't know everything. If you can't be quiet, please go wait in the car."

"I'm not leaving her alone with you."

Allison turned around in time to see the flash of pain on Erica's face. The realization that the other woman was just human enough to be wounded should have pleased her, but she was too exhausted to care.

She returned to her seat and sank down, her back screaming

with every movement. She shifted to get comfortable, but that wasn't going to happen—not on these hard chairs.

"I can't," she said simply.

"Don't say that." Summer leaned toward her. "It'll be great. You haven't met my grandma but she's really fun and she bakes. She loves kids. The house is big and there's a nice yard for Jackson." She offered a tentative smile. "It's just for a little while. Until everything is better."

Erica sat completely still, watching without speaking. Allison had no idea what she was thinking. The offer was so generous and it really did solve all her problems. But to live with Erica? How could she? Peter'd had so many stories where Erica was the villain. Only what was the alternative? The other woman's stark visual of her living in her car with two little kids, only to lose them to child protective services, was all too likely.

"I want to talk to Peter," she whispered. "I visit the day after tomorrow. Let me talk to him first."

"When is your lease up?" Erica asked.

"The fifteenth of next month." She dropped her head. "The landlord said he'd give me a bonus if I could be out by the first. The new buyers want to get in as quickly as possible."

While the money would be nice, she'd had no plans to move a second before she was required to.

"You'll need to figure out what you want with you in the house and what we'll put in storage." Erica glanced around the kitchen. "You'll want your bedroom furniture and Jackson's. Personal items, clothes, all his toys. But the kitchen could be completely packed."

She glanced at Summer. "I think there's room in the garage. In the fourth bay."

Her daughter nodded vigorously. "There's hardly anything there now." She looked at Allison. "The house has a four-car garage, so even using one of the bays to store your stuff, you can still park inside. Grandma has her own parking."

Allison felt the room start spinning. "I can't think about any of that."

Erica rose. "We should let you rest. This has been a lot." She put a business card on the kitchen table. "I wrote my cell on the back. Text me after you talk to Peter. Should you agree to the plan, we'll handle all the logistics. We'll set up a date, get packers in here, then movers. We'll have unpackers on the other end. You're too far along to be doing anything that physical."

With that, she walked out of the room, toward the front door. Summer paused to hug Allison tightly.

"Say yes," she whispered. "You'll be safe with us, plus we'll have the best time. I love you."

"I love you, too."

She said the words automatically, unable to take in what was happening. She was exhausted and confused, which meant she wouldn't do anything until she spoke to Peter. He would tell her what was right.

Allison waited in line with the other wives. Her ankles were more swollen than usual, making it difficult to walk. But she forced herself to shuffle forward so she could pause in the metal detector, then be sniffed by the mean-looking German shepherd. The air was stuffy, laced with an odor that was a combination of almost-hospital and day-old cafeteria. The lights were too bright, the walls in need of painting. Everything about being here depressed her and she only had to stay two hours. How did Peter stand living here? A plane flew overhead, the loud noise vibrating through the building.

She put her purse in her locker, keeping cash and her ID with her. Even though she was down to fifteen hours of credits at day care, she'd decided to not bring Jackson. She and Peter had to talk and their toddler would be a distraction.

At last the doors opened and she was able to walk into the main visitors' room with everyone else. There was a bit of confusion as partners found each other. She spotted Peter and rushed toward him, her arms outstretched, her face already wet with tears.

He grabbed her and held her close. For that second, for that heartbeat, her world righted itself and she knew she would be fine. Then a guard walked by and growled a quick "Break it up or the visit is over."

Peter stepped free of her then helped her into a seat. "Are you all right? You look tired."

"So do you."

No, more than tired, she thought. Worn. As if everything was too hard. Without wanting to, she thought about Erica saying that he wasn't getting out for months, maybe years. That she was in this alone and they were never getting back what they'd had.

She looked at him. "I need you to be honest with me."

"I'm always honest."

She shook her head. "You tell me what you think I can handle, but that's not good enough. When I don't have all the facts, I can't protect myself and Jackson. Why don't you have a lawyer? What have you been charged with? When will you go to trial? Can you get your bail reduced? Why didn't you tell me your bail was set at a million dollars?"

He looked at her, his expression miserable. "It's complicated and there are things I don't want you to know because it's not safe information to have."

"You told Erica about the bail without telling me?"

He turned away. "There's nothing we can do about it. I can't get my hands on that kind of money and I don't know anyone willing to guarantee the amount." He returned his attention to her. "It'll get better. Right now they're pressuring me to cooperate. As soon as I find the right lawyer, we'll work out a deal. We'll get some of the money unfrozen and reduce my bail."

"How long will that take?"

"A while."

She was getting tired of the nonanswers. "You're not making this easier for me."

He reached for her hand. "I'm sorry. You know I love you. I want you to be happy. That's how all this happened. Hearing that damned landlord was going to sell the house pushed me over the edge. We were barely making it. You work so hard and you shouldn't have to. I wanted to give you everything and it all went to shit."

He released her hand and turned away again, but not before she saw that he was crying. She'd never seen Peter cry before and the visual upset her.

"I didn't need more than we had," she said gently.

"I wanted more for you. A big house, a nice car. Security." He looked at her. "I'm going to get you that. You'll see. Once this is fixed, I'll make it happen."

The words were more frightening than comforting. "I don't need any of that. I just want our lives back." A wish that was getting more elusive.

She drew in a breath. "Erica asked me and Jackson to move in with her. I'd stay there through having Bethany and until everything gets figured out."

She'd planned on saying more—mostly that she couldn't imagine saying yes, but couldn't figure out another option—when he shocked her by laughing.

"Did she? Did she? I'd hoped she would do something, but this is better than I imagined." His entire body relaxed. "That's perfect. You'll be safe there. Erica's a bitch, but Summer will take care of you. What a relief. When are you moving? Soon, right? Once you're there, you can stop working and you won't have to pay for anything."

He looked around and lowered his voice. "Keep that money I gave you safe. I'll need it for the lawyer."

"What money?"

"The money Cappy dropped off." He frowned. "You haven't spent any of it, have you?"

"No. I've been saving it for things like food and diapers."

He waved that away. "Erica's loaded." He smiled at her. "This is great, sweetie. I'm so relieved you'll be taken care of."

She couldn't make sense of his attitude. He thought his ex-wife was a bitch but was happy to have his wife and child live with her?

"I don't know her," she said. "I won't be comfortable."

"You'll be fine. The house is big enough that you'll never see her. It's just until I get things straightened out. So when's the move?"

"I haven't said yes yet."

He leaned toward her. "You have to do that right now. Get yourself settled. You shouldn't have to worry about anything and this has been hard. Allison, I mean it. I need you to do this."

She knew she didn't have a choice, but she hadn't expected Peter to be so…*enthused*. It was as if he was abdicating responsibility.

She looked at the man she loved, the man she'd thought she would spend the rest of her life with.

"Are you a criminal?"

"What?" He drew back. "No. I'm not. Accounting can be tricky. I was helping a client. You know I'd never do anything to hurt you. Allison, I never really understood what love was until I met you. We belong together. This is going to get worked out. You'll see. Just hang in there."

His shoulders slumped. "I miss you so much. You're all I think about. Do you believe me?"

"Yes," she whispered. "And I love you. I need you, Peter. Home."

"I'm working on it."

She wanted to say *Work harder* but knew there wasn't any point. It wasn't as if he wanted to be here.

They talked until the time was up, then she kissed him once

and made her way to her car in the light rail parking lot. Her body and her spirit felt battered.

Levi would never have done this to her.

The thought came out of nowhere. She pushed it away, feeling guilty and disloyal. Thinking about him, about what he would or wouldn't have done, wasn't helpful. She had to deal with the situation she was in.

In her car, she dug out her cell phone. She carefully entered the unfamiliar phone number and typed:

Thank you for your generous invitation. Jackson and I would be very grateful to come live with you.

15

Erica placed the roasted golden beet, avocado and watercress salad on the table, along with the crispy French rolls. The cheese-stuffed shells were still in the oven. Killion was pouring the bottle of what she assumed was very expensive French wine for the three adults.

Summer waited until he was seated before passing him the beet salad. "We're having a childproofing party. A couple of my girlfriends are coming over and we're going to crawl through the house, figuring out what's at Jackson's level."

She grinned as she spoke, obviously delighted by the prospect.

After receiving Allison's text, Erica had informed Summer and Mara that they would have new roommates. The three of them had come up with a plan. Killion had come through, as always, recommending a moving consultant to coordinate everything. One phone call later, the woman had been hired and had promised to take care of it all.

"Summer and I went online," Mara said, winking at her daughter. "Childproofing equipment is more sophisticated than it used to be. We'll remove all the breakables and lock the cabinets. Our handyman is coming by on Friday to secure the big pieces of furniture to protect Jackson if he climbs."

"Kids really climb furniture?" Summer asked.

"You were more monkey than little girl," Erica said with a

laugh. "Once we found you at the top of a bookcase and we had no idea how you got there."

"I don't remember that at all."

"You were having fun. I, on the other hand, nearly had a heart attack." She pressed a hand to her chest. "I kept talking calmly while I hurried to get a chair so I could lift you down. I was terrified you'd jump."

"You should have tried gymnastics," Killion said, his voice teasing.

"I guess." Summer shook her head. "I don't think we have to worry. So far Jackson likes to run but I've never seen him climb anything."

"How are you going to like having a toddler and soon a newborn in the house?" Killion asked.

Summer grinned. "I'm excited! Jackson's so great. We always have a good time."

"You still have school and softball," Mara pointed out. "Jackson could be a complication."

"I'll make it work."

"The plan is for Allison to quit her job," Erica told Killion. "She'll be with him full-time until the baby comes."

"How will you deal with little kids underfoot?"

"I'll be fine." She picked up her wine and smiled at him. "I'm actually very good with children."

"It's true," Mara said. "If there's a crying baby at the salon, Erica's the one to calm him. Babies and toddlers adore her."

"Yes, it's not until they turn into teenagers that I get into trouble." Erica was mostly kidding, but she watched her daughter as she spoke.

Summer looked at her. "Oh, Mom."

"A secret skill," Killion teased. "You're a constant surprise."

"But only in a good way, right?"

"Of course."

She laughed. "I do enjoy babies. Not that I advertise that. I like to keep my softer side hidden."

She was joking, and yet telling the truth at the same time. She always had felt the need to protect herself. When she'd been growing up, she'd been different. A fifteen-year-old with a career plan. She'd been more interested in learning about business than trying out for cheerleading. Later, there had been the whole problem of finding a man who could be happy for her success rather than frightened of it or resentful.

After the divorce, she'd put up all kinds of barriers to keep men at bay. Peter had hurt her. She didn't want to take any more emotional risks, which was why her relationship with Killion worked so well. They were friends who slept together and were each other's plus-one. There wasn't any expectation of love or commitment. She liked him and respected him, but she didn't need him. He couldn't touch her heart.

"How are you doing?" Killion asked Summer.

"What do you mean?"

"You've been through a lot. You're coming up with plans for keeping Allison safe. You're worried about her and Jackson, you have school and it's softball season and your dad's sitting in jail. You must be scared and worried. So I'm asking, how are you doing?"

Summer stared at him blankly. "I'm fine."

Killion didn't say anything, obviously waiting out the teen. Unfortunately that gave Erica plenty of time to think about her own behavior…or rather lack of behavior. She'd been so quick to call out Allison for leaning too hard on her stepdaughter, but she'd never once sat down with Summer and asked if she was all right. She'd never thought to go into detail about what was happening with her father. Summer was so confident, so sure of what she was supposed to do next, that it was easy to forget, as she'd told Allison, she was still a child.

The teen ducked her head. "Stop staring at me."

"I will as soon as you answer my question." His tone was soft and encouraging. "Do you need anything? You know I always have a guy who can help."

That earned him a smile. She glanced from him to Erica and back. "It's hard," she admitted. "Like you said, scary. I don't know what to think about what's happening. About my dad. If he's a criminal, what does that mean?" She shook her head. "I really don't want to talk about it."

Erica glanced at her mother, who nodded.

"Was that the timer?" Mara asked brightly. "Summer, be a dear and help me with the casserole. Sometimes your mother pushes it so far back, it's hard for me to pull it out."

Summer stood and reached for her plate and her mother's. Mara took Killion's and her own. When they'd both left, Erica turned to him.

"Thanks for getting into that with her," she said quietly. "I haven't been asking the right questions."

"There's been a lot going on."

"None of it is more important than my daughter."

"Don't beat yourself up. She's doing okay."

"Because of who she is, not because of anything I did." She held in a sigh. "I hate when I'm a bad mother."

"That's extreme and inaccurate."

She waved away his comment. "You're just saying that because you like me."

"I'm saying it because it's true."

Later, when Killion had left and Mara had returned to the carriage house, Erica knocked on her daughter's half-open door.

"Got a second?" she asked as she entered.

"Okay." Summer sat up on her bed and set down her phone. "Avery's having a tough time with math. First-semester precalculus was hard for her, but now she's really struggling."

Erica angled the desk chair toward the bed and sat down. "Has she talked to her parents? I'm sure they'd get her a tutor."

"Her mom's all for it, but her dad says she just needs to try harder."

Erica couldn't remember if she'd met the man or not, but he sounded like a jerk. "Avery *is* a hard worker. She always shows up early to practice and she's the friend you study with the most."

"I know, right? I don't get it. Her dad expects all As from her but won't give her the resources to succeed. Parents can be confusing."

"We take a class," Erica said lightly. "It's part of the childbirth series. Fifty ways to confuse your child."

Summer grinned. "I wonder if there's one for kids. You know, to confuse their parents."

"Oh, you don't need a class for that. It's a natural part of growing up." She leaned forward a little. "Killion's questions tonight made you uncomfortable, but he's not wrong to ask." She grimaced. "No, let me put that another way. I should have been the one asking if you're all right. This has been a lot and you've been handling too much. You've been a rock for Allison and that speaks well of you, but as mature as you seem, you're still just sixteen. We've all forgotten that. So now I'm asking, what do you want to know?"

Summer kept her head down. Her long brown ponytail fell over one shoulder. Even from several feet away, Erica could see the ragged ends from the hideous haircut her friend had given her and her fingers itched to make it right.

Not the point of the conversation, she reminded herself.

Her daughter looked up. "Is Dad a bad man?"

Ugh. Not the question Erica had been hoping for. She'd wanted something easy, maybe focusing on logistics or timelines.

"He's done some bad things, but in his heart he loves you and Allison and Jackson. He would never hurt you on purpose." Collateral damage was another issue, but why go there?

"You think he's guilty? That he did those things? It's not all a mistake?"

"Guilty or not guilty is a legal question. Your father's been charged with several crimes including money laundering, wire fraud and threatening police with a gun."

Her eyes widened. "Dad doesn't own a gun."

"He said he kept it at work in case of trouble. That's where the police arrested him. I'm pretty sure about the money laundering." Peter had admitted to that. "So at least some of the charges are going to stick. Right now he has a court-appointed attorney. He's trying to find someone who specializes in what he's done."

"So he's going to prison?"

"I don't know. Once your dad has the right lawyer, they'll talk about him cooperating with the government. Some of the charges might be dropped, but I would guess that yes, he'll spend a little time in prison."

"Is he scared?"

Erica thought about her brief visit to the detention center. It had been a grim, terrifying place.

"I don't think he's very happy."

"Allison isn't, either. I've got you and Grandma, but she doesn't have anyone. Plus what about Jackson and Bethany? I know she's really frightened and worried right now, but at some point she'll get mad. Do you think she'll forgive him?"

"I don't know."

"Would you?"

Erica hesitated, not sure if she should lie or not, then decided avoiding the question was easiest. "Your dad and I aren't together anymore. All we have in common is you, so forgiving him isn't an issue. You're my biggest concern. After that, I'm happy to help Allison. As for your father, what he did is on him. In life there are always consequences, especially if someone breaks the law."

Summer nodded slowly. "I get that." She looked at Erica.

"Thank you for letting them live here. I know it's going to be an adjustment and stuff, but I need them to be safe."

"I know."

"I don't know how I feel about my dad."

"You don't have to decide today." Erica smiled at her. "Whatever he does, he's still your dad and it's okay to love him."

"I do. I just don't know what to think of him."

Erica rose and crossed to the bed. Summer reached for her and Erica wrapped her arms around her daughter.

"Maybe for now, you can remember how it used to be. The other stuff will still be here when you're ready to deal with it."

"That's a good plan."

Allison's life had never felt so out of control. Since Peter's arrest, she'd been reacting to events rather than driving them, and that situation only got worse. After accepting Erica's offer—something she still couldn't believe she'd done—they'd had a lengthy conversation working out the details of the move.

Given that she was nearly out of day care credits and paying for day care would take half her take-home pay, they'd decided to get her out of the house as quickly as possible. Allison had given notice at the grocery store and notified her landlord. He'd gladly agreed she wouldn't have to pay the rent for the remainder of the lease, had refunded half of her current month's rent and had given her the small bonus he'd promised. Fortunately she'd learned her lesson and had picked up the check rather than have him deposit it in her account.

The two days after her phone call with Erica, a nice woman had shown up to help her decide what to keep with her and what to store in Erica's garage. The consultant had already been to the house to see Allison's and Jackson's rooms and had come armed with floor plans and measurements.

The following Saturday, Allison dropped Jackson off at day care. He would be there much of the day, which would use nearly all her remaining credits, but she couldn't have him around for the move. She was back at her house by eight thirty. By nine the packers had arrived.

She'd never had packers before. She didn't even know such a service existed. In her world, you packed the boxes yourself, then got friends to help you move them. But not today. The team brought in dozens of boxes along with huge stacks of packing paper.

She'd carefully separated the items she was taking from those being stored. Each box was marked and put into the appropriate pile.

They worked with frightening efficiency, reducing stuffed closets to a few boxes in what felt like minutes. In less than an hour, both Jackson's room and hers and Peter's were done. She stood by the stripped bed, remembering how excited she and Peter had been to rent the house. She'd only been a few months into her first pregnancy then, and they'd both been so happy to be starting their family.

They'd brought Jackson home from the hospital to this house and she had assumed they would do the same with Bethany. There were memories here, so many of them wonderful. And now it was all gone.

Her chest ached—some from all that had been lost and some from what would never be. She missed Peter so much. Doing this on her own was hard and she wanted to be able to lean on him. She missed his warm presence, his silly jokes, the way he was always there for her and Jackson.

She returned to the living room, which was now only furniture and boxes, and sat on the sofa.

She was going to be all right, she told herself. Staying with Erica would allow her to rest before the baby was born. Jackson would have lots of attention and room to run around. She hadn't seen Erica's place but Peter had described it as "huge and cold." The latter wasn't exciting, but she was sure there was a big backyard. It was April. The days were getting longer, so Jackson would be able to play outside.

As for missing Peter, there was nothing to be done about that. He was—

"Do you think they're still here?"

The question came from just outside the open front door. Allison walked out to find a young couple standing by the porch stairs. They were in their mid-to late twenties, casually dressed and holding hands. A small SUV was parked behind the moving truck.

"Can I help you?"

They both looked at her, then at each other. The man gave her a tentative smile. "Hi. Are you the renter? We're sorry to bother you. Our broker said you'd already moved out and it was okay to come by and look at the house." His smile turned genuine. "We're the new buyers. I'm Matt and this is Greta."

Greta tugged on her husband's hand. "We'll come back another time."

Allison hesitated, not wanting to deal with them, but unable to turn them away. Because of the terms of the lease, the buyers had been unable to actually come into the house. Instead the landlord had taken several videos and posted them online. Buying a house sight unseen would be a little scary, so of course they wanted to see where they were going to live.

"There's a team of guys packing up everything," she said, waving toward the open door. "It's a mess and loud and crowded, but if you'd like to walk through, that would be okay."

Greta and Matt exchanged a brief glance.

"Are you sure?" Matt asked.

"I am."

She stepped back, waiting for them to go first. Greta led the way inside.

"Oh, look how big that front window is," she said happily. "It's much bigger than it looked in the video. I love the casing. The paint looks fresh."

"It's only two years old," Allison told them. She walked over to the sofa. "I'll stay here while you look around."

"Thank you."

The young couple explored the house. She heard cupboards being opened and closed and parts of their conversation.

"I love this closet."

"Look at the light fixture. It's perfect."

A few minutes later Greta returned to the living room. "Matt's measuring the deck," she said. "We're going to get a little grill, and my parents want to give us some patio furniture as a house-warming present."

"That will be fun," Allison said, trying not to be envious of their lives. They were in love and together, buying their first house. It was a good time for them.

Greta moved closer. "You were using the second bedroom as a nursery?"

"Yes. My son is twenty months old. It was perfect for him."

Greta sank down next to her and lowered her voice. "I'm eight weeks pregnant. No one knows but Matt. We're waiting until twelve weeks to tell everyone." Her gaze drifted to Allison's huge belly. "So this is your second? Do you know what you're having?"

"A little girl. Bethany."

"Oh, one of each. That's perfect." Greta smiled. "We're going to be so happy here."

"I know you are. My husband and I enjoyed living here."

"Are you moving somewhere bigger?"

"Yes," Allison said, knowing she was, in some ways, telling the truth. From all she'd heard, Erica's house certainly quali-fied as "bigger."

"We'll do that, too, but this is a great starter home."

Matt returned then. "I have the measurements."

Greta rose. "We'll get out of your way now. Thanks for let-ting us see the house."

"Of course. Good luck with everything."

"You, too."

When they were gone, Allison told herself she was happy for them. They weren't responsible for all she was going through. They should enjoy the house.

One of the guys walked into the living room.

"Everything's packed except for the kitchen, and he'll be done in about half an hour. We'll start loading now."

"Great."

His gaze dropped to her belly. "We'll leave one of the kitchen chairs in the house until the very end."

"I appreciate that."

Faster than she would have thought, everything she owned in the world was loaded on the truck. She walked through the empty house one more time to make sure nothing had been missed. Without furniture and rugs, the rooms echoed. She stood in the middle of the living room, trying to imagine how it had been, but the memories were already fading. That or she simply couldn't face them.

Outside the truck rumbled to life. She carefully locked the door, then left the key under the mat, as she'd promised the landlord. She got in her car, then pulled out after the truck. She would follow it to Erica's house.

When she reached the corner, she glanced back over her shoulder, at the life she was leaving behind. She'd moved into that house with Peter and a lot of hope. She was leaving it without her husband and no clear view of the future. She was dependent on the charity of her husband's first wife and the whims of fate. And she had absolutely no idea how she'd gotten here.

16

Summer and her mother lived in an older part of Bellevue. The lots were huge, the trees massive. Several properties were gated. The truck turned a corner, then drove down a long driveway. Allison followed, catching sight of a small house on the edge of the property.

"So that's a carriage house," she murmured, parking next to the truck.

The front door burst open and Summer raced out.

"You're here! I wanted to help with the packing, but Grandma said I'd be in the way." Summer grabbed her hand. "Come inside. You're going to love it here. My friends and I babyproofed everywhere! We painted your room and Jackson's room. We used that special safe paint, so don't worry about fumes."

Summer tugged her into the house. Allison had a brief impression of size and light. The foyer was two stories high and nearly as big as the house she'd just left. To the right was a formal living room and to the left was a dining room that would easily seat twenty. A grand curving staircase led to the second floor.

It was the nicest house Allison had ever seen—like something out of a movie. She couldn't imagine regular people living here, let alone her and Jackson. The tension she'd been carrying around since Peter's arrest increased and she found it difficult to breathe.

An older woman, maybe in her sixties, walked toward them. She had a little gray in her hair and looked enough like Erica for Allison to guess who she was.

"I'm Mara," the woman said, her tone warm, her smile welcoming. "Summer's grandmother and Erica's mom. How are you holding up?"

"I'm doing all right. It's nice to meet you."

"Finally," Mara said with a laugh. "I'm not sure why we had to wait until now, but it's done." She motioned to the stairs. "Summer will show you the bedrooms. I hope they'll work for you. I'll get the movers going on loading your things into the garage. They were supposed to sort the furniture and boxes based on what was going where. Did they?"

"They did."

"Excellent. All right. Let's get you settled."

Mara walked toward the front door while Allison and Summer started up the wide staircase.

"There's no way to childproof this staircase," Summer said as they climbed. "So we bought a bunch of baby gates for the upstairs and downstairs. We figure we'll contain Jackson in whatever room he's in."

Allison nodded, trying to take everything in. When they reached the landing, Summer pointed left.

"Mom's room is down there, along with her home office. The media room is through those double doors. There's a big TV downstairs in the family room, too, but this room is fun for movies. I thought Jackson and I could binge some cartoons."

She turned right and pointed to a door. "Laundry room. There's a whole wall of mostly empty cupboards you can use for diapers and other supplies."

She stood outside the last room on the right. "This is your room." Her smile turned shy. "I hope you like it."

"I'm sure I will. You've been so kind, giving up your room for me." Allison's throat tightened to the point where she couldn't speak. She fought against tears. "I'm sorry. I didn't expect to feel emotional."

Summer hugged her. "This is really hard. I get that. Mom told me I had to go slow with you and Jackson. To not think you could just jump into living here and be okay. She said you'd both have to adjust and there would be a sense of loss. That I probably couldn't understand it but I have to respect it."

"Your mom said all that?"

She couldn't imagine Erica being that insightful and sensitive, but then what did she really know about the other woman? Just what Peter had told her—nothing especially flattering. Yet action-wise, Erica had been extremely supportive. Not only with the business, but inviting Allison and her children to move in. Not many people would be willing to upend their lives like that.

"She knows things." Summer grinned. "Don't tell her I said that. It's better when she thinks I don't listen to her."

She pushed open the wide bedroom door. "Here you go. Is it okay?"

Allison stepped inside the big, empty room. The space was huge. At least sixteen by fourteen, maybe bigger, with high ceilings. There were gorgeous windows on two walls, framed by elegant floor-length drapes.

"Those are electric," Summer said, pointing to the shades that were halfway down the window. "They work off a remote control. In the summer when it gets light so early, I use both the blinds and the drapes, but in the winter, the blinds are enough. The closet is through here."

Allison stared at the walk-in closet, which was nearly the size of Jackson's room at the other house. There were built-in drawers and shelves, along with a full-length mirror at one end. She avoided her reflection, knowing these days she wasn't at her sparkly best.

"This is so big," she said, stunned at how much room there was. "You're sure this isn't the main bedroom?"

Summer laughed. "Trust me. Mom's closet is way bigger. Come on. You have to see the bathroom. Jackson can learn to swim in the tub."

The bathroom was bigger than the closet. There were double sinks, plenty of storage, a walk-in shower for five and yes, a huge soaking tub.

"The floor's heated," Summer said, pointing to a control on the wall. She opened a cabinet and showed Allison stacks of fluffy towels and washcloths. "So, do you like it?"

"It's wonderful. I can't take your room."

"I don't mind. It's no big deal. You need this more. There's plenty of room for the bed and the crib. Even the changing table. Once we get everything in, we'll see how it works. You should even have room for the rocking chair you had in the corner of the living room. The one that wouldn't fit in the bedroom."

They crossed the hall to the two other bedrooms. Summer's furniture filled the much smaller area, and the closet was half the size. Allison pressed a hand to her chest.

"No," she breathed. "Summer, no. You can't stay here."

Her stepdaughter's new bedroom was large by normal standards, but nothing like the one she'd been using. There was just one small window and the only furniture was a queen-size bed and two nightstands.

"It's okay," Summer told her. "I want this. I didn't put in my desk because I want Jackson's crib in with me. Just until he gets settled. Then he'll move next door. My desk and dresser are in storage, which is fine because the closet has built-ins and Mom suggested I use Dad's old office downstairs for studying."

Allison shook her head. "I want to move you back. I'll take this room. I'll be fine here."

"No. It's already decided. You need the extra room for Bethany and her stuff. Remember the rocking chair? Besides, this way I can watch Jackson."

She walked into the shared bathroom. There was a vanity

with a sink, separate from the toilet and shower, then a sink on the other side. Beyond that was a matching bedroom painted in a cheerful blue.

"Once Jackson's okay being in his own room, we'll move him back here. At night I can keep the bathroom doors open, so you won't have to worry. When I have sleepovers, you can use the baby monitor."

Allison continued to fight tears. "You can't give up all this for me. You can't! It's not right."

"I can and it was my idea. Allison, you're going through a lot. You're going to have Bethany soon. You need to not have so much stress in your life. I'm doing this because I want to." Her smile returned. "And because my mom said I could."

Allison looked at her. "When I was your age, I was nowhere near this together. You're so giving and thoughtful."

"My mom always taught me that we have to take care of people, especially other women. There's a sisterhood. Men are important but a lot of times, women need to take care of women. She does that with her scholarship programs at her work. Women in tough circumstances apply for the scholarships. When I was eight or nine, she had me read some of the applications so I could understand not everyone is as blessed as we are."

Summer's mouth turned down at the corners. "There were some really sad stories. Mom works with a couple of organizations that coordinate shelters and stuff so the women have a place to live while they go through beauty school."

"I don't understand. I thought your mother owned a hair salon."

"She does. But she pays for six or so women to go to beauty school every year. It's a full ride—tuition, supplies, a stipend for gas and living expenses and day care, because most of them have kids. When they graduate, they work for her. There's a special apprentice program to make sure they're successful."

She tilted her head. "I don't mean this to sound bad, but sometimes when people haven't had the same advantages, they don't understand how to talk to people or how the upscale service industry works. Mom wants to make sure the women in her program are successful, because if they are, they can make enough money to support themselves and their family. She doesn't even mind if after they're done with the program, they leave to go somewhere else or start their own business."

She smiled. "I have to do a senior service project next year. I think I want to do something with the scholarship program. This summer I'm going to figure out how I could help. The purpose of the service project is to make a difference, not just go through the motions." She paused. "I haven't told Mom yet, so if you wouldn't say anything, I'd appreciate it."

Allison felt the room shift a little. Her back and feet hurt and she was exhausted from not sleeping. The move was upsetting and now Summer was singing the praises of her mother and her generosity. Something of which Allison had direct proof.

But what about all the things Peter had said? How Erica had taken him for every penny, even cutting him out of his half of the house? It was too much to think about.

Fortunately Summer was already walking toward the stairs. "Let's see what the movers are doing. Grandma said unloading should go fast because you don't have to unpack a kitchen."

Summer's words turned out to be prophetic. Two hours later, the truck was empty and the same guys who had packed all her belongings had unpacked the things she'd wanted for the house. When they'd left, she and Summer made quick work of putting everything away.

Diapers and other baby supplies went into the cupboards in the giant laundry room. In addition to an oversize washer and dryer, there was a large sink, perfect for the baby bathtub, and acres of counter space.

"Mom said you can store whatever you need in here," Summer told her. "If you need more storage, we can figure it out."

"Where *is* your mom?"

"Working. Saturday's a busy day for her. She's usually at the salon. Unless I have a school thing, then she's there."

While Summer put away Jackson's clothes and toys, Allison loaded her and Peter's things into the large closet. His shirts and suits hung next to her more casual clothes, as they always had. She smoothed her hand over a row of ties, wondering how long before he was back with her.

Her hand stilled. Wait. What was going to happen when he was finally released from jail? Where would he go? She couldn't imagine Erica's generosity extending so far as to allow her ex-husband to live there with his new wife.

A question that was destined to go unanswered, she thought grimly. At least for now. Currently her biggest priority was putting everything away so she could pick up Jackson.

She worked as quickly as she could, ignoring her back pain and exhaustion. It only took an hour to put everything away. Summer continued to help until Allison firmly told her to stop.

"You've been so sweet to me," she said. "Now go live your life."

"Knock, knock." Mara entered Allison's room. "How's it going?"

"I'm unpacked. The house is beautiful and Summer's room is lovely." She glanced at the teen. "I wish you hadn't given it up for me."

"Oh, she wanted to," Mara said easily. "We all talked about it and she insisted. Summer can be stubborn." Mara smiled. "I wonder where she gets that from."

Her gaze returned to Allison. "I think we'd all feel better with a plan for the rest of the day. You have to be uncomfortable with all the changes, and it will take time for us to adjust."

"I need to go get Jackson," Allison said. "But first I'd like to know where the baby gates are so I can corral him."

"I can show you," Summer said eagerly.

"Don't you have homework?" Mara asked. "And dinner with your friends?"

"I was going to cancel that."

"No!" Allison and Mara said together.

Allison turned to the teen. "You're not responsible for me. I'm grateful, but I'm fine. Keep your plans, please." Erica had been right, she had been leaning on her stepdaughter too much. Starting now, that had to stop.

"Let's do this," Mara said. "Allison, you would probably like to take a long, hot shower. Why don't you do that? I'll make us a snack. After that, you can go get Jackson. When you get back, we'll take a tour of the house. I'll show you the baby gates, give you the Wi-Fi password, explain how to work the TVs. Then you can rest."

She pointed at her granddaughter. "You will do your homework, then go hang out with your friends."

"But I want to be *here*," Summer whined. She brightened. "Oh, I know. I'll invite Avery to dinner. That will be fine. Is that okay, Grandma?"

Mara looked at Allison. "Are you up for company?"

Not really. All she wanted to do was crawl into bed and sleep for three days. But that wasn't an option.

"That sounds great if it's not too much trouble. The dinner part. Or I can cook."

"I'll show you where everything is so you're comfortable," Mara said. "We'll figure out how we're going to work meals as we go. You're welcome to use any food you want. We keep a running list of what we need. The weekly cleaning service also does the grocery shopping."

"I'd want to pay for my food."

"You can take that up with Erica." Mara smiled. "She's the businesswoman in the family. All right. We have a plan. Summer, you can help me with the food after you finish your homework and text Avery. So we're set."

They went their separate ways. Allison walked up the wide staircase, telling herself she would be fine. She had a place to stay, Jackson was safe and hopefully over the next few days, she could relax enough to sleep. She needed to appreciate this unexpected miracle. Which she would, just as soon as she could shake off her sense of looming disaster.

"I want to believe you're working diligently, but my guess is you're hiding."

Erica looked up from her computer to find Killion in her office doorway. It was just after seven on Saturday. The last clients were being checked out and most employees had already left. Normally she would have headed home an hour ago, but she'd already told Summer and her mother that she would be late tonight.

"You think you know everything, but you don't. I'm not hiding. I'm avoiding. There's a difference."

"Semantics," he teased, setting a bag of takeout on the small conference table along with a bottle of Peter Michael Chardonnay and a black picnic bag.

She crossed to him. He pulled her close, then kissed her. She let herself lean into him for a moment before straightening.

She pointed at the bag. "What did you bring me?"

He turned it so she could see the Seastar logo, then pulled a receipt out of his long-sleeved shirt pocket.

"An assortment of sashimi and sushi, two orders of deviled eggs. Crab bisque, Thai chicken, black truffle mac and cheese, grilled asparagus and their bread service."

Her stomach growled. "All my favorites."

"Mine, too."

They unloaded the picnic tote. Killion, Erica had learned early, liked nice things and had the ability to always have them around him. The tote contained china plates, bowls and flatware. There were elegant wineglasses, cloth napkins and a stone chiller to keep the chardonnay at the perfect temperature.

Once their places were set, they put out the food, then sat down to eat.

"Who pulls all this together for you?" she asked. "Your assistant?"

"My personal assistant, who is someone different than my work assistant."

"Napoleon? I thought he just managed where you live."

"He handles all the details of my personal life. He arranges for the housekeeping service and tells the gardeners when it's time to prune the trees. He coordinates my travel, stocks my refrigerator and yes, keeps tracks of your favorite restaurants and what you like to order."

She smiled. "Basically, he's your wife."

Killion laughed. "He's better than a wife. In my relationship with Napoleon, I'm always right."

"Spoken like a man."

"You also like being right."

"I do," she admitted, taking several pieces of sushi while he filled two bowls with bisque. "Thank you for dinner. And the company."

"I enjoy being your distraction, but at some point you'll have to go home."

"I don't know. I could get a lovely hotel room with a water view and live there for the next few months."

"You'd miss Summer and your mom."

True enough, but they could visit her and then she wouldn't have to deal with Allison.

"It's not that I don't like her," she said, picking up her spoon. "I don't know her well enough to form an opinion. It's just so damned awkward and weird."

"That your ex-husband's second wife is now living with you?"

"And her child, although Jackson is a sweetie."

She paused to savor the bisque. The creamy texture was decadently rich, with bits of crab. She'd heard once that good bisque was in essence reduction and cream, which meant plenty of calories. Something she would worry about tomorrow.

"We're so different," she continued. "It's hard to believe the same man married us."

"Maybe the more interesting question is what you each saw in him."

She looked at Killion. "There is that. We both fell in love with a man who turned out to be a criminal. That's a little upsetting."

"He wasn't a criminal when you met him."

"I hope not. I've always thought I was a good judge of character. Given how many people I employ, it would be depressing to find out I'm not."

"Peter wasn't a criminal when you met him," Killion repeated. "You weren't the trigger."

"But Allison was? That's almost worse. Summer adores her, so I know she's nice, and she's a good mom. How can this be her fault?"

"It's not. It's Peter's fault. He's the one who chose to take those actions. It's his plan, his outcome and his responsibility. I'm saying something in their life caused him to go down that path. He would have always had the proclivity to cross the line. People who don't wouldn't have considered what he did an option."

She eyed the deviled eggs. They were delicious on their own, but Seastar topped theirs with salmon gravlax, wasabi *tobiko* or truffle-ahi tartare. After spending at least fifteen seconds trying to pick, she muttered, "What the hell," and put one of each on her plate.

"He stole from me," she said, not meeting Killion's gaze.

He was silent. She reached for her wine.

"I found out after the divorce, when the new accounting firm went over the books. He was siphoning off money. A few thousand here, a few thousand there. It added up to over a hundred thousand dollars." She looked away. "I thought he was angry and it was about revenge."

"It was more than that."

"I don't want to think that, but given where he is right now, what else could it be?"

"I'm sorry."

"Me, too." She ate one of the deviled eggs. "He totally fooled me."

"He fooled you both. That's something you have in common."

She raised her eyebrows. "Oh, please. So we should sit down over a cup of tea and discuss the man we both married? I don't think so."

"It would be therapeutic."

"Not happening."

"The more you get to know her, the less you'll worry that Summer will one day love her more."

She snapped up her head and stared at him. "What did you say?"

"What you've felt deep inside but have been afraid to articulate."

Heat stained her cheeks and she looked away. "That's crazy. You're wrong. I would never think that. Summer's my daughter. We have a bond that will never be broken. I'm hardly concerned about how she feels about Peter's current wife."

His green eyes gave nothing away as he shrugged and casually said, "You're right. I was reaching. I take it back."

"As you should. Let's change the subject."

He mentioned a project at work and she commented. The ridiculous statement about Summer loving Allison more was soon in the past. Unfortunately for Erica, it wasn't forgotten and as she drove home an hour later, she was unable to get it out of her mind.

Killion was wrong about her, wrong about her daughter. Summer was softhearted and yes, she cared about Allison and Jackson. It was her nature, nothing more. Erica wasn't going to lose her, certainly not to someone like Allison.

17

By the time Erica arrived home she'd nearly convinced herself that she'd forgotten Killion's ridiculousness. She ignored the strange car in the third bay of the garage and the stacks of furniture and boxes in the fourth as she walked toward the door leading to the house. It was nearly nine thirty and she'd been hoping to find a dimly lit mudroom and a quiet downstairs. Instead lights were on everywhere and the sound of a high-pitched toddler shriek echoed off the walls.

"Jackson, no. It's late. You need to be in bed."

Allison's voice sounded desperate and exhausted. Erica would guess that there had been too many changes for the little boy to process and he was too wound up to know he was tired.

"Go through the kitchen from that side and I'll head him off this way," Summer said, just as Erica walked in from the mudroom.

Seconds later a pajama-wearing child burst into the kitchen, spotted her and screamed happily. He barreled toward her, both arms outstretched. She dropped her bag and caught him as he launched himself.

"Did someone give you sugar?" she asked as he wrapped his skinny arms around her neck and buried his face in her shoulder. "Or caffeine? How are you, little man?"

He drew back and smiled at her, then planted a kiss on her

cheek. Immediately after, his brows drew together and he pointed at her.

She smiled. "You want to know my name, don't you? I'm Erica. Erica," she repeated more slowly.

"Rika!"

"Close enough."

Summer ran into the kitchen from the near entrance, while Allison appeared at the far end. She had stains on her too-small T-shirt and dark circles under her eyes. No doubt it had been a hell of a day. She'd been forced out of her home, her husband was in jail and the entirety of her possessions were in some strange woman's garage.

"I've got this," Erica told her, enjoying the happy feel of a toddler in her arms.

Allison blinked at her. "I'm sorry. I'm really tired, so I don't understand."

"I've got this. I'll get him settled. You get ready for bed, so when he's asleep, all you have to do is close your eyes."

"You can't do that."

"I'm actually very good with small children."

Allison looked away. "I didn't mean that." She looked back at Erica. "We're your guests here and that would be an imposition."

"You're not my guest," Erica said bluntly, careful to keep her voice calm and soothing. She could already feel Jackson relaxing as she held him. "You live here now and you're going to be living here for the next few months. This is your home."

She paused. "We should probably meet and come up with ground rules we're both comfortable with. Discuss expectations and that sort of thing. Let's plan to do that tomorrow."

Allison nodded wearily. "Sure."

Erica turned to her daughter. "Where are his books? Are they unpacked?"

"They're in the bookcase in my room." Summer grinned. "Next to my precalc textbook."

Erica carried Jackson upstairs. Allison and Summer followed. When they reached the landing, Erica pointed to Allison's bedroom.

"I was serious. I'll get him settled for the night. You go do your thing."

"I can—"

Erica cut Allison off with a stern look. Allison flinched, nodded, then retreated to her bedroom. Erica carried Jackson into the room he would share with Summer for the next few nights. His crib was in place and ready for him. She ignored that and instead sat on her daughter's bed.

Once she'd scooted them both up toward the headboard, she used pillows to prop herself up, then got Jackson comfortable reclining on her. Summer sat at the foot of the bed and handed her a book.

Erica opened it one-handed and showed him the picture. "That is a very handsome aardvark."

"Happy," Jackson said, pointing at the drawing. But his voice was low and the gesture half-hearted.

"That's what it says right here. 'Clybourne was a very happy aardvark. He was happy in his house. He was happy with his job. He was happy when he put on his favorite top hat and went to brunch with his friends.'"

She kissed the top of Jackson's head. "I think it would be very fun to have brunch with an aardvark, although I'm a little concerned about the lack of table manners. We'd probably want to have it in the backyard, just in case."

Jackson didn't respond. Instead his breathing slowed and he slumped down a little.

Summer started to get up, but Erica shook her head. "Let's give it about five minutes," she said, making sure she spoke in her storybook voice. "I want him completely out before we move him or we'll have to start over."

She continued to read, turning pages until she was sure the

toddler was deeply asleep, then she nodded at Summer, who carefully got up and took the child from her. When he was in his crib, they quietly slipped out of the room.

Erica looked at her daughter. "How are you going to manage this? Having him in your room. You're a little bit trapped."

"He'll get into his own room in a few days." Her daughter smiled. "You're forgetting, Mom. Every time I spent the night at Dad's place, I've shared a room with Jackson. I know how to do this."

Right, because she hadn't had her own room. Something that didn't seem to bother her at all.

"If you're sure," Erica said, hugging her daughter. "I'm going to check downstairs and make sure everything is locked up. You'll let Allison know Jackson's asleep?"

"I will, then I'll watch something in the media room while I text with my friends."

"Don't stay up too late."

"I won't."

Erica checked all the doors downstairs, turning out lights as she went, finishing in the kitchen, where she made a mug of herbal tea. Once back upstairs in her room, she changed into yoga pants and a T-shirt and did a quick stretching routine that always relaxed her, then sat on the small sofa in the corner and sipped her tea while doing a little online window shopping.

But her heart wasn't in it. She was too aware of Allison and Jackson in the house—something that would get better with time, she told herself. Eventually she would get used to having them here.

She finished her tea, then went into the bathroom to wash off her makeup and get ready for bed. She was about to turn out the lights when she heard a light knock on the closed door.

"Come in," she called.

Summer stepped into the room, her tablet in one hand. "I didn't know if you were still up."

"I am." Erica patted the king-size bed she'd replaced after Peter had moved out. "What's up?"

"Some logistical stuff." The teen sat cross-legged on the bed, facing her. "Allison's going to need another crib for Bethany. I've been doing some reading online about him transitioning to a big-boy bed. He's close to the right age, but they all say not to do it if there have been a lot of changes. So Bethany can't have his crib."

Erica wasn't sure why this was an issue. "Then Allison will get another crib."

Her daughter looked at her. "We're going to have to buy it."

"Yes, I know."

Along with everything else the woman needed. Hopefully Peter would get off his ass and find a decent lawyer who could get some of the money released, but until that happened, Allison was her responsibility. They'd discussed her continuing to work, but with the cost of childcare and how far along she was in her pregnancy, Erica hadn't seen the point and Allison had agreed.

Summer set down her tablet. "I want to go see Dad."

Erica stared at her daughter in surprise. "Why?"

"He's my father. I want to know he's okay."

"Sorry. I get that. It's just you haven't mentioned it before."

Summer shrugged. "I was processing. Now I want to visit him."

Erica thought about what she'd seen on her brief visit. She'd been there on a nonvisiting day and had received special treatment. She couldn't imagine how much worse it was with a few hundred other people in that huge room, with planes flying overhead and guards everywhere.

"I don't think that's a good idea. Whatever you're thinking, it's not like that. It's not like the movies. Jail isn't a happy place."

"I need to do this, Mom."

"Once you have those memories, they'll be with you forever. You won't be able to unsee them. It's better for you to think about your dad in the regular world. Those are the images he'll want you to have."

Not that she cared about Peter's feelings, but she was worried about her daughter.

"You're protecting me."

Erica nodded. "It's one of the more important rules in that set of instructions you came with."

Summer gave her a faint smile that quickly faded. "I'm not a kid."

"Sometimes you're very childish."

"Mo-om! Be serious."

"I am. That's why I don't want you to go."

"I know Dad did bad things. I know he's probably going to make a plea deal and go to prison for a long time."

Erica tried not to show her surprise at her daughter's statement. "You've been doing online reading about more than transitioning out of a crib."

"Yeah, well, it's the internet. You can find out anything."

"I hadn't even gone that far," she admitted. "I was still caught up in your dad getting a better lawyer." A plea deal? Peter had mentioned the feds were trying to get him to cooperate. That implied there would be something in it for him. But to plead guilty and go to prison?

"I want to see him."

Erica knew she wouldn't change her mind. "Okay. I'll take you."

Summer shook her head. "You don't have to. I talked to Grandma earlier and she said she would do it."

Erica wasn't sure Peter would approve his ex-mother-in-law as a visitor, but under the circumstances she would guess Mara was a better alternative than seeing his ex-wife again.

Summer picked at the blanket, then looked up. "You've done a lot." She paused. "No, I asked for a lot and you said yes. You didn't have to, but you did."

She glanced back at the bed. "I don't think many of my friends' moms would have been so open to all of this."

Erica suspected that was true. Not that she deserved a lot of credit—if there was even one other option, she would happily toss out Allison to pursue it.

But there wasn't, so here they all were.

"Allison and Jackson are your family," she said lightly. "And you're mine. This is how it's supposed to work."

With a little luck, Killion would be right and Summer would remember this for the rest of her life. That almost made it worth it.

Her daughter scrambled up the bed and hugged Erica. "Thank you, Mom. You're really good to me and I know I can be difficult."

"And childish," Erica said lightly, holding her tight.

Summer laughed as she drew back. "I can be mature."

"Yes, you can, but you often don't choose to be. Now go to bed. It's late."

Summer stood and started for the door. When she got there, she paused and looked back.

"Do you think Allison is scared?"

Erica considered various answers, then decided that the truth was usually best.

"I'm sure she is. I would be."

"Me, too. I'm glad we're here for her. Night, Mom."

"Good night."

Allison fell asleep the second her head touched the pillow. Unfortunately two hours later she woke unexpectedly, her heart pounding as anxiety poured through her. She got up and walked around her spacious room, trying to calm her body. The reaction woke Bethany, who seemed intent on kicking her way out.

As Allison paced, telling herself she was fine, that yes, she could breathe and eventually this would pass, she also had to deal with the sharp ache in her chest by herself. There was no Peter to hold her. Before he'd been arrested, when she had a panic attack he would walk with her, his hand in hers, as he offered support and reassurance. Later, when the angst faded, they would return to bed, where he stayed close, his arm around her, until she fell back to sleep.

But tonight there was no Peter to offer comfort. She was alone, responsible for her children, in a strange place, at the mercy of her incarcerated husband's first wife. The reality of her situation was nearly enough to bring back the panic, but she fought it and walked until her heart rate slowed.

Once she felt a little better, she checked on Jackson and Summer. Both were sleeping soundly. Allison returned to the hallway, not sure what to do. She'd had the movers put the TV from the living room into her bedroom, so she could watch that. Only she still felt as if she needed to keep moving.

She made her way downstairs and walked through the large, quiet house. The rooms were unfamiliar, the shadows menacing. Time, she told herself. She would get familiar with the place in time.

She paused by the French doors in the kitchen, wondering if a few minutes outside would make her feel better. Mara had said the house didn't have an alarm, so she didn't have to worry about that. But it was late and she wasn't sure about wandering around an unfamiliar backyard.

"I need to get some sleep," she murmured and turned to head to the stairs. Just then the kitchen overhead lights went on.

She turned and saw Erica standing by the far entrance to the kitchen. The two women stared at each other. Allison took in her host's loungewear set with loose but well-fitting cropped pants and a sleeveless tank, both done in a charming floral print. Erica also had on fluffy slippers that should have looked silly on a woman her age, but didn't.

In contrast Allison wore a voluminous size 3X nightgown

she'd bought at a discount store. The garment was multiple times too big for her, but she appreciated how she could toss and turn without it getting tangled around her. The nightgown was like sleeping under a tent. She'd pulled on a ratty old shawl she'd found while she'd been going through the clothes, deciding what to bring in the house and what to put in storage. Her own robe was just her regular size and in no way equipped to handle her massive belly, and she hadn't been comfortable not having anything to pass as a bathrobe. Instead of slippers, she had worn flip-flops. She looked and felt like some tragic case, sitting on the corner of an intersection, trying not to make eye contact with passersby.

"I was hoping you could sleep," Erica said into the silence. "I know you're exhausted."

"I had a good couple of hours and then I was just awake."

"I'm sure it's all the stress of what's happened, plus being here. Give it a little time, you'll settle in."

"Why are you up so late?"

Erica's smile was faint. "There's been a little stress for me, too. Plus Summer's decided she wants to go see her father."

"In jail? That's not a good idea. I know she misses him, but it's not a great environment." Allison thought about how upsetting her visits to Peter had been. "She won't like it."

"That's what I told her, but she's determined. Apparently my mother has agreed to take her."

"Mara?" Allison managed a smile. "She seems very nice."

"She's a wonderful woman. Occasionally she gets on my nerves, but that's what mothers do." Erica glanced toward the stove, then back at Allison. "Would you like some hot chocolate? I know it's a cliché, but under the circumstances, it might be exactly what we both need."

Allison hesitated, not sure she wanted to spend any more time with Peter's ex-wife. But hot chocolate did sound good and despite the fact that Erica was the last person on earth she could be friends with, right now she needed a little company to keep the worry at bay.

"That sounds nice. Thank you."

Erica motioned to the island. Allison lumbered over and slid onto one of the stools there. Erica pulled a small pan out of a wide, deep drawer under the cooktop and set it on the counter. She collected milk and what looked like a thick bar of chocolate.

She measured out milk and poured it into the pan. After setting it on the cooktop, she checked the heat, then began breaking pieces of solid chocolate into a small bowl.

"You don't use a mix?" Allison blurted, thinking of the can of Hershey's she'd put on "her" shelves in the pantry. "Jackson loves it."

"This is Spanish chocolate. Peter and I discovered it years ago when we spent time in Madrid and Barcelona. It has a lovely rich flavor and is less sweet. I order the chocolate and my favorite olive oil from a place that imports delicacies from Spain." She smiled. "They also have a frozen churro that is surprisingly delicious. You bake them for a few minutes in the oven, roll them in cinnamon and sugar and voilà! Better than a doughnut any day. We keep them in the freezer. Help yourself. Jackson will love them."

Allison knew she was operating at about thirty percent of her normal brain energy, but she couldn't grasp the concept. Erica ordered special chocolate and olive oil from *Spain*? Couldn't she just buy what was at the grocery store?

Obviously not, she told herself. The local stuff probably wasn't good enough for her.

The bitchy mental comment was immediately followed by guilt. Erica had been nothing but kind—inviting her into her home, taking care of Jackson the way she had. So far there hadn't been any evidence of the mean-spirited, evil ex Peter had always talked about.

Silence weighed on the kitchen. Allison found herself regretting accepting the offer of hot chocolate. She would rather just go back to bed, even if that meant another panic attack. She searched for a neutral topic for the next fifteen minutes.

"Your house is beautiful," she said. "I've only seen parts of it, but it's really lovely."

"Thank you. When you're feeling up to it, you should explore. There's a finished basement downstairs with a huge living area, a small kitchen and a couple of bedrooms. I think the previous owners used it as a rental. There's a separate entrance around back."

She dropped pieces of chocolate into the warming milk and stirred. "Summer talks about that being her 'digs' when she goes off to college. Somewhere to come back to that allows her total independence. Personally, I don't see her doing it. She likes to be a part of things too much."

Allison stared at the other woman. "Why didn't you put me down there? I'd be out of your way and Summer could have kept her bedroom."

Erica glanced at her. "You're pregnant, with a toddler. Living down there would be the same as living in an apartment. You need support, Allison. People around to pick up the slack. Once Bethany's born, you'll need our help. Maybe it's something to consider six months from now. I don't know. We'll have to talk."

Allison felt the room spin a little. Six months from now? Six months? She wasn't going to be here that long! She couldn't be. She had a life and Peter, plus her kids. She needed to be making plans and come up with a schedule or something.

Only just thinking about that exhausted her already burned-out brain. Tomorrow, she promised herself. Or next week. She would pull herself together and start to strategize.

"My point is," Erica continued, "you should be comfortable in the house. Get to know it. And the outside is very nice. There's lots of room for Jackson to run around." She glanced at the warming milk, then back at Allison. "If we have a hot summer, we can get one of those little blow-up kiddie pools.

There's a nice shade area by the deck where he'd be out of direct sun. At that age, they burn so easily."

"When did you and Peter buy the house?" Allison asked. "Summer's mentioned she's lived here all her life, so it had to be shortly after you got married."

Erica poured the chocolate milk into mugs. "I bought the house before Peter and I met."

Allison felt her eyes widen. "You bought a house on your own? While you were single?"

Erica walked over with the drinks and set them on the island, then took a seat and smiled. "Yes. I bought this house by myself, as a single woman. You look shocked."

"I am." Allison winced. "I don't mean that in a bad way. It's just I don't know any woman who was—what, twenty-five?—buying a house on her own." Plus Peter had implied he and Erica had bought the place together. He'd made a point of telling her how Erica had kept him from taking his half. But if she'd bought it on her own, that wasn't true.

Erica looked around. "It was a huge financial stretch for me and my mortgage broker kept trying to get me to buy something smaller." She laughed. "A starter home. I told him I didn't want to move again. I wanted a house I could grow into."

She sipped her drink. "It was in rough shape, let me tell you. The structure was sound and the plumbing and electrical worked, but otherwise, it was a mess. Run-down and dirty. No one had painted for twenty years and the carpets were worn to the backing. The kitchen and bathroom were all original. It was going to be a project."

"You sound as if you like that."

Erica smiled at her. "I enjoy a challenge. I took it slowly. Room by room. My mom was dating a contractor, and he and I came up with a plan. I saved until I had enough for the next project, then he did the work. It took about four years to get it to where you see it today."

She wrinkled her nose. "Four years and a salon. I stopped expanding while I was working on the house. I didn't have the cash flow. But once it was done, I returned to my business plan. It worked out."

She nodded at Allison's mug. "You haven't tried your drink."

Allison automatically took a sip. The hot chocolate was smooth and creamy—full of flavor but with a more sophisticated flair. Less sweet, somehow, but satisfying. It was—in a word—perfection.

"It's wonderful," she said. "Good enough that I don't care if it gives me heartburn."

"You think it will?"

"This far along, everything gives me heartburn." She returned to what Erica had told her about the house. "I don't understand how you bought this place on your own. No offense, but aren't you a hairstylist? I don't mean to be rude," she added hastily. "Peter implied you came from money but I didn't think it was…"

She pressed her lips together. "I'm sorry. I'm asking very inappropriate questions."

Erica drew her brows together. "I didn't come from money. My mother is also a hairstylist. She still has clients. I keep my hand in but I've moved to the business side of things. I can't believe Peter told you I came from money. That's so strange."

Allison was just as confused. The business side of things? How could one salon have that much paperwork or whatever? Shouldn't Erica be doing hair? Wait. What was it Erica had said about the house? It had taken four years and a salon.

"I know you own a business," she said. "It's a beauty salon so you do hair."

"Yes. I went to beauty school the second I graduated from high school and from there to building up a client base at my mom's place. I worked hard and bought her out when I was twenty-three. I grew that, opened a second salon and so on." She paused. "Have you heard of Twisted?"

Allison blinked several times. "You mean the upscale salons and spas? Of course I've heard of Twisted. They're like—"

Horror washed over her, along with an icy embarrassment bath. "That's you? You own Twisted? By yourself?"

Erica smiled. "I have many employees, but yes, I'm the sole owner of the corporation."

Allison wanted to shrink into the flooring. This couldn't be happening. Erica owned Twisted? How could she not know that? Why hadn't someone told her? Only they hadn't. Peter always dismissed what Erica did as "just hair." Summer talked about how her mom cared about things like appearance and style and had talked about her "business," but given what Peter had said, Allison had assumed she worked somewhere.

But that wasn't true. Apparently Erica had started from very little and built an empire. She'd bought this house, had grown her business. She owned Twisted!

"I'm sorry," Allison murmured. "I had no idea."

Erica smiled. "Yes, I can see that from your face." Her humor faded. "I have no idea why Peter wanted you to believe I was just a quote-hairdresser-unquote. First of all, it can be an excellent profession. A good stylist with a happy clientele can earn over a hundred thousand a year, no problem."

Something flashed in her eyes. An emotion, maybe. Regret?

"Peter and I have different business philosophies," Erica continued. "I'm ambitious and while he likes business, he doesn't share my passion for conquering the next challenge."

"He did well with his accounting business. His clients and employees all like him."

Allison forced herself to stop talking, not sure why she felt the need to defend her husband, who was currently sitting in jail.

"I'm sure they do," Erica murmured. "You've been working in a grocery store. Summer mentioned it."

Allison flushed. "Part-time. I used to have a great job at a day care co-op, but they fired me after Peter was arrested."

"What? They can't fire you for something your husband did."

Allison explained how Liz had been supportive at first, but then had told Allison they couldn't take the risk. "She was worried the other parents would pull their children out of the day care and go somewhere else."

"That's ridiculous. You had nothing to do with Peter's business. You didn't work there. It's not even community property—he owned the business before you met. She can't do that. We should talk to a lawyer and get your job back."

Allison found Erica's energy gratifying. "You're very kind, but I'm not interested in going back. At least not until after Bethany is born. Maybe then I'll take on Liz. Earning credits by working there allowed me to have the second job and not have to pay for day care. With two kids, I couldn't afford it any other way."

Erica sighed. "The childcare situation or lack of affordable childcare is ridiculous. I was lucky. When Summer was little my mom helped, and I took her to work with me sometimes. Sometimes I hired a local teen to babysit. But not everyone has that option."

Allison knew she didn't and thinking about that was depressing.

"I'm sorry I didn't know about Twisted," she said.

Erica smiled. "It's all right. I can see why Peter didn't tell you and Summer wouldn't mention it because she would assume you knew. How did you and Peter meet?"

Despite her exhaustion and the stressors in her life, Allison smiled.

"He rescued me," she said, then laughed. "I was working at the grocery store. Peter was a regular. We would chat a little, but I didn't think anything about it. One night I got off work at nine, as per usual, and my car wouldn't start."

It had been cold and raining and her car not starting had seemed like the end of the world. She'd been lonely and missing Levi and totally lost. Someone had knocked on her window.

"Peter asked if he could help."

"I never knew Peter was good with cars."

Allison grinned. "He's not, but he called a tow truck, then he waited with me. He insisted on following the tow truck driver to the dealership, where we dropped it off, then he took me home."

She held up a hand. "He was a perfect gentleman. Nothing happened. He didn't even ask for my number."

Erica's gaze was unreadable. "But he was at the grocery store the next day."

"He was. He asked me out and I said yes."

What she didn't say was that while they'd been waiting for the tow truck, he'd made her laugh. Just a little, but it had been the first time she had laughed since losing Levi. Peter had offered her hope. He'd been a few years older and not the most exciting man in the world, but he'd been steady and he'd fallen hard. His loving her had allowed her to finish healing, to open her heart again. Without realizing what had happened, she'd fallen for him, too.

"And that was that. We started dating, then we fell in love. He proposed and you know the rest."

"That's a lovely story. I'm glad he was there to help you when you needed it."

"Me, too." Unfortunately that was no longer true.

She pushed away her mug. "I can't believe he's been arrested and is in jail. How could that happen? He won't tell me anything and I'm so scared." She looked at Erica. "If he really loved me, he wouldn't have done this. He would have kept us safe. I don't know anything anymore."

Erica's expression turned kind. "The man loves you. Trust me on that. He's an idiot who made some really bad decisions, but he loves you."

"You can't know that."

Erica looked away. "Yes, I can. He told me when I went to see him." She looked back at Allison. "He asked me to help, to take care of you. If you knew what he really thought of me, you'd realize what it cost him to make that request."

Allison didn't understand but wasn't sure what to ask. "You're helping me because of Peter?" Her stomach knotted. What did that mean? Was Erica still in love with her ex-husband?

But the other woman's look of shock and revulsion quickly assured her.

"No," Erica said flatly. "God, no. I'm doing this because of Summer. She's my family and you're hers. That means we are, in some inexplicable way, connected."

"I appreciate all that you've done for me," she began.

Erica held up a hand.

"No, just no. You've thanked me enough. We need to be done with that. The situation is weird enough without you feeling you have to genuflect every time you turn around."

"I wasn't planning on genuflecting," Allison said. "Maybe a little bow now and then but not an actual genuflection."

She spoke without thinking, then immediately wondered if she'd been too flip. Only Erica's lips began to twitch and Allison found herself starting to giggle. Soon they were both laughing hard enough to bring tears to their eyes.

"I feel better," Erica said. "I hope you do, too."

Allison nodded, suddenly sleepy. She yawned. "I think I'll go up to bed."

She reached for her mug, but Erica got there first. "I'll take care of these. You go get some sleep."

"Thanks."

Allison made her way to the stairs. As she climbed she thought about what had just happened. Erica was nothing like Peter had described. Even more surprising, Allison found her very kind and likeable. An unexpected revelation. But reconciling what she'd been told and what she'd observed for herself would have to happen at another time.

18

Erica spent most of Sunday at work. She usually tried to spend the day with Summer, but given the changes at the house, she'd thought it would be easier for everyone if she absented herself. She'd gotten home around five, in time to help with dinner. Mara had joined them and Jackson had been the star of the meal. Afterward, they'd all gone to their separate corners, so to speak.

Monday morning Erica walked into the kitchen to find Summer fixing hot cereal for Jackson.

"Hey, Mom," her teen said with a smile as she added warm water to the small bowl. "Allison's still sleeping, so I thought I'd take care of this guy. She needs her rest."

Erica was torn between pointing out that Jackson was Allison's responsibility, not Summer's, and mentally agreeing that the other woman was close to collapsing from exhaustion.

"You need to get going or you'll be late for school," she said instead as she glanced at the clock. "I can feed our little man."

Summer handed over the bowl and spoon. "Great. Thanks. He likes a little banana mashed up in the cereal, and then he gets milk."

Summer gave her a fast hug, kissed Jackson's cheek, grabbed her backpack and flew out of the door. Erica turned to the toddler.

"Good morning," she said with a smile. "Did you sleep well?"

Jackson waved his arms as he grinned. "Rika!" That was followed by several nonsensical sounds, delivered in a tone of great importance.

"I hadn't heard that," Erica replied, stirring the cereal. "But it's good to know. This is rice based, by the way. Very tummy neutral."

She was just mashing in a little banana when her mother walked in.

"Good morning," Mara said, walking directly to Jackson and pulling him into her arms. "And good morning to you. How do you feel? Did you sleep well?" She sniffed him. "You need a bath. We'll do that after breakfast. Are you hungry? I'm starved."

Jackson waved his arms and kissed her cheek, mumbling something that was probably toddler for *I'm happy to see you.*

She expertly settled him back in his high chair and took the bowl from Erica. "I'll do this. You're dressed for work and I've discovered this one is a messy eater."

"Thanks, Mom." Erica crossed to the coffeepot and poured herself a mug. She held it up. "You want one?"

"I'm good."

Her mother pushed the high chair close to the table then took a seat. She checked that the floor mat was in place to catch the inevitable spills before handing over the bowl and spoon. Jackson immediately scooped up the cereal and managed to get most of it in his mouth.

"You should eat something," Mara said without taking her gaze off the child. "Coffee isn't breakfast."

"I'll grab something on the way to work."

"No, you won't."

"I promise to eat lunch."

By then she should be hungry. The disquiet of her late-night conversation with Allison had already lasted more than a day. It was time to let it all go.

"You'll get used to having her in the house," her mother told her. "In time."

"It's not her so much as the idea of her," Erica admitted, crossing to the table and sitting across from her mother. "She told me how they met." She briefly recounted the car-breakdown story. When she was done she blurted, "He rescued her," then wished she hadn't.

Mara, of course, knew exactly what she meant. "And he never rescued you."

"I don't need rescuing."

"That's not the point." Her mother wiped Jackson's face with a napkin. "You're doing so good. You're a big boy, aren't you?"

Jackson beamed at her, then returned to his eating.

Her mother looked at her. "You're capable. You've always known what you wanted and gone after it. Peter said he liked that about you until he didn't. He never played fair."

True but painful words, Erica thought. "My goal was never to be capable. I wanted to be his wife. I wish I knew what went wrong."

"You do know."

Erica wondered if that was true. "I don't think he ever loved me. He loved the idea of what he thought I was, but not the me inside." She sighed. "Maybe I wasn't completely honest when we first met. Maybe I pretended to be more what I thought he would like. Not on purpose but because I was tired of being alone."

"I'm not sure you have the acting skills for that. You put yourself out there. And you're equally guilty of loving who you thought he was rather than who he really was."

Jackson dropped his spoon. Mara picked it up, wiped it off and handed it to him.

"Or maybe you wanted him to be more like you?"

Erica tried not to flinch. "That's not true. I wanted him to have a successful business because it would make him happy."

Mara didn't say anything, leaving Erica to squirm.

"Fine. I'll say it. I didn't like him being a junior accountant with no ambition. I mean at first it didn't matter, but later…" She looked away. "I made him start his own business. He never wanted to and he resented me after that."

"He was always going to end up resenting you," her mother said flatly. "You were too strong for him. You're right—he started out admiring you, but then ended up resenting you for an assortment of reasons, most of which are on him, not you."

"Oh, I don't know."

She thought of all the evenings she'd worked late, how she'd been so busy growing her business and being there for Summer. She'd still loved Peter and had thought they would be together always, but toward the end, how much had she shown up?

"I'll accept my responsibility for what happened, but I'll never forgive him for trying to turn Summer against me."

"He does need to own that." Mara smiled at Jackson. "Did you finish your cereal?" She passed over the sippy cup filled with milk. "Here you go."

Jackson grabbed it with both hands.

"Summer's not gone," her mother added. "She adores you."

"She won't let me cut her hair. She has her friends do it. She disses what I do. Her friends would be thrilled to have me as their mother. I always thought we'd play with makeup and go shopping together. She doesn't want to."

She had once, she thought bitterly. But since the divorce, Peter had been not-so-subtly trying to turn her away from all that.

"It's one thing to resent my success," she added. "But to put Summer in the middle is awful."

"It is," her mother agreed. "And she'll come around. Just be patient. The more you resent him, the harder it is to let go."

"Let go? Peter and I are old news. I've moved on."

"All evidence to the contrary?"

"What evidence? Do you think I still care about Peter? I don't."

"You're not in love with him—I'm clear on that. But you haven't let go of past hurts. You hold yourself back."

Mothers, Erica thought grimly. Always annoying. "You're talking about Killion, aren't you? I don't know why you can't accept our relationship for what it is. Not conventional, but it works for us."

"You're holding him at bay." Her mother's gaze was steady. "You're never going to marry him."

"I'm not marrying anyone. I don't need that in my life."

"What about love?"

"I have plenty. I have you and Summer. I don't need a man."

"You need companionship, Erica. You need a life partner who is your equal. Someone to have your back. It's lonely when you don't."

Erica didn't want to talk about this. She was fine on her own. "Look at you. After Dad left, you weren't interested in getting married again. You have lots of boyfriends, but no one serious."

"Those who can, do. Those who can't, offer advice."

Monday evening Erica found herself hovering outside of Allison's closed door. It was barely eight, so the other woman should be awake. Still she hesitated, not really wanting to speak to her, but knowing they had to figure out some logistics.

She told herself to grow a pair, then knocked briskly. Seconds later the door opened.

"Oh, hi. You're home."

The faint surprise made sense, Erica thought. She'd worked late to avoid dinner with Allison and Jackson. Well, not Jackson, but they were a package deal.

"I am. Do you have a minute? I thought we should discuss some ground rules. Knowing each other's expectations should make things go more smoothly."

"Um, sure. Good idea."

Erica pointed down the hall. "Let's go in my office."

She led the way to the back bedroom she'd converted into a home office. The walls were a pale blue-gray and there was a glorious Oriental rug on the floor. The closet had been modified with floor-to-ceiling shelving for her records and office supplies, leaving the workspace serene and tidy.

As Erica gestured toward one of the chairs on the visitors' side of her desk, she remembered Peter complaining her office was never messy. He'd said it was unnatural that she didn't pile papers everywhere.

She told herself not to think about him and offered Allison what she hoped was a warm smile.

"How are you settling in?"

Allison shifted in her chair, as if trying to get comfortable. Erica eyed her huge belly and thought that probably wouldn't happen until after the baby was born.

"It's an adjustment, but again, I really appreciate you—"

"Oh, dear God! No. I don't want to hear thank you."

Allison ducked her head. "All right, but I'm thinking it."

"Think quietly."

Allison looked at her and smiled. "You don't get to control my thought process."

"I can try."

Allison's smile faded. "I'm sorry I wasn't up this morning. I wish someone had woken me up. Jackson isn't your responsibility."

"You need to catch up on your rest and it wasn't me. My mom fed him. We all adore him and he's so easy to deal with. Having said that, I promise if it gets to be too much, or if there's a scheduling conflict, I'll absolutely tell you."

"Thank you."

Erica glanced down at her list. "All right, logistics you need to know. Wednesday the cleaners are here. A team of three or four take care of the house. They scrub everything, so you'll need to let them into your room. I would suggest you tell them to do your bedroom and bathroom first and take Jackson to the park or something for an hour."

"I can clean my own bathroom."

"Not with that belly. Besides, it's what they're paid to do. They'll also change your sheets. Another team member will collect anything for the dry cleaner and bring back last week's."

Allison's eyes widened a little. "They do that?"

"It's part of what they're paid for."

"I don't really have any clothes that need to be dry cleaned."

"Fine, but if you do, they'll take care of it. They also do grocery shopping. We keep a master list in the kitchen. Write down what you need and they'll get it when they get everything else."

Allison drew back a little. "I'm not having them shop for me. I'll do that myself."

"It's up to you, but it can't be easy, shopping with Jackson. You're welcome to use the service. Again, it's what they're paid to do."

Erica looked at her list. "We've discussed the house. I hope you're using more than your room. The basement living room is actually quite large. Jackson could run around there when it's rainy. And speaking of outside, I ordered a playset for him."

She held up her hand. "Nothing fancy. Sturdy plastic construction with a swing, a slide and a little basketball hoop. It comes with a ball, but I got a couple of extras in case he loses one in the yard. And a little table and chairs. The gardener will put them together."

Allison stared at her. "You don't have to do that."

"I know. I wanted to. It will be summer soon and he'll want to get outside."

"You're being too generous." Allison blinked several times. "Thank you."

"Before you get emotional, I'm going to annoy you by asking a blunt question."

"Hardly a surprise. What do you want to know?"

"How much money do you have? I don't mean what's in the frozen account. I mean real money, cash on hand."

Allison stared at her hands. "Of course I want to pay rent," she began.

Erica cut her off. "That's not where I'm going. I want an assessment of your situation."

Allison looked at her, then away. "I have the money the landlord returned because I left early. That's fifteen hundred. I have an additional maybe two hundred and fifty dollars from before and, ah, that's it."

There was something in her tone that made Erica want to probe a little deeper, but she held back. Allison was dealing with enough crap right now. Let her have her secrets.

"What about your credit cards? I assume you've been using those to get by."

"I don't usually use the one I have. I use a debit card, which I can't anymore. But yes, I've put grocery, gas and the medical insurance payment on it. Jackson and I are on a different policy than Peter. It was something about the business."

Erica wrote that down. "So the balance is what? About two thousand?"

"With the second insurance payment? Yes."

"What about the car? Is there a payment?"

"No. We own that."

"Are you on the title?"

Allison stared at her. "I don't know what that means."

Seriously? "When you bought the car, did you sign the paperwork as well?"

"I think so."

"Good. You should always be on the title of the car you drive. Any other debts? You have a phone bill, plus your regular expenses. Is that about it?"

"I think so. I can make a list if you'd like."

"Not necessary." Erica stared at the business card next to her pad of paper. She might as well get it over with. "We have a meeting tomorrow with my personal banker. I want to open a checking account for you. It will be in my name so the government can't seize it, but you'll be a signatory and the money will be there for your use. At some point your accounts will be unfrozen but until then you need cash. I think this is the easiest way."

Allison sat wide-eyed. "I don't understand."

"It's a checking account. You must be able to grasp the concept."

"Hey, don't snap at me. You've had all the time in the world to figure out what to say. My whole life has changed and things are coming at me fast. I'm doing the best I can, but I'm tired, I'm pregnant and nothing about this situation is what I wanted, so maybe you can give me a break!"

They stared at each other. Silence crackled in the room. Erica wondered if Allison would immediately crumble, but her back remained straight, her expression defiant.

Good for her.

"You're right," Erica said quietly. "I did snap. I apologize. Let me start over. I want to open a checking account in my name but make you a signatory. I'll start with five thousand dollars. You'll have checks and a debit card."

She paused to meet Allison's startled gaze. "What you do with the money is up to you. I'm not interested in an accounting of it. If you want to blow the entire amount on a new Prada bag, that's on you."

She paused. "I'll admit I would be disappointed, but I wouldn't say anything."

"If I spent five thousand dollars on a purse, you'd better get me to the ER because I'm not right in the head." Allison slumped back in her chair. "Don't do this," she said in a low voice. "Don't give me the money."

"You need it. You have things to buy. You need to put gas in your car. The bank will notify me when the account dips below a thousand dollars and I'll put in more money."

The other woman covered her face with her hands and began to cry. "Don't be so nice to me. Just don't."

"Why? Do you speak badly of me behind my back?"

"What?" Allison raised her head. Tears still trickled down her cheeks. "Of course not. The only person I talk to about you is Summer and I'd never say anything mean about her mother." She wiped away the moisture. "I try not to talk trash about anyone."

"An admirable quality." And one that made Erica tired. "Let's be real."

"Because until now things haven't been real?" Allison sniffed. "Sorry."

"No. Don't apologize. Your instincts are good. You have the ability to be strong, you just never take the next step. Actually you back up. Let the snark hang out there. Give the other person time to realize you're someone to be reckoned with."

"I can be reckoned with? Where do you come up with that?" Allison's voice was exhausted. "I'm barely able to get up in the morning. The only reason I'm not homeless is my husband's first wife is giving me a place to live. I don't have a job or income. I'm the definition of powerless."

Erica dismissed the words with a flick of her fingers. "As long as you believe that, it'll be true. You have resources and powerful friends. That's a form of power. You have the ability to be loved. Summer adores you. More power."

"You think I'm manipulating Summer? I'm not."

"Stop jumping to the worst possible interpretation of what I'm saying. My point is my daughter loves you enough to give up her bedroom and share a room with your son. You are the kind of person other people want to love. That's a form of power."

She hesitated, not sure if she should speak the truth, then decided, what the hell. "Peter begged me to help you. When I saw him in jail, he went on his knees and begged."

Allison flushed as she turned away. "I'm sorry."

"Why? That's how much he loves you. I'm one of his least

favorite people and he begged me to help you. He would do anything for you. You are his one true love."

"I don't know what to do with that," she admitted.

"You don't have to do anything. My point is you generate strong emotion in people. They want to take care of you."

"Because I'm weak."

"Weakness generates pity, not love. Peter would never have begged for me. He didn't take care of me. Not really. I was perfectly capable of taking care of myself. I still am." She rose, signaling an end to their meeting. "Love is power, Allison. In every form."

"You're confusing me."

"You're tired. Get some sleep. I'll text you in the morning and let you know the time to meet me at the bank."

Allison stood but didn't try to leave. "I don't want the money."

"I know, but you need it and I'm in a position where I can give it to you. Maybe instead of fighting me, you can just take it and say thank you."

Allison managed a faint smile. "Make up your mind. First you don't want me to thank you, now you do. Which is it?"

Erica laughed. "Point taken. I'll text you in the morning."

19

Erica continued to be full of surprises. A week after they visited the bank together so Allison could be a signatory on a checking account with a balance of exactly five thousand dollars, she brought her boyfriend home for dinner.

Mara was the first one to tell her. The older woman had spent a couple of hours with Jackson every morning. They played, and Mara read to him and used a large set of letters to start teaching him the alphabet. This had started on Allison's second morning in the house. Mara had committed to four mornings a week for "toddler detail" as she'd laughingly called it, giving Allison time to run errands or shower without worrying about Jackson.

Now in the second week with Erica and her family, Allison had a routine. She was sleeping a little better, feeling stronger. The worry still dodged her, but she was getting good at not thinking about all the bad things that could yet happen. For now she and her kids were safe. Even her doctor's appointment that morning had gone better. Her weight was up, her blood pressure was down and her sugars were normal.

"Killion's coming over for dinner," Mara announced as she walked into the kitchen Thursday morning. "Usually she goes to his house or they go out to dinner, so this is a big deal."

Jackson shrieked and ran toward her. Mara scooped him up

and nuzzled his face. "How's my little man? You look good. It's sunny outside. I thought we'd play in the yard for a bit."

Allison continued to load the dishwasher. "Killion is her boyfriend?"

"In a manner of speaking. They have an arrangement."

"I don't know what that means."

Mara smiled as she set down Jackson. "You know, I don't, either. They go out, sometimes she spends the night. They're more at his place than here, but Summer and I have both met him." She lowered her voice. "He's very handsome and charming. I've heard he's a shark in business but around us, he couldn't be sweeter."

Allison wasn't sure what to say. "I'll keep Jackson busy upstairs." Or maybe they could go out for dinner. A fast food place wouldn't be very expensive.

"Don't be silly. It's a family dinner. Killion will want to meet you."

"Why?" Not only wasn't she family, but the whole evening had the potential to be awkward.

"He's that kind of person. Plus, he's a wonderful dinner companion. You must be there. Erica's making her famous shrimp scampi. Summer and I have worked out the rest of the menu. We'll start with homemade bruschetta and a roasted beet salad. We'll have mac and cheese for Jackson. I'm going to that lovely French bakery in Kirkland for a decadent dessert. There will be wine and—"

Mara wrinkled her nose. "Sorry about the wine mention. Summer's been researching mocktails. I'll make sure there's enough for two. We're meeting at six."

The statement sounded more like an order than a suggestion. Allison couldn't think of a gracious way to refuse. And to be honest, she was curious about the man who had claimed Erica's heart. She didn't know the other woman well, but from what she could tell, Erica kept herself a little apart from nearly everyone. She was friendly and kind and knowledgeable, but all with a slightly standoffish quality.

Which was why Allison found herself in the big kitchen at five, helping Summer wash mint and cut cucumbers for their drinks.

"I just throw a few chunks of cucumber into the blender," Summer said, peeling a three-inch section. "The fresh juice is way better. I read online that ginger beer helps an upset stomach more than commercial ginger ale, which is mostly sugar."

Mara breezed in from the formal dining room they would be using that night. She held up two tablecloths, one pure white, the other pale yellow.

"I'm using the stoneware from Italy," she said. "It's heavy but so pretty, and those flat pasta bowls work with the scampi."

"I don't know what the plates look like," Allison admitted. "Summer, which one goes better?"

"The yellow," Erica said firmly, walking in from the mudroom.

She crossed to her daughter and hugged her, then kissed her mother. She smiled at Allison. "You're looking more rested. How do you feel?"

"Good. I saw my doctor and she's happy with how I'm doing."

Summer spun to face her. "Is your weight up?"

"I weigh two pigs now instead of one and a half."

Everyone laughed. Erica set her bag on the counter and reached for Jackson, who was playing in his playpen, where he could be in the center of the kitchen and not underfoot.

"Rika!"

"Jackson!" Erica lifted him into her arms and snuggled with him. "How are you? Growing? You seem bigger and much, much smarter. Did you have a good day?"

Keeping him on her hip, Erica faced the three of them. "Thanks for all your help with this. Tell me where we are with the meal?"

"The French tart is in the refrigerator until exactly five

thirty," Mara said. "Then it comes out to warm to room temperature. I'm about to set the table. The beets are prepped and ready for the oven."

"I'm making the mix for Allison and my drinks," Summer told her. "Then we're going to start on the bruschetta."

Her mother nodded. "Good. The pesto-and-radish one and the classic diced tomato—"

"With basil and onion." Summer rolled her eyes. "Mom, I know. No soft cheese, no processed meat. I get Allison's pregnant."

Erica smiled at her daughter. "Well, as long as you get it."

She passed Jackson to Mara. "I owe you all. Let me go change and I'll be down to help. Killion's due at six and we all know what that means."

"That he'll be here at five-fifty-eight," Mara and Summer said together.

"Exactly."

Erica hurried toward the stairs. Allison turned to Mara. "How can I help?"

Mara put Jackson back in his playpen and handed him his stuffed caterpillar. "Let's set the table. Once that's done, we can figure out kitchen duty."

The next hour passed in a blur of activity. When the roasted beets had cooled, Allison thinly sliced them and segmented the oranges. Erica passed her the recipe for the dressing and told her where to find the ingredients.

Erica prepped for the scampi while Mara and Summer made the toppings for the bruschetta, and the sliced French loaf toasted in the oven. The tart came out of the refrigerator to warm up and the white wine Erica had chosen was put in an ice bucket.

Allison was surprised to find herself enjoying her time in the kitchen. There was a sense of community as they worked together at the island. The other women talked about their days. Summer complained about her friend Avery's father, who wouldn't allow his daughter to get help in calculus. Mara mentioned a client with beautiful white hair who had insisted on a dark green streak.

"I tried to tell her the color wasn't good for her. Try blue or purple, but she insisted on green, for her granddaughter's high school colors, and now she's unhappy."

"What are you going to do?" Allison asked.

"Nothing for now. It will wash out gradually over time. Once it's less bright, I can try to work with it."

"Green's tough," Erica said from her end of the island. "It goes muddy so easily. Once it's lighter, you can add blue and end up with teal."

"I think that's the plan. She wants to have the green streak for the weekend at least. There's a family get-together. Then she can start washing it out."

Allison had been worried about what to wear for the dinner, but Mara had assured her that dress was casual. Sure enough, everyone was in jeans and sweaters. She'd pulled on her nicest maternity pants and a clean, long-sleeved shirt. She was having trouble finding things that fit over her belly. She was much bigger with Bethany than she had been with Jackson. Her doctor had warned her getting bigger faster with a second child was common, but Allison hadn't expected so much of a difference.

She was refastening one of the lower buttons for the eighth time when the doorbell rang.

"It's Killion!" Summer shrieked. "I'll get it."

Allison watched her dance away. "She really likes him."

"He brings presents," Erica said dryly. "I'm not saying she isn't a fan, but there's also the thrill of the gift."

Erica and Mara both walked toward the front door. Allison stayed behind with Jackson. She felt shy and awkward, wondering if her presence would have to be explained or if he already knew about her husband and what had happened.

Seconds later, the four of them returned, Mara and Summer each claiming an arm while Erica carried in several gift bags.

Allison felt her eyes widen in surprise. Mara had said that he was handsome but somehow that word didn't come close. He was tall and fit, with dark hair, but what really caught her attention were his deep green eyes and strong jaw. He was attractive enough to draw attention wherever he went, she thought, aware of her massive belly and too-long hair. She had the sudden thought that she should have put on makeup or something—an idea so ridiculous as to make her laugh. Why did she care how she looked?

Another form of power, she thought, remembering her conversation with Erica.

Erica set the bags on the counter. "Killion, this is Allison, Peter's wife, and her son, Jackson. Allison, Killion Haugen, my, ah—" She paused, flushing slightly.

"Boy toy?" Killion offered with a grin.

"Oh, please." Erica looked at Allison. "My friend."

"Boyfriend, Mom." Summer smiled. "You can say it. No one will judge. Boy. Friend."

"Whatever." But her tone was more happy than annoyed.

Killion closed the distance to shake Allison's hand. "Nice to meet you."

"You, too."

He released her hand, then bent down to smile at Jackson. "Nice you meet you, too."

Jackson offered him a toothy grin and waved his arms. "Up!"

"Yes, sir."

Allison eyed his expensive-looking shirt and tailored jeans. She wasn't sure those clothes were toddler friendly but before she could say anything, Killion already had Jackson in his arms.

"How are you settling in?" he asked. "Is Erica taking good care of you two?"

"Of course." Allison glanced toward Erica, then back at him. "Everyone's been great. I was worried Jackson wouldn't like the change, but he's loving all the attention." She smiled.

"How can we help ourselves?" Mara asked with a laugh.

"Killion," Summer said, tugging on his sleeve. "You brought presents."

"I did. They're labeled. Help yourselves."

Summer lunged for the gift bags, caught her mother watching her, then drew back a little. "Why don't I pass them out?" she murmured, turning over a tag. "Grandma, this is for you."

Mara took it. "Oh, Killion, you shouldn't have. I'm glad you did, but you shouldn't have."

Summer gave a bag to her mom, put one in front of where she'd been working, then handed two to Allison, one of which was very large.

She looked at him, startled by his thoughtfulness. "I don't know what to say. Thank you."

"You're welcome."

"I'm going first."

Mara removed the tissue paper, then pulled out an eight-by-eight box. Inside were several brightly colored round balls. Allison stared at them, wondering what they were. They didn't look edible or—

"Bath bombs," Mara said happily. "Thank you, Killion. You know I love a long soak."

"Alone or with friends," he teased.

Mara laughed. "There is that."

Summer danced from foot to foot. "May I go next?"

Erica nodded.

The teen practically tore open her bag, then started to laugh. "I love it. Where did you find it?" She held up the package inside. "It's a gummy bear nightlight. I can't stand how cute it is."

She rushed Killion, throwing her arms around him and kissing his cheek. "You're the best. Thank you."

"Anytime."

Erica looked at Allison. "You have two to open."

Allison nodded, feeling everyone looking at her. "I'll go

next, then. Thank you." The first gift bag contained a beautiful receiving blanket and a matching onesie with the phrase Mommy's Best Girl embroidered on the front.

"It's beautiful," she told Killion. "You're very kind."

"Don't thank me yet," he said with a grin.

She pulled out a brightly colored drum with two sticks. Around the bottom of the drum were buttons.

"Those are different songs," Killion told her. "He can try to play along or do his own thing." He flashed her a smile. "You probably want to limit how much time he has on the drum. It can get loud."

Jackson squirmed to get down and walked over to the drum. Summer knelt next to him and took the toy from Allison before setting it on the floor. She showed him how to hold the sticks and touched one to the drum. Jackson's eyes widened at the sound. He grinned brightly, plopped to his butt and began banging away.

"Evil, evil man," Mara said, her tone filled with affection. "What were you thinking?"

"I was getting on his good side."

"What about the rest of us?" Erica asked, seeming more amused than annoyed.

"I have other plans for that."

Their gazes locked in a moment of intimacy—the kind well-established couples had. Allison had to look away to get control of her feelings. Of course she was happy Erica had someone in her life, but seeing them together made her miss Peter even more.

"Look," Summer said, settling next to Jackson. "These play songs."

She pushed one of the buttons and a catchy marching tune began. Jackson babbled his excitement and began banging along. His beats were enthusiastic and totally out of rhythm.

"Let's have cocktails in the living room," Erica said, over the din. "We can put Jackson in his playpen at one end. The noise won't be so bad and we can still keep an eye on him."

"Good idea. And when he's in bed, we'll take the drums to the basement." Mara looked pointedly at Killion. "Where they'll stay."

"Why are you giving me stink eye?" he asked with a grin. "None of this is my fault."

"It's all your fault," Erica told him.

Allison wasn't sure if they were kidding or not. "I can hide the drum. Either now or after he goes to bed. He'll forget about it in a few days."

Mara touched her arm. "No, no. We're giving Killion a hard time. He likes it. I agree downstairs is the right place for it, but for tonight, we'll think of it as dinner music."

Killion and Summer moved the playpen into the living room while Mara got Jackson settled—drum and all. When they were all back in the kitchen, Killion held out the last gift bag.

"Did you think I forgot you?"

Erica flushed slightly. "I would never think that." She drew out a simple white silk robe. The fabric puddled in her hand as she touched it, then flowed to the floor like water.

"It's beautiful," she said. "Thank you."

"You're welcome."

Once again their eyes locked. Summer and Mara didn't seem to notice, but Allison was acutely aware of the other couple, mostly because she desperately missed what they had.

Until he'd been arrested and taken from her, Peter and she had shared the same kind of communication. They could be in a crowd, separated by a dozen people, but if they were able to look at each other, they knew what the other was thinking. At least that was how she'd always assumed it was. Maybe she was wrong—after all, the man had a whole secret life she hadn't known anything about.

"You all right?" Summer asked.

"Fine." Allison offered what she hoped was a big happy smile. "Shall we get the cocktails and appetizers together?"

With the bread already crispy, it only took a few minutes to assemble the bruschetta. While Allison carried the trays into the living room, Summer made their mocktails. Mara and Killion put together the cocktails.

"A Tom Collins," Killion said with approval. "Classic and unexpected."

"It was her idea," Erica told him. "I've never heard of them."

"I'm sure one of her gentleman friends introduced her to the drink," Killion murmured.

"Gentleman friend. Is that what we're calling the string of men you—"

"Erica, that's enough."

Mara's tone was friendly, but Erica immediately pressed her lips together. Seconds later, she laughed. "How do you still have that power over me? I'm an adult with a grown child of my own."

"Years of training," Mara told her with a wink.

Once they were all seated, with Jackson banging in the background, Killion held up his glass.

"To an evening with beautiful women. Thank you for including me in your company."

Mara smiled at Allison. "He's very smooth."

"So I see."

She tried the mocktail Summer had put together for them. The combination of flavors was refreshing without being too tart.

"This is good," she said, holding up her glass.

"I'm glad you like it."

Killion asked about Summer's softball schedule.

"It's still two games a week."

"Unless it's three," Erica told him, then smiled at her daughter. "Don't forgot about the invitationals."

"Yes, but on most invitational weeks, those are the only games we play."

"I wonder if Jackson would enjoy watching you play," Mara mused. She turned to Allison. "Do you ever go to the games?"

"I haven't." Going by herself felt weird, plus she was always working. Or she had been. Should she start going now? "Peter and I went last season when the team made the finals."

"Erica doesn't miss a game," Killion said. "Rain or shine."

Erica brushed off his comment. "If it rains, the game is canceled. If we're lucky, they've played their five innings and the score is final."

Summer grinned at Allison. "Mom lives in fear of makeup games." She stretched out her hand and patted her mother's arm. "You're very faithful. Thank you for that."

"You're welcome."

"I'm not sure you could manage Jackson and the bleachers," Summer said, glancing at Allison. "Not with how pregnant you are. By the time Bethany is born and can go out with people, the season will be pretty much over."

"Next year," Mara said firmly. "We'll all go."

"I'll be a senior," Summer said happily. "Hmm, by this time next year, I'll be accepted at my first-choice college and Bethany will be almost a year old."

"Hard to imagine." Allison was having enough trouble just getting through the days. She couldn't imagine thinking a year ahead.

On the sofa across from hers, Killion lightly touched Erica's thigh. It was a silly thing—his hand settled on her leg for just a moment. Connection maybe. Reassurance? Like the look and the easy conversation, this was yet more proof they were a couple. Before the ache of missing her husband could overtake her, Allison searched for a distraction.

"How did you two meet?" she asked.

Erica glanced from Killion to her. "At a charity luncheon. It was what? Late last fall? I can't remember the event. We were seated next to each other." She smiled. "He charmed me."

Killion picked up her free hand and kissed her knuckles. "That is not how we met."

"What?" Erica pulled her hand free and angled toward him. "It was! I was there."

He ignored her and leaned toward Allison. "We *met* at a business connections event two months earlier. I don't remember anything about it except across the room was this stunning woman and I knew I had to meet her."

Erica stared at him. "You're making this up."

He made an X on his heart.

"But I don't remember meeting you."

"That's because you were one of the speakers and everyone wanted to get your attention. I didn't do much more than shake your hand."

She sipped her drink. "It never happened."

"It did." He smiled at Allison. "I was instantly smitten so I looked into her. Erica has a reputation for being an excellent businesswoman but standoffish. Several men had already made passes at her only to be politely shut down."

"Mom! You go, girl. Way to keep them guessing."

Erica shook her head. "He's making this more than it is."

"Shh," her mother said. "I want to hear the story. Go on, Killion."

"I found out what I could about her and bided my time. When I learned we were both going to be at a charity lunch, I made a generous contribution on the condition I was seated next to her." His smile broadened. "I made sure the man on her other side was a known jerk." He shrugged. "I didn't want any competition."

Erica looked bewildered. "I remember the lunch and you're right about the other man. He kept talking about my 'girlie business' and how much happier I'd be if I had a man running it. Asshole."

"And you won the day," Allison said. "You won your lady love."

"In a manner of speaking," Killion said. "I asked her out, she said yes and here we are."

"I honestly don't know what to say," Erica admitted.

"You were wooed," her mother told her. "Revel in it. Now I'm starved. Let's go eat dinner."

20

Erica sat on the hard bleachers, watching her daughter's team annihilate their opponents. In the last inning, they were ahead by a comfortable eight runs, with the visitors at bat. One more out and they were done.

The weather had become a little more springlike with blue skies and temperatures flirting with sixty. Practically tank-top-and-shorts weather for the Pacific Northwest.

The teen at bat fouled the ball for the second time. Erica watched the third base player run to catch it, but she missed, so the at bat continued.

So strange about last night, she thought. Killion's story about how they met. She hadn't had a chance to talk to him in private so wasn't sure he'd been telling the truth or exaggerating a little for the sake of entertainment. Not that he usually did that, but honestly she couldn't imagine him arranging to sit next to her so he could get to know her. She simply wasn't that interesting.

The sound of a bat hitting a ball drew her attention back to the game. The ball went up and over the head of the pitcher. Summer, at second base, called that she had it. The ball dropped right into the center of her glove as if that had been the plan all along. The team and most of the people watching cheered.

Erica stood with the other parents and began to climb down.

She would congratulate her daughter before going back to work. But halfway across the field, she saw a tall, lanky boy get to Summer first. He stood close, his head bent toward her, his expression intense. Summer spoke, then nodded. Erica wished she was closer so she could hear what they were saying.

As far as she knew, Summer wasn't dating. She rarely mentioned guys or going out, except in the big groups her generation favored. Had she finally found someone who interested her? Was there a way to find out without getting an eye roll?

"Erica!"

She turned and saw Crystal approaching. Erica froze, not sure if the other mother wanted to gossip about Peter or hit her up for the spa day thing. She wasn't in the mood for either.

"Hi," she said, keeping her voice and her expression neutral. "Great game."

"Yes, it was. So we were talking about our spa day and we'd like to get it scheduled. The school year will be over before we know it and summer is always so busy with vacations and that sort of thing." She named a date, then paused hopefully.

Spa day it was, she thought. A more annoying but safer topic than Peter's current situation.

"Did you all figure out what treatments you want?" she asked. "Once you know that, call scheduling and they'll get it set up. Use my name. If there's a problem, you can text me, but I'm sure it will be fine."

"Is the, ah, lunch included?" Crystal asked. "We were picturing ourselves on the terrace, overlooking the lake."

"I'll make sure it happens." Then she would charge them for every bite.

"That's so great." Crystal beamed at her. "We're excited. This is going to be our year-end party. You know, just moms." She paused, her smile becoming a little more forced. "Did you want to, ah, join us? I mean you're a mom, too. Right?"

Erica wondered about Crystal's internal battle—her need to

do the right thing by asking contrasted with her obvious desire to have Erica refuse the invitation.

"I'll be working that day," Erica told her. She gave a brief wave. "Call scheduling."

"I will."

Erica moved toward Summer. As she approached, the guy walked away. Her daughter started toward her.

"Great catch!" Erica hugged her. "That ball had your name on it or whatever the phrase is."

Summer laughed. "Oh, Mom. It's funny when you try to say jock stuff."

"I live to amuse." She glanced over her shoulder to make sure no one was too close. "I saw you talking to a boy."

"Don't even think about it. Donovan's a friend, nothing more."

"It's fine. I was just asking."

"You don't ask, you emotionally lurk and try to find out about my personal life."

"I'm interested. I can't help it."

Summer stopped walking and faced her. "He's just a friend," she repeated. "I mean that. He broke up with his girlfriend and he's been asking me what to do."

"If he wants real advice, he should talk to your grandmother. Between you and me, she's the one with the most actual experience in the dating world."

As she'd hoped, Summer laughed. "You're right, but I don't think he'd be that comfortable talking about his love life with a woman who just turned seventy."

"I'm more worried that her stories would scar him."

"That, too. I'm going to Avery's for dinner. I'll be home by nine." Summer frowned. "Is that okay? Should I be home for dinner so it's not awkward with you and Allison?"

"We're fine. Go be with your friend."

At this point, Erica was practically comfortable having Allison around and if they ran out of conversation, they could always talk about Jackson.

They took another couple of steps, then Erica stopped. "Why do you almost always go to their houses for dinner? Why don't you bring your friends home more?"

Summer blinked a couple of times. "I don't know. It's what I've always done. I guess when we were younger, you were gone working and the other moms wanted us supervised. So I went there and it became a pattern. Why do you ask?"

"I was just curious. You're all older now. Less supervision is required. I want to make sure you know your friends are always welcome."

"I know, Mom. Thanks."

Summer kissed her on the cheek, then ran back to join her team. Erica made her way to her SUV. The other mothers had already left. She was practically the last one in the parking lot.

The mothers came and went in a group. Summer had her friends. Mara had her boyfriends. Sometimes it seemed that she was the only one going through life alone. Oh, she had her family, and Killion could be counted on but there weren't any friends. She knew why it had happened and even had some thoughts on how to fix it. What she didn't know was why it suddenly bothered her. Something had changed and she wasn't sure if it was her or circumstances.

Allison sat on the hard plastic chair in the overly lit room. Around her dozens of other women, some with children, waited to see their loved ones. It was barely eight in the morning and she hadn't slept the night before. Her back hurt from being so pregnant and from the long walk from the light rail station where she had to park.

Somewhere in the distance a loud buzzer went off, followed by the sound of a gate closing. A few minutes later, inmates trickled into the room. One or two at first, then more. Allison scanned their faces until she saw Peter. She instinctively rose and started toward him, only to remember that wasn't allowed. She forced herself to stay where she was as her husband got close.

"Peter," she breathed, leaning in for the brief but precious hug that was all they were allowed.

Her hands touched his sides and she immediately felt how thin he was.

"You've lost weight," she said as she sank into the chair. "Are you eating? Are you sick?"

He gave her a weary smile. "You're so beautiful. I know you are, but every time I see you, I'm reminded of that. I love you so much. You look good. How do you feel?"

She wanted to brush away the question. What did she matter? She was on the outside, able to come and go as she wanted. He was the one trapped in here with no way out.

But of course he would want to know how she was. She was his wife and he worried about her as much as she worried about him.

"I'm doing well. I got a good report from the doctor last week. My weight is up and my blood pressure is back to normal."

He beamed at her. "That makes me happy. How's Jackson?"

"Thriving. He has a drum now and he's catching on about rhythm." She leaned toward him. "I couldn't bring him. I'm too far along to carry him all that way."

"I understand." His gaze searched her face. "I just want to look at you."

She smiled, taking in the new lines around his eyes and mouth. He looked older. She could see gray in his hair—gray that hadn't been there before he'd been arrested. What must his days be like? She couldn't begin to imagine what he was going through. Now she didn't have to panic every second, she could worry more about him.

He glanced around, then slowly took her hand and squeezed. "I have a lawyer," he said happily. "He's the right guy." He released her hand, waved to the closest guard, then pulled a business card out of his pocket. "I'm allowed to give you this because it's for legal representation."

"You have a lawyer?" She wanted to ask how that had happened, but this wasn't the place or time. "That's great."

"It is. He's going to make all the difference. He'll start negotiating on my behalf. I'm hoping he'll get some of our money released. Life can get back to normal."

She stared at him, not sure what he meant by that. Normal? He was in jail, facing felony charges, including threatening the police with a gun. They had no home, she was due in less than a month. She couldn't begin to imagine what normal would be like.

He smiled at her. "It's a new beginning."

"If you say so." She hesitated. "You know I'm living with Erica."

"You told me you moved in with her." His expression tightened. "How's that going? I know she can be difficult, but Summer's there to run interference."

"Summer's sixteen. That's not her job."

The words came out more harshly than she'd intended. She deliberately softened her tone. "I mean I've already depended on her too much as it is. She's dealing with things, too. She's still a kid."

His gaze settled on her face. "Are you all right? Is Erica being a bitch?"

"No. She's been—" Allison searched for the right word "—amazing. Peter, she's opened her home to Jackson and me. She's generous and thoughtful. I'm not saying she's warm and fluffy, but she's been incredibly kind when she didn't have to be."

She looked at her husband. "She's nothing like you described." She thought about asking about his claim that Erica had kept his half of the house even though Erica had bought it on her own, but didn't know how without risking a fight.

Peter dismissed her comments with a wave of his hand. "I'm glad she's treating you well, but don't buy into the act. At her core, she's coldhearted and calculating."

Allison wasn't convinced but nodded to keep the peace. She tucked the business card into her pocket. "I'm really happy about the lawyer."

"Me, too. I need you to call him as soon as you get back to your car and arrange to see him."

"Why?"

"He's insisting you pay the retainer." His expression hardened. "Given the charges, he doesn't trust me to pay him later."

Allison stared at him. "Pay his retainer? With what?"

"The money Cappy gave you." He glanced around, then lowered his voice. "You said he gave you cash."

"He did. Ten thousand dollars. I used some of it to pay for my medical insurance. Is the lawyer going to be more than that?"

Peter's face went white then red. "That bastard!" he shouted loud enough to cause everyone around them to turn and stare. "That fucking bastard. It was supposed to be fifty. I gave him fifty thousand. When I get out of here I'm—"

Guards hurried up and grabbed him.

"You know better," one of them told Peter. "You were warned."

Peter tried to shake off their hold. "I'm fine. I'll be quiet."

He continued to pull against their hold. Allison wanted to tell him to stop. It was obvious they were getting annoyed, but she didn't want to make trouble for him.

One of the guards looked at her. "You're done here, ma'am."

Peter glared at her. "Don't you dare leave. This is our visit and I didn't do anything wrong."

The guards half dragged, half carried Peter from the visitors' room. He shouted at them the entire way. Allison stood and quickly made her way to the exit. Her heart was pounding and she felt oddly vulnerable. Telling herself there was no reason to be afraid didn't help at all.

Once she was outside, she breathed in the cool, damp air and walked to her car. She went as fast as she could, then got inside and locked the doors. Her breathing was ragged, her body damp with sweat. Baby Bethany kicked and turned as if she sensed her mother's unease.

Allison pulled the business card from her pocket and stared at it before pulling out her phone. She would call the lawyer and find out what...

"He said it was supposed to be fifty thousand dollars," she whispered to herself. "He gave some guy fifty thousand dollars to hold for him."

Why would Peter do that? Didn't he trust her? All of this could have been so much easier if she'd had access to that kind of money. She could have actually slept at night instead of worrying. She could have made plans. But he hadn't said a word about it so there was no way to know his associate had stolen from him.

Maybe he'd been afraid the police would get a warrant for the house, she thought. If the cash had been on the property, it would have been seized.

It was the best explanation she could come up with. Anything else meant she didn't know her husband at all and she just couldn't go there right now.

She dialed the number.

"Collins, Greenwall and Smith," a female voice said.

"Raymond Collins, please. This is Allison Jenkins."

"One moment, Ms. Jenkins. I'll see if he's available."

About forty seconds later she heard a click followed by "Collins here. You're Peter's wife?"

"I am. He asked me to call you to talk about representation and pay the retainer."

"Yes. We should do that in person. I have some time this morning if you can drop by."

She glanced at the address on the card. It was in downtown Bellevue, in one of the high rises.

"It'll take me about forty-five minutes to get there. Does that work?"

"I'll be here."

"Thank you. I'll see you soon."

She hung up then started the car and drove out of the parking lot. Her visit with Peter was supposed to be two hours, but she'd been there less than thirty minutes. The law offices weren't that far from Erica's house, so she should have enough time to speak with Mr. Collins and be back around when she'd told Mara she would be.

Traffic was kind so less than forty minutes later she was being shown into a large west-facing conference room with a view of Lake Washington and the Seattle skyline. The polite receptionist offered her an assortment of beverages, but Allison refused them. She just wanted to get on with the meeting.

About a minute later, Raymond Collins entered. He was in his fifties with gray hair and blue eyes. His face was nondescript. He looked more like a high school teacher or a grocery store supervisor than a sought-after lawyer.

"Allison?" he said with an easy smile. "Nice to meet you."

They shook hands and he took a seat across from hers.

"You've obviously talked to your husband."

She nodded. "Earlier this morning. He said you were willing to represent him." She paused, not sure what to ask. "Is he in a lot of trouble?"

"It's not great. He's been charged with several felonies and there could be more to come. They want Peter to cooperate and he wasn't willing to do so until he had a good lawyer. That annoyed them, so now they're going to let him cool his heels in jail a little longer until they talk to him."

She nodded, not sure what to do with the information. "There's no way we can make bail. It's a million dollars." They didn't have anywhere near that much in collateral.

"Peter said the same thing. I'll work on getting it reduced, but I'm not sure that will help. We need to get Peter and the feds talking. Which is what I'm going to do. He told you about the retainer."

"That you'd need one? Yes. He said that." She swallowed hard. "How much is that?"

"Thirty thousand dollars."

If she'd been a fainter, she would have collapsed for sure. "That much?" she asked in a whisper.

"Helping Peter is going to take a lot of hours. Do you have the money?"

"I'll get it."

She had to. There was still nine thousand from the cash plus the few dollars she had on hand. She thought of the money Erica had given her. While she knew it was probably wrong to use that, she wasn't sure she had a choice. But even that wasn't enough.

She twisted her hands together. The movement caused her diamond engagement ring to catch the light. She could sell that and maybe her car. Combined it might be enough.

"I'll get it," she repeated.

"When you do, I'll get started."

She wanted to ask if he could start now, but already knew his answer. He didn't trust Peter and by association, her. She had to find thirty thousand dollars. If she didn't, Peter was never getting out of jail.

Allison told herself to be grateful. Being pregnant and having Jackson with her had probably influenced the jeweler who had bought her wedding set. She had forty-four hundred more dollars than she'd had two hours ago. She could take out six thousand in cash on the credit card. If she sold her car, she would have enough to pay the lawyer. She wouldn't have transportation but that was a problem for another day.

She ignored her bare left hand and weird sense of being naked. It was just a couple of rings. Given everything else happening, did they really matter? They were just *things*.

Next to her Jackson played with his puzzle. The large zoo animal pieces were scattered around him. He picked up the elephant and tried to fit it into the lion cutout. When it didn't fit, he looked at her.

"Help."

"I'm happy to," she said with a smile. "That's an elephant." She pointed to the piece. "An elephant has a trunk and a tail. Try fitting it into another spot."

He frowned in concentration then slid the piece across the board. It slipped into place. His eyes widened and he clapped his hands together.

"Me!"

"You did do it. Good for you. What's next?"

She heard footsteps on the basement stairs. Jackson looked up. When Summer came into view, he shrieked and got to his feet, then hurried toward her. The teen dropped her backpack and held out her arms.

"Hi, Jackson."

They met in the middle of the big family room. Summer picked him up and swung him around. He yelled in delight, hanging on tight. After a couple more turns, they staggered over to her and collapsed on the ground. Jackson was giggling and Summer grinned.

"Hi," she said, sitting up. "How was your day?"

Allison thought about selling her wedding ring and how much she'd cried, but she couldn't talk about that. Erica had been right to chide her about depending on the teen too much.

"We're good. Jackson's kicking butt on the puzzle front. How was school?"

"Good. It's nice not to have a game today." Summer shifted Jackson onto her lap. "I love to play, but my mom's right. The season is really busy. I can't wait for it to start, then about half-way through I'm ready for it to be over."

She pulled the puzzle close and handed Jackson the zebra. "I'm not sure I'm going to try out for next year's team."

"Why not? You'll be a senior. Isn't it a big deal?"

"I'm not interested in continuing into college," Summer admitted. "I'm okay but I'm not super talented like some of the players. This was never my dream. I do it because it's fun and most of my friends are players. But Avery's going to focus on her grades next year and there are a couple of sophomores who are really gifted. Maybe I should step back and give one of them my spot."

"That's a lot to think about. Have you talked to your mom?"

Summer pointed to the spot where the zebra fit. Jackson squealed and slid it into place. They both clapped their hands.

"I was going to wait until after the season. I know she'll support me either way." Summer grinned. "She'll try really hard to be neutral but she would be so happy not to have to go to all the games."

"It's a lot," Allison said. If Summer didn't want to play soft-ball anymore, then she shouldn't. The teen had always been thoughtful in her decisions. She was smart, funny and sweet.

Allison glanced at her. "Why don't you have a boyfriend?"

Summer handed the monkey to Jackson. "There's a shift in topic."

"I'm curious. You seem like the kind of girl the guys would be all over."

Summer wrinkled her nose. "Less than you'd think."

There was something in the way she said the words. "What does that mean?"

Summer glanced toward the stairs, then back at Allison. When she spoke, her voice was low. "I dated someone last year. Mom said I was too young to go on boy-girl dates. She wanted me to stay in groups, so I never told her."

"Or me," Allison said lightly, a little surprised Summer had kept secrets.

Her expression turned sheepish. "I thought you might side with my mom. I was only fifteen."

Allison decided not to point out Summer wasn't that much older now. "What happened?" She mentally crossed her fingers that it wasn't anything awful.

"Nothing much." Summer looked away. "We went out for six weeks, then he dumped me for a cheerleader. He said he really liked me but I wasn't girlie enough for him. I didn't wear makeup or care about my appearance."

"He's a jerk," Allison said flatly. "It's who you are that matters."

"Maybe. It's confusing. My dad's always telling me not to worry about what the other girls are doing with their hair and clothes and stuff, and sometimes I think Mom's business is so superficial. But when she talks about making people feel better about themselves, it sounds really good. You know?"

Allison always thought Peter's views were healthy and would keep Summer grounded, but now that she knew Erica better, she wondered if he was, in fact, trying to sabotage Erica's relationship with her daughter. A thought that made her uncomfortable.

"Are you making the right decision for you or are you rebelling against your mom for no particular reason?" she asked.

Summer smiled. "Rebel? Why would I do that?"

"Your mom works really hard. She's the most successful woman I know." In truth Erica was more successful than Peter had ever been. "You should be proud of her. You don't have to dress like her or want to do what she does, but she's someone to be admired."

Summer sighed. "You sound like my grandmother."

"Mara's a smart woman. So's your mom. She loves you, Summer. You should trust her with the truth. She needs to know about the guy."

"I don't want to tell her *now*."

Jackson slid the monkey piece into place and clapped his hands. Allison reached out to pat his shoulder.

"Good job," she told him. "You're so—"

"Oh my God! Where's your wedding ring?"

Summer's voice was loud enough to make Jackson spin toward her. Summer stared at Allison. "It's gone. Did you lose it?"

Allison stared down at her bare hand. The indentation from the ring was clearly visible.

Her mind went completely blank as she tried to think of what to say. Not the truth—she wasn't going to burden the teen with that, but what other excuse was there?

"I, ah, I... Oh, my hands are swollen. It happens in pregnancy. I had to take the ring off."

Summer stared at her. "You're lying. I can see you're lying. What's going on? Is it something with Dad?" Tears filled her eyes. "Are you getting a divorce?"

"What? No. Of course not. I love your father. We're fine." She held in a sigh. "I'll tell you what happened, but you can't tell your mother. I don't want her to think…well, I don't know what, but don't tell her."

"I won't." Summer held Jackson. "What is it?"

Allison quickly explained about the lawyer and the retainer. "I have some money but not enough. I sold my rings for cash. I'm going to sell my car. That's all it is. Your dad and I are totally fine. Don't worry about that."

Summer's relief was visible. "I'm glad you're not leaving him."

Allison eyed her warily. "That's it? You're okay with what I said?"

"I'm not happy, but I understand. I won't say anything to Mom."

Something was going on, Allison thought. The problem was she had no idea what, nor what to ask. She supposed given the circumstances, Summer's acceptance was the best she could expect.

21

Erica pulled the hair tight with the round brush, then used the blow-dryer to dry and set the style. She'd already finished the cut and color. She'd given Francis a few warm highlights to complement her thick brown hair.

Francis had been with Twisted from the beginning. She'd been one of Erica's first hires. Twenty years ago they'd both been much younger and a lot less experienced. Erica had just bought out her mother and Francis was a single mother of two with a fledgling janitorial business. As the salon had grown and expanded, Francis had been right there, bringing in her team every night. When Erica had bought the third salon, Francis had sold her business to her brother-in-law and had come to work for Erica full-time. She'd put together the team that kept the salons clean and sanitized. The purchase of the fourth salon had required additional staff and Francis had managed it all.

When Erica finished blowing out her hair, Francis studied herself in the mirror and smiled. "You were right about the highlights."

"They bring out your eyes and add dimension to your hair."

"Yes, and now I'll have to maintain them," her employee teased. "It's part of your master plan to get me to spend my paycheck in the salon."

Erica laughed. "Hardly. You'll need a little touch-up every

five or six months. Until you start going gray. Then we'll see you more."

Francis recoiled in mock horror. "The women in my family don't go gray."

"Then you have a very lucky family." She took off the black robe and folded it. "Thanks for letting me do your hair."

Francis smiled in the mirror. "Anytime. My friends still can't believe my boss does my hair every year or so and for free. A perk of the business."

"I need to keep my hand in. I appreciate the practice."

Francis stood, then shook her head. "I nearly forgot."

She pulled out her phone and scrolled through it, then turned it so Erica could see the picture of a handsome nineteen-year-old lounging outside of Murrow Hall on the campus of Washington State University.

"Gus is doing so well," she said, her voice thick with emotion. "He's the first in the family to go to college."

Something she'd already told Erica about eighteen thousand times.

"I'm glad it worked out."

Francis touched her arm. "It wouldn't have, if not for you. All those years ago when I could barely pay the bills, you took a chance on me. You helped my business grow and later, gave me this great job. Because of you, Gus is going to college."

"Francis, don't. We've been over this. You're successful because of your hard work. I was one of many clients."

"You were more than that. I'll always be grateful."

"As will I."

They smiled at each other. Fortunately the other woman seemed ready to let the topic go. They chatted for a few more minutes, then Francis left for the Kirkland salon.

As Erica cleaned the station, she reminded herself it wasn't Francis's fault she was tired of being thanked. Not two days ago, Allison had left her a heartfelt note of gratitude, which was lovely, but also uncomfortable. Erica simply wanted to move on.

When she'd put everything away, she returned to her office. She had several messages, including one from her financial planner. Dan didn't call often, so she returned his call first.

"Erica, thanks for getting back to me."

"Of course. I didn't think we were doing any more trades this quarter."

"We're not," Dan said, then paused. "I'm calling about Summer."

"Why?"

He paused, then said, "You know I check in with her every six months or so about her trust."

"Of course."

Erica had set up a trust for her daughter, putting aside money Summer could draw on later in life.

"We talked a few days ago. She's always surprised when I call, as if she's completely forgotten she has that money coming to her."

"When she's twenty-five."

"She called me half an hour ago. She wants to withdraw thirty thousand dollars. I explained the money wasn't available to her yet and suggested she talk to you." He paused. "I thought you'd want to know."

Erica felt all the good drain out of the day. Worry and panic instantly took over as she wondered what Summer would need that much money for. Was she pregnant? Planning to run away? Was a friend in trouble? It couldn't be for Allison—her situation was handled.

She pushed away the questions. "I had no idea," she admitted. "Thanks, Dan. I'll talk to her."

"I didn't know what else to do, but if she was my daughter, I'd want to know."

"I appreciate that and you're right. I need the information."

When the call ended, Erica tried to figure out what to do. Summer didn't want for anything so it was unlikely the money was for her. Then who?

She glanced at the clock. It was after four. Summer didn't have a game so she should be home. She reached for her phone and typed out a quick text.

Let's grab dinner tonight. Just the two of us. We haven't hung out in forever.

Dinner with just the two of them would give them a chance to talk.

Three dots appeared almost instantly.

Raincheck. I don't want to leave Allison alone. I'm ordering take-out.

Her response was a kick in the gut—more so than finding out Summer had tried to take money from her trust. It seemed at every turn that Summer preferred Allison's company to her own and she didn't know how to change that.

Erica worked until eight. She'd passed on the takeout, figuring she would eat the leftovers when she got home. She walked into the house and heard the TV in the family room.

"I'm home," she called.

"In here," came Summer's reply.

Erica went through the kitchen into the open family room and found her daughter and Allison sitting close together on the large sectional, *Mamma Mia!* playing on the television. Summer paused the movie and looked at her.

"Hey, Mom. There's Thai in the fridge."

"Thanks."

Erica tried to figure out if the teen looked any different than usual, but saw no sign of guilt or worry, which was strange considering Summer had tried to take thirty thousand dollars from her trust.

Allison smiled at her. "You work long hours. You must be tired."

"I am."

She was also confused and hurt and feeling left out in her own house, but she wasn't going to talk about that.

"I'm going to change before I eat."

She left before they could respond and hurried toward the stairs. After a light dinner, she would tackle the situation with her daughter. Or maybe they should talk first so the food didn't sit there like a rock and make her feel sick.

She left her tote on the small table by the double doors leading to the main bedroom. In her closet, she pulled off her boots and unzipped her dress. She'd just pulled on yoga pants and a sweatshirt when Summer entered.

"Can we talk?" the teen asked.

"Sure."

Erica stepped into a pair of Uggs, then motioned for Summer to lead the way. Her daughter went into the bedroom and threw herself across the bed. Erica closed the bedroom door, then took a seat on the bench by the footboard, hoping Summer was going to tell her about whatever was happening.

The teen rolled on her side, propping up her head on her hand. She sighed heavily. "I tried to get money out of my trust today."

Erica told herself to keep quiet and let the girl tell the story in her own way before starting in on the questions.

"I mostly don't ever think about it or remember that I have a trust." She shifted into a crossed-legged sitting position. "Dan called a couple of days ago to talk about the investments, which is really boring, but he reminded me there's like a million dollars waiting for me."

"Which you can't access until you're twenty-five." And even

then there were requirements to be met before funds were released, such as having an approved purpose like grad school or buying a home.

"I forgot that part." Summer looked at her. "I just need thirty thousand dollars. Can you release that for me?"

Erica struggled to keep her expression and tone neutral. "Why do you need it?"

Her daughter looked at the bedspread, then back at her. "For Dad's lawyer. The retainer is thirty thousand dollars and Allison doesn't have it."

Instant rage burned away all other emotions. That bitch! Erica had talked to her about not dragging Summer into the mess that was her life and she'd done it anyway.

"Allison didn't ask for the money," Summer added with a sigh. "She didn't say anything. I wouldn't have known except I noticed she wasn't wearing her wedding ring. She tried to lie about why but I knew she wasn't telling the truth. So I ragged on her until she told me what had happened."

Summer swallowed, her expression crumbling. "Mom, she sold her wedding ring. I know it killed her to do that. She loves Dad and it's her wedding ring."

All the mad vaporized, leaving Erica feeling foolish for jumping to conclusions. Thank goodness she hadn't said anything so she didn't have to apologize.

"She begged me not to tell you," her daughter continued. "She said you've been generous enough. She's going to sell her car. It's just so awful. Everything bad is happening to her and none of it is her fault, you know? Plus this is just for the retainer. The lawyer will need more money later and where is that coming from? So when Dan reminded me about my trust fund I thought I could use some of that to help. If I'd thought of it, I would have given her money before, but like I said, I don't walk around remembering I have it."

Erica was torn between pride that her daughter had such a

sweet, giving nature and feeling cut that Summer worried so much about her stepmother.

"It's a lot of money to give someone," she said quietly.

Summer waved that away. "It's the right thing to do. We take care of our family. I was talking to Avery today and she said her mom would never let her dad's second wife live with them. She said her mom would be happy to let her die on the streets."

Tears filled her eyes. "You're not like that. You'd never say that and that's part of the reason I thought it would be okay to pay for the lawyer."

What was that old saying? She was being hoisted with her own petard? The irony of Summer's admiration for actions she hadn't wanted to take didn't escape her. There was also the matter of the current problem. The solution was obvious but she didn't have to like it.

"I'm not changing your trust," she began, then held up her hand. "Let me finish. I'm not changing your trust, but I will talk to Allison about the lawyer." She held in a sigh. "I'll pay the retainer. She can't sell her car—she needs it. And tomorrow she can get her ring back."

Summer threw herself at her, hanging on tight. "Mom, you're the best. Seriously, I'm so glad I talked to you. Thank you for doing this."

Erica hugged her back. "When all this is done and settled, I'm going to have a serious conversation with your father about some of the very bad choices he made."

Summer drew back and smiled. "Right? Who does that? He's made it so hard on Allison and on you."

"We'll get through it. Now I'm going to eat." Not that she wanted the food, but she was interested in a glass of wine and couldn't have that on an empty stomach.

Summer scrambled off the bed. "I won't say anything to Allison. You should be the one to tell her."

Erica knew her daughter was doing what she thought was the

right thing, but she really didn't want to have another *I'm here to rescue you* chitchat with Peter's wife, although there didn't seem to be any way out of it.

She went downstairs, circling around the family room on her way to the kitchen. She put a plate of takeout leftovers in the microwave, then searched the refrigerator for an open bottle of pinot grigio. She could hear the faint sound of Pierce Brosnan and Meryl Streep singing "SOS" in the movie.

Once she'd found the bottle, she poured a generous amount, then replaced the cork. The microwave beeped. She took a seat at the island and ate her dinner. When her plate was rinsed, she topped up her wineglass, then went into the family room.

Allison saw her and paused the movie.

"Sorry, is it too loud?"

"Not at all. I thought we could talk for a second."

The other woman immediately looked wary. "Is everything all right?"

"It's fine." Sort of.

She took a chug of her wine, then set it on the coffee table and sat at right angles to Allison.

"I hear Peter found a lawyer."

The other woman immediately flushed and looked away. "Summer told you." She swung her gaze back to Erica. "I didn't want to tell her. You were right before when you called me out on burdening her. She's still a kid. But I had to sell my rings and she noticed and I tried to lie but she didn't believe me." Her head dropped. "I'm sorry. I love her. I would never hurt her, but that seems to be all I'm doing these days."

"That's certainly dramatic."

"What?" Allison's head snapped up. "I'm not being dramatic."

Erica shrugged. "You have plenty of cause, don't get me wrong. I'm just pointing out that the emotion is obviously getting to you. I'm not saying I would handle it better. I wouldn't.

For the record, you're not hurting Summer. If you were, I'd be on you in a hot second. There's just a lot of shit right now."

Allison blinked as if holding back tears. "You're right. There is. Sometimes it's more than I can deal with."

Erica eyed her glass but didn't pick it up. Instead she said, "I'll take care of the retainer. I want to meet the guy before I hand over the check, but unless he's a moron, I'll pay for Peter's lawyer."

The tears were immediate. Allison went from wide-eyed to choking sobs in less than two seconds. Erica grabbed her glass, figuring they could be there a while.

"You c-can't," Allison said, her voice thick with emotion. "You've d-done so much. You don't even know me."

"I know you better than I did. Besides, we're sort of family." A weird, twisted kind of truth, but there was no denying that they were linked through circumstances and her very idealistic daughter.

Erica got up and walked to the half bath, where she snagged a box of tissues and gave them to Allison. The other woman wiped her face and blew her nose.

"I want to say no, but I can't. I need the money."

"You also need to keep your car. Don't go selling your only source of transportation just because Peter's in jail. He did this to himself and to you. If he has to sit there a few weeks longer, then that's on him." She paused, thinking she might have gone too far. "Of course that's easy for me to say. I'm not married to him anymore."

Allison stared at her. "He said so many awful things about you. He said you were mean and thoughtless and only cared about business, but that's not true at all. You're the most caring, generous person I know."

Erica chose to focus on feeling uncomfortable with the praise rather than dealing with the ugly things Peter had said about her. They weren't a surprise but that didn't mean they didn't hurt.

"These are special circumstances," she said lightly. "Don't judge me by them."

Allison shook her head. "I could never figure out how if you were so terrible, your daughter was so sweet."

"Summer's her own person. I can't take credit for her."

"You're wrong. She's the way she is because of you. I wish I'd known that sooner."

"I'm not the good guy here," Erica protested, reaching for her wine. "I'm the one who screwed up the marriage with Peter. I pushed him to start his own business when I was pretty sure he didn't want to." She paused, wondering how much truth to tell.

"I didn't like that he worked for someone else. I never told him that, but I wanted him to be an entrepreneur like me. Driven and successful." She stared at her glass rather than at Allison. "It was never who he was and he resented me for pushing him."

"You're wrong." Allison shifted into a slightly more upright position. "He loves his business. He told me so many times. He was proud to own it and take care of his family."

"He was proud to own it when he could take care of *you*," Erica told her. "Then it was different because he was happy. You're his princess. It wasn't like that with me."

She remembered how he'd fallen to his knees and begged her to help his wife. Something she still had trouble thinking about without the gut-twisting truth of knowing he had never loved her like that.

"Why did you two split up?" Allison winced. "Is that too personal a question?"

"Oh, I think we've moved well beyond things being too personal." She paused, not sure how to answer, only to realize she couldn't answer because she didn't know.

"He never told me why," she admitted. "One day he told me he wasn't happy and he wanted out. There was no discussion, no explanation, no offer to get counseling. He was done and he wanted to leave." She faked a smile. "I had no idea he was unhappy, so it was a shock to me."

Allison stared at her. "So you were still in love with him?"

Ah, yes. That. "I was in love with who I wanted him to be. Not who he was. I see that now. We both wanted our partner to be different. Love for us was more like a theory."

Which was total crap because of course she'd still been in love with Peter. He was her husband and she'd assumed they would be together forever. Yet one more time when she'd been wrong.

But saying that would upset Allison and wasn't her life spiraling enough already?

She rose. "Finish your movie. I'm going upstairs to clear my calendar for tomorrow morning. We'll drop Jackson off at day care and go see this lawyer together."

"I can't thank you enough."

Erica held up her hand. "No more thanks. We had a deal." She softened the words with a smile. "Have a good night."

22

Erica's mid-sized SUV smelled of high-quality leather with a faint undertone of the perfume she sometimes wore. Allison perched uneasily on the passenger seat, aware of her too-tight blouse and worn maternity pants. Next to her, Erica was elegantly dressed in black pants, boots and a cashmere sweater. Her understated jewelry looked expensive. She drove with the same confidence she showed in everything. Allison truly felt like the country mouse she was and wished just once she could be the one who was capable and in command.

They'd already bought back her ring. The jeweler had tried to make her pay a five-hundred-dollar buy-back fee, but Erica had demanded to see that policy in writing on Allison's receipt. Seconds later, the rings had been hers for exactly what she'd been paid the previous day.

"I didn't make an appointment," Allison said suddenly, thinking she should have called Raymond's office first thing.

"I took care of that." Erica smiled. "It's amazing how available a lawyer can be when you're bringing in a check."

"Do you deal with lawyers a lot?"

"Every now and then. I have one on retainer for nuisance threats." She glanced at Allison before returning her attention to the road. "Sometimes clients threaten to sue in order to get their service for free. Or they'll talk trash on social media, hoping to get a payout to keep them quiet. That's when it's good to have someone around to write the sternly worded cease-and-desist letter."

Nothing Allison knew about, she thought. She'd never owned a business. Peter and Erica were the first people she knew who did. Levi had wanted a good job, so he'd gone to trade school. Owning his own business had never occurred to him.

There was something about Erica, she thought. Not just the confidence and the drive, but a willingness to do the work. When there was a problem, she got right into it and solved it. She didn't wait for someone else to figure it out. She depended on herself. Allison admired that and thought maybe she could be more like her.

She glanced at the other woman. Erica was the most self-sufficient person she knew, but she was also the most solitary. She didn't seem to have friends she went out with. Summer never mentioned her mother's friends. Except for Killion and the people who worked for her, the only social interactions she seemed to have were with Mara and Summer.

Not that Allison was one to judge. Her life was pretty much her immediate family and she'd always liked it that way. But lately, she had to admit a little more support would be nice. But first the lawyer.

"How does this work?" she asked. "Do we sign something?"

"Usually there's an agreement. You'll want to ask about his plan and how he bills. That sort of thing."

Allison stared at her blankly. "Until I met Raymond Collins, I'd never talked to a lawyer. Would you mind asking the questions?"

Erica smiled. "I'm feeling a little feisty this morning, so I'd be happy to take him on for you."

They arrived at the office and were shown right into a conference room. Erica ignored the view, instead walking over to the coffee station and studying the options.

"Did you want some herbal tea?"

"I'm fine."

Erica used the Keurig to make herself a cup of coffee, then took her seat just as Raymond walked in.

"Allison," he said, shaking her hand, but keeping his gaze on Erica. "Good to see you again." He turned to Erica. "Raymond Collins."

"Erica Sawyer. I'm a friend of Allison's."

"Here to offer her legal advice?" he asked, grinning at his own joke.

"Here to make sure she understands everything that's happening."

His gaze lingered. "It's always good to have friends."

They all sat down. Erica immediately took charge of the conversation.

"Tell us about the charges."

Raymond glanced from Erica to Allison and back. "As I told Allison when we met earlier in the week, the authorities aren't very happy with Peter right now. He wouldn't cooperate while he had the court-appointed attorney. They feel he was wasting their time. Because of that, they're being difficult now. Adding charges because they can."

"Such as?" Erica asked.

He typed on the tablet he'd brought in with him. "Assaulting a police officer. Resisting arrest. Money laundering, wire fraud, racketeering." He looked up. "There are more, but those are the basics."

Allison felt all the blood rush from her head. She swayed in the seat. "They're saying he assaulted a police officer? That can't be right. Peter would never do that."

"He pulled a gun on them when they came to arrest him. I'm getting mixed messages on whether or not shots were fired. That will make a difference."

"Is he ever coming home?"

She hadn't meant to ask the question, but the words came out before she could stop them. Erica surprised her by reaching out and gently squeezing Allison's hand.

"It's okay," she murmured. "Just breathe. We'll get through this." She turned to Raymond. "Tell me about your experience with cases like this."

Raymond closed the tablet. "Every case is different."

Erica narrowed her gaze. "Mr. Collins, that isn't an answer. Are you qualified to handle Peter's case or not? If we're trusting you with the life and freedom of Allison's husband, then the least you can do is give us honest and professional answers to our questions."

He studied her for several seconds, then nodded. "I work exclusively with white-collar defendants. Peter's charges are very common in my line of work. I know the DA and the games they play."

"And the gun charge?"

He shrugged one shoulder. "Situations get heated. My clients tend to be men used to being in command. They don't take kindly to being told what to do and they're often feeling desperate. I'm not worried about the gun charge."

"Then what are you worried about?"

"The money laundering. Even the wire fraud can be explained away. He was doing it for personal reasons, he was greedy, whatever. But with the money laundering, he's part of a group and that's never good."

Allison listened carefully, trying to absorb every word. She didn't understand half of what Raymond was saying but she knew Erica would explain it to her later.

"Any chance we can get the bail reduced?" Erica asked. "Peter's hardly a flight risk. I doubt he's been out of the country in the past five years. He has no assets, he has a wife and son whom he adores and there's a baby on the way."

Raymond's gaze dropped to Allison's huge belly. "I see that.

I can talk to the judge. Like I said, the feds are annoyed at being kept waiting, so they're not eager to make nice."

"Perhaps you could charm them."

Raymond offered her a slow smile. "I wouldn't have thought you considered me capable of being charming."

Nothing about Erica's neutral *I'm here for business* expression changed. "I'm sure you can be if you choose."

"I'll see what I can do. No promises."

Allison almost blurted out her due date, which was getting closer by the day. She wanted Peter home for the birth of their second child. She wanted him home before Jackson forgot his father. She wanted him home and their lives back to normal.

"Now about your retainer. Thirty thousand seems like a lot."

"Peter's case is going to take a lot of time. I bill at four hundred an hour. The money goes fast."

Four hundred dollars an hour? Was that even legal? Did people really make that much? Erica seemed unfazed by the amount. She passed over a personal check and a business card.

Raymond looked between them. "Who will I be contacting with information?"

"Allison," Erica said, while at the same time Allison said, "Erica."

"Both of us," Allison added, glancing at her friend. "It will make it easier when I ask questions."

"Good point."

Raymond pressed his lips together. "I have to run that by Peter. He's my client, not either of you, although as his wife, Allison has the right to know what's happening."

"Ask him," Erica said easily. "Once you explain I'm paying for your services, he won't mind at all. I'm assuming you primarily communicate with her via email?"

"Generally."

"Allison will want to be regularly informed of every aspect of her husband's case."

He shifted in his seat. "I'm a busy man, Erica. I prefer to share the highlights."

"You have staff, Raymond. Use them. Allison is dealing with enough stress in her life right now. Leaving her uninformed is not an option."

His gaze locked with hers. Allison thought she saw a flicker of respect before he said, "You're the boss."

"I'm not. She is, but I'm her advocate, so you're going to have to deal with both of us."

He glanced at her business card. "Twisted. That's the hair place, right? That's you?"

She eyed him coolly. "That's me."

He leaned back in his chair, his body language open. "So you checked me out before you came here."

Erica rose, then helped Allison to stand. "No, but I did have you investigated. I have a friend who always knows a guy. You have a reputation for getting the job done. Some question your tactics, but you stay on the right side of the law. See that doesn't change."

Raymond scrambled to his feet. "You're leaving?"

"We are. Please let us know as soon as you have something to share." She nodded at the check on the table. "I'm assuming once that clears, you'll have a lot more to tell us."

"I should know something by the morning."

"How convenient."

Raymond followed them to the elevator. He managed to get between them and angled himself toward Erica.

"We should have lunch. I'll call you."

"No, you won't."

He flashed her a smile. "Come on. You're interested."

"No, I'm not."

The elevator arrived. Erica followed Allison onto it, then faced Raymond. "We'll expect that report first thing."

His gaze lingered on her face. "You'll have it. Then you'll go to lunch with me."

"Unlikely."

The doors closed.

Allison leaned against the wall, trying to make sense of what had just happened.

"You think he knows more than he's telling us?" she asked, not bothering to keep the outrage from her voice. "Can he do that? Does he have some kind of duty to tell us the truth and stuff?"

"Once we're his client, then yes. Right now, we're just talking."

They reached the parking garage and walked toward Erica's SUV.

"I couldn't have gotten through that meeting without you. I wouldn't have known what to ask." She climbed into the passenger seat. "I'm not sure I like him. Is that bad?"

"No, it's smart. Killion says he's a bit of a player, but he's a good lawyer and he works hard for his clients. He's not cheap, but the good ones never are."

Allison wanted to ask how Erica and Killion knew so much, but suspected it had something to do with their places in the world. They were successful business owners, moving in circles she'd never been privy to.

"Raymond will do a good job," Erica said as she backed out of the parking space. "We should have more information in the next couple of days. Once the feds get over their snit, things can move forward. I'm not sure how to solve the bail situation but I'm hoping Raymond can get some of your money unfrozen."

She glanced at Allison, then turned her attention to the road. "You don't need it while you're living with me, but you'll feel better knowing you have it."

She would. Having money meant she could pay for things like day care for Jackson. He was there today, but the payment would come out of the money Erica had given her.

Allison leaned back in the seat. "You know so much. I don't know anything. I'm a small-town girl who never went to college."

"You didn't grow up in Seattle?"

Allison laughed. "Not even close. A small town in eastern Washington you've never heard of."

"Do you ever go back?"

She thought about burying her father, the only family she had. "No. This is home now."

"Want to get some lunch?"

The question surprised her. "Now?"

"It's nearly noon. I doubt you ate much breakfast. Let's stop somewhere." Erica smiled. "I'm in the mood for a really great burger."

Allison's mouth watered. "With steak fries."

"Perfect."

Twenty minutes later they were being shown to a table by the window. The restaurant wasn't one Allison recognized and seemed to be more bar than eating place, but she was willing to trust Erica's taste.

"I know it doesn't look like much," the other woman said, "but believe me. They have the best burgers." She looked at the menu. "Okay, so you're limited in what you can order, right? No soft cheese, no processed meat. You could go plant based, but that seems sad."

Allison laughed. "I'll have a cheeseburger with cheddar."

"I'll get the same and we can split the fries." Erica eyed her. "How about a milkshake? They make them here themselves. That way you'll get real dairy."

Allison glanced at the flavors. The cookies-and-cream one sounded decadent. "I don't know. They look great, but I'll be full."

"So take it with you. When we get home you can stick it in the freezer and have it later."

Allison laughed. "Fine. You've convinced me." She put down her menu and thought about their morning. "Was Peter's lawyer coming on to you?"

Erica rolled her eyes. "In a very bumbling not-smooth way. It was off-putting, but in situations like this, it's better to separate the man from the skill set."

"You shut him down. You were gracious, but you didn't give him anything."

"That was on purpose. Even if I'd been interested, which I'm not, that kind of meeting isn't the place to flirt. He needs to focus on his work." She picked up her water. "The entire gender, with one or two exceptions, is flawed if you ask me."

Their server stopped by and took their order. When she'd left, Erica looked at Allison. "If you didn't grow up here, why did you want to come to Seattle?"

Allison moved the knife and fork around. She didn't know how to answer the question. No, that wasn't true—she wasn't sure about sharing that part of her life with Erica. Silly, because the other woman had been nothing but kind.

"I was married before," she said quietly. "Levi and I married right out of high school. He was always good with his hands and could fix anything. He wanted to work for a big HVAC repair company. The ones that work on industrial buildings and high rises. So we saved for two years, then he applied to technical school here."

"What did your family think of the decision?"

"It was just my dad and me and he died the fall after Levi and I got married. Levi's family was pretty dysfunctional. His folks were more interested in fighting than caring for their kids. His two older brothers joined the military. He always said he wanted to live somewhere else, and Seattle offered a great opportunity."

Erica studied her as she spoke, seeming interested in the story.

"What happened when you got here?"

Allison smiled. "We were blown away by how big the area is. Levi got accepted into the program and I worked two jobs, supporting us." She smiled wistfully. "We were happy. Young, but there was so much we were looking forward to. We wanted to buy a house. Nothing fancy, just a small place for the two of us and the babies we would have. Every Sunday we went to open houses together to see what we liked and didn't like."

Erica's expression turned kind. "When did he die?"

"How did you know?"

"You didn't split up. There's too much love in your voice when you talk about him."

"He started feeling real tired about two years after he got his dream job. We'd been saving money, hoping to find our little house and then get pregnant. He kept saying he just needed to catch up on his sleep, but I made him go to the doctor." She paused, remembering the shock, the sense of disbelief when he was diagnosed. "It was some kind of leukemia. Not one of the good ones. He fought for the next three years and then he died."

She turned away as tears filled her eyes. "The drugs were expensive and not all covered by insurance. Nobody tells you that—at least we didn't know. Cancer's expensive. So when he was gone, I had a stack of bills."

She looked at Erica. "I paid them all. Every one."

"I know you did."

"I tried to get on with my life, but it was hard. I didn't have much, not even a baby. We'd wanted to wait until we bought our house. I wish we hadn't. I wish we'd gotten me pregnant so I would have Levi's child." She hesitated. "I don't say that to disrespect Peter."

"You don't have to explain yourself, Allison. I get it. If Levi hadn't died, you'd still be together, with three kids and a house out in Redmond. Everything would be different."

There was such kindness in her words, such understanding. "You're nothing like I thought," Allison blurted. "I'm sorry for thinking mean things about you."

Erica smiled. "You weren't my favorite person, either. I guess we know each other a lot better now." Her smile faded. "I'm sorry about Levi."

"Me, too. He was a good, good man."

She hated to admit it but she knew down to her bones he would never have done what Peter did. He wouldn't have risked his family's future. A great truth, but not one that was very comforting in her current situation because in the end, even though he hadn't wanted to, Levi had left her just as alone.

Erica lay on her back, doing her best to catch her breath as lingering shudders from her recent orgasm rippled through her body. Killion was stretched out next to her, his chest rising and falling as he, too, recovered. The bed was big and comfortable and despite the fact that it was barely seven thirty in the evening, she was tempted to let herself fall asleep.

Killion rolled to face her, placing his warm hand on her belly. She opened her eyes to find him watching her.

"Thank you," he said when their gazes locked. "That was very nice."

The understatement made her smile. "Adequately satisfying."

His mouth twitched. "A jolly good time." His hand roamed over her breasts as he leaned close and kissed her. "In fact you're nearly always a good time."

She laughed. "Nearly always? When am I not?"

"I take back the 'nearly.'"

"Too late. You said it. Now you have to be punished."

His green eyes brightened with amusement. "I didn't know you were into that. How would you like to punish me?"

She sat up. "Please don't tell me you like to be spanked or dominated. I won't judge but I swear, it's really not my thing."

"You don't want me to call you Ms. Sawyer and tell you I've been bad." He laughed as he slid out of bed. "Don't worry. My desires fall well within the ordinary range."

"As do mine."

He held out his hand. "Let's take a shower, then I'll feed you."

She joined him and together they walked naked into the spacious bathroom. Twenty minutes later they were toweling off before slipping on bathrobes and heading downstairs. While she sat at the counter, he studied the contents of the refrigerator.

"Omelets?" he asked. "I have cheese and sweet peppers, along with mushrooms."

"Perfect."

She walked into the pantry to see what treats Napoleon had left on the bread shelf. There was an assortment of muffins from a little bakery in the neighborhood. She brought the box to the island before putting out flatware and napkins, then she rinsed the fresh berries Killion had set out.

"How was the meeting with Peter's lawyer?" Killion asked.

"All right. He's not sharing much until the check clears. I told him to keep me in the loop. He'll have to get Peter's permission but as Peter begged me to take care of his wife, I don't see him saying no."

She hoped her voice didn't sound bitter. She didn't have feelings for Peter—not anymore. It was just…everything. Yes, she was successful and proud of herself and mostly pretty happy, but she had never been anyone's great love, nor was she likely to be. Yet Allison had inspired two men to love her. Peter had committed crimes for her—not exactly a recommendation of his character, but it was more than he'd done for her.

Erica paused as she rinsed strawberries. Not that she wanted Peter to have committed crimes in her name. It wasn't what she meant. It was just—

"You have scrunchy face. What are you thinking?"

"Allison was married before. We went to lunch after we saw the lawyer and she told me. Levi was her high school sweetheart."

She put the berries in a bowl, then returned to the island while he finished the omelet. "She and Levi were waiting to have kids until they could buy a house. Then he got leukemia and died." She did the math in her head. "I guess she met Peter about a year later."

"When he rescued her," Killion said as he cut the omelet in two and slid half onto each plate. He joined her at the island.

"She hasn't had it easy. I had no idea about the first husband."

"You don't know a lot about her."

"That's true." She took a bite. "Delicious as always."

"Thank you."

"The whole falling-in-love-in-high-school thing is interesting."

"Not for you," he offered.

She smiled. "I wasn't interested in anything permanent back then." She paused. "Or impermanent. I had big plans." She looked at him. "You've been married."

"Yes."

"We don't talk about your family much."

"I didn't think you wanted to."

He was right—she'd resisted sharing too much. But now she was curious. "You have an ex-wife?"

"I do. She's remarried."

"Just the one?"

He raised his eyebrows. "Yes, one ex-wife, no current wife. You're the only woman in my life."

"You have two daughters, right? They're grown?"

He nodded. "My oldest is a software engineer. Married, two children. A boy and a girl. They live here." His expression softened. "Her kids are five and three, close to Jackson's age."

That explained why he was so good with the toddler. "And the youngest?"

"She works for a venture capital firm in San Francisco. She's determined to buy me out in ten years. I'm resisting her plan."

"I never thought of you as a grandfather."

He chuckled. "Does that make me less sexy?"

"Could anything do that?"

"I like to think not but one never knows."

She smiled. "You're as sexy as you were the day I met you."

"Thank you."

"You know I mean it." Her smile widened. "Let us remember what happened about forty minutes ago."

"I'll dream about it."

She laughed, knowing he was kidding, but still, the words were nice. Killion was good to her. He always had been. Right from the start, she'd sensed that he truly *got* her. She hadn't ever had to explain or justify her work schedule or her passion for her business. If anything, he encouraged her to strive for more.

"We should all have dinner," he said, his voice casual.

"You, me and...?"

He looked at her. "I'd like you to meet my daughters."

Oh. Oh! "Why?"

"I've met Summer and your mother. And now Allison and Jackson. We could all have dinner together."

The unexpected suggestion instantly made her uneasy. Meeting Killion's daughters? That seemed so...so... Well, she wasn't sure what, but something uncomfortable. It was as if Killion thought this was a regular kind of relationship, which it wasn't.

"I'm not sure I want to explain who Allison is to your adult children," she said.

"Why not? You come out as the hero of that story."

"It's not a story I enjoy telling."

"Then we won't invite Allison." His gaze was steady. "It's time, Erica."

"But meeting family? That's not who we are."

"I text with your mother."

She stared at him. "You don't!"

"Ask her."

"Oh, God! I didn't know." Betrayed by her own mother.

She shifted in her seat, wanting desperately to tell him no. That she didn't want to get more involved. She liked what they had. But she sensed telling him that would change things between them and not in a way that would make her happy. She liked having Killion in her life. He was there just enough to satisfy her emotional needs, not to mention the great sex.

"Fine. Set up something in the next few weeks."

Even she could hear her grudging tone, but Killion only smiled.

"Thank you for being so gracious."

"You're mocking me."

"Only because the sex is so good."

23

Erica didn't have a favorite salon—each had its own personality. The Bellevue salon—her first—would always be home base. The Twisted in the U District, by the university, was edgy, with a younger vibe. Her Issaquah location was all about nature and organic and the one on Carillon Point was just plain gorgeous.

While she couldn't always coordinate her schedule with the weather, she did try to get to the Carillon Point salon when the skies were clear. Her office had a beautiful water view. When she sat there, sipping her coffee and going over payroll or orders, she felt that she had finally achieved all she'd set out to accomplish. Her little empire was the fulfillment of her dreams and that made her happy.

Despite the craziness in her life, she was in a good place. Having Allison and Jackson in the house was less disruptive than she'd ever imagined. She adored spending time with the toddler and she and Allison were getting along better than she'd expected. A bonus was how she and Summer were getting closer. They were talking more, sharing things. Last night Summer had admitted she'd changed her mind about seeing her dad. Erica had reassured her that was okay—she could go whenever she felt ready.

She was a little less sure about what was happening with Killion. She knew in her head that his request that she meet his daughters made sense. They'd been seeing each other for nearly a year and he spent a lot of time with her mother and daughter, so his request was fair.

But that was the intellectual response. Deep inside, she felt only panic and the need to run. Trust didn't come easily to her. Taking things to the next level romantically wasn't her strong suit.

"Knock, knock!"

She glanced up from her computer to see Crystal, Terry and Whitney pushing into her small office. They all looked relaxed and happy, which was great, but why were they here?

Even as she asked the question, she got the answer. Today must have been their spa day. She held in a sigh, thinking she really needed to pay more attention to that sort of thing. If only she'd been at one of her other spas.

"What an amazing day," Whitney, a curvy redhead, said with a cheerful laugh. "My masseuse had magic hands."

"I loved the facial," Terry added. "My skin is glowing. And the lunch. Seriously, Erica, we can't thank you enough for setting up the experience. It was fantastic."

"I agree." Crystal smiled at her. "All right, stop whatever you're doing. The four of us are heading over to the Woodmark Hotel and we're buying you a drink. Come on. I'm not kidding."

Erica stared at them. The Woodmark was the boutique hotel next door, so that part made sense, but getting a drink?

"It's three thirty in the afternoon."

"Uh-huh, and you work too much." Crystal pointed to the door. "We're not taking no for an answer." Her expression softened. "It's the least we can do."

Erica accepted defeat and pulled her purse from the bottom drawer of her desk. Together the four of them made the short walk to the Woodmark hotel bar. Once seated, everyone ordered. Erica chose a glass of rosé. It was her least favorite kind of wine and she wouldn't drink much—after all, she was planning on going back to work.

"I'm counting the days until the season is over," Terry said when the server had left. "There are too many games, too close together. We're always going or planning or something."

"You know the team is going to make the finals," Crystal pointed out. "So plan on at least three beyond the schedule."

"I know. It happens every year. Then it's nearly summer. Thank goodness they're all old enough to drive. At least I'm not spending as much time driving kids around. We just have to decide about buying her a car." Terry turned to Erica. "Summer has her own car. How's that working out?"

"It's been good. We have rules and she's following them. She's a careful driver."

Whitney groaned. "Essie's begging for a car, but I don't know. She's so flaky. All she cares about is fashion, guys and celebrities. You're lucky Summer's so grounded. She couldn't be less interested in clothes or looks. It's refreshing."

Crystal nodded in agreement. "She's the steady friend. That's for sure. Even when she was dating that guy last year, there wasn't any drama, no hysterics when it ended. She was sad, but her grades didn't suffer, at least not that I know about."

All three of them looked at Erica for confirmation, but she was too stunned to speak. Before she could stop herself, she blurted, "Summer had a boyfriend?"

The three other women exchanged a look. Crystal shrank back in her seat.

"I'm sorry. I thought you knew. It was just for a few weeks. It was—" She cleared her throat. "I mean it wasn't that big a deal."

Humiliation merged with pain. Summer had been dating and hadn't said anything? But these women knew, had been a part of it? When had this happened and who was the guy? No—the more pressing point was her own daughter hadn't told her about an incredibly significant event in her life.

Erica remembered telling her daughter fifteen was too young to date. Groups were okay, but one-on-one with a guy? Not until she was sixteen. Summer had said she was old-fashioned and didn't understand. Erica had refused to change her mind. She'd thought that was the end of it.

She pressed a hand to her flushed cheek and wished she could simply run away. The three women were watching her with various degrees of pity, which made things worse.

Her stomach roiled, and her body tensed. How could she not have known? How could her own child not have trusted her enough to tell her the truth? What else was Summer keeping a secret? All this time she'd thought they were getting closer, but she was wrong. She didn't know anything.

"I can't," she said, coming to her feet. "I'm sorry, but I need to go."

She walked away without looking back. None of them came after her, which wasn't a surprise. But they would be talking about her as soon as she was out of earshot. Of that she was sure.

Allison stood in the large walk-in closet in her bedroom. Her clothes hung on one side and Peter's were on the other. As she did most nights, she stood next to his shirts and lightly touched the sleeves, as if the clothing could make her feel her husband was with her.

Normally the ritual comforted her, quieted her worry and eased her mind. But not tonight. In fact not since she'd seen him last and he'd exploded about the amount of money Cappy had given her. Money he hadn't trusted her with.

Yes, she could rationalize that he'd been worried about the police raiding the house—a point she could almost accept. But not leaving it there was one thing, not telling her about it was another.

Peter had kept secrets. That was both obvious and painful, but there was no avoiding the truth. He'd had an entire secret life, most of it illegal. Which two months ago she would have said was impossible. She *knew* him, trusted him, loved him. They were married. They'd promised to love each other forever. But had she ever known him at all?

She'd been content with their lives. They'd had each other, Jackson and a baby on the way. That had been enough for her. But not for Peter, or so he'd said. He claimed to have done everything for her, which made her uncomfortable. She didn't know if him saying that meant he was trying to explain his actions or if he was passing part of the blame onto her.

There weren't any answers to her questions, no way to find out the truth. Tired of asking and not knowing, she went downstairs. Maybe she could walk off her restlessness.

It was nearly eleven and the house was quiet. Summer had long since gone to her room and Mara had been out with one of her male friends. Allison expected the family room to be dark, but several lights were on and she found Erica sitting by herself, a glass of wine on the coffee table.

In the second before the other woman noticed her, Allison had the thought that she looked sad and vulnerable. Two states of being that didn't seem very Erica-like.

"You're up late," Erica said, reaching for her wine.

"I could say the same about you."

"I'm dealing with life crap."

"Me, too." Allison sat on the sectional. "At least you get to distract yourself with liquor."

"In a few weeks, you can, too."

Allison shook her head. "I'm going to be breastfeeding, so no."

Erica put down her wine. "Now I feel guilty."

"Don't. It's not your fault. For Bethany, the sacrifice is worth it."

"I would have said the same about Summer." She eyed Allison. "Why aren't you sleeping? Is it all about how far along you are or did something else happen?"

"There's nothing new. Don't worry, I'm not going to be asking for more money." She grimaced. "Sorry. That came out more bitchy than I intended. It's just…" She held in a sigh. "I can't reconcile everything Peter did with the man I married. He told me he did it all for me. But I never wanted this and I was happy with what we had."

She hesitated, not sure how much she could say, then told herself there was no point in having secrets from the one woman helping her.

"There was money. Some guy showed up and said he had money for me that Peter had asked him to hold. It was ten thousand dollars."

Erica's brows rose. "The money would have made you feel better but having someone show up to hand it to you? Disquieting at best."

"He scared me." Allison looked at her. "I didn't tell you about it."

"I know."

"Aren't you upset?"

"Not really. Your situation was desperate. You barely knew me and you didn't trust me. Why would you share that?" She paused. "Oh, so that's why you sold your ring. You already had part of the retainer. If you added in the five thousand I'd given you, plus the car, you might have made it."

Her expression turned stern. "Forgive my French, but that's a dumbass idea. You would have been left without a penny. I know you love your husband, but you have children to think about. You shouldn't sacrifice yourself for him."

"I know you're right, but I'm not sure that's how I feel. Everything about this is hard." She felt her emotions slipping out of control and did her best to hang on. "You've told me you don't want any more thanks, but I'm going to say it anyway. I'd be homeless if you hadn't stepped in."

Erica reached for her wine. "I'm glad I could help." She

paused. "Huh. I actually mean that." She smiled briefly. "You're my lone success these days. Well, you and work. But lately my interpersonal relationships keep taking hits."

"What does that mean?"

Erica sipped from her glass. "Summer had a boyfriend last year and I didn't know. She never said a word. She went through that entire experience without saying a word. She won't even let me cut her hair. I can't figure out if she genuinely doesn't like me or if I'm the worst mother ever."

Allison felt the other woman's pain. "I'm sorry. That's really hard."

"Did you know?"

The question caught her off guard, which made her unsure of what to say. Unfortunately the silence was its own answer.

"You did." Erica turned away. "I'm not even surprised."

"No, it's not like that. I just found out a few days ago. When it was happening, she didn't say anything to me or her dad, either. She's just being a teenager. It's not as personal as you think."

"Maybe, but it feels personal. I know she loves me but we're not close in the way I had always hoped. She thinks my business is ridiculous. She doesn't confide in me."

"She told you about the boyfriend."

"She wasn't the one to tell me." Erica laughed, but the sound was bitter. "It was those damned softball mothers."

"Who?"

"The mothers of the other players on the team. Not all of them, but a few. The girls are tight, as well as the moms. They hang out and do things. They're friends. It's been going on for years now. They were at my Kirkland salon, having a girls' day out. Afterward they insisted we get a drink. It was the middle of the day, but whatever. So we went for the drink and the whole story of Summer's first boyfriend came out. It was humiliating."

Not just that, Allison thought. Painful as well. Not only for

Erica to learn about what she would see as her daughter's rejection, but to hear it from women she obviously didn't like.

"Why aren't you part of the group?"

"When Summer first started playing, they asked me to join them for lunch or whatever but I'd just bought my fourth salon. I had Summer and Peter and couldn't take off a few hours to go shopping." She put down her glass. "I'm the only one with a career. Most of them don't work, which is something I don't get. They're totally dependent on a man. But they don't worry about that. Fools."

She stood, weaving a little as she tried to stay upright. "Women need to learn to be independent. It's dangerous to need a man or anyone really. People let you down. They suck you in, then they stab you in the back, telling you they don't want you anymore. I hate that."

She drew in a breath. "I'm going to bed."

With that, she walked out of the family room. Allison lumbered to her feet, then carried the wineglass into the kitchen.

Obviously Erica had had more to drink than Allison had realized. The pain of the revelation about Summer had hit her hard. But it wasn't just that, she thought. It was how Erica had sounded when she'd talked about being unable to join the other women. Oh, she'd dismissed them, but those words had come from a place of pain. She'd felt left out—with them and with her daughter.

Erica worked hard and took care of everyone around her. Family, her employees, even her ex-husband's second wife. But who took care of her? Who had her back?

Killion seemed supportive but he was a man, and as such, he might not get the importance of female friendships. There were things women shared that guys just didn't get. Erica was lonely. She needed a friend—a good friend—and that was something Allison knew she could be.

★ ★ ★

Erica walked into the kitchen close to eight at night, expecting to find it empty. Instead Allison sat at the table, her tablet open in front of her, a pad of paper next to it. She glanced from the screen to the paper and frantically scribbled notes.

"Hi," Erica said, her voice coming out more weary than she expected.

It had been a long, complicated day. Her product order had been delayed, then what had arrived hadn't been what had been ordered. A level-one stylist had dropped a bowl of hair bleach down the back of a client, effectively ruining a vintage Roberto Cavalli sweater that, based on a brief internet search, seemed irreplaceable. Why someone would wear something so precious to get her hair colored was beyond her, but the client had and now it was Erica's expensive problem.

She still had a daughter who hadn't bothered telling her when she'd had a boyfriend, and while she wanted nothing more than to call Killion and beg to curl up in his bed, preferably also in his arms, as he promised her everything would be all right, she couldn't. Or rather, wouldn't. She was stronger than that. She took care of herself and didn't need a mere man to right her ship, or whatever the saying was.

"Hi, yourself." Allison put down her pen and smiled at her. "How was your day?"

"Sucky."

"What happened?"

"Nothing earth-shattering. Just a bunch of little things that piled up in what shouldn't matter but does because there are too many of them."

"Nibbled to death by ducks." Allison shrugged. "My dad used to say that to me."

"It's a good enough description."

Erica set her tote on the chair and unzipped her boots. She walked barefoot to the cupboard for a wineglass, then paused and thought maybe food was a better option. But the thought of pulling something together exhausted her.

"Sit," Allison said in a surprisingly firm tone. She rose and pulled out a chair. "I'll get you dinner."

Erica stared at her in confusion. "You're like a thousand weeks pregnant. You shouldn't be on your feet."

"I'm fine. It's less than a yard from here to the counter. I'll go slow. Summer and I made a chicken casserole. It's good, but it has a lot of pasta in it, so we also made you a big salad. I knew you'd prefer that. Let me get it for you."

Erica was too surprised to protest. She sank into the chair and watched as Allison pulled out a covered dish and a large bowl from the refrigerator. She put the covered dish into the microwave, then added dressing to the bowl and tossed the salad. After plating the salad, she grated a little cheese, then put it in front of Erica.

"Do you want wine? I think there's a nice merlot in the rack."

"Just water."

Before Erica could add *And I'll get it*, Allison was scurrying away. She returned with a large glass of ice water. When the microwave dinged, she took out the covered dish and scooped the contents onto another plate before setting that in front of Erica, as well. She poured some milk into a glass and brought it with her.

"I'm behind on dairy," she explained as she resumed her seat, taking a sip and trying not to shudder.

Erica stared at her dinner. The salad was fresh, with several kinds of lettuce, along with kale, spinach and vegetables. There were sliced heirloom tomatoes on the side of the plate and a light dusting of parmesan to complement the balsamic vinaigrette.

She took a bite and realized she was starving. She ate nearly half the salad without stopping before turning to the creamy chicken pasta dish.

"How much of the cooking did Summer do?" she asked.

Allison grinned. "She refused to deal with the chicken carcass. Your mom stopped by with a couple of rotisserie chickens. She was keeping one for herself and offered us the other." She lowered her voice. "I got the impression she would be having company tonight."

"I'm not surprised. Lately she's been out of the game. I'm sure her gentlemen friends miss her." She nodded at the table. "What are you working on?"

Allison looked away, then back at her. She seemed to square her shoulders before speaking. "Taking your advice."

"I don't remember giving you advice."

The smile returned. "It wasn't directed at me, exactly. The other night you said you didn't understand how the softball moms were so comfortable not having jobs. That they were completely dependent on their husbands and a divorce would leave them in financial trouble."

Erica groaned. "I was ranting. Don't listen to me."

"Why not? You're the smartest person I know. Look at the mess I'm in because of Peter. Not just him being in jail and the frozen bank accounts, but all of it. I have no skills. Not ones that can get me a good job. I worked part-time in a day care and a grocery store. I'll have two kids to support. How am I supposed to find a job that allows me to cover day care and my monthly expenses?"

That job doesn't exist. But Erica knew not to blurt out the depressing words. Allison already lived the dilemma of not being able to afford to work because day care cost as much as her paycheck.

The other woman nodded at her tablet. "I've been researching ways to earn money from home."

"Don't fall for one of those envelope-stuffing scams. No one uses direct mail anymore. We all advertise online."

"I was thinking more customer service, either by chat or phone. I was doing research and a lot of them have their employees take calls from home. I could work nights while the kids sleep."

"When would you sleep?" Erica asked dryly.

"I'd work it out."

"It's a short-term solution. Eventually you'd crash." She paused, wondering if Allison was figuring at some point Peter would get out of jail and join her.

Now there was an uncomfortable thought. Peter was married to Allison so if he got out of jail, he would expect to live with her. Here. In Erica's house.

She had the brief thought that she should have accepted that glass of merlot, then sighed. There was no point in worrying about that before it happened. Right now Peter's bail was set at a million dollars. No way Erica was putting up her house as collateral and she didn't think Peter knew anyone else with those kinds of assets.

"You need a plan," she said, returning to the topic at hand. "Goals. I think the idea of a call center is—" Well, duh.

"What?" Allison asked. "Are you all right?"

"I'm a moron."

"Hardly."

Erica rubbed the bridge of her nose. "No, I mean it. I'm so stupid. I have a call center and the employees work from home." She paused. "Okay, there's a couple of weeks of training, then four weeks of supervised working from the Bellevue store, but then you work from home. The job starts at twenty-seven dollars an hour and the shifts are six hours." She looked at Allison. "I have no idea what a babysitter costs these days but I'm sure my mom could take a few hours and I could tell Summer it's part of her summer job."

Allison turned away. "Stop. You're not offering me a job."

"Why not? It's exactly what you were talking about doing. Why not do it for me?"

"Because you've already done too much. With you, I'm a permanent mercy case and that's not who I am."

The other woman's distress was palpable. Erica lightly touched her hand. "You're dealing with a truckload of shit that isn't your fault. Maybe I started out helping because Summer guilted me into it, but this is different. I think you should take the job."

"Do you even have any openings?"

Erica smiled. "The call center is down by two. We're about to lose a receptionist, which sucks because I always want to inspire those young women to go to beauty school, then come back and grow into stardom. I need a couple of level-three stylists, one in Issaquah and one in Bellevue, but those are the hardest positions to fill. My operations clerk is about to get her second warning, so we'll be replacing her soon. The cleaning staff is never a problem because Francis runs a tight ship. So yes, I do know if we have any openings in the call center."

Allison stared at her. "Holy crap. You know everything."

"No one will ever love my business more than me. Training is online but happens in the salon. You'll be paid for your time and I'll cover Jackson's day care. If you're interested."

She eyed Allison's huge belly. "If we hurry, you could finish before you go into labor. You in?"

"I would genuinely be living in the gutter if it weren't for you."

"Don't be dramatic. You'd be in a shelter. No one lives in the gutter."

Allison laughed. "Fair. I'll owe you forever, but I can't help it. The job is perfect. Thank you. When does training start?"

"I'll let you know tomorrow."

24

"So you're like Edward in *Pretty Woman*?" Allison asked, sounding doubtful.

"No, I don't buy companies and sell them for parts. I buy companies in trouble and make them better. Then I sell them for profit." Killion smiled at her. "It's all about the profit. Sometimes a company has a good idea but can't get it to market or can't get the financing for manufacturing."

"But wouldn't the bank just loan them the money?"

"Banks are picky."

"You're picky, too," Erica pointed out. "Just in a different way."

"But with the bank, there's only a loan, right?" Allison frowned slightly. "But when you get involved, you own part of the company. They have to do what you say."

Killion grinned. "That's the part I like. My job is to make money. I look for cheap companies with potential. I make them profitable, then sell at the highest price. I don't want to hold on to anything permanently. I'm not looking to acquire. I want to get the most I can, then move on."

Allison looked doubtful. "That sounds ruthless."

"You've just made his day," Erica teased. "Killion loves when people think he's ruthless."

They were seated in the kitchen at her house. Summer was out with friends and Mara was "entertaining," so it was just the three of them. Erica and Killion had talked about going out to dinner, but had decided to stay in instead. He'd shown up at about six thirty, in time to entertain Jackson with a rousing half hour of chase and play with trucks. While Erica had popped the white-sauce lasagna in the oven, Allison had bathed her son and read to him until he'd fallen asleep, then she'd come downstairs for dinner.

Killion picked up his wineglass. "It's business. I'm in it for a profit."

"But do people get hurt by what you do?"

"Some will get fired. Others will make a lot of money."

"What about the ones who lose their jobs? What if they have families?"

"Most companies have a severance policy. There's unemployment."

"You know that's not enough."

His gaze was steady. "I do."

"But you're so nice, to me, to Erica."

"That's personal."

Erica could see her friend struggling with the concept. Yes, Killion was a good, kind man who cared about those in his world. But in business, he was, as Allison had said, ruthless.

"People are complicated," Erica told her. "How is training going?"

Allison had been going to the Bellevue salon for her customer service training for a few days now. Allison looked at her, obviously aware of the not-so-subtle shift in topic. She looked at her plate, then back at Erica.

"It's great. I'm enjoying the program you use. The lessons are clear and easy to understand." She smiled. "They're a bit repetitive, but that's probably the point."

She turned to Killion. "Have you been to the Bellevue Twisted? It's so beautiful. The reception area is so open and inviting. There are these large cabinets filled with product and plenty of seating. There's one person whose whole job is to ask you if you want something to drink. They make lattes and cappuccinos. Everyone wears black. Seriously, head-to-toe black. They do hair and nails on the first floor. All the other treatment rooms are upstairs. When the elevator opens, this lovely scent wafts in. Kind of a vanilla-and-eucalyptus combo."

She stopped talking and looked at her plate. "I went on and on, didn't I?"

Erica smiled. "I love your enthusiasm. Plus you're bragging on one of my favorite places, so say more."

They all laughed.

"It's an amazing place. We got to observe a facial. One of the staff was the model and the esthetician talked us through everything she did. It was so interesting." Her tone turned wistful. "Working at home with soon-to-be two kids makes the most sense, but there's something about the energy of the salon I really like."

"That makes me happy." Erica smiled at her. "The Bellevue salon is where it all started. Whenever I have a problem to work through or a hard decision to make, that's where I go to think things through."

"It's your sacred space," Killion teased.

Erica laughed. "In a way."

Killion glanced at Allison. "How's Peter now that he has a new lawyer?"

Erica saw Allison's mouth tighten.

"I haven't really talked to him since Erica hired him. I know it makes me a coward, but I'm to the point where I really don't want to know what's happening. All I hear is bad news."

"That's going to change," Erica told her. "Once all the charges are on the table, Raymond can start negotiating. Peter will cooperate and things will get better."

"He's not going to be home in time to see Bethany born." Allison sighed. "I think I've always known that but now it's impossible to even pretend."

"Can you ask one of your friends to be with you?" Killion's voice was kind.

"I will."

"A solution," he said. "But not the one you want."

"No."

Erica was more concerned about whether or not Allison really was going to ask one of her friends. So far no one had stopped by to hang out with the pregnant woman and she rarely went anywhere socially. Were there friends or was Allison in her position—living her life for something that, in the end, turned out not to be enough?

After dinner, Killion helped with the cleanup, then excused himself. Erica walked him to the door, where she promised to come stay with him in a few days, then returned to the family room.

Allison was trying to get comfortable on the big sectional.

"He doesn't stay the night?" she asked.

"Not here. It's easier for me to go to his house. It's one thing for Summer to know Killion and I are together and another for her to see him in his bathrobe."

"I think she knows you've seen each other naked."

Erica sank onto the sofa and smiled. "Yes, but there's no need to make it obvious. She's very mature for her age, but still only sixteen."

"Killion really cares about you."

"Killion likes me and finds me convenient."

"What does that mean?"

"What it sounds like. He enjoys my company and my lack of expectations." She smiled. "We're each other's plus-one. Monogamous, but without expectations. The relationship isn't going anywhere."

"You're not in love? You don't want to get married?"

Erica laughed. "You're such a dreamer. No, I don't want to marry him or anyone and I'm not in love with him."

"But you sleep with him."

"Yes, I do."

"Without love."

"Apparently."

Allison frowned. "I could never do that."

"I know and that's fine. We're all different. All my life men have judged me for being too ambitious, too successful. They've been more afraid of me than attracted to me and some who have wanted me have done so for the wrong reasons. Killion gets me and I get him. We're both busy and driven, which makes being together easy. But neither of us expects happily-ever-after."

"I don't know." Allison looked at her. "I'm pretty sure he's in love with you."

"What?" Erica sat up straight. "Why would you say that? He's not."

"He acts like he is, the way he takes care of you. Plus you haven't seen how he looks at you."

"What do you mean *how he looks at me*? What a ridiculous thing to say."

She could feel herself getting annoyed, which made no sense. They were just having a conversation and Allison was wrong. Killion was like her—he enjoyed what they had and would never want more.

Allison surprised her by smiling. "You're right. Don't listen to me. I barely know the man. I don't think I could handle your relationship, but I respect it. Besides, it's working and that's the whole point."

Which all sounded right but left Erica feeling oddly unsettled. A sensation she didn't like at all.

Summer walked into Erica's home office, her tablet in her hand and a determined expression on her face. Erica braced herself for conflict.

"I'm almost afraid to ask what you're thinking," she said, her voice teasing, hoping to avoid whatever fight they were about to have.

"I have a list," her daughter admitted, flopping down on the sofa. "For summer and other stuff."

"Ah, the summer-activity dance." Erica typed on her laptop and pulled up her daughter's calendar. "You're scheduled for softball camp, as per usual. Last we talked, you weren't sure if you want to spend the rest of your time volunteering or getting a job. It's kind of late to get a volunteering gig. Won't most of them be taken?"

"I've decided to work," her daughter said, studying her tablet. "Not just for the money, but to learn some skills. I've applied a couple of places."

Erica waited, but Summer didn't offer any specifics.

"All right," she said slowly. "Softball camp is in the morning and—"

"I don't want to go to camp." Summer sat up and set the tablet on the coffee table. "I'm done with softball."

Erica stared at her. Sure, she'd mentioned she didn't want to play in college and was thinking about letting the sport go, but this seemed sudden.

"What happened?"

"Nothing." Summer smiled. "I'm serious, Mom. Nothing big. No revelation. I've been playing for a long time. I'm good but not great. I don't want to play in college. It's a lot of work and the schedule ties me down. I want to be free to explore other things. Avery isn't going to play, either, so it's not like all my friends will be doing it."

She sighed. "I told you about the younger players. They're really good. Competitive good. They'll probably get college scholarships. So let them have my spot."

Erica thought that if the other players were that good, they would have beaten Summer for her spot and she wondered if that was part of her daughter's decision. Better to quit on top than be forced out.

Was that the right lesson to learn? Should Erica force her to practice this summer and then try out in the new school year? But to what end? Summer was a good kid. If she was done, then she was done.

"You'll finish out the season," she said.

"Of course." Summer rolled her eyes. "Mom, I would never let down the team."

As she spoke, she pulled the band from her ponytail. Her long brown hair tumbled over her shoulders. Erica tried not to wince at the split ends and uneven cut. Her fingers itched to get in there with a pair of scissors and take off about three inches and add some layers. Maybe a couple of highlights. Nothing wild, just a subtle brightness here and—

"Stop mentally doing my hair."

Erica held in a smile. "I have no idea what you're talking about. What else is on your list?"

"Allison needs baby stuff. She's weeks away from Bethany being born and she doesn't have anything. Shouldn't she have little clothes and diapers and wipes and those jumpy-chair things?"

"She should have all those things," Erica said slowly, typing into her computer. "I've been so caught up in getting her settled and everything else, I wasn't thinking about the upcoming birth."

She searched for a generic list for "what do I need when I bring home a baby."

She carried her laptop over to the sofa and sat next to her daughter. They both stared at the long list.

"We're going to need a moving van," Summer murmured. "And a bigger house."

Erica laughed. "It's not that bad. You gave her the big bedroom, and the laundry room has tons of storage. She can use that. I'm not sure what she has from when Jackson was born. If she was planning on having more kids, she would have kept all that stuff."

Summer looked at her. "Did you keep my stuff?"

"I did. For at least five years." She remembered the boxes full of tiny clothes, most of them so girlie, with ribbons and bows.

"I dressed you in pink. Oh, there was the occasional trim in teal or white, but otherwise pink. It was all so pretty and delicate." She smiled at her daughter. "I'm sure you hated it."

"I've seen the pictures." Summer leaned against her. "I did hate it but I looked cute."

"The cutest."

"Why didn't you and Dad have more kids?"

"I couldn't do it, time-wise. I wanted another child, but with you and work and Dad, I was already scrambling every second of every day. I was afraid I couldn't be there enough, and no kid wants to feel like their mother doesn't have time for them."

Summer drew back a little and angled toward her. "You come to every softball game."

"I do."

"That's a lot of time."

"You're worth it." Erica smiled. "I pray for rain a lot."

Her daughter laughed. "Sometimes we do, too. But only if we're winning."

"Sure. Why would you want to take the loss?"

Summer stared at her. "Are you mad about Allison?"

"In what way?"

"That she's here, that I guilted you."

"I'm not. Surprisingly, I like her very much. She's a good person. I'm sorry for what she's going through and I'm happy we can help." Peter was a total douchebag, but that wasn't news.

"I like having her and Jackson here, too. I'm excited about Bethany being born."

"Oh, a newborn isn't necessarily the thrill you think she's

going to be. They can be loud. My bedroom's far enough away, but you're right next door. I hope you can get enough sleep."

"I'll be fine. If it's too bad, I'll sleep on the sofa in the family room. I can take Jackson with me." Her daughter grinned. "We should get a dog."

"No."

"Come on, Mom. Jackson would love a dog."

The dog request wasn't new, but the use of Jackson as a reason was.

"Nothing about our lives has changed. I'm gone too much and you're gone too much. A dog needs human contact."

"Allison's home."

"With two small babies and starting a new job. Trust me, she's not looking for more responsibility." She closed her laptop. "If this is very important to you, I can get you one of those fluffy mechanical ones. They walk and bark and I think there's some kind of heater in them so they feel warm."

Her daughter laughed. "That's so horrible. Don't offer me a fake dog."

"Then be realistic and think about the life the poor dog would have with us. It's a firm no."

Summer leaned against her again. "You're right."

"I usually am. No wonder you find me annoying."

"You're not annoying. Just mom-like. Can I go shopping with you for the baby stuff?"

"You are absolutely going shopping with me. I'm not doing that alone."

"What about Allison? Should we tell her what we're doing?"

Erica considered the question. "Let's wait until she asks about it. If she knows we're basically outfitting her for her newborn, she'll feel awful and then she'll start thanking me and I'll feel awful."

"I get the Allison part but why don't you like being thanked?"

"I don't know. The first time is nice. The second time makes me feel funny. Guilty about having too much."

"But you worked hard for what you have."

"Guilt doesn't always make sense. We'll surprise her. That will be better."

"We can have a reveal party. With snacks."

"Hungry again?"

Summer pushed off the sofa. "Always. Let's raid the refrigerator."

While Allison found the walk from the parking lot to the prison more difficult every time, she was getting used to the indignity of checking in, being searched and having to talk to her husband in a large public room with a hundred or so other people and several dozen guards.

"You look better," she told him, noting that he seemed more rested and less worried.

"Raymond's doing his magic," he said happily. "He's working to get money released to you, plus some of the charges have been dropped."

That was news to her. "Which ones? Does that mean you'll be able to get out?" *Before Bethany is born?* But she didn't ask that. He'd already told her that wouldn't happen.

Peter glanced around, as if judging how close the guards were, then he reached across the plastic table and took her hand.

"I'm not getting out. Not for a long time. I'll have to plead guilty and serve my sentence. They'll count the time served so that shortens it some—"

He kept talking, but she couldn't hear him. There was a rushing sound and a sense of the world shifting off its axis. The tears immediately followed as a protest rose up inside of her.

"You're not getting out?"

She tried to keep her voice down, remembering what had happened when Peter had started shouting. But the broken part of her wanted to scream out a protest.

"You're not getting out?" she repeated in a whisper. "I thought we'd have time. I thought you'd fight the charges. Isn't that what Raymond is for, the reason you waited for him? So he could help you?"

Peter sat in his chair, obviously uncomfortable. He looked at everything but her.

"You really thought I was coming home? Allison, I can't. The charges. Didn't you know?"

"Know what? You kept saying it was a mistake. A misunderstanding. What does this mean? You're cooperating. So you know stuff? Are you guilty? Did you do those things?"

"Oh, baby, I'm so sorry."

He reached for her hand again. She wanted to snatch it back, but that would cause a scene and despite everything, she didn't want the visit to end. If only she could ignore the sick feeling in her stomach.

"I wanted everything for you," he said desperately, his voice low, his gaze intense. "I need you to remember that. Things weren't going well and you were pregnant and I got frantic."

She tried to understand what he was saying. Or maybe the real information was in what he wasn't saying.

All this time she'd assumed he was an innocent man. That circumstances had forced his hand, or he'd been tricked or something. But she'd been wrong.

"Are you a criminal?"

"What? No." He drew back. "Why would you ask that? You love me. I'm a good husband and father. I'm not a criminal."

"But you're in jail and you're going to plead guilty."

"It makes things easier." His gaze locked with hers. "I love you, Allison. For always. This is just a bump in the road. We'll get through it."

A bump in the road? "Do you have any idea what this has been like for me? I believed in you. In us. Was it all a lie?"

"No." His voice was strangled. "God, no. I hate what I've done to you, but you have to understand why."

She didn't. She couldn't. Nothing about their situation made sense.

"Did it really start in the past few months or have you been doing stuff like this for longer?"

He looked around again, as if conscious of listening ears. "No, no. Of course not. It was just a one-time thing. I got tripped up and things spiraled."

She wanted to believe him. Despite everything, she missed him and she wanted him home with her and Jackson. She'd seen herself growing old with Peter.

"There was nothing wrong with our life," she told him. "What we had was special because we loved each other. We had a family and a future."

"Baby, all that's still true. Give me some time."

Time wasn't the problem, she thought as she studied him, looking for the person she'd fallen in love with three years ago. The problem was that she was finally figuring out he wasn't who she'd thought. And while it was easy to say it was all his fault, what if it wasn't? What if she was just as much to blame?

25

"I'm not hungry," Allison said, avoiding Erica's gaze. "I'm going to my room."

Erica had spent the day dealing with a quirky HVAC system and a training class that had gone off the rails when a stylist had accidentally set her blow-dryer on fire. She was tired, she was cranky and she'd driven out of her way to bring home the best fried chicken on the Eastside of Seattle.

Mara was busy with a man friend, Summer was out with the girls, so it was just the two of them. Most nights that happened, Allison put Jackson to bed about the time Erica got home and they hung out together. Like friends. Sure, they were thrown together by circumstances, but Erica had started to look forward to their evenings and she wasn't in the mood to be understanding.

"What has your panties in a bunch?" she demanded, her tone snarky.

Allison slowly turned to face her. "Excuse me?"

"Panties. In. A. Bunch. You heard me. It's fried chicken. You have to be hungry. If nothing else, you have to eat. I got the damned kale salad even though we both hate it because it's the healthiest thing on the menu and in case you haven't noticed, you're seriously pregnant."

Allison glared at her. "You're in a mood."

"You're acting like a sulking teenager."

"My husband's in jail!"

The words came out as a shout. Erica didn't react.

"Hardly news," she said, pouring Allison a glass of milk and herself a glass of wine. "The man is a total loser. Why on earth we married him is beyond me."

The second the words were out of her mouth, she realized she'd gone too far. Allison immediately began to cry and Erica instantly felt like a monster.

"Shit. I'm sorry." Erica hurried to Allison and pulled her close. "I'm such a bitch. That was uncalled for. I was only thinking of myself. Jeez. It's not you, it's me. I swear."

Only when she stopped babbling did she realize she and Allison had never hugged before. When she'd moved in, they'd barely been beyond the saying-hello stage.

But her friend didn't pull back or slap her, so Erica hung on a few more seconds. Allison drew away, wiping her face.

"I've got to stop crying," the other woman said, her voice shaky. "I'm always a mess. It's not attractive."

"At least there's no one around you want to impress."

"Very funny."

Allison grabbed several tissues from a box on the counter. "My life is shit."

"Yes, it is."

Despite everything, Allison laughed. "You don't have to agree so quickly."

"Except for your kids, my daughter and the fact that I'm so amazing, it's hard to find the good."

The tears returned. "You're right." She started to sob.

"No!" Erica hugged her again. "I'm so stupid. I was going for humor. I suck at this."

"I'm glad you suck at something. Your perfection gets annoying."

"I'm far from perfect."

"You dress really well."

"I'm not twenty-seven months pregnant and I have money."

"You also have style. I don't have that."

Allison sniffed as she stepped back.

"Thank you for bringing home dinner."

"You're going to eat."

"Asking or telling?"

"Both."

"You're right." Allison moved to the table by the window and sat down. "I hate my life. I can't sleep, I'm uncomfortable all the time. Jackson's a sweetie and I have you and Summer and Mara, so I'm not alone, but it's hard."

"I know."

Erica set their drinks on the table and brought over the take-out bag. While she got flatware, plates and spoons, Allison opened packages.

When Erica was seated, Allison looked at her. "Why did you marry him?" She held up her hand. "I know what you said before about other guys avoiding you because you were too ambitious and not willing to cater to them, but why Peter? Was he just convenient, or did you really love him?"

"I loved him."

"Why?"

The blunt question. Erica took a chicken thigh and some potato salad. After the day she'd had, she refused to eat kale.

"He was funny and sweet," she said, peeling off the skin. "Smart but not scary smart. He seemed interested in what I did. Some of the other people on my accounting team wanted to talk more than they listened. He wanted to understand my process. He was impressed by me."

She thought about how lonely she'd been and how much she'd wanted to fall in love. She'd wanted a family in addition to her business and had been worried it would never happen.

"I was ready to fall in love with someone and Peter was ready to be loved," she added. "He was a little goofy, which I liked. A couple of years younger, but that was okay, too. We could talk about things. We were comfortable together."

Until he'd decided he was done with her.

"I'm not saying it was a great love, but it was enough."

"Did you know he was a criminal?"

Erica was as surprised by Allison's bitter tone as by the question itself. "He's not a criminal," she said automatically, then held in a wince. "I mean he wasn't. Circumstances and—"

"Do you believe that?" Allison asked, cutting her off. "Do you really think that out of nowhere Peter came up with this plan to launder money and commit wire fraud?" She paused. "I don't even know what that is, but it's bad, right? A felony. He's in jail right now and he's not getting out."

Erica's heart sank. "You saw him today."

"I went after work, so I owe you for the extra childcare."

Erica waved that comment away. "What happened?"

Allison wiped her fingers. "He said the lawyer is negotiating to get some money released and some charges dropped. Peter said he'd be cooperating and that would reduce his sentence. I didn't get it at first, but he's not getting out. There's no bail. He'll plead guilty to a lesser sentence and serve his time."

She swallowed. "My husband is a criminal. There's no other way to describe it. I trusted him with my heart, my life. I wanted him to father my children and he's a con man. I was fooled. I admit that. I never had a clue, so I'm a moron, but you're really smart and if I'm right, how come you didn't see it? Because there's no way this is new behavior. He didn't just wake up and decide, 'Hey, let's defraud some people.' It had to start somewhere. So what do you know that I don't?"

Erica didn't know what to say. She wanted to protest Peter wasn't a criminal, but the evidence was hard to dispute.

"He loves you."

"So it's my fault?"

"Of course not. His feelings for you drove him to do things he shouldn't have. You didn't marry a criminal. It just happened."

"Things like that don't just happen. Did he ever do anything to you or the business?"

Erica had a bad feeling her expression gave her away.

"What?" Allison demanded.

"After he said he wanted a divorce, I moved the business to a different accounting firm. They audited the books. They found out Peter had taken over a hundred thousand dollars from me in small amounts, over time. I told myself it was because he was angry at me."

Allison face went white. "He stole money from you? While you were married?"

Erica wanted to excuse the actions by saying a case could be made that the money was community property. Only Peter had signed a prenup so he had nothing to do with the salon.

"He really is a criminal," Allison whispered. "He took advantage of both of us. He probably chose us because we were vulnerable. In different ways, but still marks. We were marks."

"Don't say that. We weren't. I genuinely believe he loves you. I stood in that jail and looked into his eyes. He begged for you, Allison. He hates me and he begged me to help you. He would do anything for you."

Erica wasn't sure why it was so important for her to convince her friend, but she knew she had to.

Allison shook her head. "I know you're trying to help and that's sweet, but you're wrong. He risked everything. He took a chance, and now we're all paying the price."

She pushed away her plate. "The worst part is I still miss him. I touch his clothes in the closet. I close my eyes and pretend he's there. I tell myself he'll be home soon. But he's never coming home and we're never getting our life back. Worse, I don't know him anymore. Or trust him. So what happens now?"

"Nothing," Erica said quietly. "Because you don't have to

decide. You're upset and you should be. He did put everything on the line and you're the one paying. But you're safe and what matters is focusing on staying healthy for Jackson and Bethany. The rest can take care of itself."

Allison nodded. "Let's talk about something else. How was work?"

Erica groaned. "That's not a cheerful topic. Know anything about HVAC systems?"

"Not really."

"Then let me tell you. They're pure evil."

"What about diapers?" Summer asked as she pushed the cart through the large baby store.

"We'll have those shipped to the house." Erica looked at her daughter. "She'll need ten to twelve a day."

"Diapers?" Summer's voice was a yelp. "Seriously? How is that possible? I remember from when Jackson was born. I even changed him when I was there, but I didn't realize how many diapers." She glanced at the list on her phone. "Babies need a lot of stuff. It's kind of poor planning, evolution-wise. They're helpless. Newborn puppies can smell and sense heat."

"And crawl. Babies can't even do that. But we're stuck with what we have. What's next?"

"A crib."

They walked over to the furniture department, where Erica immediately felt overwhelmed. There were dozens of faux rooms set up with cribs, dressers and changing tables, along with rocking chairs. The options ranged from dark wood to painted furniture covered in dancing unicorns.

Summer stared at the too-happy unicorns. "Not that."

"I agree. Let's go simple. I'm thinking a bassinet. It takes up less room and when Bethany outgrows it, she can take the crib and Jackson can move into a toddler bed."

She walked over to a display of well-made furniture in light pine. "She'll need a changing table. I'd totally blanked on that." She smiled at Summer. "That's a lot of furniture, so it's good you gave her the bigger bedroom."

"It's working out. Do you like this one?"

"Uh-huh. There's lots of storage in the changing table. She'll want supplies right there in the room with her."

They pulled out drawers and made sure the shelves were sturdy. Erica made a note of the model numbers and they continued to the clothing and bedding.

"We want real cotton," Summer said. "It's breathable and washes well. Or a cotton jersey knit. And organic is better. That means the cotton was grown without chemicals."

Erica grinned. "Apparently I'm not the only one who went online."

"You're not but I never thought to look up diapers."

They started going through the clothing. Summer pulled out simple, gender-neutral styles and colors while Erica found herself drawn to the pinks and purples with lots of detail.

"Oh, Mom. That little dress isn't practical."

Erica fingered the soft lace. "I know, but it's pretty. The girl clothes are so cute."

"Maybe Bethany's like me and doesn't want to be dressed like a doll."

"When she can tell me that herself, I'll listen."

She expected her daughter to laugh or tease her. Instead Summer's big eyes filled with tears and the teen rushed toward her and hugged her.

"Why am I so mean to you?" she asked, her voice thick with emotion. "I'm horrible."

The shift in tone and subject was startling. Erica stroked her daughter's hair.

"Sweetie, why are you upset?"

Summer wiped her face as she stepped back. "You really like all the girlie stuff. You think it's fun and helping women feel good about themselves makes you happy. I know that but sometimes I diss you anyway, and that's not fair. I was talking to Grandma about Dad and should I go see him or not and how he always said bad stuff about you, and she pointed out that he really influenced me."

"He's your father and you love him." She deliberately lightened her tone. "Sometimes I influence you, as well, although you do seem to fight it."

"But you're the better person. Why don't I listen more?"

"Because you're a teenager and I'm your mom." Erica thought maybe she should push back against Summer saying she was the better person, but then reminded herself Peter was in jail so maybe it was a fair assessment.

"Honey, I love you and I want you to be happy. Would I do the happy dance if you were a tiny bit more interested in what I do at work? Sure. Let's talk mascara and go clothes shopping." She smiled. "But is there any way I could love you one drop more than I do? Not possible. You're my daughter and no matter what you're in my heart."

"You say that now." The teen shook her head. "But I've done stuff. Bad stuff."

Erica ignored the cold that swept through her, telling herself not to panic. Summer was a good kid. She trusted her. Facts first, freak later.

"Can you be more specific?"

Her daughter looked at her. "I had a boyfriend last year and I didn't tell you."

The relief was instant but before she could say anything, Summer continued.

"It was only for a few weeks and the whole thing was silly. You said I was too young to date and you were right. But I thought he was great and I felt special and then he dumped me because I wasn't girlie enough, which hurt. But I couldn't doubly tell you because I'd gone behind your back and he wanted me to be more like how you wanted me to be."

She wiped away more tears. "I'm sorry I lied."

"Me, too. You can always talk to me. I'm your biggest fan."

Summer rushed at her again. They hung on to each other. Her daughter looked up at her.

"Maybe I have too much freedom. You trust me so it was easy to keep the guy from you. I might need more boundaries."

"Do you want more boundaries?"

"No."

"Are you going to hide a new boyfriend from me?"

"I don't have one but if I did, I would tell you."

"Then I think we're okay."

"Don't you want to punish me for lying?"

Erica held in a smile. "It was a long time ago and you feel really guilty. I think we'll go with that."

"Thanks. I do feel bad." She sighed. "And the guy thing was complicated. I mean shouldn't he have liked me for me?"

"Absolutely. If a man wants you to change, he's not the one."

"That makes sense. I should find someone like Killion. Not the money and stuff, but how he treats you. He respects you, Mom. Plus the way he smiles at you."

"How does he smile at me?"

"Like he's always happy you're around. He gets this look when you walk in the room. I want that someday."

There was no look, Erica told herself. Summer was being silly.

"Take your time," she said. "But for now, let's get the plain onesies, but this perfect pink dress as well. Compromise."

"It has lace."

"I know. That's what makes it the best."

The hundred-foot yacht came with two living rooms, or "salons" as the captain called them, a large formal dining room and enough outdoor space to play football. Although it was May and summer didn't really start in Seattle until July 5, the night was unusually mild. A warm front had brought temperatures close to seventy and the lows would barely crack the midfifties. Heaters provided warmth as the guests circulated.

Killion had gone all out for the celebration. There was a band up by the bow, a photo booth with boas and funny hats, two bars serving top-shelf liquor and a seafood buffet that included lobster and crab.

Erica had no idea how much it cost to rent the amazing yacht, but she could estimate the price of everything else, then multiply that for a party of nearly thirty people.

She waved her glass of Dom Pérignon. "Are we drinking up your profits?" she asked, her voice teasing. "Should I switch to club soda?"

Killion, handsome as always in a custom tuxedo, smiled at her. "This party doesn't begin to touch one percent of my profits. Drink as much as you'd like."

The evening—a formal affair celebrating the sale of one of his companies—had started at six when the yacht had sailed. They'd spent the evening circling Lake Union and Lake Washington, with views of the Seattle skyline.

The captain walked over and spoke quietly to Killion. When he'd left, Killion smiled at her.

"We'll be docking in fifteen minutes. An hour after that, we'll have the boat to ourselves."

The yacht rental was twenty-four hours. The caterers had boarded at one to set up. Once the guests disembarked, the staff would clean up, but Killion had possession of the boat until one tomorrow. He'd asked Erica to spend the night with him.

"Are we going to just sail around the lake all night?" she asked with a laugh.

"I thought we'd take one last lap, then dock and settle in the main cabin."

She'd left her overnight bag in the large space so knew about the king-size bed, the view from the windows and the skylight.

"I've never spent the night on a boat," she admitted. "It should be an experience."

"I hope so."

The yacht approached the marina. Killion excused himself to say good night to his guests. Erica went downstairs to the main cabin, where she took off her uncomfortable heels. She pulled yoga pants and a sweater out of her suitcase, then unzipped the simple black gown she'd worn. Once she was in comfortable clothes, she stepped into her Uggs and hung up the dress.

By the time she returned to the main deck, the guests were gone and the catering staff was cleaning up. One of the women saw her and smiled.

"We left some food in the refrigerator in case you were hungry. Sometimes it's hard to eat at an event like this."

"Thank you."

She found Killion on the rear deck. He smiled when he saw her, then pulled her close.

"How is it you look more beautiful now than you did when you were all fancy?"

"All fancy?" She laughed. "I dressed as per the invitation."

"Yes, you did. You always do the right thing."

"It comes from years of practice."

He kissed her. "Hungry?"

"For food or lovemaking?"

Humor brightened his green eyes. "Both."

"Then yes. The caterers left us some food."

"Good. We'll eat while we circle the lake and take care of that other thing later."

They stood together, staring out onto the lake. Lights twinkled from the shore. Tall buildings stretched to the sky. It was a beautiful night and she was enjoying herself, but her mind kept circling back to her conversation with Allison.

"You sighed."

She leaned against him. "I'm distracted. I feel so bad for Allison. I can't seem to let it go."

"You don't like problems you can't fix. Nearly everything about her situation is unfixable. That makes you uncomfortable."

She glanced at him. "I thought you were going to say it's because I care about her."

"You do, but you don't mind that."

How did he know her so well? She thought briefly about what her friend had said about Killion and his feelings for her, then dismissed the concern. There was no way he was in love with her. They were convenient and they liked each other's company, nothing more.

"I think Peter's a total shit and now it turns out he's also a criminal, which is surprising, but oh well." She turned to Killion. "But me thinking that is one thing. Allison loves him. She's the kind of woman who needs to be in a relationship to be happy. He was supposed to take care of her and he didn't. He's in jail and he's not getting out anytime soon. She's totally alone with a toddler and a baby due in a few weeks. It sucks and I'm just pissed at Peter for screwing up her life."

Killion touched her cheek. "She's not alone. She has you."

"It's not the same."

"No, but it's a good substitute. You won't let her down and you're unlikely to be arrested."

That made her smile for a second. Then she sighed again. "You're right. I want to fix things, and I can't. Summer wants to throw her a baby shower."

"I can give you the name of my party planner. She can pull it all together."

"It's a baby shower. I think I'm capable. Besides my mom said she'll help and that means she'll do most of the work."

"How about if I have Napoleon call her and they can work out the details together?"

She smiled. "I like that idea. You always know someone."

"Yes, but more important, I'm someone you can trust to take care of you."

What? She glared at him. "I don't need taking care of. I'm perfectly capable of—"

He silenced her with a brief kiss. "You know what I mean. Don't make what I said more than it is. You handle things for me and I do the same for you."

She let her mad fade. He was right. From arranging movers to finding out where Peter was being held, Killion was someone she could count on. Funny how she'd never really seen that before.

26

Allison spent her break with Emmy, the salon's general manager. They'd hit it off the first day of training.

"Not every salon has the training programs that we offer here," Emmy said as they sat in the break room. "Beauty school teaches a lot, but most graduates need real world experience. We pair our graduates with a mentor and offer additional training. How long varies from department to department."

Allison sipped her mug of warm water and wished her feet weren't so swollen. But she was too far along to expect to be comfortable.

"There's also ongoing training for all departments," Emmy continued. "Our suppliers bring classes to us or offer slots for classes they're teaching elsewhere. We can also earn slots through product sales and contests."

"There's a lot more to running a salon than I'd realized," Allison admitted.

"If we were just doing hair, it would be easier, but we're running a spa as well."

One that was always busy, Allison thought. She knew that from both the calls she was taking and the number of cars in the parking lot.

"I like the program that helps new employees get established," she said. Clients who went with someone new got their service at a discount, regardless of the department.

"Erica believes that well-trained employees are happier and clients are more satisfied."

"You like working for her."

"I do." Emmy grinned. "I wanted to beg for the job when I interviewed here three years ago, but I did my best to play it cool. I was coming from another salon. Nothing this big or well-run. Erica has a reputation in the industry. She has high standards, but she treats her employees fairly and pays them well. Just as important, she gives them the tools to succeed."

"She's an amazing woman." One Allison had grown to admire. Not just because Erica had rescued her but because of how she lived her life.

"Are you thinking of switching careers?" Emmy asked.

The unexpected question caught Allison off guard. "What do you mean?"

"You're interested in the business. I wondered if you'd like to be a part of it."

She hesitated. "I've toyed with the idea," she admitted. "Not doing hair. I think that's a bit like being an artist. I don't know that I have the talent. But I wonder about being an esthetician. Everyone feels so much better after a facial."

Emmy nodded. "It takes about seven hundred and fifty class hours and eight hundred apprenticeship hours to be licensed in our state. If you're serious, I can connect you with admissions at the local school we prefer."

Allison thought about how she didn't have any money for something like beauty school. Even if she got a scholarship, what would she do with her kids?

"I think I need to have Bethany first," she said lightly. "Then I'll look at my options."

Emmy eyed her huge belly. "I agree. Newborns take precedence. But I would encourage you to think about being an esthetician. You have a good personality for it. You're friendly, smart and just nurturing enough for clients to feel comfortable."

The kind words were unexpected. Allison wanted to ask how Emmy could be so sure about her. They barely knew each other. Then she reminded herself to accept the compliment graciously. Having a breakdown would be so awkward for them both.

Erica walked directly from the garage to her mother's carriage house. Two hours earlier she'd gotten a cryptic Come see me before you go into the house text from Mara.

She knocked once, then opened the front door. "It's me. What's going on?"

Her mother walked in from the kitchen, her normally happy expression tight and worried.

"Something's going on with Summer. When she got home from school, she was upset. She tried to say she was fine, but I don't believe her. Allison doesn't know anything, either. We decided not to push and let you deal with it."

Erica didn't understand. "She was fine two days ago when we went shopping and yesterday after the game. She was her normal self all evening and this morning at breakfast. Something must have happened at school. I'll talk to her."

"It might be nothing."

Erica shook her head. "Mom, you know your granddaughter. If you're worried, I'm worried. I'll let you know what she says."

She entered the house through the garage, as always. A thousand thoughts—none of them good—swirled through her brain. What could have happened? She didn't think it had anything to do with a guy and she doubted Summer would be so withdrawn if she'd had a car accident.

"It's me," she called, careful to keep her voice cheerful. It was still early and Jackson would be awake.

Sure enough, fast footsteps thumped on the hardwood floor as he flew toward her, arms outstretched.

"Rika! Rika!"

She swooped him up and nuzzled his neck. "How are you, little man? Did you have a wonderful day?"

He giggled and gave her a kiss on the cheek, then began to babble about maybe a puzzle or a book.

"Is that what happened? Were you okay with it?"

He beamed at her, then dropped his head to her shoulder. Erica turned to Allison.

"You okay?"

The other woman frowned. "I'm fine. Why?"

"Worry isn't good for you. You're getting bigger by the day and the last thing you need is one more stressor."

"I'm not stressed. I'm concerned. She was so quiet when she came home from school." Allison twisted her hands together. "No, it was worse than that. She came straight home. She didn't stay to talk to her friends or go to practice. She was here by two-fifty. That never happens. She barely said hello to Jackson, then she locked herself in her room. She won't tell me anything. She says she's fine."

Allison shook her head. "I didn't want to push her too hard, so I texted Mara. She couldn't get anything out of her, either. She looks okay, so I don't think it's anything physical."

"I'll talk to her."

Erica handed back Jackson, then went upstairs. She quickly changed into jeans and a sweater, then knocked on her daughter's closed bedroom door.

"It's me," she called.

"The door's open."

She found her daughter lying on her back, staring at the ceiling. Her backpack was sitting, unopened, by Jackson's crib. Erica sat down on the bed.

"Hey. What's going on?"

Summer opened an app on her phone and then turned it toward Erica.

Guess who's a jailbird?

The fancy font covered a photoshopped picture of Summer's face on a dancing crow. The bird was behind bars.

Erica scrolled through the posts. There were mean comments about criminals running in families and accusations of Summer stealing a car. Someone had posted Peter's arrest warrant. Several videos had the song "Bad Boys" playing in the background.

Erica's stomach immediately clenched. With everything going on with Allison and what to do about her situation, she'd somehow forgotten about Summer. In this digital age, nothing was private—certainly not in a high school. She should have helped prepare her for when the information inevitably came out.

"Oh, sweetie, I'm so sorry."

Summer rolled on her side, facing her. "It's not that bad," she whispered. "I know some kids have it worse. But it's never been me before. I'm not super popular, which means I don't get a lot of attention. Sometimes people get on the whole softball team if we're losing and I've been called out for missing a catch, but that's easy, you know."

She blinked away tears. "This is about my life and my dad. I didn't realize what was happening for a while. I walked into class and I could hear 'Bad Boys' on someone's phone, but I didn't think it was for me. Not until Avery showed me. By then it was everywhere."

She rolled on her back and wiped away tears. "It's not a lot of kids. My friends are totally supportive. I know they'll be there, but people I don't know are saying things and posting things. I'm so ashamed."

Erica stretched out next to her and took her hand. "This sucks. I'm sorry. I should have realized word would get out. When I was in high school, you could go home and forget about it. The worst that happened were some prank calls. With social media, there's no escape."

Summer shifted close, put her head on Erica's shoulder and started to cry. "They're so mean and they're saying stuff about my dad."

Erica stroked her back, her heart breaking for her daughter's pain. "I know."

"It's so personal. Why do they care? The kids that are doing this don't even know me. Why does my life matter?"

"They're small people with small lives. They've decided it's fun to torture other people. It's a game to them. They're too self-absorbed to know or care they're hurting other people. What they think of you isn't who you are. You're stronger than they are."

"I don't feel very strong."

"I know. We can talk to the administra—"

Summer sat up. "No! We're not escalating this. No meetings. I don't want to make it bigger. If someone had hit me or something, I would be all in on grinding them to dust, but this isn't that. You're right—this is a game to them. I can either do it better than them and be a total troll on social media or I can pretend to not care."

"Do you want to be a total troll? No offense, but I doubt your techie skills are up to it. But we could ask Killion. He probably knows a guy."

That earned her a faint smile. "I'm sure he does. And I thought about it. I nearly texted him earlier."

Summer wiped away more tears. "Like I said, it's never been about me. Except for my circle of friends, I'm pretty much ignored. Some kids are bullied constantly. We all see it. There's this one girl." She shrugged. "We let her eat lunch with us when she wants. Not really brave, huh? But it's something. I just didn't know it could happen to me."

Erica struggled to find the right words to help her daughter. She was grateful Summer didn't want to go the revenge route. Erica would be thrilled to see those kids' social lives destroyed but it wasn't exactly the mature response. In this neighborhood, this school district, not a lot of fathers went to jail. It was news. Torturing Summer because of it was simply what teens did. It wasn't right, but she was more concerned about her daughter's feelings and mental health.

"So no going to the administration," she said lightly, just to confirm.

"The videos are stupid and I never stole a car, but aside from that, they aren't lying. Dad really is in jail and I guess he did those things. I don't want to get into a big deal about bullying. I'll deal."

Brave words, Erica thought. But hard to execute.

"What does 'dealing' mean?" she asked. "This is painful. You need a plan."

"You and your plans."

"You're going to school every day. You have a couple more games. You drive your own car so you don't have to worry about something happening on the bus or while walking home. If one of them showed up here, your grandmother would so take them on."

Summer managed a faint smile. "They're not coming to the house, Mom. Their world is online. They'll post mean memes. Then they'll move on to another victim."

She drew in a breath. "I think I'm okay at the games. The last two are away ones. My team will be there."

"As will I and the other moms. We'll look out for you."

"I know and I'm grateful. School's a drag, but there's nothing to do. They don't want the teachers finding out, so they won't be obvious. I guess I just have to get through it."

Erica tapped her daughter's phone. "You could stop looking at this so much."

Summer stared at her. "I'm not giving up my phone."

"No one's saying you should. But maybe a little less time on it. Turn off notifications. Stop scrolling a couple of hours before bed so the bad stuff isn't in your head. Start looking at videos of puppies and kittens."

"Then I'll want a dog."

"I'd rather fight with you about getting a dog than see you so unhappy." Erica cupped her face. "You're my best girl. I'd do anything for you."

"I know. Thanks, Mom. This totally sucks."

"It does. I really want to do something to those kids."

Summer drew back. "But you won't, right? Having one parent in jail is enough for me."

Erica smiled. "I promise to be lawful in every way, but I will hate them in my heart."

"Thank you."

Erica glanced at the clock. "It's nearly seven. Want to go downstairs and get something to eat?"

Summer perked up a little. "Grandma ordered in Italian but I wasn't hungry. Lasagna sounds really good."

"Is there garlic bread?"

Summer grinned. "Mom, Grandma placed the order. There's everything."

Allison tried to watch Summer without making it obvious. The teen seemed in better spirits. She was talking and laughing with only a faint hint of wariness in her eyes. But about twenty minutes into the meal she realized that Summer had left her phone upstairs.

Allison held in a sigh, thinking she'd never seen Summer without her phone nearby. It was practically a new limb for her. Erica was firm—dinner was family time. During those meals, her phone was usually on the big island, where its regular beeps and tones would cause her to glance at it longingly. Annoying but normal.

But not tonight.

Allison didn't know the kids who were bothering her, but she wished she could confront them. She wasn't sure what she would say, or why her opinion would matter, but she burned with a need to do *something*.

Some of that energy came from her affection for Summer and the natural worry the situation created, but some came from guilt. The teen was suffering because of Peter's actions.

She tried not to let her discomfort show. She was friendly, joining in the conversation. It was only when Summer retreated upstairs that she turned to Erica.

"This is Peter's fault. If he hadn't been so selfish and stupid, none of this would have happened."

Erica raised her eyebrows. "I agree that this is on him, but what's happening with Summer seems like the least of his sins."

"How can you say that? She's his child. Did he ever once think about how this would affect her? He says he loves her, then he commits a bunch of crimes and goes to jail."

"I doubt jail was one of the goals." Erica studied her. "You're really upset about Summer."

"Of course. This is horrible. We have to do something. Talk to the school or those kids' parents. And I'm going to put this all on Peter when I next see him."

Erica motioned to the family room sofa. "Waddle over there and have a seat."

"I don't waddle."

"Want me to take a video? Regardless of how you get there, you need to get off your feet. You're so huge, it's painful to look at you."

"Imagine how it feels from this end, and don't try to distract me. Someone needs to suffer." She collapsed in a chair.

Erica's expression remained calm. "While you and Summer were heating dinner, I scanned the school's bullying standards. I don't think what they're doing qualifies. Are the memes awful and mean? Yes. But unless this continues for weeks or they get worse, I don't think talking to the administration is the right thing to do. Mostly because Summer doesn't want it."

"But she's in pain."

"She is, but she's tough and she has a lot of support. We'll both keep an eye on her, as will my mom. If I think for one second she's hiding something from me, I'll call her on it. We can be on alert, but I think fire-bombing someone's house is a little extreme."

"I never suggested that," Allison grumbled. "That's going too far."

"I'm glad you think so." Erica's glance fell to her belly. "About the childbirth classes…"

"No." If Allison could have jumped to her feet for emphasis, she would have. "Stop talking about it."

"One of us has to."

"Yes, and you've decided that's you. It's not your problem. I'm fine."

Two days ago Erica had suddenly started going on and on about Allison going to a childbirth class, which was ridiculous.

"I remember everything I'm supposed to do," she said sharply. "Jackson was born less than two years ago. It's not like anything has changed."

"Why are you being difficult? You need a refresher course and you need a coach. You can't have the baby alone."

Words Erica no doubt meant to be helpful but every one of them felt like a slap.

"Would you get out of my business, please? I know I owe you, but I don't want to talk about this. No. Just no."

"I can see this conversation is upsetting you," Erica began.

"Oh, can you? How perceptive."

"You're in a mood."

"And you're not listening. We are not having this conversation. It's none of your business."

"You're having a baby. You need to take a class and—"

"I'm not taking a damned class," Allison shouted. "Not by myself and not with a friend. Peter is my husband, this is his baby and he needs to be there."

Erica stared at her wide-eyed. "He can't be. He's in jail."

"I'm incredibly aware of that, but thank you for reminding me. Yes, my husband, the father of my child, is in jail, so he can't go with me. I will not walk into a class and have to explain where he is. I'm having a felon's baby. I'm not proud of that, but it's what's happening." She pointed at her belly. "This is a felon's baby."

Erica shrugged. "You probably shouldn't put that on a T-shirt."

Allison stared at her, prepared to tell her off for being so insensitive. But instead of yelling, she found herself laughing. It started with a little uncontrollable giggle, then grew. The more she laughed, the more she wanted to give in to the humor. In the back of her mind, she was braced for the tears that would inevitably follow, but for a few glorious seconds, she just laughed.

Erica watched her warily. When the chuckles had faded, she asked, "Are you having a breakdown? Should I call 911?"

"Shut up. I'm fine." She drew in a breath. "No birthing classes. I'm not doing it."

"It's your decision. Just don't blame me when you forget what to do."

27

"You okay?" Killion asked as he carried plates to the kitchen sink.

"Fine."

He looked at her. "'Fine' isn't an acceptable answer. When a woman says she's fine, she either means *I don't want to talk about it* or *Now you have to guess what's bothering me and if you guess wrong, you'll be punished.*"

Erica laughed. "Have I ever done that to you?"

"No, but the potential is always there."

She rinsed the plates and stacked them by the dishwasher. "I refuse to be judged by your past relationships. I have my flaws but playing games isn't one of them."

She looked at him. "I meant it, I'm fine. Summer's doing better. You heard her at dinner. The harassment seems to be dying off. Hopefully it was short-lived and she won't have to deal with it much longer. It didn't go viral, thank God, so there's that."

She paused, glanced around to make sure they were still alone in her kitchen, then lowered her voice.

"She's sticking closer to home. I'm a bad mom, but I'm liking having her around more."

"That doesn't make you a bad mom. You wouldn't wish the problem on her in the first place."

"Of course not. I'd much rather they came after me."

"Then they'd have both of us to deal with."

She groaned. "Don't protect me. I'm very capable."

"Yes, you are. I'm not questioning that. But I'd still get between you and any harasser."

She told herself not to read too much into his words. He was being a guy, nothing more.

They finished clearing the table. While Killion loaded the dishwasher, she wiped the counters. They'd just finished when Summer burst into the kitchen.

"I said I'd help! You did everything!"

Erica leaned against the counter and smiled. "You said you'd be back in five minutes. You were gone football time five minutes."

"Sorry." Her daughter grinned. "I really did go upstairs to read Jackson one story, but then I got a text from Donovan."

Erica struggled to put the name in context. Who was— "Oh, the friend who's a guy and having trouble with his girlfriend."

"That's the one." Summer danced from foot to foot. "They're fully broken up and he's sad, but he still wants to go to prom. He's a senior and he said he doesn't want to spend the rest of his life explaining why he didn't. So he asked me."

She held up both hands. "As *friends*, Mom. I'm serious. Don't make it more than it is."

Erica tried to hide her pleasure. Her little girl going to prom. She was thrilled. But all she said was, "That sounds like fun. Are any of your friends going?"

"Portia and Tyra."

Friends from softball, Erica thought with relief. Summer would have backup if anyone said anything about her dad.

"Sounds like fun. What do you want to do about a dress?"

She asked the question casually, not wanting to push. This was Summer, after all, the teen who didn't believe in being girlie.

"Go shopping, of course! Mom, it's prom. I know I'm not into all that, but I have to look killer. Donovan's ex will be there with her new boyfriend, and the guy I dated for like five minutes is a senior, so he'll be there. I have to look totally epic. A dress, shoes, hair and makeup."

Erica kept her body language relaxed. "I'm pretty good at epic. It's kind of my thing."

Summer clapped her hands. "Exactly! So the full treatment." She paused. "Nothing that hurts, though. And I want my hair to stay long. But otherwise, go for it. Highlights, layers, whatever."

"Self-tanner," Killion teased.

"All of it." Summer danced around the kitchen. "They will bow before me and tremble in my company."

Killion chuckled. "I like your confidence. I know a guy who has a Bentley. Want me to rent it for you and Donovan for the night?"

"No," Erica said.

"Absolutely," Summer said at the same time, then spun to face her. "Mom! A Bentley!! It's not like we'll be driving it."

"I don't want you throwing up in it, either."

"It's prom. There won't be drinking."

Erica rolled her eyes. "It's prom. Of course there will be drinking."

"Well, I won't. I'm an athlete. At least for now. I promise, we won't throw up in it."

Erica thought about mentioning they shouldn't have sex, either, but didn't think that conversation should occur in front of Killion. But if Summer was going to start dating, it was definitely time to get her on birth control.

Killion smiled at her. "So yes on the Bentley?"

"I suppose," Erica said, "only why haven't you taken me out in it before?"

"I didn't think you would be impressed by a car."

"I might be. I don't know. I've never driven in a Bentley."

He leaned forward and lightly kissed her. "Consider it done."

Napoleon, Killion's assistant, and Mara pulled together Allison's shower in a matter of days. Bouquets of balloons in every shade of pink provided a thematic background. There were stacks of presents, posters of the first ultrasound, a buffet worthy of an upscale wedding reception, a guy doing card tricks and making balloon animals, songs with the word *baby* in them, and a frothy pink drink made with ginger ale, lemonade and strawberries, which looked disgusting but tasted delicious.

Erica was pleased with the size of the crowd in the large basement rec room. She and Mara had put out the word and people had responded. The softball moms and daughters were there. Liz, the evil boss from the day care center, and the other women Allison had worked with. Emmy from the Bellevue salon, a couple of people Allison had known from her grocery store job. Even Hillary, the only employee to stand by Peter, had come. Killion was the lone man to brave the sea of pink and all the women. As usual, he was totally at ease, talking and laughing as if this was how he always spent a Thursday evening.

Mara had hired a sitter to watch Jackson, so while he was downstairs with everyone and enjoying plenty of attention, someone was ready to whisk him away should he get fussy or need a diaper change.

A little before five, Erica went upstairs. She'd said she would wait for Allison and bring her down as soon as she got home. Her signal to the group would be to turn the stair lights on and off a couple of times, warning them to be quiet and be prepared to shout "Surprise!" Unfortunately the second Allison walked into the kitchen, Erica realized the giant flaw in their plan. Her friend might not want a surprise baby shower.

Allison's face was blotchy, her eyes red from an obvious bout of tears. She saw Erica and immediately started crying.

"I can't do this," she said, her voice thick with emotion. "There's too much change, too much uncertainty. I love Peter and I miss him but I'm so angry at him. He did this to me and Jackson. He broke the law and left his family stranded. I'm totally dependent on you. I work at a job you gave me, live in a house you own. I eat your food."

She wiped her face. "I'm not saying thank you. I know you don't like that and I really appreciate everything you've done, but I want my life back."

She swallowed and sniffed. "But even as I say that I'm hearing a voice in my head saying my life was a lie. Because while I was happy, Peter was lying to me and being a criminal and I had no idea. I never thought he could do that to me."

Erica wrapped her arms around her. Allison sagged against her—at least as much as she could with her massive belly.

"It's not your fault."

"I married him."

"So did I."

Allison stepped back and looked at her, wide-eyed. "It's true. You really did. You married a criminal."

"He wasn't a criminal when I knew him. That's on you."

She figured there was a fifty-fifty chance that Allison would start crying again or slap her. Instead her mouth twitched and she smiled.

"You're saying I'm a bad influence?"

"I'm not the one he's crazy in love with." She softened her tone. "I'm sorry about everything that's happened. I know this isn't how you saw things going. For what it's worth, we all like having you and Jackson living here."

Allison waved a hand. "Don't be nice. I barely have these tears under control."

"About that." Erica pointed to the hall bathroom. "I need you to wash your face, then think happy thoughts."

"I don't like the sound of that." Allison looked around. "Where's Jackson? Summer said she wanted to pick him up from day care."

"She did and he's fine. He's downstairs." Erica hesitated. "You're having a surprise baby shower. There are about twenty people in a sea of pink down there. You're going to have to face them while faking happy and shocked."

The tears returned. "You're throwing me a baby shower?"

"It was a group thing. My mom and Killion's assistant did all the work."

Allison rushed over and hugged her again. "I can't believe you did that. You're the nicest person ever. Peter was a fool to let you go."

"It's weird you're saying that while you're knocked up with his kid."

"I know."

Allison walked past the family room as casually as she could, just to make sure she hadn't been wrong the first time. Nope, they were still at it. Summer and her friends were sitting on the floor, playing *The Game of Life*. And not some digital, online version. They'd pulled out the actual board game and were rolling dice and moving pieces. On a Saturday night!

The only thing she could figure was Summer was still lying low because of the social media attacks, and her friends were hanging out to show solidarity. Which was very sweet and supportive, only it seemed like they were too quiet. Four teenage girls should not be anything close to silent—not when hanging out. Where was the music and the shrieking?

She thought about going into the family room and suggesting Summer turn on the complicated stereo system. She couldn't figure it out but she was sure the teenagers would have no problem. Only this wasn't her house and Summer wasn't her daughter. But Erica seemed content to leave the girls alone. She'd greeted them, then had disappeared upstairs. Was she giving them space or did she not know her place with them?

Under any other circumstances Allison wouldn't have dared consider that Erica might be unsure. The other woman was one of the most confident, capable people she knew. But when it came to her daughter, Erica was always careful and sometimes seemed hesitant. Some of that was probably from the natural minefield that was a mother-daughter relationship when the kid was a teenager, but some of it probably came from how Peter had undermined her with their child. Yet one more issue she had with her husband, but not the point tonight.

She walked to the stairs, only to pause. Getting involved seemed...fraught. Except Erica was her friend and she cared about her.

"I'm doing this," she whispered and went upstairs.

She found Erica in her home office, laptop open.

"Have a second?"

Erica smiled. "Of course. Is Jackson asleep?"

"He was out in three seconds. I wish I could sleep like that."

Erica eyed her belly. "I want to say you will after Bethany is born, but we both know that's not true."

Allison sat in one of the chairs. "Summer is downstairs with her friends. It's too quiet."

"You're complaining they're not making noise?"

"There should be music and laughing. Plus they're probably hungry."

"It's eight. They would have eaten dinner before coming over."

Allison groaned. "Seriously? Teenagers are always hungry."

Erica looked uncertain. "You're suggesting I talk to them?"

"You could offer to bring in pizza or something."

"I don't want to get in the way."

"You're not joining the game. You're doing the mom thing."

Erica worried her lower lip. "Summer doesn't invite her friends over very often. She said when they were younger, it was because I was always at work. Now it's just a habit. I don't want to mess up the evening."

"You won't. Offer them food and see what happens."

"Come with me?"

The request surprised her, but Allison nodded. "Of course."

Together they went downstairs. The teens were talking, but it was still too quiet. The four of them looked up. Summer sat up.

"What's up, Mom?"

"I wondered if anyone was hungry. We could order pizza."

"That would be great," one of the friends said eagerly. "I'm starved."

"Me, too."

Summer grinned. "I guess we're interested."

Erica pulled out her phone. "Then I'll place an order. Who wants what?"

There was an intense discussion of toppings, vegetarian versus meat and an extra-cheese debate. In the end Erica ordered four pizzas, a dozen chocolate chip cookies and soda.

"I'll let you know when they arrive," Erica said, slipping her phone into her pocket.

"Thanks, Mom."

"Anytime."

Allison turned to leave when one of the teens, Varina, said, "Ms. S, can I ask you a question about waxing?"

Summer groaned and sank onto her back. "No. Ripping out your hair by the roots is not natural."

"Ancient Egyptians waxed," Avery said, her tone mild.

"You're making that up."

"Maybe but women have been removing hair from their bodies for thousands of years."

Varina ignored them both. "I want to wax my brows but my mom says I'm too young. Plucking takes forever and it hurts. I'd rather get all the pain over with at once."

"Brow waxing should only be done by a professional," Erica said. "It's easy to mess up. You want the right shape for your face."

Avery leaned toward her. "Is it true that if you keep waxing or plucking, eventually the hairs don't grow back?"

Erica nodded. "You can damage the follicle, so you want to

be careful. You're not going to be sixteen forever and when you're in your fifties, you'll want eyebrows." She looked at Varina. "We do consultations. Make an appointment and bring your mom. She can ask all her questions. Once she's comfortable, she might be more likely to say yes."

Varina sighed. "She would never agree to that."

"Offer a compromise. If she really listens to the consultation, you'll respect her answer. If it's no, you won't bring up waxing for at least six months." Erica grinned. "Moms will do a lot to not be bugged."

"That might work."

"I'd love some makeup tips," Avery said eagerly.

Erica glanced at Summer, then back at her friend. "You probably want to get back to your game."

"No! Don't say that."

"This is fun."

Summer groaned. "I knew this would happen. You can't help it, Mom. What you do is interesting to my friends. I'm okay with it if you are."

Allison had no idea what they were talking about. Erica had been doing great with Summer's friends. The conversation had been fun and organic. Did Summer really hate the whole beauty thing that much?

Summer scrambled to her feet. "Everyone grab a chair from the kitchen table. We're going upstairs."

"Are you sure?" Erica asked.

"Yes, but give me your phone to monitor the front door. Everyone will be so mesmerized by 'the room,' they won't notice the pizza guy is at the door."

Erica handed over her phone. The teens all grabbed a chair. Allison followed along, into Erica's huge bedroom.

Allison had never been in it before. There was a large bed with what she would guess was custom bedding that coordinated with beautiful floor-to-ceiling draperies. She wanted to pause and admire all of it, but everyone else was walking into the bathroom, so she went with them, only to come to a stop and stare in amazement.

The bathroom was at least triple the size she'd expected. There was a big walk-in shower and a stand-alone tub, along with the obligatory double vanity. But the showpiece was a wall of mirrors with a makeup station. Erica flipped a switch and lights went on around the table, providing what Allison would guess was professional lighting for any occasion.

Summer had her friends sit in a semicircle. Erica insisted Allison take the padded chair by the vanity.

"You'll be my model."

Allison started to protest. "Do one of the girls. They're all so young and beautiful."

"You're hardly old. I'll do you first, then each of them. We can bring the pizza up here and have a makeup party." Erica looked at her daughter. "If that's all right."

"I'm always up for a party. Plus, I can figure out what look I like best for prom."

Erica pushed one of the mirrors. It swung open, revealing shelves filled with foundations, eye shadows, mascaras, blushes, all unopened. One shelf was filled with brushes, sponges and a few things Allison didn't recognize.

"It's like a fancy department store," she said.

"I get a lot of samples. I used to bring them home for Summer and me to play with, but she outgrew the game. But the sales reps still drop off products for me to try."

By the truckload, Allison thought, even as she tried to remember the last time she'd bothered with makeup. Around her, Summer's friends looked equally amazed and delighted.

Varina looked at Summer. "You're so lucky. You have all this at home and your mom knows exactly what to do. She can teach you everything."

Summer smiled at Erica. "I guess I am kind of lucky."

"As am I," Erica said with a laugh. "All right. Allison first. I'm thinking something sultry."

"I'm a few weeks from giving birth and not sleeping. No one needs to see me sultry."

"It'll be fun. Trust me."

Summer's friends didn't leave until nearly midnight. Erica dropped each of them off before driving back home. She expected to walk into a dark downstairs—Allison had gone to bed nearly two hours before—but the kitchen lights were still on and Summer was waiting at the island.

"Why aren't you in bed?" Erica asked.

"I was waiting for you."

"It's late."

"I'm not sleepy." Summer traced a pattern on the quartz. "Tonight was fun. Thanks for doing everyone's makeup."

"I had a good time."

The teens had been good company. Tomorrow she would thank Allison for suggesting pizza. That simple act had allowed Erica to spend time with her daughter and her friends. She wasn't looking to join the group but appreciated the chance to check in with all of them.

Erica sat next to her daughter. "You have great friends."

"I know. They've all been totally there for me while other kids at school have been so mean about Dad."

"You'd said it was getting better. Has that changed?"

Summer shook her head. "No. I get a few comments, but not every day. I told Donovan what was happening, in case he wanted to take someone else to prom."

That was news, Erica thought. "What did he say?"

"He told me he would take on anyone who messed with me." Her daughter looked at her. "As a friend, Mom. We're not dating."

"So you've told me."

"I want to make sure you believe me."

Erica smiled. "I do." She made an X over her heart. "I promise I'm not secretly hoping you fall in love with Donovan. But I'm curious if there's anyone you like."

Summer shrugged a couple of times. "I don't know. Sometimes I think a guy is cute but I'm not sure that's enough. The good-looking guys are so self-centered and the jocks can be jerks. The nerdy guys all run away when I say hi."

Erica tried not to laugh. "Wow, that's a lot of generalizing and making assumptions. I know stereotypes exist for a reason, but a lot of times it's not for a *good* reason. Maybe you'd like to get to know a few of these guys rather than lumping them into groups."

"Oh, but that's so mature. You know I hate that."

They smiled at each other.

"You don't have to date," Erica said. "If you're not interested or don't feel ready, then it's fine. Take your time. It's like the whole hair-and-makeup thing we did tonight. Your friends love it, but it's not your thing. Embrace that."

"Sometimes I feel out of step."

"I always felt that," Erica told her. "Sometimes I still do. The softball moms are great, but we have nothing in common. They don't have jobs, let alone a career. They're all married and I'm single."

"You're not single. You have Killion."

Erica remembered too late that she'd never explained her somewhat transactional relationship with the man and it was probably best she never did.

"Killion and I aren't serious," she said instead. "We like each other, but we're not madly in love."

Summer looked at her as if she was an idiot. "Mom, the man's crazy about you. Of course you're in love."

Erica leaned back in her chair. "I'm not. We're friends and have similar interests."

Summer rolled her eyes. "I can't believe you won't admit how you feel. Plus, Killion is so in love with you. We can all see it." She frowned. "Are you holding back because of me? I think he's great. He supports you and he's not intimidated by your success. You can marry him, Mom. It's totally fine. He would be a great stepdad."

"No one is getting married." Erica heard the shrillness in her voice. She consciously breathed and spoke more softly.

"No one is getting married," she repeated. "We're not in love. We have a convenient relationship. Nothing more."

Summer didn't look convinced. "Uh-huh. Sure. You're scared. That's so strange. Nothing scares you."

"I'm not afraid. I'm not anything. We're not getting married."

As if she would ever do that. She also wasn't in love but repeating that seemed to be belaboring the point.

Summer got off the stool. "So you've said. You seem extra weird tonight. Maybe you need some sleep." Her daughter hugged her. "Night."

"Sleep well."

Summer waved, then headed for the stairs. Erica got up, then sat back down again. Married? Married! No and no. There was no commitment, no expectation and certainly no being in love. Not by either of them. She'd been very clear with Killion from the start. She liked what they had and didn't want it to change, but if he pushed her, she would push back. Hard.

28

Allison paced the length of her bedroom, then turned and walked the other way. She told herself she was fine, to keep breathing. She was imagining what was happening. She wasn't feeling any pain and she certainly wasn't in labor. She still had two weeks to go.

"Relax," she whispered as she walked, ignoring the cramping in her back. "I'm fine. It's a false alarm."

She put her hands on her belly. "Stay in there, little girl. You need time to grow more. I know two weeks doesn't seem like much, but every day is important. Not yet. Not yet."

She had more to say but a contraction claimed her, reaching across her belly and nearly making her cry. She sank onto the bed and did her best to breathe through it.

"No," she whispered when she could speak again. "You can't come early. You can't."

"You've been quiet since you arrived," Killion said as he minced a shallot.

"Have I?" Erica ran her fingers up and down the stem of the cosmopolitan he'd made for her that she had yet to taste. "I don't mean to be. Tell me about your day."

Because getting him to talk was a whole lot easier than trying to explain what was happening in her head. Normally she was so calm and rational. She thought things through, made plans. She used logic and experience, and if she didn't feel comfortable with her own knowledge, she hired experts. She was cool, calm and always in control. Until two nights ago when her daughter had oh so casually announced that Killion would make a great stepfather and Erica should marry him.

Since then, she'd thought of little else. The horror of it had started small but it consumed her now to the point where she was nearly frantic. Love? Love? No. Not her, not ever. She'd loved Peter and look what had happened. He'd hurt her more deeply than she had known possible. Worse, she hadn't seen it coming. She'd been happy and in love and planning the rest of their lives together when he'd already been gone.

She'd been a fool, which she could accept, but she'd also been devastated, which she wouldn't allow to happen again.

"I heard from Cari," Killion said, drawing her back to the conversation.

Erica struggled to place the name. "Your youngest?"

"Yes. She and her partner, Melonie, are planning a trip to Seattle. I thought it would be a good time for us all to get together."

Yes, the infamous and frightening *I'd like you to meet my daughters.* Scary then and even more terrifying now.

Some of what he said sunk in. "Is Melonie a woman?" Because these days, one was never sure.

"She is."

"You never said your youngest daughter was a lesbian."

He used his knife to push the shallots into a small bowl. "I never said my oldest daughter was straight, either."

"Fair enough."

His gaze settled on her face. "Is that a problem? The lesbian thing?"

"What? God, no. Love is love."

Honestly his daughter's sexual preferences had absolutely nothing to do with any of her problems. She could be involved in some dinosaur romance for all Erica cared. Which apparently was a thing in the erotic world. She'd stumbled on one by accident, browsing on her e-reader. The sample she'd read had possibly scarred her for life.

Which was neither relevant nor the point but was instead an example of how undisciplined her brain was right now. She needed to deal with what was wrong so she could start acting and thinking normally again.

She picked up her drink, put it down untasted, then looked at Killion.

"I'm not in love with you and we're not getting married."

Nothing about his expression changed as his dark green gaze met hers. "So we're done talking about my daughters and getting together for brunch."

"Apparently."

He wiped his hands on a towel. They were in his kitchen, the island between them. Erica appreciated the physical barrier—in some strange way, it made her feel more secure. Not that she was afraid of Killion. Of the two of them, she knew she was the more emotionally dangerous.

"I don't recall proposing and I've never told you I love you," he said, his voice calm and reasonable. "What brought on your announcement?"

She felt her face flushing. "Several things. Mostly Summer. The other night she mentioned she thought you would be a good stepfather and that we should get married." Erica paused. "Actually she asked me if she was the reason we weren't married."

"I hope you explained that marriage was never on the table for us. Neither of us needs the financial connection and socially, there isn't a reason. You enjoy your independence."

"Don't you enjoy yours? Are you saying this is all on me? That if it were up to you we'd be married and then what? Sharing a house? Having more children? That's not happening. I'm forty-eight years old. I'm not interested in having more children."

"Why are you angry?"

His voice was so calm and reasonable, which made her want to throw something.

"I'm not. I'm telling you where I am. I don't want to marry you. I'm sorry if that hurts your feelings."

He studied her, as if trying to figure out what was going on. She hoped he didn't ask, because she didn't have any answers. She understood she was overreacting. Killion had never proposed or even hinted he wanted more—so why was she so mad at him? But logic ended there. While her brain continued to process and point out she was making a fool of herself, every other part of her was six emotions past terrified. She lashed out to protect herself. She wanted to throw something at his head, then bolt for safety.

"Are you afraid you're in love with me, or could be?" he asked.

He sounded more curious than concerned, which should have made her feel better but didn't.

"I want to say you'll be safe if you love me," he continued. "I would do my best never to hurt you, but being that close to someone means the hurts are inevitable. Signals get crossed or misread. Emotions bump into each other in the night. There's pain.

"I wouldn't leave you," he added, again as calmly as if discussing adding capers to the sauce. "I've often thought the suddenness of Peter going was as much a part of what damaged you as the pain of it. He was cruel and he knew how to hurt you where it wouldn't show."

The flush returned, deeper this time. "You don't know that. I never told you the details."

"I know enough to guess the rest."

"I wasn't damaged."

"We're all damaged. For what it's worth, you would hurt me, as well. It happens. But we would talk about it, learn from the experience and do better. When it's good between people, that's what they do."

He continued to watch her. "I am in love with you, by the way. In case it matters."

If she'd been capable of speech, she would have shrieked. Or screamed. As it was, she could only stand there, probably not breathing, telling herself he hadn't just said what he said.

"You just went completely white. Not the sign I was hoping for."

Sadness flashed in his beautiful eyes and then there was no emotion at all. She would guess he'd retreated somewhere safe because Killion knew her as well as she knew herself and he could guess what she was going to say next.

"Don't," she breathed. "Don't love me. I don't want that. I want what we had. It was nice, but not important. We were convenient and we got along and nothing about our relationship mattered."

He stiffened slightly, as if the words wounded, but she couldn't deal with that. Or him. Or anything.

"There's no love," she said. "And now everything's ruined. I can't be with you anymore." She turned, searching for her handbag. It was where she always left it—on the small desk by the pantry.

She ran toward it, circling around to avoid Killion, but he didn't try to stop her. Instead he watched her with unreadable eyes. She had a brief thought she was being cruel, that later she would regret her words and her actions, but the need to escape was too strong for her to listen to her better angels.

She was halfway to her car when her phone buzzed with an incoming text. She almost didn't look at the screen—whatever he had to say, she didn't want to listen. But the text wasn't from Killion at all.

Allison's in labor. Meet us at the hospital.

Erica stared at the message. "But she's not due for two weeks. This is too early."

Which was a stupid thing to say. The baby was coming now and Allison needed her.

On my way, she texted before driving away without once looking back.

Erica shoved the bag of tennis balls behind Allison's back. "Better?" she asked.

"No."

The pathetic, nearly mewing sound of Allison's voice worried Erica a whole lot more than the early labor. The pregnant mom-to-be had mostly been crying since Erica had arrived, barely responding to questions and not reacting to much of anything except when a contraction caused her body to arch as if she were being electrocuted.

According to the medical staff, her vitals were acceptable and she was progressing normally, albeit slowly.

Erica had arrived to find her mom with Allison as she was being admitted to the hospital. Allison had been pale and shaking, moaning that it was too soon. The baby couldn't come this soon.

Erica had taken charge, announcing that she was the birthing coach and getting Allison through the tedious paperwork she should have already filled out but hadn't.

"You should have taken your imminent delivery date more seriously," she said as she pointed to yet another place for Allison to sign.

"I'm taking it seriously now," Allison had snapped before straining against a contraction.

Once she'd been admitted, Erica had asked Mara to bring her more comfortable shoes, a pair of yoga pants and a couple of T-shirts. At the rate Allison wasn't dilating, she could be here for a while.

Five hours later, the two of them were still in the labor room, waiting for Baby Bethany to make her appearance.

"I have ice chips," Erica said, trying to sound upbeat and cheerful.

Allison lay on her side, her back to Erica. "Go away, leave me alone."

"Not happening. You're stuck with me. Once you pop out that kid, I'm outta here, so if you really don't want me around, then that should be an incentive to move things along."

"I can't do this," Allison whispered.

Erica walked around the bed to face her. "What can't you do?"

Tears leaked out of her tightly closed eyes. "Have this baby."

"All evidence to the contrary? What's going on with you? I know things suck but you've always been excited about Bethany. She's going to be your little girl. You love her."

Allison's eyes opened and she half sat up. "This is my fault. She's early because of the stress. What if something's wrong? I did that to her. Me! I'm her mother and I've already hurt her."

Erica had tried being nice. Maybe it was time for a little tough love. "Stop whining. You heard the doctor when she was in here before. She said Bethany's heart rate is strong and she's not in any distress. There's no reason to think there's a problem, so let's not create one. You're in labor. Like it or not, you're having that baby tonight if I have to dig in there myself and pull her out."

Allison glared at her. "You're not putting your hands any-where near my girl parts."

"It's not like I want to, but one of us has to be the grown-up here and it sure as hell isn't you."

"What happened to compassion?"

"You've annoyed it right out of me."

Allison struggled into a sitting position. "You have no right to act like this. Your life is perfect. Fucking perfect. You have everything. I'm homeless and pregnant and my husband's in jail where he's going to stay for a long time."

Her voice rose with every word. "He's not here. He's not here! He's supposed to be with me and he's not and I don't know when he's going to see his daughter. He did horrible things and he broke me."

Allison covered her face with her hands and began to sob. "He broke me," she repeated. "There's nothing left."

With that she collapsed on the bed and turned away. Another contraction ripped through her, causing her to gasp and writhe, but she didn't cry out.

Erica stared at her friend. She was at a genuine loss as to how to deal with what Allison was going through. Obviously everything had hit her at once and having the baby come early had pushed her over the edge. So what was the solution? Loving support or yet more tough love?

She circled the bed and pulled up a chair, then got in Allison's face.

"Don't you dare say he broke you," she said, her voice soft but forceful. "Don't you dare. He doesn't get to break you. He's a weak, cowardly asshole who fooled both of us. You didn't do anything wrong. All this is on him. All of it. But you know what? You're going to get through it because you're strong, you're smart and you're not going to let that poor excuse of a man mess up your life. You have two babies who need you and you're not going to let them down, either."

Erica took her hand and squeezed her fingers. "I'm right here and I swear to God, I'm not going anywhere. No matter what happens, I'm here. We'll figure it out as we go. First, you need to deliver Bethany. The rest of it will take care of itself."

More tears spilled onto her blotchy cheeks. "What if she's not okay?"

"Then we'll deal with that. Both of us. You and me. Honestly, is there anything you think I can't do?"

That earned her a faint smile. "You're not that spectacular in the kitchen."

Another contraction claimed her. Allison whimpered as she squeezed Erica's hand hard enough to snap bone.

"I would think the epidural would be working by now," Erica muttered when the contraction passed and she could pull her hand away and massage it.

"I think it is. This is just the extra pain."

"Yet another reason I'm glad I stopped with just the one kid."

Allison stared at her. "I'm so scared."

"I know and I'm right here. Even when you're pushing out poop and other gross things, I'll be telling you what to do and staying through it all."

"I miss him, which makes me a fool, but I do."

Erica was less sure what to say to that. "You're going to have quite the story to share with him when you finally see him." She touched Allison's head. "It's going to be all right. I promise."

"I'm holding you to that."

"You should. I'm someone you can count on."

Allison shuffled down the corridor toward the NICU. She was sore, she was exhausted and she was alone. After Bethany had been born, when the doctor on duty had assured them that while the newborn would need a couple of days of extra care, all signs were good and she should be going home in about seventy-two hours, Allison had insisted Erica leave and get some sleep. Erica, being Erica, had protested, but had finally agreed with the understanding she would be back in a few hours.

Allison had tried to rest herself, but she was on call for feedings every two hours. She was going to try to get Bethany to breastfeed, but if that didn't work, she would pump her breast milk so her baby girl had the best start to her new life.

She stepped into the entrance to the NICU and smiled wearily at the nurse.

"Reporting for duty," she said lightly.

"Right on time."

The nurse got Allison settled in a large, comfortable padded chair with big arms to offer support. Bethany was brought over.

She looked good, with plenty of color and a shock of brown hair. She was getting oxygen and being kept warm, but other than the monitors attached to her, she looked like any normal, albeit small, newborn.

The nurse pulled several curtains so Allison had privacy as she opened her robe, exposing her left breast. She settled Bethany in her arm, shifting her so they were skin-on-skin.

"Let's see if we can get her to latch on," the nurse said quietly. "If not, you can pump, so there's no pressure."

Allison nodded as she moved her breast so her nipple was by her daughter's tiny mouth. She stroked her cheek, then tickled the corner of her mouth.

"Come on, sweetie," she whispered. "Aren't you hungry?"

She knew there was milk. Her breasts were full and ached. She kept encouraging Bethany to start nursing, blowing softly on the top of her head, then offering her her nipple again. Finally the baby's tiny mouth parted. Allison eased her nipple inside and waited. Seconds later she felt the first tug.

"She's doing it," she whispered, looking at the nurse. "She's nursing."

"Excellent. Keep her on that breast until she stops, then switch her to the other side. She may not latch on twice, but she's getting something, which is great. Right now her stomach is about the size of a cherry, so don't worry about volume. When she's done, you can pump the rest. Her stomach will get bigger over the next few days. Within a couple of weeks, you'll figure out how long it takes her to nurse. Some babies need thirty minutes, others are done in fifteen. As long as she's growing and putting on weight as we expect, then you're doing great. If you start to have trouble, we have lactation resources."

The nurse smiled. "That's enough for now. I'll check back in a few."

She left Allison with her baby. Bethany continued to breast-feed for several more minutes. Allison watched her, feeling love fill every cell in her body. What had seemed so hopeless a few hours ago was now possible. Bethany had been born and she was going to be all right.

"You have a big brother," she whispered, stroking her daughter's cheek. "His name is Jackson and he's very excited to meet you. He's with Grandma Mara right now."

The older woman had promised to look after him until Allison was home. Summer was pitching in, as well. Erica would also be there. Erica who had bullied and cajoled and supported Allison through one of the roughest days of her life.

"You're going to meet Erica," she continued, her voice soft. "And Summer, and you're going to love them so much. They're good people with big hearts."

Tears burned, but she blinked them away. "Your daddy can't be with us. He's in jail because it turns out he's a bad man. I'm sorry about that. I know it makes for a more difficult start. The thing is, I didn't know him at all. The man I fell in love with was so different. Kind and gentle and caring. He rescued me and allowed me to believe in love again. I trusted him and he betrayed all of us."

She wanted to say he'd broken her, but Erica was right. She was a little shattered, but she wasn't broken. She would heal from all this and be stronger than she had been before. Oh, there would be scars—she would be a lot less trusting and a lot more wary, but maybe that wasn't a bad thing.

Bethany drew back a little and looked at her.

"All done with that one? Let's try the other side."

She shifted her newborn carefully and got Bethany in position. Her baby immediately latched on to her breast and sucked hard.

"You're hungry, huh? That's good."

She closed her eyes and told herself she would sleep soon. Maybe just for an hour, but at least it was something. For a second she allowed herself to pretend that she wasn't holding Peter's baby. That Levi stood right outside the door, watching her, thrilled that they had the baby they'd always wanted.

If only, she thought, then shook her head. No if only. Levi was gone, taken by a cruel quirk of DNA, and he was never coming back. She had to stay in the real world. She had her kids to take care of and a life to start over. She might not have Levi anymore and she still had to deal with Peter, but she wasn't alone. She had a family and she knew that no matter what, they would be there for her.

29

"You know you can go the speed limit," Allison said from the back seat, where she sat beside Bethany's car seat.

"Shut up."

Erica gripped the steering wheel with both hands. The short drive from the hospital to the house seemed fraught with danger. Too many drivers were idiots and she had special cargo.

"You're going what? Twenty? Cars are backing up behind you."

"I'm being careful. We have a newborn in the car. Be grateful."

"I'd rather be home."

Erica shot her a look in the rearview mirror. "You have a lot of attitude for someone who gave birth three days ago."

"They gave me a vitamin B12 shot. I'm ready to take on the world."

"For real?"

"No. I have to pee, but at the rate you're driving, it's going to happen in the car."

"Cross your legs. We're nearly there."

She stayed under the speed limit and in the right lane the rest of the way, then made a wide, slow turn onto the long drive-way. When she pulled into the garage, the door burst open and Mara, holding Jackson, and Summer rushed out to greet them.

"Mommy, Mommy, Mommy!"

The little boy was frantic. Allison unfastened her seat belt.

"You take care of him," Erica said, turning off the engine. "We'll get Bethany."

Allison hurried to her son, who threw himself at her and started crying.

"I know," she said, holding him. "It was too long. But I'm home now."

Summer joined her mother. "You're back. I can't wait to see her." She opened the back door and studied the sleeping baby. "She's so beautiful."

Summer carefully unfastened the car seat, then lifted it out of the car. Erica grabbed all the bags Allison had collected during her short stay in the hospital. The baby furniture had been delivered, so everything was ready for the little family.

Still holding Jackson, Allison came over to them. "Thank you so much for taking care of him."

Mara lightly touched Bethany's cheek. "He was so good. He ate well and we played a lot and ran around outside."

"He was in day care in the mornings," Summer added. "Mom took him and Grandma picked him up. We thought keeping him on a regular schedule was important." She tickled the little boy. "He slept great."

They all went into the house. Allison tried to show Bethany to Jackson but he was more interested in demonstrating how he could climb the stairs with only a little help.

"We've been working on that every morning," Mara said with a laugh. "It was good exercise for me."

"You're growing up so fast," Allison told her son. "What a big, big boy."

He beamed.

Summer handed Erica Bethany in her car seat. "You take her upstairs, Mom. I think I need a little more baby practice before I'm comfortable doing that."

Erica hadn't carried a newborn in nearly sixteen years, but she told herself it was like riding a bike. At least she hoped it was.

Plus, Bethany was all strapped in and there was a handle from the removeable part of the car seat.

They made it to the second floor. Jackson broke free of his mother's hand and started shrieking.

"New, Mommy. New!"

"What's new?" Allison glanced at them. "Tell me you didn't buy Bethany a pony."

"Not yet," Mara said cheerfully as she pushed open a door. "But the furniture fairies did put in an appearance."

Erica hung back as everyone else pushed into the room. It was more crowded, but all the new things fit. There was a bassinet by the bed and a fully stocked changing table along the far wall. The rocker was tucked in the corner. A few wall hangings neither she nor Summer had been able to resist brightened the space.

"Look!" Summer raced over to a small refrigerator tucked next to the dresser. "It's for when you pump breast milk. That way you don't have to go downstairs in the middle of the night."

Allison had only been using one side of the bathroom vanity for herself. Summer and Mara had set up the other side with baby supplies.

"Plus the extra stuff is stored in the laundry room," Summer said. "Mom set up a diaper delivery service. You just let them know how many you want each week, and the size, and they'll show up on the following Tuesday. It's cool. Come look at the closet. We put all her clothes away. The normal stuff is from me and Grandma but Mom bought too many girlie things. She's a newborn. How many little dresses does she need?"

Erica kept her gaze on her friend and knew the exact moment Allison started to lose it. She dropped Jackson's hand and crumpled onto the bed, covering her face with her hands. Harsh, ugly sobs shook her body.

"What did I say?" Summer asked, looking scared.

"Nothing. You were perfect."

Erica crossed to the bed and sat down, then put her arm around

Allison. "She's dealing with pregnancy hormones and having a newborn. She's sleeping fifteen minutes at a time. It's a lot."

Allison sniffed and took the tissues Mara offered. "You know I can talk for myself, don't you?"

Erica lowered her voice to a mock whisper. "Sometimes new moms are cranky."

"I'm not cranky. I'm overwhelmed. I can't believe you did all this for me."

"Not just you," Erica pointed out. "Actually very little of it is for you. Most of it is for the kids. When did you get so self-centered?"

Allison managed a shaky smile. "Thank you."

Jackson watched her cautiously, then tugged her hand. "My woom."

"Is he stringing words together?" Allison asked as she wiped her face. "Are you learning sentences?"

He beamed at her, then pulled her to her feet and went across the hall. Allison started toward the room he shared with Summer, but Jackson pointed the other way. Erica hurried to catch up with them.

"Yes, well, we were at the baby store and there was a sale and things got out of hand."

"It's Mom's fault," Summer said cheerfully. "It was her credit card. I'm collateral damage, so you can't blame me."

"You're throwing me under the bus."

"You taught me to put on my own oxygen mask first. That's what I'm doing."

Allison stared at the half-closed door. "What did you do?"

"Oh, it's just a picture or two, and the odd rug," Mara murmured. "A bit of furniture."

Allison pushed open the door and gasped. Jackson ran in and flung himself on the low toddler bed in the shape of a race car. The bright primary colors of the bed were reflected in the racetrack carpet on the floor. The windows were covered with checkered-flag curtains. There were bookshelves, a tiny desk and a toy box that looked like the car engine.

"How did you do this?" Allison asked in amazement. "I was only gone three days."

"Everything was already on order," Erica told her. "The setup took no time at all."

"It kind of happened right after you went to the hospital," Summer said. "Yesterday Jackson took his nap in here. We thought that would be the best way to start him in his toddler bed. Just naps. In a few weeks, when he's ready, he can sleep in here at night. I can leave the bathroom doors open, so he knows I'm right there."

Allison hugged the teen. "You're so amazing. Thank you."

Summer smiled. "He's my brother. I want to be a part of everything in his life. Plus by the time he's ready to sleep here all the time, you'll want the crib for Bethany. Everything works out."

Erica saw Bethany stirring. "I think she's waking up. Is it time for a feeding?"

Allison smiled wearily. "She eats every two hours. It's always time for a feeding."

Mara distracted Jackson with the promise of a game in the yard and took him downstairs. Erica took the car seat into Allison's room and put the newborn on the bed.

"You going to be all right?" she asked.

Allison nodded. "I'm a pro. I'll be down when she's asleep."

"Why don't you get some sleep yourself? We'll wake you for dinner."

"I need to spend time with Jackson."

"We'll keep him busy for as long as we can, then we'll wake you."

Allison glanced longingly at the bed. "I know I should be strong, but I really need sleep. Thank you."

Erica and Summer walked out, closing the bedroom door behind them.

"This is so great," the teen said as they went downstairs. "Bethany's tiny. I know Jackson was small, too, but it feels like a long time ago."

"It's easy to forget how they start out. You were once that small."

"I've seen pictures, but even so, it's hard to imagine. Were you scared when you brought me home from the hospital?"

"Terrified. Your grandmother stayed with us for two weeks, which made all the difference. Although when it was time for her to go, I cried and begged her to stay."

Summer grinned. "That will be me one day."

"You're planning on having kids?" Erica asked. "You've never mentioned it."

"I've never *not* wanted kids. I'm sixteen. I'd like to wait to think about it for a while."

Erica touched her shoulder. "I promise I won't try to guilt you into having grandbabies. I'd like them, but it's your life. You have to do what feels right."

Summer sat at the kitchen table. "I want to believe you," she teased. "But I'm not sure you'll be able to hold back."

Erica settled across from her. "You'll be amazing. But speaking of having babies—"

Her daughter's eyes widened. "We weren't. Not really."

Erica ignored that. "We need to get you into your doctor for your annual. While we're there, let's talk about getting you on birth control. There are a couple of low-dose options that are easy for a young woman your age to manage."

Summer's eyes widened and her cheeks flushed. "OMG! Mom, what are you talking about?"

"Birth control."

Summer looked around, then lowered her voice. "Stop saying that out loud."

Erica hid her amusement. "So I should text the words."

"I don't know, but you don't just say that stuff in front of people."

"Allison's upstairs and Mom's out with Jackson. It's just us mice."

"Ugh. Does anything bother you? I don't need to be on— you know."

"You don't now, but things change. Better to be protected. I know they cover this in sex ed, but to be clear, birth control doesn't protect you from STDs. That's a whole different topic." She paused. "I'll get you some condoms, too."

Summer's blush turned scarlet. "I can't believe you said this. We're not talking about this. It's too humiliating."

"It's just sex and staying healthy."

"For you!" Her voice was a shriek. "I'm sixteen. You're my mother! You're not supposed to know about sex or do it or talk about it. You're just not."

Erica couldn't help smiling. "You shock me. I thought you were so together and mature."

"I am. But not about—" she lowered her voice "—that."

Erica patted her hand. "I see we have more work to do on this topic and this really isn't the time. In a few days when no one's around we'll a have a heart-to-heart. In the meantime, try to avoid contact with a boy's penis."

Summer sprang to her feet and threw up her arms. "Stop!"

"Saying penis?" Erica couldn't hide her amusement. "You're weird, kid. Should I call it a pee-pee? Is that better?"

"Why do we have to talk about it at all?"

"Because most girls like to play with them and they can be dangerous."

Summer covered her face with her hands. "Fine. We'll talk. Just not today when anyone could walk in. Please. I beg you."

"I'll stop."

"Thank you." She sank back in her seat. "You're a nightmare.

Although I'm not sure talking to Allison would be that much easier. She sleeps with my dad. Maybe Killion, except he's a guy, so no." She frowned. "We haven't seen him in a while. Is he coming over tonight?"

The unexpected question landed like a body blow. Erica wanted to crumble to the floor, where she could pull her knees to her chest and hold in the pain. Because of course Killion wasn't coming over for dinner. He wasn't ever going to see her again. She'd made it clear they were finished, and he was the kind of man who listened.

Breaking up with him had been the right thing to do but living with the consequences sucked. She missed him. A thousand times a day she thought of something to tell him. After Allison had given birth, she'd automatically phoned him, barely stopping the call before it went through.

"No, Killion's busy with a business deal."

She didn't usually lie to her daughter but she wasn't ready to admit what had happened. She didn't want the questions, less so from Summer than from her mother. Mara would see through to the real reason she'd done it.

"I wish he could be here tonight," the teen said. "We'd have the whole family together." She hesitated. "Except for Dad. Does he know Bethany was born?"

"I haven't asked Allison."

"It's got to be hard for him, knowing his daughter was born but he can't see her and he wasn't there. Allison's really strong, you know? The way she's handled this. It's because she has us. Well, mostly you, but us. I like having them live here."

Erica smiled at her. "I do, too. When you suggested it, I was furious and unwilling and a bunch of other negative things, but it's worked out. So how about dinner? I'm thinking takeout. None of us wants to cook. We could overorder so Allison can eat the leftovers all night. We'll get healthy starting tomorrow."

She waited for Summer to start suggesting places but instead her daughter stared at the table.

"I have a summer job."

There was a change in topic. "All right. You said you wanted one. It's probably a good idea, if you're not going to softball camp."

"I'm not. I meant what I said about letting that go." She glanced at Erica. "So I applied at this company that has a summer program for teens. It's for eight weeks and you rotate through different departments, learning about the business. I'm not sure how much I'm going to actually help the place, but I'll learn a lot."

"That sounds great. Is it like what we do at Twisted?" She'd started a teen program about ten years ago. Students applied and were chosen based on a series of interviews.

"Mom, it *is* at Twisted. I applied and was accepted into the program." She wrinkled her nose. "I have Dad's last name so I got through the preliminary discussions without anyone knowing who I was, but Emmy does the final interview and she's known me since I was a kid."

Erica tried to understand. "I don't understand. You applied at Twisted for the summer?"

Summer nodded.

"But you hate what I do."

Her daughter slumped on the table. "I don't hate it. I don't understand it or respect it." She sat up. "Sometimes it was easy to dismiss what you did. Dad always said kind of mean things. I didn't get it before but since he's been in jail, I've had time to think. I'm not saying I want to do hair, but you run a really big business. You're successful and strong and stuff. There's a lesson there."

Now it was Erica's turn to fight tears. She felt like one big emotional mess.

"I didn't know you'd applied."

"I asked Emmy not to tell you and I told her to hire me or

not, based on merit. I don't know if she listened. I mean I am your daughter." She smiled. "I'm kind of excited to see what all you do there. Allison's always talking about how she enjoys her work and how great the salon is. She really loves it there. So does Grandma."

Erica told herself not to make a big deal about it. Her daughter working at Twisted. She would take that as a win.

"So takeout," Summer said, pulling out her phone. "Does Allison have any food restrictions? She's nursing so there's that." She looked at Erica. "If I do a search on what nursing mothers can't eat, is it going to gross me out?"

"I doubt they're going to mention the word *penis*, so you'll be fine."

"Mom!" She looked over her shoulder. "Stop saying that. It's wrong coming from a parent."

Erica smiled. "Sometimes you're so mature, I worry you won't be my little girl anymore. It's nice to know you still have some growing up to do."

"Whatever. Just stop saying that word!"

30

Allison knew she had to get some sleep. She was exhausted and her daughter's next meal service was in an hour. But while her body was ready to surrender, her brain was too busy swirling and dipping, trying to process all that had happened.

It was nearly one in the morning and the house was quiet. Still she got up and pulled on her robe, then tucked the baby monitor into her pocket. She walked barefoot down the hall.

Erica's door was shut, but a light was on. She knocked lightly.

Seconds later the door opened and Erica looked at her, brows drawn together with concern. "Are you all right? Is it Bethany? Are we—"

"We're fine," Allison said quickly in a low voice. "Nothing's wrong. I just thought... I don't know. Can we talk?"

"It's one in the morning."

"I know. Is this a bad time?"

Erica stepped back and let her in, then closed the door. "No, I was awake. I guess I was just stating the obvious."

They looked at each other, then glanced away. Allison thought about the surprises she'd come home to—the new furniture, Jackson's room.

"You've done too much," she said.

Erica returned to her large bed and got in one side. She patted the other side, then settled back against the stack of pillows.

"I've done just the right amount. How are you feeling?"

"Tired. No, exhausted, but happy. Bethany's doing well. She's eating great and sleeping and pooping."

"Every mother's dream," Erica teased.

Allison slid into the big bed and leaned against the stack of pillows. "These are nice. Very comfortable."

"I'm a pillow person. The more the better."

Allison thought about her bed at the house she'd shared with her husband. "Peter hates pillows. Give him one flat one and he's happy. He thinks any extras are silly."

"The man is flawed."

Allison didn't want to think about that. At some point she was going to have to deal with her husband and what had happened between them, but not tonight.

"Does he know?" Erica asked. "About Bethany?"

So much for not talking about it. "I haven't told him." She hesitated. "I wasn't sure how to get a message to him, then I didn't know what to say when he made his usual call. She's early so it's not like—"

"Stop," Erica said quietly. "You don't have to explain to me. I just wondered."

"Not yet. I'll go see him in a few days and tell him."

"How are you feeling physically? Not just the tired part, but the rest of it."

"You mean passing a baby the size of a bowling ball?" Allison did her best not to shift on the bed. "Sore. Bleeding. Puffy. Slightly beat up."

"So good?"

She laughed. "Better every day." Her humor faded. "I need to get my life together."

"You have a healthy newborn and an adorable little boy. I'm not sure things can be better than that."

"I've been drifting."

"You've been dealing with a ton of crap. Give yourself a break."

"I need a plan. When I put one together, will you look at it and be honest with me? I really want your thoughts."

"Hey, when have I not been blunt? It's kind of my thing."

Allison looked at the woman who had rescued her from what could have been a hellish disaster. During the long hours of labor, Erica had been at her side, encouraging her, yelling when necessary. She'd been the one to cut the umbilical cord and place Bethany on her bare belly.

"Where's Killion?"

Erica's expression immediately tightened as she turned away. "It would be awkward if he were with us right now. The bed just isn't that big."

"Why wasn't he here tonight? It was a big family dinner. He's family."

She already knew what had happened—oh, not the particulars, but she'd guessed the second Erica had started talking about what they'd done to Jackson's room. It had all been about her, Summer and Mara. There'd been no mention of Killion at all, and a project like that was something he would happily take on. He liked doing things for Erica—even if his participation was simply to call a guy he knew.

"Killion's busy with work."

Allison continued to watch her friend. "I think that's the first time you've lied to me. What happened?" She held up a hand. "Wait. You broke up with him, didn't you?"

Erica swung back to stare at her. "How did you know?"

"Because he's crazy about you and when it comes to giving your heart, you're a stinking coward."

"I'm not."

Allison thought about what she knew about the end of Erica's marriage to Peter. She was sure it was much worse than she'd been told. As she'd recently learned, her husband had a selfish streak she'd never known was there. There was also a myopic cruelty that if turned on a woman who was still in love with him…

That combined with how Erica had been so out of step with her friends in high school when she'd been more interested in her future dream than in the football captain. Even now, she had trouble connecting with women. She held herself apart, pretending it was because she was busy and they had nothing in common when in truth, she was afraid of rejection.

"I suppose the good news is you're as flawed as the rest of us," Allison said lightly. "Just as frail and broken. It evens the playing field."

"I'm not frail. Why would you say that? I'm a kick-ass bitch. Ask anyone."

"What happened?"

Erica picked at the blanket. "I told him we weren't ever getting married. That ours was a relationship of convenience, nothing more."

Allison winced. "Not exactly what he wanted to hear."

"That's not my problem. We had a deal. He's the one who violated it."

"How?"

She sighed. "He told me he was in love with me so I broke up with him."

"Wow, was that a smart decision."

Erica glared at her. "I don't need a man in my life. I'm fine without him. Better than fine. He was weighing me down."

"Then why do you miss him so much?"

"I don't."

"Two lies in a night. Don't make me think I don't know you."

"Whatever." Erica stared at the far wall. "I might miss him a little, but I'll get over it. I don't love him and I don't want him to love me."

"Of course you do. The man's amazing. He's kind and funny and he thinks you're the most incredible woman ever. He's proud of what you've accomplished, he'd never think less of you. He wouldn't dare give you the world because he knows you'd have more fun winning it yourself. Why wouldn't you be in love with him?"

"Then you date him."

"Erica, be serious!"

Her friend seemed to crumple a little. "I can't do it. I won't. I'm never giving my heart again. You don't know what it was like. Levi was taken from you and I'm not saying that wasn't tragic. It was. But you didn't have a choice and he loved you to the end. Peter didn't love me. When he said he wanted a divorce, he laid me bare and humiliated me. He belittled me. Not just me, but everything I was and wanted to be. I was left with nothing. I can't risk that again."

Allison ached for her. "Killion isn't Peter. He would never hurt you."

"Of course he would. That's what people in relationships do. They hurt each other."

"You know what I mean. He's a different kind of man." A better man, she thought sadly. She could see that now. "He would always be there for you. Trust me on this, Erica, being alone is the worst. Life happens and when it gets bad, you need support. You have your mom and Summer and me, but you need more. If you throw him away, you're going to regret it for the rest of your life."

"That's not true. I barely think about him."

"Three for three," Allison whispered. "I didn't think you were like that."

"Don't say that."

"Then don't lie to me."

Erica looked away then back. "Fine. I miss him, but it will pass."

"And if it doesn't?"

"I don't have an answer for that."

★ ★ ★

Allison sat on the hard plastic seat and waited for the man she was married to. Even after nearly a half-dozen visits, she still hated the sounds and smells of the prison. Everything was too much. Too bright, too stark, too loud, too fraught. It was not a place any sane person wanted to be. Even the visits had a hopeless, desperate quality to them that made her uncomfortable.

After waiting for a few minutes, she saw him walking over to the table. He moved more confidently, as if he was a man expecting only good things to happen. He smiled as he sat across from her.

"Have you talked to Raymond? He's making progress with the feds."

"So he said. Some of the charges have been dropped and he's hopeful about getting some of our money released."

She'd gotten a call that morning from the lawyer. She would be getting half the money in savings and the checking account, along with a mature CD that she planned to cash out as soon as it was released.

"You're going to need some of it," he said as he reached out to touch her hands. "The rest has to go to my lawyer."

"What? He has a thirty-thousand-dollar retainer."

Peter shrugged. "He's spending a lot of time on my case. The money goes fast."

Too fast, she thought bitterly, withdrawing her hands and tucking them on her lap.

Peter didn't seem to notice. Instead he spent the next few minutes talking about his case. She waited, growing more impatient by the second. Okay, yes, she was sitting down and she still had her postpregnancy belly but surely her own husband would eventually notice she'd had the baby.

"Did you want to ask about me?" she asked, interrupting him. "How I am? What's happening in my life?"

He looked at her in surprise. "Allison, what's wrong? I thought you'd want to know what was happening with my case."

"I thought you'd want to know that I had our baby a week ago."

"What? You did?" His gaze dropped to her belly, then returned to her face. He grinned at her. "You had Bethany."

He jumped to his feet and waved over one of the guards. "Allison had our baby! I'm going to hug her now."

The guard shrugged in obvious disinterest. "You've got thirty seconds, then sit back down."

Peter circled the table and pulled her to her feet. "How is she? How are you?" His smile disappeared as he pulled her close. "I wanted to be there. I can't believe I missed our little girl's birth. Are you all right? I'm supposed to be taking care of you, but here I am, putting you through all this."

His arms were familiar. He was thinner than he had been, but still her husband. The man she'd loved and married. The man she had children with.

She pulled the pictures she'd printed from her back pocket and handed them to him. He traced Bethany's face and smiled. "She looks like you. She's so beautiful. She's all right?"

"She's doing great. Jackson isn't sure what he thinks of her, but he's being so good about everything."

They sat back down and he reached for her hands again. "Tell me everything." He turned away, clearly fighting tears. "Who was with you?"

"Erica."

He swung back to stare at her. "Erica was with you in the labor room?"

"Yes. Every second. She was amazing. She took care of me."

"That should have been me." He squeezed her fingers. "I love you, Allison. Just give me a little more time to get this straightened out and we'll be a family again."

He leaned closer. "Remember that place in Astoria where we went on our honeymoon? That little B&B."

She nodded. It hadn't been very fancy, but it had been right on the river. They'd stayed up late every night, sitting on their balcony, watching the water flow by in the moonlight. Being there with Peter had been the first time she'd felt whole since losing Levi. By the time they'd driven back to Seattle, she'd known she'd made the right decision marrying him. She'd believed he would always be there for her, would always love her. She'd known she could depend on him.

She'd been wrong about all of it.

"We'll go back," he said. "Back to that B&B. When I get out."

She wanted to ask how they would pay for it. After all she was raising two children without him. She had minimal skills and expensive childcare. She'd spent three months being afraid, confused and adrift. She needed direction in her life and that meant coming up with a plan.

That was what she thought about while she nursed Bethany. Her family's future. How she was going to take care of them.

She looked at the man she'd loved and no longer knew. "I've spoken with a divorce lawyer," she said quietly. "You'll be served in a few days. It would be better for all of us if you just signed where they said and let me go."

He stared at her, his expression blank. "What did you say?" He half rose, then sank back onto his chair. The tears returned. "No. Allison, no. Not a divorce. Don't do that. Don't cut me off. I love you. You're my world."

"You keep saying that. You tell me how much you love me but what you did to me, to our family, didn't come from a place of love. It came from selfishness and carelessness. You don't care about me. You want to blame me for what you got yourself into, but that's as far as it goes."

"That's not true."

She ignored that. "I could deal with all of it if it was just me, but it's not. Do you know in all the times I've come here you've never once asked about Summer? She's your daughter and it's as if you don't know who she is."

He looked away. "She hasn't bothered to come see me."

"She's sixteen. It's up to you to be the adult. You don't ask about Jackson, you didn't notice I wasn't pregnant. I can't figure out if you've always been self-absorbed or if this is a prison thing, but it doesn't matter. I'm done."

His expression turned pleading as tears slipped down his cheeks. "No. Don't say that. I didn't mean to end up here. I'm sorry. I did it for you. All of it."

"Really? What makes you think I wanted to be married to a criminal? What makes you think I wanted a husband who would risk our future on some stupid scheme? I was happy with what we had. I was content. But you didn't care about that. You thought we should have more and you destroyed what we had. This is on you."

He cried harder. "What about the kids? I'm their father."

"I want you to sign away your rights. When you get out of here, I won't come after you for child support and you won't ever see them again."

"No. Allison, I can't. I love them."

"Not enough to be their father."

The tears dried up as he glared at her. "You're different. You were never like this before. It's Erica, isn't it? This is all her idea."

"She doesn't even know I've talked to a lawyer. She has nothing to do with this." Allison stood. "You were right about one thing. You said she'd take care of me and she has. She's the best person I've ever known and I will always be grateful to her. But more than that, I'm proud to be her friend."

She looked at Peter and knew she would always wonder if he'd really changed that much or if she'd never seen him for who he was.

"Sign the papers and let me go. If you ever loved me, let me go."

She turned and walked away.

"Allison. Allison!"

She ignored the shouts and kept walking. She didn't have to worry about him coming after her—the guards would never let him get away.

Erica stared at the large bouquet of flowers on her credenza. They'd been delivered two days ago, but they were still fresh and beautiful. She'd tucked the card that had come with them in her desk, but she didn't have to get it out to know what it said. She'd memorized the words.

I won't pretend to understand your decision, but I will re-spect it and you. I miss you. Always.

He hadn't called or been in touch. He'd only sent the flowers. It was a very Killion thing to do. He didn't invade her space, but he let her know what he was thinking.

Always. What did that mean? He would always miss her? He would always love her? The latter was completely unacceptable because she didn't want or need his love, but still she wondered.

He'd left a bigger hole than she'd anticipated. There were no funny texts, no quick calls, no delicious meals, no nights in his bed. She kept herself busy—easy enough to do with four salons and all her personal commitments—but she was always aware he wasn't there.

The door to her office opened suddenly and her mother stepped inside.

"Where's Killion?" Mara demanded. "I was finishing with a cut and I realized how long it's been since he's been over. His business trips are always only a few days and he wouldn't go anywhere else without you."

She started toward the desk, then stopped when she saw the flowers. Her mother frowned.

"Did you fight? I can't imagine him messing up so much that he needed to send those."

"We didn't fight."

"Then what?" Her mother settled across from her. "I'm done for the day so I can sit here for as long as it takes."

Erica didn't know what to say. Okay, sure, she could tell the truth, but that would cause her mother to lecture her and she just couldn't handle that right—

"Dammit, Erica. You broke up with him."

"Maybe he broke up with me."

She expected her mother to snap at her, but instead Mara stared at her with what could only be described as pity.

"When?"

"A little before Allison had Bethany."

"That long?" Her mother sighed. "What set you off?"

She thought about protesting she didn't have to be "set off" to make a decision about her life, but knew there wasn't any point. Mara knew her well enough to see through any lies or pretense.

"Everyone thinks I'm in love with him and I'm not. He's convenient, nothing more. I don't care about him."

"But you still miss him."

An excellent point. "He's like a habit. I'll get over him."

"Do you remember when your father left?"

The shift in topic was unexpected. Erica thought back to that time. She'd been young. Barely nine. One day he'd been there and the next he'd been gone. She'd been so confused, so scared and had missed him desperately.

"I cried myself to sleep for nearly a year," she whispered, remembering the pain.

"So did I." Her mother shrugged. "I knew he was a player and not the type to be tied down, but I thought I could change him. I thought what we had was so special that he would want to be a part of it forever."

"But he didn't."

"No. He told me ten years was the most he could give. That he'd tried to make it work, but he couldn't. So he left and we never saw him again. It took me five years to stop missing him and get on with my life."

That long? She hadn't known. "But you acted like you were fine."

"You were my daughter. You didn't need to know about my suffering. You were dealing with your own broken heart. Eventually my game of pretend turned into reality and I was all right." She paused. "But here's the thing. He hurt me so much, I vowed to never risk love again and I haven't."

"There are tons of men in your life."

"Casually, yes, but I don't let them stay. I don't get serious. I'm seventy years old, Erica, and I've lived most of my adult life alone. It was a stupid decision to make then and it's still stupid. The problem is, this is all I know and I'm too old to change. You still have time and you have a wonderful man who loves you. Don't be a fool and don't let Peter win."

"This isn't about Peter."

"Of course it is. He hurt you so badly, you're afraid to take another chance. But Killion is three times the man Peter ever was. You're equals. With him you can be yourself fearlessly. That's a gift. Don't waste your life like I wasted mine."

31

Erica got home a little after ten. She expected the downstairs to be dark, but lights were on in the kitchen, and Allison was rummaging in the refrigerator.

"Your timing is perfect," she said with a laugh. "I just fed Bethany and I'm starving. There's leftover pizza. I'm preheating the oven. Want some?"

Erica wasn't hungry, but she knew she had to eat. She dropped her bag on the island and sat at the kitchen table. "Sure. I'll take a couple of slices." Then she would figure out how to tell her daughter about Killion. Everyone else knew, so it was time.

After school tomorrow, she promised herself. Summer would be devastated, but that couldn't be helped.

Allison opened the oven and slid several slices on the pizza stone, then set the timer. "Five minutes should be enough."

She poured herself a large glass of milk. "Want some wine?"

Erica pushed herself to her feet. "I'll get it."

"Sit. I'm fine. All I've done today is feed the baby and sleep."

Erica eyed her. "And look after Jackson. Plus, weren't you visiting Peter? You must be exhausted."

"I can open a bottle of wine."

Erica sank back in her chair. "Thanks. It's been a long day for me, too."

"Such is the burden of being a tycoon." Allison set a glass of wine in front of her. "Or is something else bothering you?"

Erica held up her hand. "Please don't talk about Killion. I beg you. My mom lectured me earlier. I can't take any more."

"Then I won't mention his name except to say we all miss him."

"I'm sure he misses you as well."

The timer dinged. Allison plated the slices and set them on the table.

Erica inhaled the scent of tomato sauce and oregano, and her stomach growled. She polished off two slices, barely stopping to breathe, then wiped her mouth with a napkin.

"I was hungry."

"I can see that. Did you eat today?"

"No."

"But we're not talking about how much you regret breaking up with Killion?"

"No, we're not."

Allison grinned. "You don't scare me."

"Why should I? You're a nursing mother with a toddler. It's not like I'm going to beat you with a stick if you bring him up again, but I will take my pizza and wine and leave."

"The adult equivalent of taking your marbles?"

"Yes."

"I'd prefer your company so I won't mention him again. At least not on purpose."

"Thank you."

"I have news," Allison said. "I heard from Peter's lawyer. He's getting some money released by the bank."

"That's good." Erica knew Allison worried about not being able to pay for things. She was happy to take care of her friend, but she understood the need to feel at least somewhat independent.

"There's also a CD I'm going to cash in," Allison continued, not meeting her gaze. "It's not a huge amount but between that and the savings, plus the cash I still have from the ten thousand that guy gave me, I could probably pay up-front for a six-month lease on a small apartment."

"No!" Erica blurted. "You're not moving out. Why would you say that? You can't live in a tiny apartment with two kids. Plus you'd be on your own. It's a complete waste of the money."

Her chest got tight and she found it a little difficult to catch her breath. Emotions swelled inside of her but she was unable to name any of them. Worry maybe. A strange sense of loss and abandonment.

Allison looked at her. "I can't live with you forever."

"Why not? You can stay. The house is big and we're all here to help." Of course Allison had to live here. It made sense. "We work. The five of us. Six if you count my mom. Jackson loves living here. Use the money for something else." Her eyes began to burn. "Just don't go."

Allison stood and walked around the table. Erica rose and rushed toward her. They hung on tight.

"I love you, too," Allison whispered. "You're the sister I never had. I'm not trying to scare you because I know you have a whole *I don't love* thing going on, but you have been such a blessing for me."

Erica blinked away tears. "No. I'm the lucky one. I like having you around. I've been so lonely for a friend for so long, but I didn't know how to break out of my shell and trust someone. I didn't want you to move in, but now I don't want you to go." She swallowed. "You're like my sister, too, and I do love you. I can love people. Just not, you know, men."

"I'm sorry Peter did that to you."

"Let's not talk about him, either."

They resumed their seats. Erica took a gulp of her wine.

"Moving to an apartment is a really bad idea. I can't believe you said that."

Allison raised her eyebrows. "Really? We just had that great emotional moment and you're telling me I'm an idiot."

"Not you. The idea."

"I have to move forward with my life. I can't sit around and do nothing forever."

"You just had a baby. You get to take a breath."

Allison leaned forward, then sat back. She put her hands on the table, opened her mouth, then closed it.

"Just say it," Erica told her, fighting worry again. "Whatever it is, we'll deal."

"I want to go to beauty school. I want to be an esthetician. I've been talking to Emmy about it and I've done some research. I can apply now and start in the fall. I'd use the money from the CD and savings to pay for it and—"

"Don't be ridiculous," Erica told her. "Why waste the money? There are scholarships. You can apply through the school. You're going to qualify and you're exactly who they want. You're an older single mother with a clear idea of what it takes to be successful. Women like that do the work because they know they can't afford to fail."

Allison sagged back in her chair. "I thought you were saying going to beauty school was a waste of money."

"No. It's a great idea. I'd tell you that Twisted gives out scholarships, but I have a feeling you'd refuse that. But when you graduate, you can join our apprentice program. You'll learn the right way to do things. When you're licensed, you can stay with the company or go work elsewhere. Although I have to tell you, we're absolutely the best place to work."

"Thank you."

Erica waved away the words. "We had a deal. No more thanking."

"You're giving me a job."

"No, you're earning the job. I'm not giving you anything. If you're lousy, you'll be fired."

Allison grinned. "Now there's the Erica we all know and love."

"I'm not keeping a crappy employee just because we're family."

"I'm happy to hear that." Allison looked at her. "I want to move into the basement."

"No. It's cold and damp."

Allison rolled her eyes. "It's beautiful and it's a walk-out so there are windows to the backyard." She softened her tone. "Summer needs her room back and the kids and I need our own space. I want to stay here, don't get me wrong, but let's have a little separation so we don't ruin what we have."

Erica knew she was right. Currently everything was new and shiny but over time, there could be issues. "Let's wait until Bethany's a month old, then make the move."

"Agreed."

Erica smiled. "I feel like we're on a roll here with the problem solving. We should tackle something really tough."

"Like you and Killion."

She glared across the table. "We aren't talking about him."

"I'm just saying, you're making a mistake."

"I can't hear you."

But the words were said automatically. In truth, she missed him enough to wonder if she really did have feelings for him. At least more than she'd first thought. But so what if she did? Getting involved was too much of a risk.

"I told Peter I want a divorce," Allison said, grabbing the last slice of pizza on her plate.

Erica would have thought the threat about moving out would have been the most shocking event of the evening, but she would have been wrong. She heard the words, but couldn't process them. When they finally made their way into her brain, she couldn't believe them.

"You didn't," she breathed. "But you love him. You're happy together. He's the father of your children. He begged for you."

Allison set down the pizza slice. "He risked everything for something I didn't want. He didn't give me a choice about any of it. He lied to me, he abandoned me and our children. He's a criminal and not at all who I thought. What I don't know is whether the problem is I didn't know him ever, or if he changed and I didn't notice."

Erica didn't know what to say. "Are you still in love with him?"

"I don't know. I'm not sure the man I loved ever existed. I talked to a divorce lawyer yesterday. Assuming Peter doesn't contest the divorce, it could be over in three or four months."

"I thought you were happy with him."

"My happiness was an illusion." She blinked away tears. "Sometimes I lie awake at night and wonder how I got here. How could I have been so wrong about so many things?"

"You weren't. You were wrong about one."

"Yeah, and it was a big one." Allison picked up her pizza. "So let's talk about Killion."

"Don't make me slap you."

"You are so full of cheap-ass talk."

"Prom is Saturday," Erica said as she drove toward the high school. "I'm worried."

"You know you're not going, right?" Allison asked, which earned her a sharp glare.

"I'm worried about Summer and someone saying something mean."

Allison understood her concern. The social media frenzy had died down, but hadn't gone away completely.

"She'll be around her friends and she's a strong young woman. She'll get through it."

"I know, but still."

"You worry."

Which was so Erica-like, she thought. On the outside she was tough, standoffish, even, but on the inside she had a soft emotional marshmallow center.

"Prom will be good for her," Allison said. "She'll have a lot of fun. Donovan will take care of her."

"He'd better."

Erica pulled into the athletic field parking lot. Today was the softball team's final game of the season. Allison had pumped breast milk so she could be away from Bethany and join Erica to cheer on Summer and her friends. Mara was looking after Bethany and Jackson, and even though the other woman would take good care of her children, Allison still felt odd about leaving them behind.

Just as uncomfortable was her bare left hand. She'd taken off her wedding set the night after she'd told Peter she wanted a divorce. In a few weeks, she would sell the rings and put the money in her day care fund for when she went to beauty school.

They got out of the SUV and walked toward the stands. There were dozens of parents and other supporters heading in the same direction.

"I didn't know the team pulled in such a big crowd."

"There aren't usually this many," Erica said. "There are more people showing up for the last game." She paused and glanced at the stands. "If you're not bothered by heights, we should head up to the top. We'll have a great view."

"Works for me."

They'd just started up when someone called out to Erica. They both turned. A pretty blonde woman headed toward them.

"Last game of the season," she said. "We're so excited." She laughed, then lowered her voice. "That they're going to be over."

Erica smiled. "It does get long. Crystal, this is Allison. Allison, Crystal. She's one of the softball moms."

Allison started to say hello but stopped when she saw Crystal's stunned expression.

"But you're…you're…"

"Summer's stepmother?" Erica said briskly. "Yes, she is."

Crystal flushed. "Oh, right. Of course. Nice to meet you."

"You, too."

"We should get to our seats," Erica said. "Good to see you, Crystal."

Allison followed her to the top of the bleachers. When they were seated, she said, "I shouldn't have come."

"Of course you should be here. You wanted to see the game. Plus except for going to the doctor, you haven't been out of the house since Bethany was born."

Allison glanced to where Crystal was in a very intense discussion with two other women. "They're talking about us."

"Their lives are small. Ignore them. I do."

"But you want to be friends with them."

Erica stared at the empty field. "I don't need them in my life."

"It's nice to have friends."

She said the words fully expecting a sarcastic response, but Erica only shook her head. "We're too different. We have nothing in common."

"You and I don't have anything in common and we managed to make it work."

Erica surprised her by smiling. "You're wrong. We have Peter in common. Sort of."

"And look how that turned out."

Allison spoke the words lightly, as if saying his name didn't hurt. Just then the team walked out onto the field, everyone stood and cheered, and the subject was dropped. But the little stab to her heart lingered.

She was brave enough to tell him she wanted a divorce and smart enough to be furious at how he'd upended their lives, but she couldn't turn off her feelings as quickly as she would like. Yes, his actions had gone a long way to killing her love for him, but it wasn't fully dead yet and she knew she would always regret how things had ended.

Summer's team was ahead by enough runs that the game ended after five innings. Erica had a feeling the parents in the stands were cheering that as much as the victory. They all went onto the field to congratulate the players. While Allison was hugging Summer, Erica felt a tap on her shoulder. She turned to see Crystal behind her.

"Oh, hi," Erica said. "Great game."

"Could I talk to you for a second?"

Strange, but okay. "Sure."

They walked toward the stands. Once they were away from the crowd, they faced each other.

"I didn't mean to be rude before," Crystal said, not quite meeting her gaze. "About Allison. I was just so surprised."

"That we're friends? She lives in my house."

"I know and that's part of it." Crystal looked directly at her. "I don't know how you do it. All of it. The business, raising a great kid. That's enough to make all of us hate you, but then you took in your ex-husband's second wife. And you didn't just let her live in your house, as you put it. You're friends with her. I could never do that. If Braedon and I split up, I'd want to kill whoever he married after me. Or at least maim her. I could never be so gracious or forgiving."

Erica smiled. "I appreciate the praise, but don't make what happened more than it was. I didn't want Allison to move in. I only did it because Summer guilted me into it. The friendship thing…" She glanced over at Allison, who was talking to Summer's teammates. "That just happened. Neither of us expected to like the other."

"You can downplay it all you want, but you did an incredible thing." Crystal paused. "We're having a potluck Friday night at my house. The team and some of the parents. I'd like you to come. You and Allison."

The invitation was a surprise. "Are we the entertainment?" she asked dryly.

Crystal laughed. "Only for the first few minutes, then it's just friends hanging out."

"Can we bring a toddler and a newborn?"

"The more, the merrier."

"Then we'll be there. Does taco salad work?"

"It's perfect."

They walked back into the crowd. Erica hugged her daughter.

"You did great today."

Summer grinned. "I caught the final out. That's always exciting. Okay, I'm going to go grab my stuff, then I'll meet you at home."

"Hey, aren't you going to celebrate with your friends?" Allison asked.

"That's for Friday. There's a potluck. I'd rather be home with you guys tonight." She looked at Erica. "You doing all right, Mom?"

Erica held in a groan. Ever since she'd told Summer about the breakup, her daughter had been checking in on her.

"I'm totally fine." Which she was, except for missing him.

"Good."

Summer hugged them both, then hurried toward the dugout. Erica watched her go.

"About that potluck she mentioned. We're invited."

"As a couple?" Allison asked.

"Ha ha. Crystal apologized for weirding out about you being here and she invited us to join everyone Friday night. Jackson and Bethany, too." Erica looked at her. "Is Bethany too young to be in a crowd?"

"She is, so I'll stay home with her, but you should go."

"By myself?"

"Yes. Summer will love having you there. And next year, you need to sit with the softball moms."

"I won't be sitting with any of them. Summer isn't playing next year."

Allison sighed. "You know what I mean. Don't lose touch with them. If they ask you to go somewhere, say yes. They want to be friends. Accept the invitation and expand your social circle. It'll be good for you."

"I hate change."

"Now you sound like your daughter."

"There are worse things."

32

"Oh, Mom."

"Don't cry. If you cry you're going to mess up your makeup."

Summer blinked a couple of times. "I'm not going to cry. You are."

Erica laughed. "I can appreciate the moment without tears."

"Then I'll cry for both of you," Allison said, already sniffing.

"I came prepared." Mara handed over a tissue, then dabbed her own cheeks. "Summer, you're stunning."

"I want to point out that I do really good work," Erica said, smiling at her daughter. "But I had a lot to work with."

Jackson, playing with his farm toys, and Bethany, asleep in her car seat carrier, didn't seem to have an opinion.

They were all in Erica's bathroom to watch the transformation. She'd started by giving Summer a decent trim and adding a few layers. Once that was done, she'd applied makeup, going for a more natural look with just a little sparkle. She'd finished by using her large barrel curling iron and creating a head full of beautiful beachy waves.

She touched one of the curls. "I used a lot of product so these should last most of the night. Now let's get you into your fancy clothes."

Summer had wanted a short dress. They'd found a pretty, deep blue tank dress that shimmered. The simple style flattered

Summer's athletic shape while allowing her to move easily. The hem was high enough to be sexy and yet not so high that she would be flashing the world.

Her daughter had shocked her by saying she wanted to pair a high heel with the dress. They'd bought cute strappy sandals with three-inch heels and Summer had spent the past four days walking around in them.

They went into the large closet and Summer stepped into the dress. Erica zipped it up, then steadied her while she slipped on the sandals.

Erica looked at her daughter and sighed. "You're stunning. Grandma is going to want pictures."

"Aren't you?"

She laughed. "Yes, I want pictures, too." She glanced at her watch. "What time do Donovan and his friends arrive?"

"I'm the last stop so not for a while. We're going out to dinner, then to prom."

Donovan and two others had gone in together to rent a limo to take them to and from prom.

"I want you to keep in touch if there's a change in plan."

Summer shook her head. "Mom, I'm not going to any party after. Donovan and I already talked about it. I know him way more than I know his friends. If there is a party, they'll drop me off first." She held up her hand. "But I promise, if they push back on that, I'll call you to come get me."

"I'll be sitting here, my car keys in hand."

"I really hope that isn't how you spend your evening."

They went back into the bathroom, where Allison and Mara wept over how beautiful Summer was, then everyone, including the kids, went downstairs for pictures.

There was an intense discussion about where to take the photos. The curve of the staircase won and Summer dutifully posed. They were nearly done when someone rang the front doorbell.

"It can't be Donovan," Summer said. "It's too early."

Erica looked at Allison, who shrugged.

"I'm not expecting anyone," she said.

Erica opened the door and found a man in a dark suit on the doorstep. "Can I help you?"

"Yes. I'm here to take Summer Jenkins and her young man to their prom."

Erica looked at her daughter. "I thought you said they were picking you up last."

Summer stepped outside and gasped. "Mom, this isn't Donovan's car."

Erica followed her and saw a gleaming black Bentley parked in the driveway.

"But how…"

How could this be? Yes, Killion had told Summer he would provide her with a Bentley for prom, but that was before they'd broken up. Except they hadn't broken up—she'd dumped him, and he'd still arranged for the car.

Mara joined them. "What's all the fuss? Oh, my. Look at that." She glanced at Erica. "Killion sent the car?"

"He must have. I never thought he would. I mean why would he bother? We're not together."

"He kept his word."

Summer clutched her arm. "It's a sign, Mom. A really big one. Look how much he cares. He didn't want to let me down so he did this and I'm not even the one he's in love with."

"It's not a sign."

Allison came out, the carrier in one hand and Jackson clinging to the other. "What am I missing?" Her breath caught. "Is that what I think it is?"

"A sign," Summer said.

"Or just a man who keeps his word." Mara patted her arm. "My daughter, the fool." She picked up Jackson. "I'd like to play a game. Would you like that, too?"

"Yes!"

They went inside. The driver hovered nearby.

"Shall I be taking Miss Summer and her young man to prom?"

"Of course you will." Summer laughed as she started texting. "I'm letting Donovan know I'm coming over in a ride he won't ever forget." She sent the text, then grinned at Erica. "Now you don't have to worry about me getting home if there's a party. I have my own wheels and very responsible driver."

The man nodded. "I'll take care of you."

Killion had sent the car. He'd remembered and then he'd had Napoleon make arrangements. Because he'd given his word? Because that was simply who he was? Or was he sending her a message? She honestly had no idea.

Summer hurried inside for her coat and clutch. She hugged Erica and Allison, then followed the driver to the car and, when he'd opened the door for her, slid onto the back seat.

"She's going to have the best time," Allison said as they watched her drive away.

"I hope so."

They went inside. Allison set Bethany down.

"You should call and thank him."

"I'm not doing that. Summer can text him a thank-you tomorrow."

"Why don't you want to call?"

Erica exhaled. "It would be awkward and confusing and I wouldn't know what to say. Besides, I don't want to talk to him."

"I hate it when you lie to me."

"Fine. I don't want to talk to him very much."

"Still lying. Call him. Call him!"

She found herself tempted. Hearing his voice would be nice. No, better than nice. She missed him so much more than she'd thought. The longer they were apart, the more she felt like a piece of her life was missing. They'd been good together. If she called...

She pulled her phone out of her pocket.

"You're going to do it? I can't believe it." Allison practically danced in place. "You never listen to me. This is exciting."

"I'm not calling him." She opened her calendar. "He's not home. There's a charity event tonight." Her voice turned wistful. "I was supposed to go with him."

"That's even better." Allison gave her a little push toward the stairs. "You should go to the event. Put on something sexy and go talk to him."

Erica stepped out of reach. "I'm not crashing a fundraiser for children with cancer."

"Give them some money. They won't mind. It's not like you're going to steal a meal. You just go in and find him and thank him for the car. Easy peasy."

"Are you out of your mind? Nothing about that is normal behavior. He'll think I'm stalking him. It's creepy."

"He'll think that maybe you're regretting your actions and you'd like a second chance." Allison's stare turned pointed. "Because you would."

"I…"

"You're in love with him. We can all see it. You're moping around like a teenager after her first breakup. Killion is great. You married the wrong man the first time. Why not get it right the second time?" She pointed to the stairs. "Go. Go now. Get dressed and go to the fundraiser."

The idea was ridiculous, Erica thought. She wasn't going. Crashing a charity event simply wasn't done. She would wait and maybe call him in the morning. Or next week. Either way she would make sure Summer texted a thank-you. And maybe that was enough.

"Stop thinking!" Allison put her hands on her hips. "Stop talking yourself out of it. Erica, I swear you're the most amazing person I know but when it comes to Killion, you're a moron." She paused. "No, you're scared. Terrified maybe. But he's worth it. I know he is. Trust him and trust yourself to be strong enough to handle it. And get your bony ass upstairs and get dressed for the party!"

Erica had a whole lot she wanted to say, but somehow instead of speaking, she found herself rushing upstairs. Allison called for Mara, grabbed Bethany and hurried after her.

Once again everyone—minus Summer—crowded into her bathroom.

"I don't know what to wear," she said as she tried to apply eye shadow, only her hands were shaking too much. "I can't remember how formal it is."

"Tell me the name," Mara said, whipping out her phone. "I'll look it up."

"I'll look it up," Allison said, grabbing the phone. "You do her makeup. She's making a mess of it."

Erica collapsed into the chair. Her mother washed her hands, then picked up the shadow brush.

"I assume we're going for the super sexy, this-could-be-all-yours-sailor look."

Erica shifted back in the chair. "Not the sailor part, but yes to the rest of it."

"Black tie," Allison said, reading from the phone. "The annual event, blah, blah, blah, six million raised last year, black tie event. Women in evening gowns." She looked up. "Do you own any evening gowns?"

"Several."

"Really?"

Allison disappeared into the closet. Seconds later she yelled, "Holy crap, you have a lot of clothes and they're mostly black."

"That's the work side of the closet. Turn around."

"Oh, jeez. You have dresses. Oooh, I love the red one. With your coloring, it's perfect. Plus, he'll see you coming."

"Not that one. It's really tight, so I can't eat a week before I wear it."

"You haven't been eating," her mother said, carefully applying false eyelashes. "It'll fit just fine." She chuckled. "We should call back the guy with the Bentley. After he drops off Summer and Donovan, he can come get you."

"I'll drive myself. The event is at a hotel. There'll be valet parking."

In less time than she would have thought, her mother was done. Mara rubbed some hair product on her hands and refreshed Erica's spiky hairstyle. When she was done, Erica dug through her lingerie drawers, looking for the right shapewear and bra.

When she stepped into the red gown, she sucked in her breath, hoping it would slide up easily. Apparently her mother was right because it slipped over her body with no problem. Allison stepped behind her to pull up the zipper.

The dress was a simple silk, off-the-shoulder style that clung from breasts to hips before falling straight to the floor. It was dramatic and elegant, and while Erica knew she looked good, she couldn't shake the growing sense of trepidation.

"I have no idea what I'll say to him," she said as she took a pair of diamond and ruby earrings out of her jewelry box.

"I miss you and I was wrong," Allison offered. "Then suggest you go to his place and have—" she glanced at her son playing on the carpet "—s-e-x."

"It's a fundraiser. I'm not suggesting that."

"As long as you leave a check, they'll be fine."

"You're surprisingly cynical."

"I'm being practical. Yay charity, but for me, this is about you and Killion."

Erica had just finished transferring her car fob, wallet and cell phone to her small evening bag when her mother walked down the stairs, a small overnight bag in her hand.

"Just in case," Mara said.

Erica took it, both excited and nervous. "This could all end badly."

"Or it could end very well."

★ ★ ★

Erica was still unsure about the plan and what she was supposed to tell Killion even as she handed over her key fob to the valet. She followed the signs to the grand ballroom. It was barely seven, so the cocktail party and silent auction would be going strong. Dinner wasn't until seven thirty, which gave her enough time to find Killion and—

She came to a stop, horror sweeping through her. What if he was here with someone else? What if he was over her and on to the next conquest? What if he hadn't meant it when he said he was in love with her? She could be about to make a huge fool of herself in public. Witnesses to her humiliation would make things worse. Better to head home and reach out to him another time. Or not at all. While she missed him, she would eventually be fine. Wasn't it easier to simply not take the chance?

She turned and started for her car only to stop a few steps later. Indecision gripped her. The fear was strong, but so was the need to see him. She honestly didn't know what to do.

Trust him and trust yourself to be strong enough to handle whatever happens.

Could she do that? Be that brave? Did she have a choice?

"Dammit, I'm not going to regret letting him go for the rest of my life," she muttered, turning and walking purposefully toward the ballroom. Maybe this *would* all end badly but she was going to make the effort. She'd spent her whole life going after what she wanted—that was who she was and it was time she started acting like it.

She easily found the crowd of well-dressed donors. She circled the check-in area, joined a group of women coming out of the restroom and walked in with them. In her dress, with her obviously expensive beaded clutch, she fit right in. Once she was past the check-in area, she stepped away from them and began her search.

Fifteen minutes later, she wanted to shriek in frustration.

There had to be seven hundred people there, half men dressed in black tuxedos. Finding one man who may or may not be with someone else was nearly impossible. Once everyone started in for dinner, she would be stuck with nowhere to sit. It wasn't as if she wanted to spend the evening walking around the dozens of tables, hoping to spot him.

"Hello, Erica."

She spun and found Killion standing next to her. Relief was quickly followed by a need to throw herself at him. He looked so good—handsome, as always—but also steady and possibly a little bit happy to see her.

"I've been looking for you," she told him.

"Here I am." He offered her a slight smile. "I wasn't expecting to see you tonight."

"I know. Coming here was a last-minute decision." She glanced around then returned her attention to him. "Are you with someone?"

The smile widened. "No."

"Why is that funny?"

"Less than a month ago I told you I was in love with you. Why would I bring a date to something like this so soon after that?"

"People don't want to come by themselves. Or maybe you're over me. I can't read your mind."

"You're getting defensive, which means you're nervous." He took her hand and drew her toward a quiet alcove. "Erica, why are you here?"

She glanced at the carpeted floor, then back at him. "You sent the Bentley. For Summer. I never thought you'd even remember that, let alone do it."

"You know I didn't make the arrangements."

She waved that comment away. "Yes, yes, it was Napoleon. I know, but that's not the point. You remembered."

"I keep my word."

She looked into his green eyes and saw affection. No, she

thought, knowing she had to be honest. Love. She saw love there and while it still terrified her, it was also very nice to see.

"You scare me," she admitted.

"I know."

"I don't like that."

"You've made that very clear."

She drew in a breath. "But it's also possible I'm in love with you."

"When will you know for sure?"

She tried to laugh, then nearly started to cry. Too many emotions churned inside of her.

"When Allison was having Bethany, she was missing Peter and was scared because the baby was a little early and she said she wasn't strong enough to deal with everything. She said Peter broke her."

"Did he?"

"No. She's really strong and I got in her face and told her that. I said whatever happened, I would be there. I never thought he broke her, but I do think he broke me."

Killion watched her as she spoke. "He shattered your confidence, Erica. He made you doubt who and what you are. But then you picked yourself up and took care of whatever crap there was to deal with. You raised your daughter, grew your business and thrived. Proof no one can break you. Be proud of that."

"I avoided men. I never wanted to hurt that much again. I wasn't willing to trust anyone."

"I know. I knew you wouldn't be easy, but that you'd be worth it."

"I'm less sure about that." She took a step toward him. Now was the time for the truth. "I love you, Killion."

Something hot and bright and happy flared in his eyes. "I love you, too."

She pressed a hand to her chest. "That was hard and I feel a little nauseous, but I think I'll be okay."

He chuckled as he pulled her close. "I've missed you more than I can say. Every day, with every breath. Promise you'll never leave me again."

She stared into his eyes and felt the last walls around her heart fall away. "I promise. I do love you."

He kissed her then, a soft, welcoming kiss that quickly grew into something much more intense. When he finally drew back, he was breathing just a little hard.

"All right," he said, taking her hand in his. "We're going to stop by the registration desk, where I'll put a sizeable donation on my credit card, then we're going to my place."

"Yes, we are."

When they got there she would text Summer and tell her where she was. She would also let Allison and her mother know that everything had worked out and that she and Killion were back together.

As they walked toward the front of the hotel, Killion asked, "Is everything all right with Allison and Bethany?"

"They're both fine. The baby is thriving. Jackson's still a little unsure about her, but I think he's going to like being a big brother."

There was so much more to tell him. About how Allison was going to be staying with her for at least the next couple of years and that Summer would be working at Twisted. But that was for later. Right now the most important words had been said.

As they waited for the valet to bring their cars around, she smiled at him.

"I really do love you."

He smiled. "Those words will never get old."

And they didn't...not for the rest of their lives.

★ ★ ★ ★ ★

SUSAN MALLERY

FOR
THE LOVE OF
SUMMER

READER'S GUIDE

SUGGESTED MENU

Creamy shrimp scampi with vegetables (recipe follows)

Green salad tossed with olive oil and vinegar

A light-bodied white wine, such as chardonnay

QUESTIONS FOR DISCUSSION

Please note: These questions contain spoilers about the story, so we recommend that you wait to read them until after you have finished the book.

1. How did you feel about Erica in her first scene, when she was dealing with a hair color emergency caused by an inexperienced stylist? How did you feel about how she related to her employee and to her client? What would you have done differently? Why do you think Mallery started with this scene? Did your impression of Erica evolve as you read the book and, if so, in what way?

2. In chapter two, just as Allison is introduced, her life is immediately thrown into chaos with one hit after the next. How did you feel about her and her circumstances? Did your feelings change as the story progressed? Discuss her relationship with Peter and how it evolved in the story.

3. Why do you think Erica agreed to bring Allison and her son, Jackson, into her home? Could you ever invite your ex-husband's current spouse to live with you and your family? Why or why not?

4. Do you think *For the Love of Summer* is a fitting title for this book? Why or why not? What did you think of Summer? Discuss Erica's complicated relationship with her daughter, and how their relationship evolved in the book.

5. When Allison moved in, the women had a very unbalanced relationship—Erica had the house, the money, the knowledge and the connections to help Allison, which put Allison in a position of gratitude and subservience. At what point did the balance of the relationship change? What brought about the change? Did it feel believable to you?

6. With which character did you identify most closely? Why?

7. Discuss Erica's relationship with the other softball moms. Did you empathize with Erica's feelings toward the other women? Both Erica and Allison had a difficult time making friends, but for different reasons. Discuss. Do you find it easy to make new friends? Why or why not?

8. How was Erica's relationship with Killion affected by her divorce from Peter? What did you think about Killion? Do you think it's possible for a person to be ruthless in business but kindhearted in his or her personal life?

9. Erica's salon chain, Twisted, was named by one of Susan Mallery's readers on Facebook—and Mallery gave Erica that reader's last name, Sawyer, in her honor. If you were going to open a salon and spa, what would you name it?

10. As the book opened, Allison was happily married while Erica was divorced and determined to remain single. By the end, they had essentially swapped relationship statuses. How did you feel

about the ending? What other direction do you think Mallery could have taken the story? Do you want there to be a sequel, or are you happy with *For the Love of Summer* as a stand-alone?

CREAMY SHRIMP SCAMPI WITH VEGETABLES

16 oz uncooked linguine
2 Tbsp olive oil
1 pound uncooked shrimp, peeled and deveined
1 cup asparagus spears cut into 1-inch pieces
¼ cup red bell pepper, diced
¼ cup onion, diced
6 cloves of garlic, minced
½ tsp red pepper flakes
¼ cup white wine
½ cup frozen peas
1 cup cherry tomatoes, cut in half
½ cup cream or half-and-half
½ cup fresh parsley, minced
Salt, pepper and parmesan cheese to taste.

Cook the pasta according to directions. Reserve one cup of liquid for the final step.

While the pasta is boiling, heat the olive oil in a heavy-bottomed pan. Add shrimp in a single layer, then asparagus, bell pepper and onion. Cook two minutes. Flip shrimp and cook another two minutes. Add the garlic and red pepper flakes and cook for another thirty seconds. Add wine, peas and tomatoes, and cook until the wine is reduced by half, about two minutes longer. Shrimp should be opaque. Remove from heat. Stir in cream and parsley. Toss with cooked pasta, salt and pepper, and about one-quarter cup of the pasta water. Add more water as desired. Sprinkle with salt, pepper and parmesan cheese.